AVRIL MARIA SERENE

THE HODIN CABAL: CHOICES

A DEBRA ANN WYNN MYSTERY

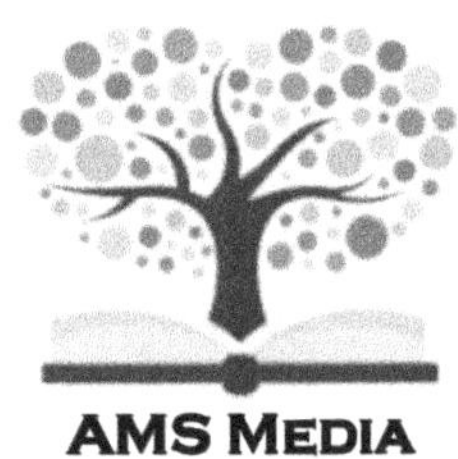

AMS Media
1646 East North Street #1H
Springfield, Missouri 65803-4357

First printing, April 2025

https://AvrilMSerene.com

AMS MEDIA is a registered trademark of AMS Media, LLC.

Printed in the United States of America

10 9 8 7 6 5 4 3 2 1

ISBN (paperback): 979-8-9928602-5-2

(continued from previous page) like the gripping intrigue of Dan Brown's novels and the layered character development seen in Gillian Flynn's work, yet it stands apart by intertwining speculative science fiction elements with real-world societal concerns.

"… The plot intricately combines mystery, crime, and speculative fiction, creating a rich narrative landscape. Unlike traditional mysteries that often revolve around solving a crime, this story delves into the prevention of global-scale atrocities, evoking a sense of urgency and moral ambiguity not always present in its genre counterparts.
"… The character development, especially of the protagonist and Spector, is nuanced, allowing readers to explore their complexities. This depth ensures characters are not merely vehicles for the plot but integral to the thematic exploration of the story, much like in Flynn's 'Gone Girl,' where character complexities drive the narrative.

"… The varied settings, from urban landscapes to the tense confines of a psychiatric hospital, are well-utilized to amplify the story's mood and themes. This effective use of setting mirrors the atmospheric tension found in Raymond Chandler's Los Angeles, though 'The Hodin Cabal' employs a broader canvas to explore its complex plot.

"… The narrative's pacing and structure maintain suspense and engagement, weaving between personal stories and the overarching conspiracy. This balance of personal narrative depth with plot-driven suspense is reminiscent of Brown's 'The Da Vinci Code,' though 'The Hodin Cabal' leans more into speculative fiction territory."
—*BKS (reviewer), Pleasanton, CA. (9/27/2024)*

See all the reviews submitted to Avril's website at https://avrilmserene.com/product/the-hodin-cabal-choices/_.

See all the reviews submitted to Amazon's website at https://www.amazon.com/product-reviews/B0F628CBLM /ref=cm_cr_dp_d_show_all_btm?ie=UTF8&reviewerType=all_reviews .

For Terry and Bill

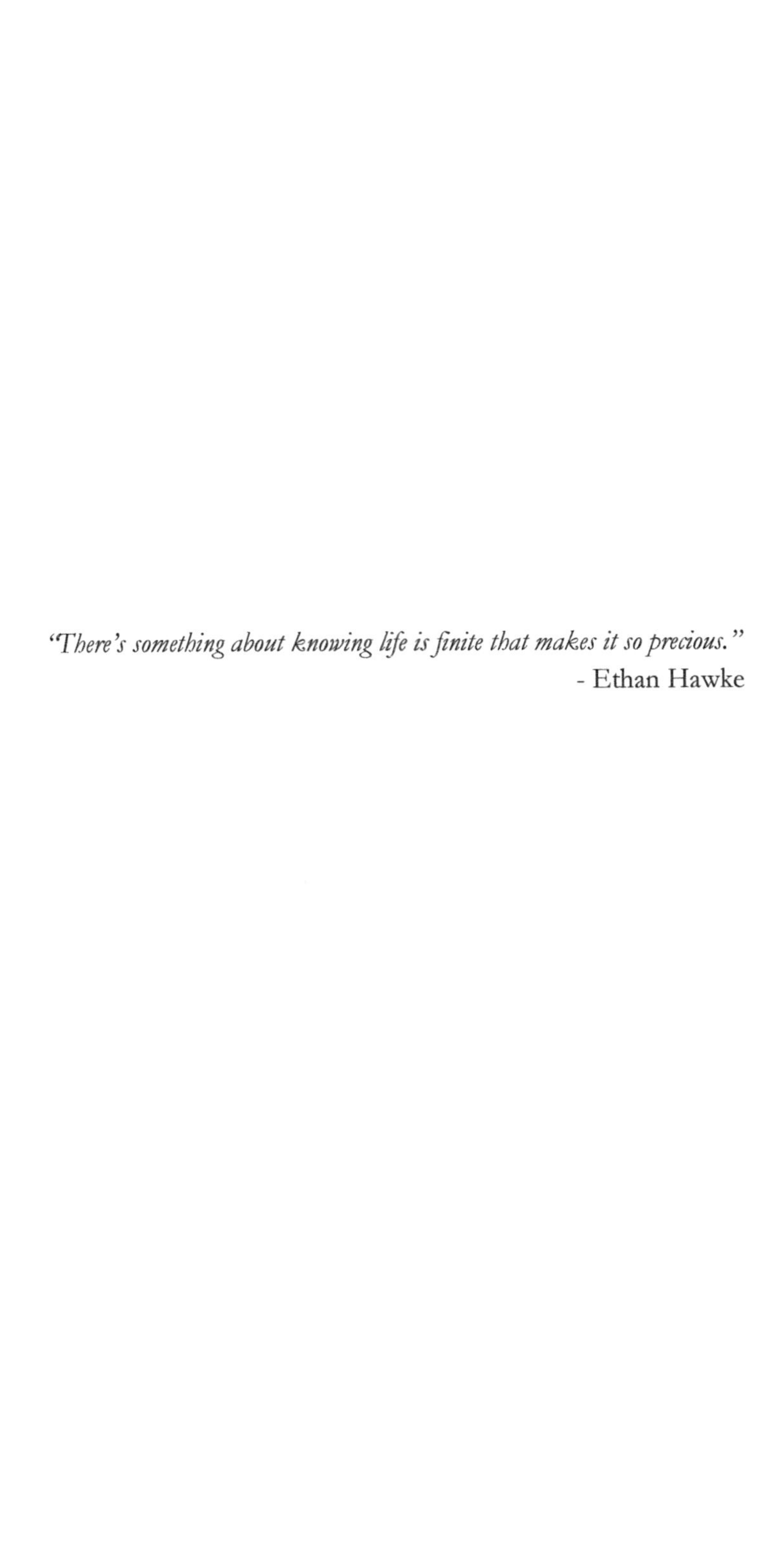

"There's something about knowing life is finite that makes it so precious."

\- Ethan Hawke

BOOK ONE

THE WRITINGS OF
AVRIL MARIA SERENE

BOOK ONE — PROLOGUE

NEAR BORREGO SPRINGS, CALIFORNIA

Hovering high in the arid atmosphere above the barren wasteland in San Diego County's northwest corner, the soft whirring of the drone's rotors went unnoticed. Wavelets of heat escaping the desert floor into the rapidly cooling night warped and slightly wrinkled the camera's images. Still, the view of the distant white duty van and two uniformed officers was unobstructed.

Three powerful LED floodlamps on leggy tripods illuminated the area to the sides of the police transport vehicle's headlights. Ahead of the van, several mounds of loose rocks, sand, and soil, each roughly a foot high, encircled a broad, shallow pit.

The taller, older man in the center of the excavated depression stabbed a four-tined pitchfork into the ground. He stood waiting, his hands on his hips and a scowl on his face. He'd filled the hole behind him with a dozen plastic-wrapped, drab tan bundles of various shapes and sizes arranged in a single layer. The harsh white light glinted off their shiny surfaces and highlighted the perspiration on his face and forearms. His voice's strong bass resonated through the dry air.

"Will you quit fucking around, Reynolds," he grumbled, "and get your ass back to work?" Wiping a sleeve across his forehead, he intercepted a rivulet of sweat trickling from his dark blonde crewcut. "Just once, I'd like to get home before midnight."

Half-heartedly jamming the back of his damp shirt under his belt with one hand, he yanked the pitchfork back from the rocky earth.

His partner, short and hyperactive with a wiry build and an unkempt mop of curly black hair, danced in front of the van's headlights outside the wide trench.

He batted a vaguely round object between his feet like a soccer ball. Someone had wrapped the lumpy package in brown butcher's paper, then swathed it in layers of clear shrink wrap. Greenish blotches and irregularly shaped stains of dark maroon were visible through the plastic. They spread with every kick, releasing small puffs of cloudy stench as the tiny colored droplets sparkled in the headlight beams.

With his arms held wide and a slow-motion windup of his right leg, Reynolds swiped at the package using the side of his boot.

It bounced and then rolled over the lip of the dug-out area.

"Check it out, it's a 'header!' And the crowd goes wild!"

He loudly cheered his macabre joke, both fists in the air, face to the sky.

Dropping his arms, he stood idly, watching his companion work.

"Lighten up, DeVance," Reynolds said dismissively, looking his partner up and down with his head tilted. "We're getting *paid* for this, and a lot more than our city paychecks."

DeVance snorted, unsold.

"You're just pissed because you banged your head coming up here," Reynolds called over his shoulder, walking back to grab another package from the van's rear deck. This bundle was larger, roughly shaped like a seat cushion, but with bumps and bulges.

"Serves you right for bitching about getting back home to your precious 'Diana'…." Reynolds' tone turned derisive as he made air quotes with his fingers. "*Jesus*, man, pussy-whipped or what? You wanted the pedal to the metal; you got it. Not my fault there ain't any paved roads out here."

"Yeah, yeah, yeah… from the guy who has to pay to get laid," DeVance retorted. "How many we got left in the van?"

"Say six or seven for each complete one, maybe three more."

"Every time we do one of these runs, they add more bodies. They ought to give us a bonus — we should ask the next time that mouthy little shortshit comes to the precinct. OK, give me that. Grab the other shovel out of the van. We'll have to dig some more."

"Fine, you asked for it," Reynolds replied mockingly. Swinging his bundle behind him and to one side, he slung it at DeVance with a mighty heave.

"Goddammit, Reynolds!" Devance yelled, dropping the pitchfork just in time to catch the package. As it hit his chest, he flung his hands wide to let the parcel drop at his feet.

"These fucking things leak, asshole. I'm *not* fighting with my wife tonight about how the hell I got bodily fluids all over my uniform. Again."

"Take them to a dry cleaner — we're making enough; you don't *have* to be such a tightass." Reynolds carried a shovel and a large green garbage bag from the van's rear into the light.

"C'mon, Reynolds, tell me you're not so fucking stupid you're taking shit to a dry cleaner after one of these jobs...." DeVance stared at his partner, anger in his voice. "Are you *trying* to get us locked up?"

"Chill out, man. My guy knows I'm a cop. You get stains and smells when you work crime scenes — it goes with the territory. He cleans for a lot of officers. What, you think he'd rat us out and give up all that business?"

"You know, Reynolds, you're a fucking idiot. Let's get this crap done so we can get the hell out of here and breathe some fresh air. This place stinks like a meat packing plant in the middle of summer."

Dropping the garbage bag into the pit, Reynolds leaned over, grabbed the two corners opposite the opening, and yanked on them to dump its contents. Belts, dentures, eyeglasses, dirty clothes and underwear, battered shoes, cheap costume jewelry, the occasional ratted-out handbag or hat, and the paper contents of wallets and purses spilled out.

"Wasting your time, Reynolds," DeVance scoffed as he rested his cheek on his hands, crossed atop the pitchfork handle. "They've already gone through that crap; took anything worth a damn."

"Hey, never know, one man's trash is the next guy's treasure...."

Reynolds held out a cracked and yellowed Polaroid of a uniformed recruit; the original colors had faded into dull sepia tones.

"Well, I'll be damned — that's *too* ironic. One was a cop back in the day."

"Don't be screwing with karma, jackass," DeVance replied. "Drop it, and let's get this done."

Pulling his hand back, Reynolds glanced at the other side of the print.

"Robert E. Perkins, huh? Never heard of him. Well, rest in pieces, buddy."

Standing up and flashing a sardonic grin, Reynolds spun the picture by its corner as he tossed it onto the pile of trash.

THE WRITINGS OF
AVRIL MARIA SERENE

BOOK ONE — CHAPTER 1

SAN DIEGO, CALIFORNIA

I couldn't wait for the publication notice to arrive in the mail. It marked a watershed event — my one-hundredth freelance article — and I was so excited. It'd been five years since I left my lead investigative journalist position at the *San Diego Union-Tribune*. And, despite my editor's threats when I departed, this milestone meant I'd made it. The Debra Ann Wynn byline had found a home among my accomplished peers.

I planned a celebration with the friends who'd made this moment possible, but not everyone could attend. Harry Sanderson, a rumpled walking version of *Bartlett's Familiar Quotations* and my favorite private investigator, was always too busy to socialize. Doug Stein, the *Union-Tribune* reporter who'd taken me under his wing when I was just a cub, wasn't available. A confidante for so many years and in many ways still a mentor, he'd taken his wife to Hawaii on vacation.

Emma Woodson would come. I'd met the inspirational supermom of three during the Seaver case, my first significant investigation after Dad passed, and we'd become close.

Lindsay Barnes, my best friend from junior high, has been my go-to hair stylist for years. She'd talked me into growing out my short bob to show off my naturally red curls — she was begging me to add highlights for the event. I'd agreed, but not to the bouffant style she wanted to try. Already five foot nine, I didn't want to be any taller. But Lindsay would be there.

And commemorating my published pieces made no sense without Marci.

Besides being a dear friend, Marci Robbins, an up-and-coming sergeant in San Diego's Major Case unit, has been a quotable source for many of my articles since I first interviewed her a decade ago. Blonde and tall like a model, she had a beautiful face and an engaging personality; you'd never know she was a breast cancer survivor or that she'd once lost custody of her children when struggling with personal issues.

TWELVE YEARS AGO

San Diego Police Officer Marci Robbins, recently demoted after four years working Vice's undercover unit, scowled as she and her partner pulled up to the curb. Neither of them wanted to deal with the homeless encampments lining the sidewalks of Fifth Street downtown.

Needing to stay under the radar added to Robbins' stress. Three weeks ago, her sergeant had laid it out in plain English.

"Listen, whatever's happening in your personal life, get a handle on it! Have your union rep hook you up with the Employee Assistance Program. Do the twelve-step thing, whatever, but you can't drink on the job.

"I get that half the officers here want to jump in the sack with you, but that won't save your badge. The rest would like to see you fired — people are talking, so take care of it; I can't cover for you anymore. If the situation makes it into a written report, you're through. Are we clear?"

"Yes, Sarge," Robbins replied, her voice resigned rather than enthusiastic. "I'll make the call, get it straightened out."

I can drink vodka, she thought. *Something people can't smell.*

Her day wasn't starting well — this morning, she was assigned to ride with that Bible-thumping prick, Andrews. When his wife was pregnant with their second child at the end of last year, Andrews asked Robbins for a date. They were doing crowd control for Governor Newsom's campaign swing through the city. She'd left Andrews no wiggle room when she shut him down in front of their team members and passersby — *that* pissed him off.

He'd nursed the grudge ever since. Robbins avoided working with him for months, but her luck ran out today. At their shift's start, Andrews took the keys from her; he'd drive, saying he didn't want their squad car pulled over for a DUI.

Folding her slender frame, shapely even in her uniform blues, into the passenger seat, Robbins scrunched close to the door — she didn't need Andrews putting his ham-sized paw on her knee.

A radio call commanded their presence at the homeless sweep, and Andrews cursed. "That's the third one this month! The wife and kids won't have anything to do with me tonight until I shower. When will these empty-suit political types figure out these people need *somewhere* to go? Instead, they anoint us St. Patrick for the shift and tell us anyone who sleeps on the street is a snake. We're supposed to drive them out into the open ocean and hope they drown."

Robbins was glad Andrews picked a topic they could agree on; avoiding conflict with fellow officers was paramount.

"You've heard the rumors," she said wryly, tightening the bun she'd made of her long blonde hair. "They've told some of us to dump them off in other cities around here, but quietly. Especially Oceanside and Chula Vista, or up north to rural Riverside County. Internal Affairs is hassling Daniels for loading them up and dumping them on the cartels across the border in Mexico."

"The suits think if we harass the homeless enough, they'll go away on their own." Andrews sighed. "But every time we do a sweep, something nasty happens to *us*. Last month, I got stuck with a needle and cut by broken glass. We've been bitten by rats and diseased dogs and torn up by cats. You get tired of fighting the schizophrenics, PCP users, … and drunks."

Despite that last dig, Robbins couldn't help noticing her partner was keeping to the straight and narrow. Andrews was a big man with a dark Italian complexion that made him seem more intimidating. He had a deep voice, and he'd drop it a notch lower in frequency when hitting on someone. He wasn't doing that today.

Did someone talk to him about the touchy-feely stuff? Robbins was already under the microscope and hadn't made a complaint — that'd end any female officer's career despite what the brass advertised, especially hers. Maybe his wife heard something — either way, he'd dropped the every-other-sentence sexual innuendos.

"Try tangling with one on speed who outweighs you by fifty pounds." Robbins gave a little snort. "Me, I'm scared of catching an infectious disease."

"We bitch about it every time, just like now," Andrews griped. "But nothing changes. When I was a rookie, I told my sergeant I'd take it to the union. He said they'd fire me before I made my next roll call."

"Insubordination — the last thing any officer wants on their record." Robbins flashed a crooked smile. She was playing along to stay on Andrews's good side but had no love for their civilian overlords.

Andrews shifted in the driver's seat, conflicted but unable to resolve anything. "Besides dealing with the nasty smells and sanitary conditions, now they tell us to run off anyone with cameras. They don't want the department getting sued again!"

"I don't get it. The department lost the class-action lawsuit last year." Robbins was hesitant, unsure of her footing. "Didn't that give the homeless *some* rights — or respect the rights they already had? Either way, I thought we'd be off the hook...."

"Yeah, the department settled, but it was a big joke. All they did was hang up that list of things we're not supposed to do, like rousting them during nighttime sleeping hours. Have you read the whole thing? I know *I* didn't."

Robbins rolled her eyes. "Sarge says legal posted it for show."

"They never intended to act in good faith. The district attorney turned around and ordered us to keep doing the homeless exactly how we always have."

"Oh, yeah, the new thing about repurposing the encroachment law," Robbins snorted. "Whoever decided that was the right thing to do had to be an asshole. That ordinance was supposed to keep homeowners from putting garbage cans on the sidewalk. It's been around forever, but now they're saying 'trash' means 'people.'"

"The brass says that's how the law reads; there's nothing they can do," Andrews agreed. "The homeless and their worldly possessions are legally garbage. Literally."

"I don't remember writing anyone up for it when I had beat duty. Maybe warned somebody if a neighbor complained, but that was all."

Robbins's body had relaxed as the fear of unwanted advances melted away. Today, Andrews was open and expressive, showing he shared her frustrations and accepting her more as a fellow officer than the object of his affection.

"I thought they were kidding when they told me to ticket a homeless guy so we could take his stuff," she added. "The tent he slept in crossed a few inches outside the asphalt. It's the same place we're going now, on Fifth.

"But they were serious. Twenty minutes later, the bulldozers scraped that tent, and everyone else's, into a dump truck."

"I have to go to church and listen to sermons about Jesus being homeless," Andrews complained. "It seemed like the preacher was directing them at us. So I told him, 'We never wanted this. We're just the tools the suits use.' Then my youngest daughter tells me a little girl in her Sunday school asked why the police don't keep their word.

"We end up stuck in the damned middle."

Robbins found it interesting that Andrews cared about what civilians thought of him.

"They didn't teach us about *any* of this at the academy," Robbins observed.

"What, they didn't tell you how thankless it would be?" Andrews' smile was cynical. "Tomorrow, we'll get the riot act at roll call because street crime's up again. Nobody'll admit we couldn't stop it because we were doing this horseshit. You can't be in two places at once. But as boots-on-the-ground grunts, we gotta do what they tell us, so we get hit from both directions."

Pulling up behind another cruiser, Andrews ended the conversation with another dig. "But you know, Robbins, if you want anyone to hear you, you gotta clean up your act. I'm serious. People in glass houses…. You need to get your ass to AA, get some guidance through the Lord."

Mind your business, Robbins thought, nodding slightly and looking away. She surveyed the scene: three patrol units onsite, a Republic Services garbage truck, and a Streets and Maintenance dump truck backed up to the sidewalk. Yellow end-loaders emptied their buckets into the dirt hauler. A black-and-white skid-steer loader scurried back and forth, scooping up the homeless' tents and possessions.

Officers had queued up camp residents, some handcuffed, behind a transport van and were herding them into the back.

Nearly stumbling as she stepped out of their unit, Robbins hoped no one noticed or would remember the bobble. With smells, commotion, and destructive behaviors diverting attention, Robbins could hide her intoxication easily. Other officers, rendered nose blind, couldn't smell anything against the general stench. If they detected alcohol on anyone's breath, they'd blame a detainee.

Still, Robbins had to acknowledge that Andrews was right. *I'm glad I'm working a homeless sweep — because it means I won't lose my job today? It's time for me to get my shit together. Christ, I'm turning into such a hypocrite. Watch me have to tag somebody today for drunk-and-disorderly whose blood alcohol level is less than mine.*

— ◦ —

Seven hours later, their shift ending, Andrews and Robbins climbed into their cruiser. They'd had a long day chasing down, sobering up, and identifying and processing the homeless. New rules required inventorying the detainees' possessions of value, further slowing the work.

The sidewalk and the surrounding area were now clear, with some trash, broken glass, and aluminum cans still to be gathered.

Though exhausted, neither officer had suffered injury.

"What a klusterfuck," Andrews groused. "Another political shit show."

"Hopefully, that'll be it for a while — with the election in two weeks, the campaigning will be over." The effects of Robbins's morning drinking had worn off, and she was trying to ignore her growing thirst.

"It seems like more than just that," Andrews responded. "The last time I worked a homeless roundup, I overheard my lieutenant and one of the mayor's crew talking. The press wasn't there yet — this aide was walking around, readying things for the photo op.

"Something had him riled. He was going off about him and the mayor being victims of the homeless, screaming at the lieutenant.

"Like the people in their tarps, torn tents, and toothlessness were doing it on purpose. Intentionally being poor, miserable, and disenfranchised out in the open solely to piss off these elected officials. 'Why the hell can't they crawl into a corner and flip over on their backs like the rest of the cockroaches — just leave us the fuck alone?' That's their thinking."

Robbins agreed. "Like it's personal, some kind of vendetta entitled assholes are waging." She leaned her head against the window, tired and wanting a drink.

"I was cuffing a guy for the prisoner van," Andrews continued, tightening his grip on the steering wheel. "I turned to see what this suit clown was ranting about – he was glaring straight at the man I had sitting on the curb. The look on his face was pure hatred, something you don't usually see politicians showing publicly. I didn't expect to see anything like it again.

"But days later, I saw a retweet of an OAN interview with the white supremacist Stephen Miller. Somebody in the White House said Miller's Waffen-SS — he sure looks like Joseph Goebbels. But Miller was saying in words what the empty suit was saying with his facial expressions. And my dad says that's how it was in Germany in 1938 for anyone who didn't fit in."

Robbins grimaced, nodding. Too many times already in this job, she'd seen the willingness to kill someone over almost anything.

Telling that some things are a step too far, even for Andrews.

"As a starry-eyed recruit, I thought I'd spend my career helping people." Robbins's smile was ironic. "But sometimes it seems more like we're just muscle for powerful politicians who'd prefer these people dead."

Her sigh was more of exasperation than acceptance.

"I keep thinking the day's coming when they'll have us out here gassing the homeless."

Book One — Chapter 2

PRESENT DAY

Harry Sanderson and I hadn't spoken for months — hearing the disheveled private detective's raspy voice was a pleasant surprise. I'd been finishing up a deep investigative piece on San Diego's mayor and his cronies cleaning up financially from our once-in-a-lifetime hurricane. I'd done the writing, and it was ready for the editor; an excuse to take a break was welcome.

"'Darling, the legs aren't so beautiful; I just know what to do with them,'" the caller solemnly intoned. Harry's penchant for secrecy made Caller ID unreliable. But Marlene Dietrich's quotes were my guarantee I was talking with the genuine Harry. It'd been that way since working our last case together, a mystery of misdirected letters that exposed several murders.

"Harry, it's been forever — what *have* you been up to?" I asked, idly twirling a strand of hair with my forefinger.

"I keep chasing the women and the money," he answered, "but they're getting faster. Quit smoking so I could catch up."

"*You*, not smoking? That's a big change, but it's good to hear! How's it going?" An unsettling image flashed through my mind: his fifty-something, way-less-than-svelte figure bouncing along after nubile beauty queens.

"Like giving up sex, good food, thirty-year-old Irish whiskey, or featherbeds."

"That bad?" I stifled a laugh. "Sorry, but don't give up the fight, Harry."

"I'll make it — I just need to find another great vice to take its place."

"It's always interesting to hear from you, but you're not about chitchat. So, … ?"

"Well, Debra Ann, since you insist… I called wanting a favor."

"Perfect timing, Harry — just put an article to bed, looking for my next project. Ask away."

"Got a request from an old friend I trained with at the academy. He contacted our Boston office to inquire about security for his son. The kid's gotten himself tangled up in something pretty crazy.

"There've been some changes in his life recently, and he wants to extricate himself from his present situation. He anticipates having problems doing that. I've looked into parts of it, but the boy's very independent — former Navy intelligence — thinks he can handle it himself. I'm not so sure.

"We'll protect the son, with or without the boy's help. I'm concerned about the narrative he's telling us. If his account's true, I'll keep him safe for the short term, but I think the kid's longevity depends on getting his story out. You're the best investigative reporter I know. For publishing this to work protecting my client's interests, the writer has to have an audience and credibility."

"What's he saying?" I was intrigued.

"I don't want to get it wrong in the retelling; I'll just say it's a doozy, and I've seen it all. Would you meet the young man and listen to what he says? Nothing more than that."

"Color me sold, Harry." Curiosity alone made me eager to do it. "I'd never question your judgment about a case. You've been up to your elbows in some bizarre things. If this is one of those, so be it. When and where?"

"The subject's sister is getting married in Oceanside. That's the cover he'll need for the three of us to meet. There's enough time for an introduction, not much more. The client will make the arrangements. Just let me know what you need.

"We've got a safe house near San Marcos — I don't want him spotted around my office. I'll drive us there and return you when we finish. We'll have a chance to catch up and talk about how the interview went heading home."

"Any precautions I should take?"

"No, I have a man in the house and two in the residence across the street. I'll make the introductions and remain for the duration."

"Okay, Harry… when?"

"Does next Tuesday work?"

"That'll be fine — it'll be good to see you again."

Hanging up, I reflected on how things had changed since I'd last seen Harry, especially in my personal life.

***

It was three months ago when I first noticed the stranger. I'd come in from the rain through my apartment's tenants' entrance. Walking the common hallway between the units, I saw him standing in the doorway of the apartment catty-cornered from mine. A tall Hispanic man, clean-shaven, in his early to mid-forties, he had an athletic physique and a full head of closely trimmed black curly hair. He stood in a hoodie, sweatpants, and deck shoes between two open cardboard boxes filled with picture frames and trophies. The man seemed familiar, even from a distance.

He'd bent over slightly in the doorway, fumbling with a large ring of keys, trying to find one to fit his door.

And then came, *"Mother Mary, full of grace!"* as his keys fell, something I'd heard a hundred times in my first postgraduate year at USC Annenberg. *Oh, my God, could it be?*

The man I'd called "PJ" was attractive. The neighbor in the doorway still was some fifteen years on — enough that I was grateful I'd hit the gym early this morning. But his face had aged beyond his years, and I didn't recognize the tiredness about him. The intervening time had been kinder to me than to him.

I was a few dozen steps away when he found the right key and opened the door. Stooping down to pick up a box, he lost his grip on the cardboard, prompting another split-second of exasperation. Distracted as he became aware of me, he turned his head my way. When he did, his eyes lingered, realization sinking in.

I quickened my pace; my heart was pounding. *"PJ?* PJ Castro, is that you?" I called out.

PJ stood upright, the box still on the floor, flashing me that oh-so-familiar quick and easy smile. *"There's* a name I've not heard in fifteen years… *Debra Ann!* Well, I'll be — aren't you a sight for sore eyes!"

I threw my arms wide, rapidly closing the distance. We hugged — PJ laughed and picked me off my feet as I shrieked joyfully.

Finally, we let go of one another, saying simultaneously, "What are *you* doing here?" Again, we laughed, stepping back to look one another up and down with approving glances.

"I live here," I said. "For six years since my divorce."

"Ahh, I see. Me too," PJ replied. "I mean about the divorce, not living here. Everyone calls me Paul now — *nobody* knows I got locked out of the dorm in the 'Mission: Impossible' pajamas Mom packed for me."

I couldn't help but smile at his infectious grin.

"So, what brings you here?"

His expression quickly turned serious. "Things went south in a hurry when Suzanne and I split. Finding a place in this town is hard — I spent a year in a real dump. This apartment was the first nice, affordable place available; the landlord signed the lease yesterday."

Suddenly, I regretted the wind and rain outside making a mess of my hair.

"I'm so sorry your marriage ended." I wanted to sound sincere even if I didn't mean it.

"One of those things. Our situation would be hard to understand if you weren't in it. The important part is that our daughter, Cindy, has had cancer for four years. She's in Stage 4 now, but she's a real fighter. You'd like her."

"Oh, no." My stomach suddenly tightened, and I felt a flush of guilt that hearing of Paul's failed marriage had pleased me.

The vitality had suddenly gone from his face, revealing an emptiness in his eyes I'd never seen those many years ago. But I *had* seen that look in my bathroom mirror for months after Dad passed. I recognized the signs of profound sadness, even desperation. I knew of only one thing that could help — I could sense it'd been some time since anyone listened to what Paul wanted to say.

"You tell yourselves you won't let it come between you, but it does." Paul's eyes went toward the far wall as he bit his lower lip.

"When they first told us her cancer was gastrointestinal. They hadn't caught it quickly enough. The fight's been debilitating and drawn out, for Cindy, of course, but also our marriage. The downward spiral it causes is beyond anything you can prepare for. Cindy's young; she surprises you with her toughness, so you have moments when you think it'll improve.

"And then it doesn't.

"One day, in the middle of another running argument, Suzanne screamed that she couldn't stand my face anymore. And that was that. I doubt she meant it the way it sounded. But I'd become just another daily reminder of Cindy's suffering and the unfair, bad things that had invaded our lives."

I couldn't process his words quickly enough to avoid an awkward moment.

"Oh, I apologize; what am I thinking?" Paul shook his head. "We used to talk about everything, just you and me. I forgot where I was. My bad.

"I wanted to say I'm so happy to see you and ask how you've been. Can you stay a moment to share what's been happening with you? The furniture hasn't come yet, and all I have are folding chairs, but I have a Keurig and some Styrofoam cups in the kitchen…."

"You won't believe this," I said, pointing with my finger, "but my home sweet home is the next door down."

Paul didn't miss a beat. He threw his hands up in mock surrender, saying, "I swear, Officer, I wasn't stalking her; really, I wasn't!"

Putting my hand over my forehead, I shook my head, chuckling.

"Look, you were in the middle of something here." I glanced down at the boxes on the floor. "Why don't you finish what you're doing? That will give me time to straighten up the joint, and you can come over for coffee. We can talk then."

"Sounds like a splendid plan." Paul seemed enthused by the prospect. "Give me a half-hour, and I'll knock on your door."

"Catching up will be fun." I grinned. "I still drink that Italian roast you used to like — I'll put on a fresh pot."

⁂

PJ — short for either "Paul James" or "pajama bottoms," depending on whether you knew that story — was six months older than me. He'd taken a semester off after high school to consider his options, eventually signing up to join Navy ROTC. He chose Cal State LA, eventually getting his master's degree in criminalistics.

I was in the second semester of pursuing my master's in journalism. Introduced by a mutual friend, we began dating the day we met, and it lasted a year and a half. We spent most of our relationship sharing a tiny apartment off the 101 near the Los Angeles River, which split the distance between our campuses.

Old memories flooded my brain as I straightened up for Paul's visit. As I checked the kitchen counters for crumbs, an insignificant thought, apropos of nothing, made me smile. Paul taught me to toss my tub of ice cream in the microwave for thirty seconds to give it a velvety smooth texture, something I still do. Little things truly matter.

For me, our time together had epitomized not knowing how good you have it until it's gone. When I got my offer from the *Union-Tribune* in San Diego, the Navy shipped Paul off to Annapolis for his post-ROTC tour of duty at their service academy. We were deeply in love, so of course, I was despondent, crying for weeks. We made promises to see each other when we could.

But life got in the way, and it just didn't happen. In my naïve heart, I comforted myself with the belief that surely another relationship would come my way once the sadness ended. It'd be different, of course, but uniquely wonderful in its own right.

I've learned since that wasn't a reasonable expectation, even in theory. Truth hurts — my next long-term relationship ended in three broken teeth and a radial fracture of my right arm. My attacker spent two months in the hospital, courtesy of three construction workers employed by my father.

For me, Paul would become that one who got away, or so I thought — something I'd long ago filed under life's lessons learned.

Perhaps that class wasn't over yet.

Book One — Chapter 3

THREE MONTHS AGO

My head was giddy; still, I was a little nervous hearing Paul's *tap-tap-tap* on my door. Quickly glancing in the hallway mirror, my choice of a black sweater and tan slacks pleased me — my figure looked almost as trim as a decade and a half ago. The legs he once adored were still as long and slender as ever. The freckles may have faded, but the smile on my face would cover for the sinister beginnings of crows' feet.

Hugging again when I invited him in reminded me how broad his shoulders were. We took positions on either end of my couch, and I poured out java from the service on the coffee table. Out of practice from when we'd finish each other's sentences, both of us tried to start the conversation together. I relented.

"You've done well." Paul pushed up the sleeves of his gold cable-knit sweater to just below the elbows. "Looks like you've taken good care of yourself." He chuckled as I blushed. "I've followed your career. You did some fine work at the *Union-Tribune*, but you've blossomed since you went solo.

"Your pieces about the serial killer James Seaver and his cohorts were page-turners. The idea of you damn near getting killed — twice — freaked me out. I never saw that side of you all the time we were together. But once I realized you were okay, I ran around the office for weeks afterward, telling everyone you used to be my girlfriend!"

He winked, his smile wide.

"So, what's been happening that the public doesn't know?"

"Well, we lost Mom six years ago, Alzheimer's. Dad passed almost two years ago from pancreatic cancer. Before he left us, he'd found letters lying around the grounds while visiting Mom at her resting place. That's how the Seaver story started."

"I'm sorry to hear they're gone." A look of genuine compassion crossed Paul's face. Paul had the kindest eyes, his black eyebrows a little higher in the middle than at the ends, giving him the natural look of someone paying attention. When he showed sorrow, I wanted to comfort him. But his face brightened as he tapped into old memories.

"Your parents were always good to me. Remember the first time they visited you after we rented that little apartment? Your friend Lindsay let you borrow her dorm room and make it look like you lived there. But your dad wasn't having it. Your parents were so cool with us living together once we 'fessed up."

Those memories were food for the soul.

"Mom and Dad both liked that you looked out for me while I was away from them. They assumed we'd tie the knot someday and make them some grandkids. Greatest parents ever, but they kept to the traditional values."

I grinned as a remembrance streaked through my mind.

"Mom had a lucid moment near the end and blurted out in front of me, Dad, and her caregivers, 'Paul looks so damned sexy in his uniform!' Then she nudges me with her elbow, giving me this over-the-top wink. Not sure who was more surprised, me or Dad…."

"You were pretty hot yourself in college." Paul had a sly smile, raising and lowering those long lashes I've always thought were *so* cute. "I see you still have it going on. You've kept the same slinky shape I couldn't get over back then. I know you're independent by nature — one thing I've always liked about you — but I thought you'd have settled down with someone."

"There've been opportunities," I said in a lilting voice, giving him a coy look, then going solemn.

"But ten years after you left for Annapolis, I felt that biological clock ticking. Doctors hadn't diagnosed Mom yet, but Dad and I knew something was off, and it wasn't improving. There were a lot of rationalizations. I thought I should be more responsible and, using your words, 'settle down' to please her. You bargain with yourself, trying to stave off facing the truth."

"Something close to that brought me and my ex together." Paul rested his elbows on the knees of his jeans. "Though I've no regrets, even with Cindy's challenges. I assume you found someone to help with your little sperm-and-egg experiment?"

"I met a guy through a social function at the paper. I knew it wasn't ideal. Still, I thought about the success of arranged marriages in Asia. I figured the rough edges would smooth out with a little work and patience. And I had my career, which, in retrospect, mattered to me most. So, what would it hurt to roll the dice?"

Paul nodded.

"The military can be like that — a safety net letting you try new things, so long as you paint within the lines."

Honesty required touching on a less pleasant topic.

"I can't remember you and me ever raising our voices in anger at one another when we were together. I was so spoiled. I had no clue what abusive relationships looked like, even when I found myself in one. Your lover hits you once under stress. You make excuses for him and blame it on the situation; he profusely apologizes and makes amends. You don't realize it's a cycle until it comes back around. Let's say it ended badly."

I still knew Paul well enough to understand the protective side of his nature. Now wasn't the time to upset him with the details.

"By the time everything healed, I was too aware of the risks. No one's come along since who was worth taking that chance again."

"Oh, Debra Ann, that's just not right," Paul said, a concerned look on his face. "I shouldn't have been flippant calling it an experiment."

"No need to be sorry. I didn't warn you about how that episode ended. But honestly, my experiences pale compared to horror stories I've heard and reported. I only endured that one relationship. My parents helped me through it. While it did affect how I look at the world, the important things remained intact."

"Abuse shouldn't happen to anyone." Paul's expression had turned serious. "But as you know, only too well, our society flails in trying to stop it. Bad enough, the changes the abuse forces on the survivors, punishing the victims further. But we have no answers for damaged people who can't recover on their own. Much of the violence I see on the job reflects abuse propagating itself forward as some victims become offenders.

"Sadly, the cruelty often amplifies as it's passed along."

The room went silent for a moment, and I considered the irony. The jobs Paul and I had were necessary because of the harm people did to one another. When we lived together, we'd talk about the downsides to our chosen careers — most of our work comes after the hurt to someone, the damage already done. I've frequently wished that wasn't so, but I've found comfort in knowing what I do forewarns others and helps preempt future injuries.

By helping bring criminals to justice, Paul's efforts more directly righted wrongs — stern warnings to potential future criminals. I knew those things were important to him.

Still, I wanted to change topics.

"Tell me about you and your family, especially your daughter, beginning when you left for Annapolis." I twisted my hips to put one hand on his knee.

"The academy's rigid military structure was a major change from college." Paul turned more toward me. "In ROTC, we'd just been playing dress-up. That first year at the Naval Academy was such a whirlwind.

"Once I'd graduated, the Navy assigned me to NCIS, and I got my first real promotion in rank. The military has systems, especially data, which overlap with its civilian counterparts. Nonmilitary contractors helped us navigate everything digitally, from case files to exemplar comparisons. I dated an analyst. But before anything meaningful developed, I spent a year with the FBI in Quantico for training. Mostly profiling and evidence evaluation — eight hours in class, then eight hours in the field daily, no time off."

"That training had to be awesome for your career."

"Oh, absolutely," Paul agreed with a smile. "Intense as it was, I enjoyed learning new skills. I hadn't realized how much I wanted — needed — to be someplace like Quantico. I'd hoped to return there for more before I separated from the Navy.

"When I returned to Annapolis, the same girl, Suzanne, was still there. We picked up again, but more seriously this time. When I first met her, Suzanne seemed practical, the sensible-shoes type, very goal-oriented. She liked to keep lists. But she had a great sense of humor — it came out once you got to know her. We married and had Cindy that next year."

"Dad forwarded me your wedding invitation." A slight smile crossed my lips. "I appreciated the thought, but I was heads-down in a story — couldn't spare a weekend for a cross-country flight."

"Honestly, I'd have been surprised if you came." Paul pursed his lips and raised his eyebrows. "Once we were married, the Navy moved Suzanne to another sector, and we no longer worked side-by-side. Not being together all the time contributed to our problems afterward."

"How so?" I *was* curious; I'd always considered more autonomy in relationships a good thing.

"You know me — I'm pretty independent." Paul's flash grin just as quickly faded away. "I don't need handholding when there are challenges to meet. When you and I dated, that worked because you were the same way. We went to different schools, and being together evenings and weekends was perfect for us.

"Suzanne's not that way. She's calm and collected when everything moves along like it should. But she doesn't have the tools to deal with disruptions and falls apart. When together pretty much 24/7, I didn't notice. We'd take care of the little things as they came along. Nothing built up to the point of a major event."

"So, you'd become her primary support when the unexpected happened?" I tried to tread carefully.

"Initially, anyway, and after the dust settled, she'd impose her will. That wouldn't become an issue until later. But the baby changed Suzanne as much as it did me. I became more responsible, while her emotional side came out. She went through serious postpartum depression. Still, the military and her employer provided great resources, and she pulled through."

I nodded my understanding. "That's one area where medicine has advanced, especially recognizing symptoms as a serious problem."

"Absolutely. We were grateful." Still, Paul's expression had become pensive. "Things were stable for a long time after that. We were as happy as any modern working couple with a child can be. Then Cindy got sick, the first time when she was eight.

"It was one of those perfect storms. A kid with an upset stomach or diarrhea isn't a big deal if it goes away. You wouldn't take a child to an emergency room as your first option. But Cindy was constantly ill and began losing weight. Pediatric gastric adenocarcinomas are rare and not what the doctors initially looked for. Stomach cancer symptoms are all over the map; it's easy to mistake them for acid reflux or peptic ulcers.

"By the time the doctors identified it, the cancer had spread, making her survival chances less than one in three."

Paul's phone was buzzing in his front pocket. He pulled it out, checked the Caller ID, and explained, "It's my movers. Hang on."

"While you're doing that, I'll refill the coffee." I grabbed the pot and headed to the kitchen to give him some privacy.

The container filled, I felt anxious to finish our discussion — it shouldn't end on such a sad note. I crossed my fingers that Cindy's story would have a happy outcome.

THE WRITINGS OF
AVRIL MARIA SERENE

Book One – Chapter 4

Paul ended his conversation as I returned to the living room with the fresh pot.

"The movers are finishing up at the old place," he informed me.

"They should be here in half an hour. So, we still have a few minutes. I'm sorry for the horrible timing — I didn't mean to leave Cindy's situation at an unhappy moment.

"After the diagnosis, friends, family, doctors, everyone pitched in. In some ways, it's good not to know everything you're up against. Stopping to think about it frightens you, so you keep going, clinging to this innocent belief that it'll turn out okay."

"You have to, right? What kind of a life would we have denied hope things will improve?"

"Exactly." Paul held my hand, nodding as he smiled. And yet, I could see sorrow, perhaps fatigue, in his eyes.

Please, please let this part of the story turn out well.

"Cindy fought tooth and nail." Paul pursed his lips. "You're admiring your child for courage most grownups don't have. And yet, it all seems so natural.

"Then, one magical day, they told us she was in remission."

Paul smiled again, still with that trace of sadness.

"That had to be great news for your family…."

"Yes, couldn't have come at a better time. Even so, the damage to our only child, our finances, and our marriage was tremendous. We started therapy so Suzanne and I could heal, too, knowing it'd be a long road ahead. Still, we were *so* thankful Cindy would recover; we'd have done anything."

His eyes were bright with moisture — he was looking at me as if to find an answer in my face.

"We had about six months of relative calm before it came roaring back. Probably not so much different than the abuse you described — the second coming of something that surprised you the first time seems much worse. Unlike before, now you *know* how bad it can get. It was too much for our marriage. All I knew to do was put my head down, try to work through it, and find new ways to fight back.

"But Suzanne had nothing left. She wanted to be anywhere that this thing couldn't get to her — no talking about it or anything or anyone reminding her of it.

"But not dealing with it wasn't an option for me; that would mean writing Cindy off. Quantico had invited me back, but Cindy's health was far more important. I had to pass. For reasons I'll never understand, putting Cindy's challenges above my career triggered Suzanne."

Paul broke off, his voice trembling.

My heart welled up with feelings. It's incredibly emotional to see someone strong — especially a man you'd once loved — biting his lower lip to fight back tears. I'd just watched Paul age ten years from when he first entered my apartment. He looked exhausted.

Both Paul's hands were palms downward, resting on his knees. I slid over on my short couch to be closer to him, placing my other hand over his. He folded his thumb over the top of my hand — the way he'd shown me years ago that he was comfortable with me there.

"Suzanne blamed me for constantly reminding her of negative things." Paul became more composed. "And I felt I was dealing with all the challenging problems alone. We fought constantly.

"Then I found a respected oncologist at Moores Cancer Center in UC San Diego Health who specialized in cancers like Cindy's."

"Was it coincidental the doctor you found worked here?"

"I'd have gone anywhere I had to. However, teaching hospitals associated with major universities have the best access to new, aggressive treatments and trials, especially in California. I wanted her close to the ocean, mountains, and fresh air from her wheelchair or gurney."

"Things the rest of us don't think about until we're in the same position."

"It's a learning experience. I got the Navy to assign me to the San Diego base, and Cindy and I came here. Suzanne stayed in Annapolis, ostensibly to finish out her contract. Lord knows we needed the money, but I was upset about Suzanne not being here for Cindy. Then, once Cindy and I settled and had a mailing address, Suzanne served me with divorce papers. Stone cold, just like that."

"Wow," was all I could say, stunned anyone could be so heartless with their child still fighting for life.

"This was three years ago," Paul continued. "My dad passed the summer before — I always felt guilty I couldn't be there for him. My mom had her struggles, so I didn't have much support around me then. The Navy had been great, but it *was* the military, and you couldn't expect that favored treatment to last forever.

"My résumé was pretty strong — I'd worked for NCIS throughout my military career, other than the year at Quantico. A Navy buddy got me an offer from the California Bureau of Forensics Services. I had enough accrued time to take an early twenty-year retirement, so I went for it."

"Was the offer from the Bureau's main lab in Sacramento?"

"Yes. It was tough for a couple of months. We were flying back and forth to San Diego so Cindy could get her radiation treatments. Eventually, Suzanne sold the Maryland house and moved to Huntington Beach. Her mother raised her there, and she has family. We alternated taking Cindy to her treatments, though I couldn't always trust Suzanne to follow through on her part."

"How'd you end up here?"

"Two years ago, the state agreed to loan a staff member to the San Diego Police Department when they formed the San Diego Joint Terrorism Task Force. I jumped at it, and they gave it to me — a good thing, too, because Cindy's condition had worsened enough she couldn't leave the hospital.

"That position evolved into a stable situation, helping SDPD catch up on its backlog of cold cases. I wanted a nicer place for Cindy to stay once she beats this thing, so I gave notice last month at the rat trap I was renting. That's pretty much it."

I was relieved — Paul still sincerely believed in a positive outcome.

Paul's phone had been vibrating for several moments. "Time flies, I guess." His look was apologetic. "It's the movers again." He held a forefinger in the air. "I gotta take this."

"This is Paul Castro. The back lot? Okay, I'm heading your way."

Signing off, Paul turned to me.

"I'm so sorry, Debra Ann, to have dumped all that on you and then leave like this. It's been unbelievable to see and talk to you again. Can I have a raincheck to finish talking later?"

Paul did that thing where he bats his eyes with a goofy ear-to-ear grin on his face. That took me years back to when we were just kids. It was the perfect break from a deeply emotional conversation for both of us.

I couldn't have refused him if I'd wanted, and I certainly didn't.

"I can't wait; let me know whenever you have time — I'll be around."

We walked to my door, heads down in silence. As we got to the entryway, Paul turned, and for barely a nanosecond, I wanted to peck him on the cheek — decades-old habits hadn't gone anywhere. As I realized the moment, I saw he did, too. We laughed, hugging instead, and I reluctantly let him go. Turning to walk down the hallway to his place, he looked over his shoulder, giving me a finger wave.

I could only smile back and then softly close the door.

My head was swimming in the sorrow of Cindy's situation, the warmth of comfortable old memories — and an occasional bracing splash of new fantasies.

BOOK ONE — CHAPTER 5

SAN MARCOS, CALIFORNIA: PRESENT DAY

Harry was almost unrecognizable when he picked me up at my apartment complex. His hair was thinner, and his comb-over less convincing. He'd slimmed down, and his face was not as florid as when I last saw him. Still disheveled as ever, he confirmed he was not only off cigarettes but dropped fifty pounds at the same time. I'd ask him how he pulled it off if I could catch him when business wasn't so pressing.

While driving, Harry explained more about the circumstances around this morning's trip.

"The son's name is Dennis Whitcomb — his father's my paying client. The young man says his employer has him doing things that'll hurt too many people to count, circumstances that could fall back on him. He claims he could be in real danger personally just for trying to extricate himself from the situation.

"But you need to hear the whole thing from him; honestly, you do. I think there's fire behind the smoke. Today is mainly introductory — we've got to get Whitcomb back to Boston before they miss him. Hopefully, you'll get enough to know if there's something worthwhile there.

"By the way, they presented us a new wrinkle this morning — another player. It turns out Whitcomb's girlfriend also works for the same organization. With Whitcomb acting on his concerns, she's decided to get out, too. Her name's

Jennifer Carlson; she's twenty-six, stylish, with dark brown hair, and very attractive. Despite that, she seems intelligent."

I had to give Harry some side-eye for that last little dig.

"By the way, do you have issues with dogs, allergies, that kind of thing?" Harry stopped for the light and turned toward me.

"No, I like dogs and cats — a lot. What brought that to mind?"

"Jennifer's got this poodle — cute little thing; takes it whenever she travels. She says an airline refused to let him stay in his crate in the passenger compartment just once — a JetBlue flight. So, she booked with a different carrier. The JetBlue plane aborted midway to its destination for a mechanical issue.

"Now she thinks the dog is the earthly incarnation of her guardian angel."

As Harry and I chatted, he pulled the car into the drive of a light gray, two-story stucco home at the end of a cul-de-sac.

Once we'd entered, Harry made the introductions, beginning with a young woman in her late twenties holding a poodle mix in her arms. My first thought was that Jennifer and her dog shared a salon stylist — they had the same curly brunette hair.

I realized something else when Jennifer stood again after setting the dog down to explore. Harry had mentioned "changes" to his protectee's life in our first telephone conversation. At least one source of those was readily apparent — Jennifer had a pronounced baby bump.

Harry addressed the fit, early-thirties Black male in the well-tailored business suit beside her as "Jeremy." Seeing the confused look on my face, the young man explained.

"I'm Dennis Whitcomb by birth, but the Hodin federation gave me a new identity. The people I work with know me as 'Jeremy James Hansen.' My job's so much of my life, it's easier to go with that name."

"'Hodin federation?'" My eyebrows rose quizzically.

Jeremy glanced back at Harry with a questioning look.

"I haven't told her anything," Harry explained. "I thought it should come from you."

"The organization I work for prefers that you believe it doesn't exist," Jeremy explained. "So it has no official name. Partners, associates, and outsiders refer to us as the 'Hodin cabal' — internally, we use 'federation' or 'coalition.' It's a secret subset splintered off from the Bilderbeck Group, the international think tank, just before the turn of the millennium."

He narrowed his eyes. "Before we start, I need to ask you a question."

"Okay…" I replied, albeit skeptically. "I'll play — what would you like to know?"

"We've not met before, so I'll assume some things. You present yourself well, have a profession, and seem alert and aware. I'll presume you're intelligent, well-educated, and live in a respectable manner of your choosing. You and those around you can afford decent medical care — through insurance, if nothing else. You try to eat well. And you don't overindulge in alcohol or medications, legal or otherwise."

"Most of those statements apply, or at least I think so." I wondered where he was going.

"I'll go further and assume you're popular, stay in touch with an extended family, and socialize with several coworkers and associates, personally and professionally. I doubt you're a sociopath or even a narcissist. In other words, you care about those people — some, a lot. Your instincts are to like and empathize with strangers. You enjoy people — they appreciate you. Nobody you know of wants to kill you. All in all, you're pretty normal."

"Again, most of that's true." I found myself bemused.

"So, my question, in four parts: Why are so many people you know sick and dying? Why did those who've passed go so early, so painfully, succumbing to such extreme diseases or disabilities? When did you last hear of anyone dying of natural causes? Lastly, why have there been so few babies around you?"

Though I'd expected questions, I hadn't prepared for the onslaught or the subject matter. It took a moment to gather my thoughts.

"Sure, I know people who have health issues. I've lost family members and friends. It's just a normal part of life. I doubt there are more or less of those things in my circle than anyone else's. Who knows how many babies were *supposed* to be around me?"

"Hold on to those thoughts, Ms. Wynn. Those shared general experiences are crucial to what's going on. And FYI, that much suffering surrounding you is *not* 'normal' for someone your age."

What's this guy peddling — happiness insurance? I accepted long ago that life is not perfect; I make my living by reporting bad things to the world.

"Just what's the point you're trying to make, Jeremy?" I posed my challenge straight up, finding the subject matter irritating. Death wasn't a comfortable thought in the context of Paul's circumstances and not the topic I'd choose for introductions.

I glanced at Harry, but his face was uncharacteristically stoic. Jennifer's had that forced smile spouses display to hide boredom hearing the same spiel too many times.

"The point, Ms. Wynn," Jeremy replied confidently in the face of my doubts, "is I know the 'whys' to my first questions and the reasons behind the last.

"I also understand why the questions annoy you. They connect to things bothering you in the back of your mind, things you'd rather not deal with. That preference to avoid harsh realities, even when obvious, is part of the human psyche. The shared reluctance — some would say 'denial' — is a reason you know nothing of the coalition or what we do."

Perhaps not insurance, but I'm getting a feeling Jeremy's selling me a bill of goods.

His self-assuredness was grating on me. Still, something he'd said had caused a chill to run through me, and I couldn't explain why.

"Jeremy, as you said, you don't know me. That includes what I think or believe. So, let's hear it – what is this 'cabal,' and what purpose does it serve?"

"The Hodin federation's entire reason for being is to depopulate the planet to save humanity from itself." Jeremy paused, seeming to study my reaction.

He met my moment of silence by expanding his statement.

"They created the conditions behind the questions I asked you. They support and constantly develop more challenges to human survival. They've been doing it for more than two decades now."

He'd caught me completely unprepared for his revelation, and I'm sure my face showed my surprise — and disappointment.

I'm supposed to believe there's some sinister plot against humankind? That's *what we're all here for?*

I looked over at Harry, who raised both palms upward, arching an eyebrow as he offered a crooked smile. Yet I sensed he was toying with me — there *had* to be more to this. And yes, on first impression, Jeremy appeared intelligent, earnest, and self-aware, even if a little presumptuous.

But still…

"I've heard the conspiracy theories for years." I made my resistance obvious. "Look, I don't mean to offend you, but I write off that kind of thing to the nutzoid MAGA and QAnon crowd. Those contrivances always seem to involve some fringe group lurking in the shadows to kill off a bunch of people. The group wants you to believe they're preventing a disaster they claim would be worse than everyone living. At first blush, that's hard to deal with seriously."

"No offense taken, Ms. Wynn. I don't doubt that's how it looks from thirty thousand feet up — the first time I heard it, I thought the speaker was off-the-wall bonkers. Even after working there for a while, I sometimes wondered what the hell I'd gotten into.

"But the devil's in the details. For three years, the last one spent in the trenches, I've seen these things through my own eyes. And the facts visible at ground level paint a much different picture — depopulation is real. It's gaining traction daily."

I pursed my lips, unmoved.

"Unless you're living in an igloo on the North Pole," Jeremy continued undeterred, "you've been affected by the Hodin federation's behaviors. You don't realize just how much.

"Whether you see it or not, Ms. Wynn, you've lost loved ones and friends and acquaintances way too early to all kinds of cancers, dementia, diseases, strokes, organ failures, and technological threats. The Hodin federation is a big part of 'why,' and their capabilities grow daily."

There was no way I'd fall in with an elaborate fabrication. Still, I had to admit that, for just a moment, a slide show of everyone in my life who'd suffered or moved on prematurely flashed through my mind: my little brother Eddie's unstoppable brain tumor. Mom's dementia and Dad's pancreatic cancer; Marci's loss of a breast; Cindy's battles fighting adenocarcinoma. A dozen friends and coworkers lost to aggressive diseases with long names.

Common sense quickly reeled me back in — anything behind Jeremy's claims would have to be of enormous scale and yet unseen; at its core, an oxymoron. *I'm out in the world every day. Yet, I've not once heard of anyone treating depopulation as anything other than a sick joke.* That I could be completely unaware of anything *real* struck me as ridiculous; I quickly shook off my twinge of genuine concern.

Feeling a little sheepish, I returned to the conversation in full doubting Thomas mode.

"You can call me Debra Ann, Jeremy. I'll give you that depopulation would make for an interesting conversation.

"But honestly, it'd be an enormous climb to convince me. And that's only a quarter of the battle. I've been doing investigative work for close to twenty years now. Even if I could prove this cabal's existence and its nefarious intent and behaviors, I've no clue how to get the average reader to buy into something like that on my say-so."

As I spoke, I persuaded myself I was on a fool's errand, ever-so-briefly questioning whether I'd misplaced my trust in Harry's judgment. Still, I'd get paid for this and had several hours to kill. I might as well take in whatever craziness Jeremy put forth.

Suddenly, the little brown poodle at Jennifer's side barked sharply. The dog's coal-black eyes glared at me in reproach.

I grinned back. "I didn't mean to ignore you," I apologized to the little pooch, my glance up at Jennifer contrite. "Or you, Jennifer. The premise was so engaging I lost my manners. Now, who's this?" I knelt and offered the back of my hand for the dog to sniff.

The young woman's shoulders relaxed, her smile gracious. "This is Danny Boy — he keeps me safe whenever Jeremy's not around.

"Thanks for coming today to hear what we have to say."

"You're most welcome. Oh, and I see congratulations are in order. If I may ask — how far along?"

"Sixteen weeks." Jennifer beamed.

"Oh, my – do you know yet if it's a boy or a girl?"

"She's on our team." Jennifer winked at me with a wide smile. "We just had the ultrasound Tuesday." Her expression turned solemn.

"She's one of the reasons we need your help."

"I'm here to see what I can do about that. I must confess that I wasn't expecting to see a couple so youthful and full of life discussing eliminating people from the Earth. And with a little one coming…"

Jennifer's face colored. "In college, I was into that altruistic make-the-world-a-better-place vibe. A friend laid out the Hodin proposition as an intellectual matter. There was no mention of harming or killing anyone perforce; it was more like prevention — getting people to stop bringing unwanted children into a world that has too many of them. I know that seems naïve now that we need protection from them eliminating *us*."

"Oh, I get the attraction — as a philosophy, unmindful of the blood and gore," I mused. "And I certainly understand why you'd feel differently now. What's your role with the cabal?"

"I serve the federation as a recruiter and facilitator. Until I met Jeremy, I never thought about the ugly parts. Out of sight, out of mind.

"The federation's operations have grown — existing member recommendations don't generate enough help. They need to bring in, incentivize, and educate new members chosen from the public without sacrificing coalition secrecy. My job is to scope out a candidate's trustworthiness, character, and motivations. If those pass muster, I approach them with my pitch."

"The Hodin cabal has recruiters? Hmmm. Not just a few guys out in the desert wearing aluminum foil hats, then…. "

"You're going through the viewpoint adjustments we all had to make," Jennifer said generously. "Once a candidate's committed to the federation's mission, I set them up in their new role. I assist with the logistics — getting them acclimated in their new identities, moved if necessary, and into new homes and cars."

"Aliases? Relocation? *Seriously?*"

Jennifer and Jeremy both nodded.

I was starting to think maybe I'd had the wrong take. The idea of large numbers of people organizing to pursue something can be newsworthy by itself, even if that "something" makes no sense. I shot Harry a look of apology for the thought that he'd lost his ever-loving mind, and he nodded sagely back at me.

"Is that how the two of you met?"

"In a way," Jeremy replied. "Technically, Jennifer didn't recruit me. I was already working for the coalition's security team. That was more of a straight forty-hour-a-week job. I met Jennifer while on the clock three years ago. Eventually, she talked me into and set me up with an embedded assignment. I work in a federation partner company's chemistry research lab. We've been dating ever since."

"We tried to keep our relationship secret," Jennifer put in. "But we've been together long enough that people in the organization know." She looked down at her tummy. "And now, of course…"

Crouching down, Jennifer stroked Danny Boy's dark fur — he seemed her go-to for stress relief.

"If Jeremy leaves or openly disagrees with them, they'll come after me, too. The coalition represents the same threat to me as to Jeremy." She straightened up, catching her boyfriend's eye.

"We don't need to remain standing for this," Harry interjected. "This will likely become a long and interesting conversation. Why don't we take our seats and get comfortable?"

I wanted to know how tenuous the young couple's situation was. "Why can't you simply walk away?" I asked as Harry ushered us into the living room.

Jeremy shook his head. "Because of our roles in the federation, who we work with, and what we know, they'd never just let us go. We may have already attracted suspicion."

We settled on the sofa and matching wingback chairs.

"What's the immediate upshot?" I wanted to know the urgency.

Jeremy's expression was forthright.

"I think our lives are in extreme danger. Every instinct the military honed in me says they'll kill us."

THE WRITINGS OF
AVRIL MARIA SERENE

Book One — Chapter 6

Our host had arranged the wingback chairs in a semicircle facing the couch in the center of the living room.

We were seated in pairs across from each other; Jennifer held Jeremy's hand on the sofa, with Danny Boy in her lap. Harry sat in the chair next to me, which, given death threats as a context, felt comforting — more so in a room darkened by heavy drapes. Those covered the picture window near the front door to provide security.

Jeremy's last comment had dampened the conversation, and I set up my digital audio recorder in silence before starting my formal interview.

"I'm here because Harry's concerned there's truth in what you believe, and your survival depends on getting your story out." I looked Jeremy in the eye. "Harry doesn't get these things wrong."

I hope.

Almost as though he'd heard my last thought, Harry narrowed his eyes and cocked his head.

I half-smiled before continuing. "Please explain why you feel threatened and the nature of that threat. You mentioned you're an embed with one of the cabal's partner businesses. How does your job inform you about the cabal's wider activities or put you in danger?"

"The partner gig is the lesser of two positions I hold in the federation," Jeremy explained. "The second job poses the more significant threat — I assist one of the most powerful men in the coalition, John Masters. Only the founder's council has more say about the federation's operations. He calls himself a manager. That title belies how much influence John has over the federation's daily activities.

"I doubt they meant it to be that way; it's something that evolved. My role touches everything he does. I don't have the authority he has to act on my accumulated knowledge. But merely knowing makes me a risk for the coalition under the right conditions."

"And because I know the real identities of some of the members," Jennifer added, "and we're in a relationship, Jeremy's potentially a bigger threat, making me a target, too."

Harry jumped in, his face showing genuine concern. "That added component, the ability to ID the players, is a bigger security issue than any other element. The cabal would consider that threat existential."

I chewed on my upper lip, acknowledging the new twist.

"You believe those conditions have become 'right,' or soon will?"

Jeremy nodded. "Recently, I've sensed things are changing. Something's up with John; I think his relationship with the federation is about to go south. Maybe he's acted against the coalition's interests or is about to.

"But leaving the federation and breathing are mutually exclusive. And anything negative John does, or the coalition does to him, reflects directly back on me because of my position and what I know."

He exchanged a worried look with Jennifer.

"You'd have to understand how the federation works and what John does to appreciate the danger I'm in."

"Could I contact John Masters for verification later, if necessary?"

Jeremy's face blanched, and there was panic in his voice. "Oh, no — you'd likely get both of us and yourself killed, and sooner rather than later."

"That's one of our challenges." Jennifer's face showed she was distressed. "Ask questions of a real-world actor behind a cabal pseudonym, especially those involving Jeremy's work, and the Hodin federation will assume *I* gave up the member's information."

"Understood. I presumed confirmation was unlikely, but my role here requires that I ask. Reporters always want validation, occupational hazard."

I was eager to get back to less menacing topics.

"I know of the Bilderbeck Group. Over the years, I've heard rumors about powerful members of the think tank itself depopulating the planet in evil ways. I've not heard of an independent entity formed specifically to manage the Earth's human numbers. How did this Hodin cabal originate?"

"As you mentioned, depopulation's been an undercurrent within the Bilderbeck Group for ages." Jeremy seemed calmer. "Usually, it comes up as something tactical and purpose-driven."

"In college," Jennifer offered, "they presented it as a way to reduce poverty worldwide."

I nodded, and Jeremy continued. "Reducing large populations weakens a country's military power; less cannon fodder for India or mainland China to throw into a conflict. Something the U.S. learned in Korea when McArthur foolishly crossed the Yalu River, chasing the North Koreans into China. The sheer number of troops the Chinese pushed onto the battlefield, pumped up by nationalist fervor after defeating Chiang Kai-shek, overwhelmed him."

"But the depopulation I know of has been internal to a country." I wondered if I'd missed something. "Pol Pot and other genocides, or the Chinese voluntarily adopting their one-child policy."

"And the Chinese doing that on their own," Jeremy jumped back in, "pushed depopulation discussions within the Bilderbeck Group to the back burner for decades."

"So, why the formation of the Hodin cabal?"

"Ours is a greed-driven world," Jeremy replied, "so the stimulus for that was the bursting of several financial bubbles, beginning in July 1997 with the collapse of Thailand's currency. That event flagrantly exposed the flaws in wealthy Western markets. It surprised the U.S. and Europe that Asian economies had grown so large."

"In their internal communications," Jennifer interjected, "they're careful to rationalize depopulation using other concerns — restoring the ozone layer, drought in Africa, pollution, and, especially lately, global warming."

After watching her as she spoke, Jeremy returned to me. "A small set of world leaders realized that minimizing global population would solve all these problems in one fell swoop.

"And I'm sure it's no coincidence that reduction makes it easier for people with power to control those who have none. I didn't think about that until recently, but it bothers me."

"So, that subset within Bilderbeck became the Hodin cabal?" I asked; I'd revisit his new concerns later.

"Eventually," Jeremy replied. "There was serious conflict within the Bilderbeck Group about the idea. That encouraged supportive members to split off, secretly creating the Hodin federation to pursue their ideology independently."

"Can you describe their core beliefs? Those that inform cabal management's decisions, actions, and goals?"

"Stripping out the effects of modern technology," Jeremy explained, "and ignoring the powdered wigs and the preference for parfum over bathing, the federation considers the pinnacle of human achievement to be the historical period known as the Enlightenment. Say, roughly 1750, nine years before François-Marie Arouet published *Candide,* writing as Voltaire."

The intelligence of the explicit response struck me as unusual. "You're a student of history?"

"I admire courage. Arouet was a prominent voice opposing slavery at the peak of the colonial period."

"I can see why you'd make a good assistant. Please, continue; I didn't mean to interrupt."

"The lofty ambitions to return to humanity's glory days come from positive influences within the federation. Recently, negative forces began fighting for control, claiming ancestry from those who fought in the Crusades. They hide their hyper-fear, gross ignorance, and illiteracy under the religion they wear on their sleeves. They'll leverage any excuse to destroy anyone who doesn't look, act, think, or — especially — worship as they do."

"I've seen pointed messages from members about dating outside one's race," Jennifer said, her eyes round and brows arched. "Given what they're capable of, it scares me."

"The same influences began taking over general society in 2016," I murmured, and the rest of the group nodded in agreement.

"No surprise those federation members would make themselves visible now." Jeremy sighed. "Like interbreeding cockroaches — once they've filled your walls, they no longer hide. They're everywhere you look these days."

"A subject for another discussion. Hopefully, better minds will prevail."

A silent pause followed my comment, accentuating the pervasive doubt that would happen. I needed to push things along.

"Can we get back to the coalition's original goals?"

"While we can't roll back technology," Jeremy replied, "the adverse side effects of unfettered 'progress' have been disastrous to society.

"Of those, the worst has been explosive growth in population. That growth multiplies harmful, yet otherwise manageable, aspects of the Industrial Revolution. Crushing demands on the planet create a vicious cycle, driving the need for new technologies to support everyone. The result is horrific damage to the environment and our future."

His voice became more emphatic.

"But once you remove excess population, *every problem goes away,* even if all else, including technology, remains in place! The federation wants to reset the numbers, carefully applying lessons learned to maintain reasonable future population sizes. They're shooting for a billion."

"' Reset the numbers' is a pretty sterile label for 'kill most of us,'" I mentioned. "But why one billion specifically?"

"Again, 1750. The positive achievements of humanity relative to the population had reached their zenith. The world was then home to one billion people; therefore, that's become the coalition's ultimate goal."

"From anecdotal history, then. Is there a scientific basis for that number?"

"I presume there's supporting science. But management made that decision long before I joined the federation. Coalition leaders claim that once, as few as ten thousand individuals were available in the human gene pool, from whom everyone alive today descends; the hardiest survivors of a volcanic eruption of seventy-four thousand years ago."

"Scientists have debunked most of the 'Toba Catastrophe,'" I pointed out.

"True; the tale is meant only to illustrate that populations have been way below one billion for most of human existence with the gene pool remaining robust."

"In our economic system, you'd still need human bodies for labor," I mused, "and consumer markets to sell into, right?"

Jeremy's look was dismissive.

"Computers, robotics, 3-D printing, hydroponics, genetic engineering, and artificial intelligence have advanced to where enslaving people, virtually or literally, to perform work makes no sense economically. Feeding and housing the uneducated to perform labor was failing as a model long before the Civil War."

"I'll give you that. But regardless of how things get produced, somebody's got to buy them…."

"Plenty of markets are available in and between a billion people," Jeremy replied. "But capitalism as we practice it today — nothing more than unfettered greed — doesn't function well without new markets or undiscovered resources. 'Growth,' what supporters call the avarice that capitalism relies upon, is cancerous to a closed system — gains can only come from consuming healthy tissue.

"Still, we could make a heavily regulated version of capitalism work. Economic and planetary health projections show everything scales nicely."

Danny Boy whined, wriggling in Jennifer's lap, and she set him down. He looked at me but stayed close to her. "Hush, now," she murmured. "Go on, hon," she urged Jeremy.

"The *only* rational path forward," he continued, "is to rid the world of excessive numbers and create social and political systems that prevent future overpopulation, as the Hodin federation originally planned. I have problems with how they want to do it now, but even so…."

Harry discreetly looked at his phone. "I'm sorry to interrupt a good conversation," he interjected. "But we'll need to adjourn. The men must return Jeremy and Jennifer to the airport for their flight."

Once we'd said our goodbyes and Harry and I were on our way home, I turned in my seat, facing him.

"Harry, sometimes you can be an ass."

He kept his eyes on the road.

"Now I know why you wouldn't tell me anything before we arrived."

Harry took it well, keeping his mouth shut and a sheepish expression on his face. He had to know this was coming.

"*Global depopulation?* Seriously, Harry? You could have warned me — I'd have brought a propeller beanie…."

"So, you're not interested in pursuing this?" he asked cautiously, cutting off my rant.

I gave in with a grin, letting him off the hook. "The whole thing pushes the boundaries of 'preposterous.' Still, there's some logic — uncomfortable, but it's there — behind why they'd want to do this. I had my doubts early on, but I have to say, I'm intrigued. Unfortunately, we didn't have enough time to hear their grand scheme for pulling it off. I'd want to know that before making any promises. Let's do at least one more interview and see how it goes."

"Fair enough. I can make that happen."

I reflected for a moment.

"I'll admit that Jeremy's a compelling source. But I keep reminding myself that in the early going, that's what the moth thinks of the flame."

BOOK ONE — CHAPTER 7

SAN DIEGO, CALIFORNIA

I'd have a few days before meeting Harry, Jeremy, and Jennifer for a follow-up. Meanwhile, I'd hunt down quotes I needed to humanize my next article on San Diego's homeless population.

I wouldn't have to twist Marci Robbins's arm to get the interview, one of the benefits of having been great friends for so many years. Invitations from either of us to coffee, lunch, or dinner were always welcome, and choosing the Cheesecake Factory made it a lock.

Marci needed to drop her car off at the mechanic, so I offered to drive her home afterward. She arrived first, waiting on the cushioned bench facing the check stand. Blonde and attractive as ever in a knit sweater and dark skirt, her preferred civilian attire, she drew attention from other patrons merely sitting there.

She stood when I walked in, and we hugged — I could tell she was in an excellent mood.

"Debra Ann, I'm so glad you called; just the person I wanted to see. I got my five-year recovery chip at the meeting last night!"

Marci offered me the medallion. Handcrafted by a jeweler, it featured a unique rendering of the tree of life in gold, inlaid into carved jade.

"Congratulations, Marci! You put *so* much into getting this." I stepped to the window to check it out under natural light. "Oh, an artist made it — the carving is intricate, beautiful work. Did Danny have this custom-made for you?"

Marci nodded, uncharacteristically bashful in her moment.

"Playing with it in your hand feels good... and it's sturdy enough to last until you get your ten-year chip," I added with a wink, handing the coin back to her.

"You know the best part? Danny ordered it and had its holder engraved three months ago. The chip is lovely and all, but knowing he had no doubts that I'd make it means everything."

"Danny's a nice guy anyway, and the two of you supporting each other is as good as it gets."

"He took me out boot-scooting after — I had a great evening. You and Paul should go with us sometime."

We'd arrived at the tail end of the noon rush. The restaurant was half full, and the hostess gave us our choice of tables. As we took seats near the window, Marci resumed.

"'But wait! There's more!' Like the late-night TV commercials." Her face was all smiles. "My ex increased my visitations with Matt and Mike. He says he recognizes the positive changes, and the boys are at an age where they need to see more of their mom. Just like that, no strings."

I was honestly surprised.

"Whenever I've seen Steve, he seems angry; I didn't think he'd ever let it go."

"He's been trying harder to get along. After marrying Marsha, he sees more of the mother's side. The lawyers filed the paperwork with the court Tuesday, and Steve's giving me an extra weekend with them starting Friday night."

"Okay, we need to *party* then." I gave her a sly grin. "Wanna share a slice of tiramisu cheesecake?"

"Oh, yeah. That'll be plenty, though Danny and I *did* burn some calories last night." Marci snickered.

"TMI, Marci, TMI — it's a family restaurant; little ears may be listening!" Doing my best to look horrified, I tilted my head toward the family on our left. "Any big plans for the weekend?"

"Matt's competing in a video game tournament Saturday morning. There's an old-school carnival at the fairgrounds afterward. Sunday, we'll hang out at Pacific Beach. What's going on with you?"

Our server took our orders before I answered. It was now midafternoon at the restaurant, and the clatter of dishes, bustling about of servers, and background murmur of other diners had quieted with the end of the lunch hour, making conversation more comfortable.

"I'm looking for the right opportunity to ask Paul if I can tag along when he sees Cindy," I confided. "I'm treading carefully — I just have to cross my fingers.

"Doug Stein, my old friend from the *Union-Tribune*, and his wife invited us over Saturday night for dinner. Paul's working the late shift on Sunday, and I planned on getting some couch potato time. Might binge on some of the old *Bones* episodes on Roku, brush up on my forensics."

Marci snorted

"Hey, since you're buying, I should ask what you're interviewing me about. I'm guessing it's not *Bones.*"

"I need your field experience. Gannett, the USA Today publisher, wants a localized piece, part of a series on homelessness nationwide."

I pulled the voice recorder from my purse.

"They've published articles describing what's happening in California cities people consider liberal. San Diego's more traditionalist and, some say, cruel — conservative elites have run this city most of my life. Gannet wants to juxtapose what's happening here against the situations in those other places."

"I'll sum it up in one sentence," Marci offered. "No one in San Diego city government's doing anything to fix any problem until they figure out how to line their own pockets — otherwise, all you'll get is that 'thoughts and prayers' crap right-wingers dish out."

"Marci, as usual, you have cut straight to it." I shook my head. "You *do* know I'm a writer? Somehow, I need to wring more than one sentence out of this. And I doubt that's a quote you'd want your name attached to."

I flashed Marci a grin, then turned serious again.

"I hoped you'd be my source inside the department. I know you're close with people on the street from your days driving a patrol cruiser. And the officers doing those homeless sweeps now still confide in you."

"I'll help you with your piece," Marci agreed, "but you need to keep me anonymous — too many alt-right Neanderthals in the department. To them, anyone who sees the homeless as human beings is a tree-hugging liberal. In other words, a target."

Marci sighed, her smile disappearing. "I can't deal with their behind-your-back 'owning the libs' garbage ... Most don't even 'own' the single-wide trailers they live in or the septic tanks in their front yards."

What happened? Marci's ebullient mood had suddenly faded. *Was it the topic or something else that got under her skin?* I decided to let things play out before I asked.

Marci and I met back when I, then a newbie reporter, researched my first article on all the problems within the San Diego Police Department. She was in Vice staging undercover stings, and she'd agreed to be a confidential source. The strength of our connection was a big reason the piece turned out well — Marci knew what I needed. Our worldviews were close enough that we quickly leapfrogged toward the same understanding.

To me, she wasn't just my friend but my Radar O'Reilly. Marci knew everything going on in the department — they'd assigned her as the charging documents and evidence liaison between Major Case and the DA's staff.

I turned on the audio recorder, placing it between us to capture the rest of our conversation.

"Okay, Marci, I'll edit this later, and you'll get final approval. So, go ahead, let fly as it comes to you. Maybe start with background describing the city and how it sets up the homeless beat-down."

Marci jumped right in.

"Police officers see firsthand how the homeless problem has worsened because we deal with it daily. We have the same issues other jurisdictions do with everything driving homelessness — alcohol and drug addiction, gambling and other economic problems, mental and physical health challenges, crime, and domestic abuse. However, homelessness hits California cities harder because of the beautiful weather and scenery. Those draw people who don't have — or lose somewhere along the way — the resources necessary to survive the nation's highest cost of living."

I nodded, and she continued.

"San Diego is even worse because of the conservatism. Unfortunately, in the modern age, cowardice-slash-denial, corruption, and collusion have become synonymous with that brand of politics — its extremists, of course, but also its enablers."

Our interviews functioned more like conversations, and I didn't hesitate to inject my thoughts.

"The hypocrisy of it all gets to me," I complained. "For one thing, conservatives have always branded themselves as fiscally responsible. But long before Trump demolished the myth altogether, they were bankrupting San Diego with their corruption. One scandal after another. People here see through their BS but won't hold their feet to the fire."

"That's a sore point that hits home in the department," Marci agreed. "Officers are angry about politicians using the city employees' pensions as a slush fund. They've done it for decades, and they're still doing it. But it doesn't stop there. First, they bail out their buddies, paying $100 million for a building at 101 Ash that's worthless and unusable because of asbestos contamination. Then give the mayor's cronies another $100 million as kickback contracts to 'fix' it."

"How about transferring $275 million in Petco Park debt to taxpayers?" I added. "They built the stadium promising it wouldn't cost citizens a dime. The city now owes over five-and-a-half billion dollars at high interest but only has two-and-a-half billion in assets to back the debt. Then there's the runaway annual budget deficit — over $350 million this year alone.

"I'll write in other examples if they don't come up later in this interview."

Marci nodded and took us back to homelessness.

"The city's virtual bankruptcy is one of their excuses for refusing to devote meaningful resources to the homelessness problem. And they make things worse. After looting the city's coffers, the politicians have only one way out. They raise property taxes by any means, legal or otherwise. Grossly inflating individual property valuations is their method of choice.

"That attracts less attention than raising the millage rates for everyone, and they don't need anyone's permission."

"City employees do that through appraisals, right?" I assumed the simple answer.

"They also control zoning enforcement, construction permit issuance, and policing resources allocated to neighborhoods," Marci replied. "They approve those permits and rezoning requests that destroy affordable properties in favor of replacements that generate more taxes. It's the same with requests for new construction or renovations — it's all about more money. If anything else, you're out of luck. Landowners of lower-end properties get mostly harassment."

"How does policing fit in?"

"As an officer, it pains me to admit this — but most people don't realize the department provides two types of policing, allocated by property values. The poorer neighborhoods get after-the-harm-is-already-done policing, if any, and the delivery is less than enthusiastic. As opposed to the proactive, preemptive, and protective police services given wealthier neighborhoods paying those higher taxes. Lower neighborhood crime rates boost property values."

"The city pulls bureaucratic levers the public doesn't see or consider, then, to keep their thumb on the scale," I concluded.

"When officials artificially pump up property values to drive higher tax collections, the percentage of affordable living spaces falls. Buyers at every level get priced out of the home they could have afforded five years ago. Neighboring property valuations increase, and the higher rents and taxes evict those on fixed or marginal incomes. As the evictees get bumped into the homes once owned by the class beneath, the people at the bottom rung of the ladder get kicked out of having *any* home. Repeat as needed to fill the politicians' pockets."

She paused, her brows furrowed.

"Worse, the city goes out of its way to screw the homeless. They promise shelters and treatment but renege if a single homeowner says, 'Not in my backyard!' Lip service — for every homeless shelter promised but never built, they first tear down an existing one.

"The number of accessible homeless beds keeps declining in proportion to the need."

"And the requisite mental health and other resources never materialize," I filled in, exasperated. "Where does that leave us?"

"The victims' families, jobs, schools, friends, churches, neighborhoods they know, and social networks are still here," Marci added. "They've nowhere to go. With minimal resources and at risk of losing any support they *do* have if they leave, they stay here, forlornly hoping things might get better. Some end up living outside."

"Nothing ever trickles down to lower classes in a conservative-run economy except upper-class urine." The smile I offered was cynical.

Marci nodded her agreement as our server topped off her iced tea.

"I've dealt with the housing crunch myself. Steve and the kids got the house in the divorce. When I came out of rehab, there was nothing decent or safe a single person could afford on a cop's salary. It's tough when a city employee doesn't make enough to live in the town she works for.

"Luckily, I got a 287-square-foot studio for half my after-tax monthly salary, and I was *thankful* for it. Lots of the single younger officers have roommates to get by.

"That easily could have been me out there on the streets, back when I was drinking, after they took custody of the boys from me. Just one step away. Had the department fired me rather than gotten me some help, I'd have been sleeping in my car, maybe even on the street. I see how my life has turned around since and realize I'd have nothing if just one person had been a little more mean-spirited."

Now I understood why Marci's demeanor had turned uncharacteristically downbeat, even sarcastic. I nodded in sympathy — I'd seen Marci struggle through tough times rebuilding her life.

"I don't mean to brag, but I've done a lot of good since." Her voice exuded defiance. "Maybe it's not a big deal to society, but I've put some nasty people away before they did worse damage. My sons might never have seen any of it.

"Many important and powerful people in history have been homeless at some point, or damned close to it. Rising from nothing to success is supposed to be the great American story. Assuming they're not committing real crimes, we shouldn't add to anyone's suffering during the worst chapter of their life. No one's written the rest of their book yet."

I had to respect Marci's point.

"When I see the homeless today, I think about Cindy's situation if Paul didn't have the resources he does. Are any of us that far removed from losing it all?"

The question wasn't hypothetical; Marci was only one of many people in our orbits to face down that possibility. The thought was almost *too* close to home.

"You know, Marci, I think it's the 'why' to the harassment that galls me the most. I've filled my notes with similar stories from talking to homeless people.

"The politicians make this big show every few months, rousting them from any place they sleep or gather for peer support — all to deflect public attention from crimes committed by city leaders. Merely because they exist, they're visible, and they make easy targets, the homeless get used. There isn't a park, an underpass, a sidewalk, or an alleyway where persons experiencing homelessness are safe. Their crime? Waking up still breathing each day."

"And the bullies have doubled down." Marci's expression was combative. "Think the assholes running this city aren't abjectly cruel? Check out the vehicle habitation ban the city passed in 2019. Bad enough, the law tasks police with kicking out anyone sleeping in a vehicle during evening hours — but impounding their transportation and the possessions in it? The owner loses access to the few things they have and any way to get to work, take their kids to school, or go to a doctor.

"They don't want these people to live in affordable homes, in homeless shelters the city refuses to build, in their cars, in the streets, or on the sidewalk." She was spitting mad now.

"Let's be honest — they don't want them alive, period." I was irritated and couldn't let it go without one final thought.

"A person gets caught in a down moment, and for that alone, the city intentionally puts their very *life* in peril?"

THE WRITINGS OF
AVRIL MARIA SERENE

Book One — Chapter 8

Once the waitress had refilled our drinks, I stared at the remnants on my plate, mentally stepping back and taking a breath. Our conversation had proven more upsetting to me than a professional could allow. A reporter never wants to be too emotionally entangled in a story they're covering.

"We've discussed the how and why of the problem," I resumed, my attitude adjusted. "And we've started to explore what the city's doing about it. I want to follow that train of thought. But first, let's establish your bona fides. Tell us how you've become familiar with San Diego's homeless community and how you maintain those contacts. I won't use any details that would identify you."

"They kicked me from Vice down to patrol officer back in my dark days," Marci reminded me, her tone solemn. "With my relationship problems, losing the boys, and dealing with chemo after breast cancer surgery, I'd been drinking — a lot. My superiors were eyeballing me, and I was barely hanging onto my badge.

"The department treats desk or traffic duty and homeless sweeps as punishment for underperforming officers. They'd regularly send us to demolish homeless encampments downtown, under the overpasses, and in the sports arena parking lots. I never got the sense we were out there to protect and serve. Or help anyone, for that matter — not the homeless, not society, and obviously not ourselves.

"We weren't supposed to *solve* the problem; our assignment was to eliminate it from the sight of anyone influential."

"Given the power differential, it wouldn't have been natural for officers to reach out to the people they were locking up or separating from their meager belongings. How *did* you develop relationships with members of the homeless community?"

"I'd always felt like a total hypocrite making their lives more miserable than they already were — badly enough that I finally got myself to treatment and then AA after one of those raids. Once I did, I eventually reached that ninth step — facing people you hurt and trying to make amends. I wanted to do what was right for that community and my family, friends, and coworkers.

"I started going to food pantries and shelters to help on my days off whenever I didn't have the boys. I became familiar with several of their clients — I knew their names, they remembered mine — and helped them when I could. I keep up with those who are still around."

"So, back then, you were regularly in touch with the homeless?"

"I'd see the old-timers out and about because I recognized them. Otherwise, without a connection to anyone outside their group, they tend to get ignored by the general public and us unless there's an infraction. We'd talk during those sweeps, and I developed trust with a few.

"There's a certain range of things you can talk about and find common ground. You can have an honest conversation if you stay within that range." She sighed. "But not many of my old contacts are around anymore."

"I imagine there are many challenges for them on the street; I can't see how they'd last very long. I've interviewed several for this article. They always mention the ones they've lost or haven't heard from lately."

"They're disappearing at a higher rate than before." I detected bitterness in Marci's voice. "So many are gone now."

"*You don't think this is all by chance,*" I realized, feeling the tingle of a story heading off in a new direction. "Those I spoke with, I wasn't focusing on that aspect, so I didn't catch a pattern among the missing."

"And as an outsider, you wouldn't." Marci shook her head. "You'd have to understand how it is with the homeless.

"There've always been these core personalities who've got it figured out — more vocal, still have their wits about them, fewer addictions and mental health issues. They know how to survive and work the system. They pass what they know on to the new arrivals and band everyone together when trouble's coming for them as a group. The weaker tend to cluster around the stronger leaders.

"From my first days in uniform, I've suspected city officials were getting rid of the mentors in ways that weren't legal. There were lots of rumors. Back then, I didn't consider the possibility of murder. Now I'm not so sure. So many of those leaders are turning up missing. Yes, bad things certainly happen on the streets. But too many have disappeared over the last few years, way more than normal. The others are sitting ducks without anyone they can turn to in that community for guidance."

"Have you said anything to anyone about this?"

"I started asking around the department," Marci answered, "and the way people were clamming up told me questions weren't welcome. When I passed my detective exam, my lieutenant took me aside and said, 'Robbins, you've got yourself straightened out and on a good path around here. Now's not the time to make waves. The homeless situation is what it is. Leave it be. Not your problem to solve.'

"So, taking my suspicions further means putting my career on the line. That's tough because I'm up to make detective when there's an opening."

"You know, Marci," I said slowly, giving it some thought, "I asked you here so I could finish off my homeless piece. But a journalist never wants to rush a story past the important parts. Let me ask you straight up: do you think the city might be 'disappearing' the homeless?"

She hesitated. "I can't prove it." Marci was deliberate. "And I'd lose my job if I tried. But yes, my gut tells me something's going on.

"Somebody's figured out how to make their problem go away quietly, with the blessing of those in power."

THE WRITINGS OF
AVRIL MARIA SERENE

Book One — Chapter 9

Honesty requires an admission: pre-coffee, I'm not the most desirable of morning companions. Or so Paul's gently told me, and he'd know. The date I'd agreed to yesterday afternoon had Marci picking me up two hours before I usually drank my first cup. I knew I'd need an entire pot before I climbed into her car, so last night, I set the alarm clock a half-hour earlier than necessary.

During our lunch yesterday, I offered to have Harry Sanderson or Paul run down any illegal directives from local officials meant to reduce the homeless population. That would protect Marci from risking exposure by digging around on behalf of my story. But they'd need some leads to work with.

"Can you think of anyone who could kickstart this thing? Someone who'd know specific details but wouldn't reveal their questions or the answers to the department?"

"I might know just the guy," Marci replied. "His name's Arlo Daniels. He and I weren't that close, but the department tried to screw him back in the day. We've had a change in administration since then. But he may still have an axe to grind and know some current players."

"What's his story?"

"Daniels always claimed he was under direct orders from the mayor's aide, but Internal Affairs busted him for kidnapping several of the homeless after giving them alcohol and drugs. He'd take them in his Black Maria across the Mexican border and dump them off there at the mercy of the cartels."

"'Black Maria'?"

"The Ford Expeditions the department uses for prisoner transport. An auditor discovered Daniels was turning in high mileage numbers off-duty. When IAD tracked him crossing the border with unauthorized passengers, Daniels claimed it was at the mayor's behest. But the aide threw him under the bus. They fired Daniels, but he'd been smart; he kept receipts, e-mails, and texts. The union represented him in court and eventually won — full reinstatement, back pay, attorney's fees, the whole nine yards.

"Daniels wasn't back long when something happened — I don't know what — and Daniels turned in his badge. A few months later, the Oceanside Police Department hired him. If he talks to you and keeps up with friends in San Diego, he could point you in the right direction."

If true, what they'd accused him of was abominable — *and* the basis for a monster story.

"Thanks, Marci, that should give us plenty to start with."

She'd become thoughtful as we were leaving the restaurant. "You know, Debra Ann, there is something else I can do to help if you want to dig deep. It'll cost you a day of sleeping in, but I'll buy you breakfast to make up for it."

Wait, there has to be a reason Marci's bribing me with a morning meal.

"Okay, I'll bite," I replied cautiously. "What do I have to do?"

"I'll meet you at your place tomorrow morning at five. You'll want to dress down for this."

"*Five?* As in, '*a.m.*'?" I was startled. "Marci, you *know* I love you, but there *are* limits. Me being a trust fund baby comes with certain benefits you're not grasping…."

I let out an over-the-top sigh as Marci snorted.

"Fine, say my common sense flew completely out the window. Paul's working nights, so at least I won't be waking him. Marci, this better be a damned fine breakfast. Denny's or IHOP, none of this Jack-in-the-Box drive-through garbage…." I frowned, my lower lip protruding.

Marci wouldn't need me to chauffeur her home from our lunch — the mechanic brought her car to us during the test drive after the repairs. After we'd said our goodbyes, I gathered my purse and headed to my vehicle. But something caught my eye, and I paused a moment. I pondered the ragged man at the corner with his bucket and squeegee, dodging traffic to swipe at the windshields of cars stopped for the light.

I had to wonder — would I see him at all if not for our mealtime conversation? It's always bothered me how little we value human lives other than our own, but would I notice if he wasn't there one day?

Does anybody besides Marci know or care how many are already gone?

As Marci pulled into the tenant parking lot this morning, I wrote Paul a quick note explaining why I wouldn't be there when he got home. My mad dash out the door to greet Marci hinted I might have overdone the coffee.

Anticipating a need, she'd brought me a Venti-sized Starbucks. Five minutes into being peppered with my nonstop questions, Marci reclaimed for herself the cup intended for me.

"Okay, Chatty Cathy, you've had enough caffeine — you're way too up for this." Marci grinned as she shook her head.

"So, what's our big plan?"

"First, a little background for our field trip today...."

"I'm all ears. Well, and coffee."

"... I'll introduce you to someone the homeless gravitate to. It'll be quite the education, I promise. And getting that community to trust you will grease the wheels for your story. The woman you'll meet calls herself 'Alma,' probably not her real name. Hopefully, we'll catch her starting her morning run, and you can get to know her."

"Alma? Morning run?"

"Alma's one of the homeless group leaders I mentioned yesterday," Marci replied. "She starts collecting aluminum cans once there's enough daylight to see inside dumpsters.

"Alma's something of a matriarch for her group. She's got an old pull-behind trailer and SUV. She lets her members use them for shelter when it rains and during cold winter days. One can sleep in the Caravan with her, and up to four can bunk in the trailer."

I nodded solemnly, Alma's realities counterpointing the safety and warmth of Marci's car.

"Alma's a sharp old gal — she's still got most of her marbles, with one glaring exception. Right up front, she'll show you a picture of her son. Just accept whatever she tells you. Show sympathy, say nice things, and try to get her to move on. Otherwise, she'll go into her shell, and the interview will end."

"What's the story behind that?"

"Her son was Bobby Perkins," Marci answered.

"'Was?'"

"It's been a long time. Most people wouldn't remember his name if they ever knew it. A good cop — he's on the Wall of Honor. He died working undercover in 2002, a drug bust gone wrong. If you tell Alma he's gone, she'll start screaming, 'Why does everyone keep making excuses for him? Tell him it doesn't take that long to write me something!' Then she'll start rocking back and forth. Shuts down completely."

"Thanks for the heads-up. Otherwise, I'd surely have stepped in it."

"We're almost there. I can't park too close to Alma's trailer. In that neighborhood, the gangs will at least take my wheels if they don't strip the entire car. We'll walk up and catch her outside — don't ask to go inside, and politely decline any invitation to enter. You'll understand why once we get there."

I first saw Alma hunched over a shopping cart, rearranging its contents. My eyes went to the tall arrangement of dusty plastic lilies and baby's breath standing outside the fray in one corner of her cart. She'd fenced it off from the clutter with a barrier made of torn cardboard.

For all the grime and disorder surrounding her, she devotes precious space to pretty things.

Alma was in her mid to late fifties. Her posture and movements suggested she had osteoporosis and, as I got close enough to see her hands, arthritis. Her gray and white hair was long and wild — it bushed out from under a gardener's straw hat with the crown missing. Her features were weathered and wrinkled, and she wasn't wearing her dentures. Using all the muscles in her face, she squinted at us as we approached — I guessed she needed glasses, if not cataract surgery.

She wore several layers of worn and ragged clothing. Her footwear was a beat-up pair of vintage men's hiking boots, high-top Doc Martens without the laces.

She stood near the driver's door of a battered maroon Dodge Caravan from twenty years ago, the plates four years out-of-date. The nose of the vehicle tilted upward at a rakish angle, and it wasn't hard to see why. The rear tire nearest us lay flat, and its rear trailer hitch bore the weight of a two-axle, tow-behind travel trailer.

The trailer, far too heavy for the light van to pull, sat at a similar angle but in the opposite direction. It, too, was old and dingy, with a big dent visible in the side facing the curb. Rust had eaten away at the bottom of the side panels. A faded logo and labeling on the side read, "Four Winds Express Lite." It seemed too small to sleep four people, but that likely depended on the desperation.

The close quarters were doubtless an inviting option if the only other choice was standing out in the cold rain.

THE WRITINGS OF
AVRIL MARIA SERENE

Book One — Chapter 10

As we approached Alma's vehicle, the unpleasant smells coming our way grew intense. I suddenly understood Marci's warning about entering any enclosed spaces.

"Alma!" Marci called out to get her attention. "I'd like you to meet Debra Ann. She's an investigative reporter — she'll help me find your missing friends. You know how afraid people around here are of the police. Debra Ann can get answers without scaring anyone off."

"Well, Debra Ann, it's nice to meet you," Alma said. "I'm sorry if it's hard to understand me — I've lost my upper denture somewhere, and I can't wear either if I don't have both."

She still had a sense of dignity; she seemed bashful, even embarrassed, about her predicament.

"You're fine; I understand you perfectly," I offered.

"Everyone believes we're on drugs or alcohol all the time," Alma explained. "I didn't want you to think I was."

"Oh, I knew better," I replied. "Marci told me you care for the people here, and they depend on you."

"Marci, did you tell her I used to be a paralegal back when?" Alma wanted me to know there was more to her than her situation. "It was before they called it that. But I did most of the uncomplicated legal work myself — simple bankruptcies and divorces, wills, traffic court, forms, that kind of stuff. I help when someone gets a citation, needs to fill out paperwork, or has legal problems.

"Did Marci introduce you to my boy?"

Without waiting for an answer, Alma pulled out a small, yellowed envelope from her bra, extracting a cracked and worn Polaroid edged with brown stains. The faded image, taken during the late nineties, was of a young policeman in uniform, a studio photo celebrating the recruit's graduation from the police academy.

"This is my son. One of San Diego's finest." Alma cackled to a joke that only she understood. "I'm mad at him — he never writes anymore. All I hear are excuses. If you see him, will you tell him to stop by, or at least write me a letter? But I know he's got important things to do."

"He's a handsome young man. I don't know him, Alma, but if we run into each other, I'll be sure to tell him," I answered, heeding Marci's warning.

"His letters might be coming back to him." Alma's face showed concern. "I had to give up my post office box — couldn't afford it anymore. Tell him to send them to the Father Joe's on Seventeenth. They know me there."

"I'll do that," I promised as Marci nodded.

Alma began shuffling down the street without further ado, pushing her cart. She carried an empty garbage bag in one hand, with another tucked into a rawhide belt around her waist. We trailed after her.

"Marci and I talked about how much you do for your little flock." I tried to change topics. "Tell me something about the people you care for."

"People on the street divide up," Alma replied. "Half of us join in bunches to watch out for each other. The other half are the loners, the ones you'd call the outcasts of the outcasts. They make most of the trouble, but we all pay for it.

"Being in a group protects everyone from them — mostly, they steal our stuff. We get support from each other. It makes us stronger when we have turf wars with other groups over good panhandling corners. We have to fight for the best restaurant dumpsters and over the cherry routes for picking cans out of the trash and off the street."

She looked around as if for an example, but there weren't any other early birds. "It helps to have everybody here when cops come to hassle us. They keep trying to take my van and the trailer, like leaving us without anything is a big moral triumph for them. Fuck them."

For a split second, I was surprised, maybe even frightened, by something I hadn't expected. In Alma's brief flash of defiance, of irrational strength in the face of terrible circumstances, I saw a tiny bit of … *me.*

And maybe not so tiny, once past the implications of Alma's situation, which promised few rewards for being her. Were it not for knowing bad things happen to good people, the thought that she and I were not so different would have driven me away in denial. Instead, I felt an odd kinship with Alma, the closest affirmation I'd experienced personally for the old saw, "There, but for the grace of God, go I."

It took me a moment to break out of my reverie.

"So, how many are in your little group?"

"When nobody was locked up, we used to have six, including me," Alma answered. "But it's always changing; the regular people I started with keep disappearing. When it rains, new ones show up, wanting someplace to sleep. I try to keep some room open in case my friends come back. But they never do."

I sighed — I hoped it came across as sympathetic. "Tell me about the ones who disappeared."

"I miss Pops Bird the most. It's tough as I'm getting older, and he used to help me out a lot. The battery's dead on my van, and my tire has a hole. I can't move my trailer. He'd fix things like that and straighten people out when we had squabbles."

"How'd he get the name 'Pops Bird?'" I hoped I could identify the man within the system.

"He's a good handyman. Sometimes, he sells birdhouses he builds from old license plates. He makes cute little hummingbird feeders out of two-liter pop bottles he finds."

"What else can you tell me about him?"

"Pops is a Gulf War veteran; got hurt in a forklift accident at a Sam's Club warehouse. An ambulance chaser took all his money to sue them but didn't get a dime back. He became addicted to painkillers. The VA got him off them, but now he drinks up his disability check when it comes.

"He sobers up for a while doing odd jobs. Then the first of the month comes, and it starts all over. What're you going to do?" Alma raised her shoulders, both hands out to the side, palms up. "When they stole his tools, he kinda slid downhill."

"I took up a collection from the squad room," Marci stepped in, "and we got him permission to store his new tools behind a restaurant."

"Pops is doing better lately," Alma said. "He got a part-time job assembling bicycles for a local shop. Pops likes doing it, and they like him. They're teaching him e-bikes, so he thinks there's a future. They let him go when he didn't show up for work. I hope they'll take him back when he comes home."

At first, I thought the word "home" odd, but then it came to me — *if not there, where?*

A frown on Alma's face showed her apprehension about Pops Bird.

"Pops and I got along well," Marci added. "He's personable, talkative, intelligent. He knows a lot of the other homeless. The jury's still out, but he could be one of the success stories coming from this community if we could find him."

"Can you tell me about others who've gone missing?" I asked Alma.

"Ryan's one of my newer ones." Alma was rooting through a garbage bin outside a Chinese restaurant. "When he's on his meds, he talks like a stockbroker. Ryan has an MBA and used to work in financial services. He overdosed on cocaine. Maybe he had schizophrenia before and hid it. But the overdose made it worse, or maybe his mind just came apart. The paranoia and the voices get pretty wild when he's off his prescriptions."

"I've talked to Ryan a lot," Marci told me. "Cleaned up, he can get a good job with references and support. But he self-destructs — starts thinking about family he lost, rebels against the routine he needs to manage his mental health problems."

"Who else hasn't been around?"

"BamBam's just a good-ole-boy lay-about," Alma answered. "Tells quite a story, likes his alcohol and drugs, not particular about either. He's harmless when he's sober. But a mean drunk, and when he's that way, you have to keep him away from the girls.

"Sarah's one of the younger ones; pretty typical of how homelessness goes these days. She was raped years ago and never got over it — terrible choices in men. She had two kids along the way; both fathers left her. Sarah tried the supermom thing but couldn't hold it together. She can't keep a job. CPS took her kids when they found out she was living out of her car. Eventually, her wheels got towed, and no money to get them back — spiraled down from there."

"What do you mean when you say, 'spiraled down?'"

"No drugs or alcohol, just a total emotional wreck; the years on the streets took her physical health. She's just skin and bones — spends most of her time huddled in a corner, whimpering. Sometimes, she'll get out of her funk and try to make an effort — a different person when she does. But it won't last long. Any mention of kids or a boyfriend sends her back into the corner. The last that anyone knew, they were loading her into a police van for loitering two months ago."

"Any others?" I flipped over a page in my paper notebook; the battery in my digital recorder had given up the ghost.

Alma's face wrinkled in concentration.

"Those are the ones I can think of where nobody knows what happened to them. Happy Fitz OD'd on fentanyl, the Cartman hopped a bus to beat an assault and battery beef, and Shifty Reynolds got hit by a truck."

Alma filtered handfuls of garbage through her unprotected fingers, releasing a cloud of nasty odors.

"Thanks, Alma." I was anxious to go. "I'll get started on this and leave you to your work. I'll let you know what I learn. It's been wonderful meeting you, and I hope you have a great day."

Walking back to the car, Marci and I discussed Alma's situation.

"You were right," I said. "Alma's as together as any of the homeless I've interviewed. It's tempting to think she could get off the streets and make it with a little help for some of her problems."

"You wouldn't be the first to reach that conclusion," Marci agreed. "But when you try to change her circumstances, she falls apart. Alma thrives in her tiny part of the world. Her little tribe makes her feel important — like she belongs. Starting over in the straight world, she loses that right from the beginning.

"I worry about her. Now and then, I see glimpses of early-onset dementia. If the group loses her, they're out an irreplaceable resource. Most won't survive."

"I caught that, too. But without knowing Alma better, I wasn't sure."

As Marci drove toward the IHOP, I called Harry. When he didn't pick up, I left him a message with the skeletonized version of what Marci and Alma told me about those missing from the streets.

I considered calling Paul, but he'd be sleeping now. And with all he was going through around Cindy's illness, I'd rather see in his face whether he was ready for further distractions.

THE WRITINGS OF
AVRIL MARIA SERENE

Book One — Chapter 11

HENDERSON, NEVADA

Harry Sanderson picked me up from the Las Vegas airport for my second round of interviews with Jeremy Hansen and Jennifer Carlson.

"Have you spoken with Arlo Daniels yet?" Harry asked. "I gave Claire what you'd told me about the disappearing homeless. You've piqued her curiosity."

Claire Brennan was Harry's longtime lead detective, now a partner in his agency. A unique character in her own right, only Harry was better at the job. Even so, the competition was pretty close.

"I'll talk to Daniels tomorrow. I'm glad to know Claire's interested. I'll fill her in once that interview's finished."

"She's highly motivated when it comes to the marginalized. I'll tell her to expect your call. You're quiet today… Everything okay?" Harry glanced at me as he drove.

"Oh, sorry, Harry — I've a lot going on. My personal life was boring for a long time, but things changed recently."

Harry listened attentively to my history with Paul, how he'd come unexpectedly back into my life a few months ago, and a little about Cindy's struggles.

By the time I finished, he'd pulled up to a ranch-style house on the west side of Henderson. The home was in a quiet, older, lower-middle-class neighborhood. I'd spotted motor homes and boats in driveways and alongside curbs as Harry drove, a testament to the proximity of Lake Las Vegas. Likely built in the early eighties, the mint green dwelling had a carport rather than a garage on one end. Its primary feature was being nondescript, indistinguishable from its neighbors — probably why Harry chose it as a safe house.

Jeremy, Jennifer, and Danny Boy were already present with two of Harry's operatives. The little poodle gave me an "I know you" wag as the rest of us exchanged greetings — Harry's men, though cordial, revealed only their first names. Taking our seats in another darkened room, this one a den off the living room, my mindset returned to work mode. I reflected on what Jeremy had revealed in our last session and chose the path I wanted to follow.

"Given what you've told me, Jeremy, my first question is the immense effort required to depopulate most of the world. Separately, the immediate threat to you relates to the Hodin cabal's structure — specifically, from your boss's role. To address both, I'd like to understand the group's organization. That'd give me an appreciation of their capacity to achieve their goals and some grasp of the risks you face." I gave him a measuring gaze, still not convinced of anything. "Can we work our way down from the top?"

"The Hodin federation's an autocracy," Jeremy began. "At the head sits the founder's council, members for life. Not quite what you'd think — if a founder falls out of favor, the coalition ends their existence, not just their membership."

"And they're transparent about this? It requires total commitment, then. But why join an organization that might kill you someday?"

"The question tells me you've never served your country," Jeremy replied.

"The answer is in the fact that so many good people do.

"They serve for two reasons. First, no one focuses on the bad part happening to them. Secondly, if they consider the downside, the potential gain to themselves, their loved ones, their country, or their beliefs outweighs the possible harm. It's the same for those who join the federation. They believe overpopulation is destroying the human race, and they'll do whatever is necessary to stop it, even risking their life. It makes sense once you've experienced believing in something bigger than yourself."

I didn't know how to take that last sentence, so I moved past it.

"What are the founder's council's responsibilities?"

"Current founders appoint new council members and establish depopulation count targets by period and region. The founders also control enforcement, fundraising, and research and development.

"The coalition uses the term 'initiative' to identify a discrete task or project implemented to accomplish their broader goals. They monitor the progress of depopulation initiatives through the topmost implementation director, known as 'the principal.' The founders arbitrate disagreements around the development or deployment of initiatives."

"Do you know any of the founding council or the principal?"

"No. Members get a new identity upon joining. The federation doesn't permit the use of real names by any associate. Communications are point-to-point through encrypted devices and methods.

"However, I repeatedly deal with the same members and partners in my work, and I've learned some of their real-world occupations and titles. For example, if something requires participation from the VP of advertising for Ringwald-Stone, his public name's no secret. But if you looked it up on the Internet, the coalition's security would be at your door, and you'd be missing by the next morning."

"I recruit new members," Jennifer spoke up, "so I know their real names before they join. I facilitate getting their alias identities and lives. Since I know both old and new, I'm at risk if they go after Jeremy." Her grip on Danny Boy had been loose; now it tightened. The dog snuggled deeper into her lap.

"A hierarchy of implementation directors headed by the principal sits below the council," Jeremy continued. "Eight top-level directors are each responsible for a population segment of one billion people. Lower layers equate to the geopolitical borders and subdivisions on a globe. The directors of the second tier down would represent countries, for example.

"Each director reports to, takes instruction from, and has an annual budget assigned to them by the director above or the principal. They allocate their resources, supervise subordinate directors, and hire and monitor managers to oversee the physical work, mainly implementing green-lit initiatives."

"Do you know how many people each director supervises?"

"I wouldn't, no," Jeremy replied. "Even between members, they keep these things secret. I think John deals with roughly a thousand people worldwide, researching and creating implementation scenarios for initiatives. But I couldn't tell you who are federation embeds and who work for partner organizations. Maybe two hundred managers and assistants work directly for the coalition under John."

"I work with payroll," Jennifer offered, "helping mitigate identity issues for tax reporting. Around eleven thousand active members draw some of their paychecks through the federation. About the same number get paid solely through the partners they're embedded in or don't get paid anything.

"About twice that total are passive members — those who donate money or other resources but don't get involved in the coalition's day-to-day operations. I don't know how they assign members to directors."

I keep underestimating this — how can I verify what they tell me?

I glanced over at Harry, who, with a slight frown, raised and dropped one shoulder.

"Is there anyone you know or a resource I can access that could tell me more about the size of the cabal?"

"Only founders would know," Jennifer answered, "and they wouldn't talk to you even if you learned who they are. Simply asking would be risky. There's no way for you to know all the relationships the person you're interviewing has with the federation. They could take it as threatening to themselves or the coalition."

I paused, sorting through my doubts. The claim a vast syndicate was working in the background meant nothing without validation.

"Somebody has to say this…." I pursed my lips. "There's no way tens of thousands of people can keep secrets like these for that many years. Surely someone's talked. How does the Hodin cabal control the damage?"

"You're right," Jeremy replied. "The federation's security team can't stop every leak. But it's like getting probed by a UFO. It may have actually happened to someone. But if it did, nobody'd buy it because of all the tinfoil-hat whack jobs making the same claims over seventy years. You can thank old rumors around the Bilderbeck Group's activities and new ones spawned by Trumpies and QAnon for giving depopulation a cover of ridiculousness. People won't believe something the media publicly debunked decades ago."

Ah, cynical but plausible, I thought, the irony not lost on me.

Danny Boy was restless, and Jennifer let him down to sniff my legs and, especially, my shoes. Tongue out and tail wagging, he wanted me to pick him up. I looked over at Jennifer for approval, and with a smile, she nodded. He was a chunky boy and was not easy to lift onto my lap.

"That covers implementing initiatives — what about the cabal's other functions?" I asked as Danny Boy furiously tried to lick any part of my face he could get to.

"Those include fundraising, enforcement, and Process Development, or PD, the unit John Masters and I work for," Jeremy replied.

"Recruiting's under the enforcement director," Jennifer added, "because the trustworthiness of new members is paramount."

"Interesting — better organized and more mature than I expected." I was beginning to understand what Jeremy meant by "the devil's in the details." I set the writhing Danny Boy down, and his nails clicked away across the laminate floor.

"That much hierarchy — serious overhead," I observed, "which means costly. How does the Hodin cabal fund all this?"

"The fundraising director reports to the founders," Jeremy answered. "The Hodin federation generates revenue in two ways. They get donations from passive members — I'll describe those in a moment. But most revenue is from cybercrime."

Just months ago, I'd written an in-depth article about cybersecurity threats, and what I'd learned in the process frightened me. Often, there was little you could do as a victim of cybercrime, and over time, being victimized by digital criminal activity was inescapable. The subject surfacing in this context startled me, awakening some of that fear. That new dimension suddenly made all this seem much more… *relevant.*

Jennifer raised her hand as if in grade school. "We didn't stop on the way over after my flight. Is this a good place for us to take a break?"

"I'm sorry, Jennifer, I should have asked," Harry apologized, rising from his chair. "Let's take ten. Fresh coffee in the kitchen, baked goods on the counter, and cold drinks in the fridge."

I rose, with my mind still on digital theft. Writing that article taught me where cybercrime money comes from, but I wondered where the cash went.

I thought, "Let's see what bad guys do with it," heading for the refreshments.

THE WRITINGS OF
AVRIL MARIA SERENE

Book One — Chapter 12

We filtered back to our seats with fresh drinks and snacks. I was anxious to follow up with Jeremy's last comment.

"You said cybercrime funds the Hodin cabal. How does that work?"

"According to *Deaver on Cybersecurity*," Jeremy answered, "adding costs of the crimes, money wasted on ineffectual cybersecurity products and services, and revenues from downstream crimes funded by cyber theft, the impact upon the world economy exceeds $20 trillion annually.

"Cybercrime funds not only the Hodin federation but also oligarchs, drug cartels, and rogue governments. Digital fraud and theft are so lucrative that authoritarian nation-states — North Korea, Iran, Russia, and China — use it to augment their national budgets, avoid sanctions, fund cyber warfare, and discreetly surveil and manipulate both friends and enemies. The money, often as cyber currency, also props up the mob, individual hackers, financial institutions, independent criminals, elites, and corporations."

"You used the word 'impact,' not 'losses' — wouldn't cybercrime negatively influence the economy? And you meant crooked corporations, right?"

"No, not at all. Most businesses you'd call 'honest' exploit cybercrime extensively — in their advertising, especially, and now through artificial intelligence, or 'AI.' Digital crime contributes to inflation, which skews numbers on the profits side, masking its actual effects. So, cybercrime's impact also includes ill-gotten gains, although ultimately, the consumer and taxpayer pay dearly. It's like Al Capone funding soup kitchens in poor neighborhoods with crime proceeds — mixed effects mean cost estimates are all over the map.

"The US government pinned losses at $8 trillion in 2023, roughly twenty-five percent more than the US government's entire annual budget. Those damages will grow to almost $24 trillion in 2027."

"Our *entire* national budget? I had *no* idea...." I was caught off-guard. Things had gotten worse since my research.

Harry broke his silence. "The fraudulent 'cybersecurity' software sold for protection is itself cybercrime."

He watched my eyes narrow in disbelief.

The detective went on, "That software takes money for products and services that, at most, sweep floodwaters from one corner of the room to another. That lack of effectiveness is by design. Stopping cybercrime would end the profits and benefits corporations derive from it. For example, the theft and sale of personal data used to SPAM you — all digital advertising depends upon stolen data for its content or delivery. AI pilfers every byte of data it uses to generate output — it belongs to someone else; AI neither pays for nor attributes the intellectual property it leverages, consumes, or plagiarizes. Silicon Valley would wither into dust without data theft.

"Therefore, more than four decades of exponential growth in cybercrime continues. You could call it unstoppable; it'd be more accurate to say no one wants to stop it. And the motivations have changed. Hackers used to show off with nuisance attacks, but these days, it's all business."

Jeremy nodded slowly. "When I served in Naval intelligence, cybercrime was a huge problem. Digital forensics could eventually chase down a hacker's access point for a single incident, but it's costly and time-consuming. Some NSA facilities fend off hundreds of thousands of intrusions *daily* — you can do the math.

"Bottom line? The Hodin federation could meet their financial needs through cybercrime profiteering alone."

So, paying for the cabal's overhead wasn't a problem.

"We've covered management structure and funding." I switched topics. "You mentioned termination as punishment several times. Who polices the coalition?"

"Enforcement," Jennifer put in. "Where Jeremy worked before becoming an embedded operative."

"The enforcement director answers only to the founder's council," Jeremy added. "'Enforcement' broadly covers anything of a security nature. Agents monitor partners and members, directors, managers, and supervisors. They ferret out and eliminate threats of any kind. Depopulation is the mission, so they'll engage wet work."

"'Wet work' meaning 'killing?'"

"Yes. Some security personnel learned the trade through spycraft," Jeremy explained. "Others are ex-military, paramilitary group members, or former police officers. Some still work for their local military, clandestine services, or law enforcement agencies while also serving the coalition."

"Your potential termination by the cabal is the specific threat that brings us together today," I summarized, "and cabal enforcers are the direct source of that threat."

"Yes, and yes," Jeremy replied.

"I get the problem with knowing identities. I understand your immediate supervisor's hinky behaviors casting negativity upon you. Can you tell me specifically why they'd kill you now but didn't, say, a month ago?"

"Sure. As I mentioned, I work for John Masters...," Jeremy started.

"That's his cabal name?" I hadn't checked when he came up earlier.

"Yes. John's probably the most critical person in the federation for getting things done. Understanding why requires knowing more about how the coalition works, but if you accept for the moment that he is, you'll get my situation."

"I'll take your word, assuming you'll circle back later and tell me the why."

"Agreed. So, something's up with John lately; some personal legal problem he can't control. I've overheard snippets — not sure what, why, or how, but it threatens his position in the federation. He's not showing up at work or gung-ho anymore about the mission, and he's evasive. I sense he's looking for a way out. But if I can see it in such a high-security environment, others can too."

"Like enforcement?"

"Exactly," Jeremy replied. "You'd be surprised what I had to do to keep this interview off their radar. My military service was in intelligence and is relatively recent, so I'm up on the latest technologies. Whatever training John's had isn't current. Plus, there are more eyes on him because of his responsibilities and importance.

"And John's a loner by nature, not the personality type you usually see in a leadership position. He avoids socializing whenever possible, preferring to engage in transactional exchanges bearing on a specific problem he wants to solve. He doesn't schmooze. His history and accomplishments speak for themselves; he thinks that's sufficient."

"Why do you believe that's going to change?"

"Human nature. His job has enormous power, more than anyone other than the founders. Members with influence in their own right envy him. They want that degree of visibility and control within the federation. John might be untouchable for the moment, but only until he screws up. Once he does, he's vulnerable — he's got no political support inside the coalition.

"I've seen these situations before — I understand how they play out. John knows too much; his fingers are in every pie. If they perceive him as disloyal, the federation will kill him for the disciplinary message it conveys."

While not life-threatening, the politics of the *Union-Tribune* gave me enough background to send a shiver down my spine.

"And whatever happens to him also happens to you," I surmised.

"I'm John's righthand man. I'm a party to everything he's touched this past year. If they can't trust him, they won't rely on me. I'm through once he's gone, regardless of whether John leaves me holding the bag."

"Okay, I get it. That paints a clearer picture. Earlier, you mentioned cabal managers as responsible for seeing work done. How do they fit in?"

"PD, John's and my unit, is unusual. They terminated our director sixteen years ago when John was PD's North American manager. John took over, but without assuming the director title — he just added the duties to his original responsibilities. Other PD managers handle lesser trade areas, generally following John's lead and adapting his creations to their region."

"And the managers for the other directors, the ones who implement depopulation initiatives…?"

"Their managers make green-lit initiatives happen," Jeremy replied. "Those that PD develops, tests, approves, and sends them. The managers disseminate products, services, and information required to support the initiative, modifying them for language and culture.

"They also monitor and tweak continuing deployments of older initiatives. They'll make suggestions or requests for specific initiatives tailored to their geographic region or politics and pass those up to their directors. Those then go to the founder's council for consideration."

"Understood. But whose hands get dirty performing the actual work described in the initiative?"

"Underneath the managers are Hodin federation members," Jeremy answered, "who come in two flavors. I mentioned passive members earlier — they primarily provide additional funding and occasionally resources for the coalition's operations."

"The federation recruits many of the new active members," Jennifer offered, "but the passive members usually come to us of their own volition."

Jeremy saw my quizzical look and added, "A passive member's interest in the federation is buying their family's way into the one billion planned survivors."

"Their stairway to heaven…," I summarized.

He nodded. "That's why passive members don't get respect. But knowing how much the federation's doing to eliminate others and the opportunity to become a survivor is a compelling incentive to contribute — it makes for a significant revenue stream. It's cynical, but if necessary to achieve their ends, the coalition would gladly assure several billion passive members of their survival. Who'll check the federation's math afterward or slap their hands if promises go unkept?

"Passive members don't implement the coalition's initiatives. A passive member might inject themselves into a pet project. But there's no compensation, and the fund-raising director must babysit them. Passive members stay outside the loop for the proposal, planning, and execution of initiatives; they're considered a potential security threat. Enforcement aggressively monitors passive members' communications and relationships to avoid leaks or misbehavior."

Harry leaned forward, his open collar and loosened tie starkly contrasting Jeremy's crisp, dark suit. "I assume that's because they don't have skin in the game," Harry surmised. "Passive members could cut ties with no blood on their hands the cabal could hold over them."

"Differentiating them from active members," Jeremy agreed. "The actives are the true believers. They're the boots-on-the-ground soldiers making all of this work.

"They're usually young with long futures ahead of them that will be directly affected by the world's problems. Often, they're intelligent, educated, well-read, and passionate, many from college campuses. They may be less vocal and less attention-seeking, yet they're committed to their idea of the right thing to do — willing to work hard toward their goals. They believe in everything this country promoted itself as being after World War II. Still, they despise the hypocrisy delivered as substitutes for those old promises.

"Active members earn respect within the federation. Their value to the coalition is in their work or access they provide to certain things the federation needs. There are tens of thousands of active members across the globe."

They are you, Jeremy, I thought to myself as I heard the intensity in his voice. *And who you'd still be if the cabal hadn't become a threat.*

"The federation embeds active members into every significant company, governmental unit, and nongovernmental organization across the planet," Jeremy added. "Managers train and reserve some to implement planned future initiatives. Others contribute daily. For example, suppose an initiative calls for adding an off-the-record ingredient to a store-branded version of a famous cracker. The active member embedded with the food manufacturer makes that happen."

"Would you describe most active members as fanatical devotees or simply earning a paycheck?"

"Some of both. The federation compensates many active members, perhaps most, but not always financially — their rewards could come as access or power."

There wasn't much limiting the cabal's reach, then. And as Jeremy and Jennifer laid it out, that reach was already long.

BOOK ONE — CHAPTER 13

Danny Boy needed out and had become insistent about it. Jennifer stood and patted her thigh to call him.

"I'll take him to the backyard and play with him for a while."

I began anew after the rest of us had stretched our legs and returned to our seats.

"You've explained the basics of the Hodin cabal's structure. Now, I'd like to get into the sausage-making — what the cabal does, the impact on us, and your role in everything. I want to learn how information and decisions flow through day-to-day operations. Maybe start with a high-level overview and drill down?"

Jeremy took a moment to compose his response. "The federation's mission has two major phases. The first is to reduce the population. The second establishes governance for the survivors, tuned to their new world."

I'd bought into Jeremy's presentation enough that whenever he used the word "survivors," I'd think of the seven billion of us who wouldn't be, giving me goosebumps.

"There are two principal components to the first phase. The founder's council lays out broad courses of action, which come to us on the PD team. We break their directives into actionable initiatives.

"We realize proposed initiatives in two stages — the first identifies the resources, tools, and methods required, develops and tests an implementation plan, and, if necessary, creates countermeasures to protect those we spare. Twenty years of practice has perfected the procedure."

"You do this by assembly line?"

"Not necessarily — projects vary in complexity. We don't want more complicated initiatives slowing the delivery of others in the queue. For example, binding carcinogens to microplastics and chemicals already in human bloodstreams is very promising — we've had early success — but protecting intended survivors from them is complicated.

"At the other extreme, erythritol's an artificial sweetener. Coincidentally, it causes strokes and heart attacks in healthy people at the same rate as having diabetes. Getting it onto grocery store shelves took no effort. It's sugar alcohol occurring naturally from stevia; no problem getting backing from the federation's moles at the FDA and WHO. We were good to go once we notified survivors about avoiding it."

"How do you put the word out if no one knows who other members are?" I asked.

"The federation distributes encrypted messages to portals our members frequent," Jeremy answered. "Members pass them out to others they regularly associate with. The coalition's managers give the information to their direct reports. We broadcast messages, if necessary, using steganography."

"'Steganography?' I'm not familiar."

"It's a way to embed secret information into something digital, say, a photo. You can pass the picture around anywhere — to the rest of the world, it's just an image. Members use a secret app to extract its message."

"Ah, I see. How many initiatives are in production?"

"We're independently developing a dozen at any given time, enough to keep the pipeline full."

"Once an initiative exits your process, what happens?"

"Work on the next stage — implementation of green-lit initiatives — overlaps the first for expediency," Jeremy explained. "The world's inability to address global warming sped up the clock. That's because downstream environmental issues affect the quality of the world we'll leave to survivors. The sooner we meet our target depopulation goals, the better.

"Once research shows an initiative and its defenses are doable, we send it to implementation directors for fulfillment prep. Once PD notifies directors that R&D is complete for an initiative's final form, managers assign that initiative to active members who put it into practice."

"Suppose everything works and you achieve your population goals. Then what?"

"The Hodin federation's second phase governs survivors and sustains population levels. Some of the 'how' is still being negotiated," Jeremy answered. "I know the high points. A single world government will stabilize the number of citizens and protect the environment. Other functions will include fixing prices and wages and managing markets."

After Trump and his idiot minions mucked everything up, you'd think the failings of authoritarianism would be apparent. Still, I'm not here for confrontation.

"So, more controlled than things are today?" I deliberately understated the issue.

"There'll be differences from our world. Law enforcement will treat manifestations of greed — any improper transfer of wealth — as harmful to the whole and punish them according to degree. Public statements for gain containing untruths or omissions will be considered attempted fraud, with severe penalties.

"Smaller subordinate councils will have limited autonomy over unique local issues. But the world government will maintain oversight, veto power, and the only military."

These statements would have made my younger blood run cold. But they weren't that much different than what any group seeking power today desires. The focus on eliminating greed and untruths *was* an interesting wrinkle.

"So, citizens will surrender what we consider basic human rights today…?"

Jeremy drew back into the sofa cushions. "Don't look now, but I'm a Black man trying to survive the racist MAGA age. To some law enforcement, my right to *breathe* is an open question." His tone had become testy. "But yes, there'd be changes, even sacrifices. Nobody wants to repeat the mistakes that caused the mess we're in today."

Seeing questions in my eyes, he elaborated. "Here's an example, something I've thought a lot about lately: Conceiving a baby would require marriage, a birthing license, insurance, proof of means and parenting ability, and surrendering the option to divorce. Raising a child poses too many risks to society if it goes badly, so the state would treat having a newborn as a privilege, not a right."

He straightened in his seat.

"That's how we treat driving cars, and for the same reasons — society must manage unilateral behaviors that risk causing significant harm to themselves or others."

"I'd worry about partner abuse and marital rape when divorce isn't an option…" I'd agonized over those real-world threats on a near-daily basis in my marriage.

"Look, depopulation's necessary because we don't respect life for the privilege it is." Jeremy's voice became intense. "Within a state treating life as a gift, not an entitlement, the death penalty would always be on the table, even for crimes we trivialize now.

"So, no more cavalier attitudes towards 'he-said, she-said' crimes like rape or any form of abuse. The state would investigate and punish those far more stringently than today. Those who no longer exist can't abuse anyone; the same is true for the other side of that coin, making false accusations."

"A big adjustment from what people are used to." I cut a look at Harry, whose neutral expression reminded me that our interest in this was to protect Jeremy's life, nothing more. Buying into what Jeremy believed wasn't required. A good thing — I'd never accept that abandoning the ideals of freedom, even if illusionary, made sense. The hope of better lives, realistic or not, drives humans forward.

"Will citizens have a right to vote?" I wanted to move on; I found Jeremy's fervor unsettling. I'd almost forgotten that perceived threats, not changes in his core beliefs, were why he was ditching the cabal.

"Governance will be through a two-tier meritocracy," Jeremy answered. "Everyone starts at the lower level, except for federation-designated appointees to staff required positions until the government has matured. The lower tier will be a cooperative — sharing community property, no individual ownership of anything, and all voices equal.

"The upper tier will be a meritorious democracy. For elections, auditors will multiply each person's vote according to a weighted score representing their economic and non-economic contributions to society. Community members suggest and appeal weighting adjustments through an online rating system monitored and corrected by government auditors, themselves subject to merit ratings."

"How do private citizens move between the two tiers?" I kept my voice from betraying my intense disagreement.

"The state will promote individuals from the lower level to the upper for good works and behavior. People will move downward as punishment for crimes if their merit scores fall below a threshold or if their work performance or conduct is otherwise substandard.

"In sports, there's a concept they call 'value over replacement player,' comparing the athlete's contributions to the past production of average players in the same position. Are you familiar with the idea?"

"Generally, yes. Are you saying that's how merit scoring would work?"

"Same basic idea. The legal system will assert the death penalty when crimes, performance, as shown by merit score, or certain behaviors cross prescribed boundaries. It will reserve some leniency for children and those elderly with exemplary past histories, but only when population levels are at or below acceptable limits."

He sat back against the cushions. "That's all I know about the federation's plans for future governance."

I wanted to hear some examples of specific cabal initiatives, but we were interrupted.

"We've got a lone female, early twenties, Hispanic, approaching the sidewalk to the front door," Harry's operative called out from the living room.

"How do you want this handled, Boss?"

THE WRITINGS OF
AVRIL MARIA SERENE

Book One – Chapter 14

The room went quiet.

"What's your read on her, Jim?" Harry hurried to the window.

Hunched over, his man peered through the blinds with a scope.

"Looks like a campaign worker, maybe a college student pushing magazine subscriptions."

"Got an N-95 mask with you?" Harry asked. "Good, put it on. Step outside and intercept her before she gets to the door. Tell her your wife's too ill to have visitors in the house, long COVID, and you need to get back to her."

We waited for Harry's operative to dispense with our visitor, Harry silently keeping an eye on both.

We heard two muffled voices in pleasant tones. Then the agent returned, handing Harry two brochures for inspection.

"She's canvassing to get out the vote, local Democratic party worker. Seemed legit." Harry nodded, and the agent returned to his window post.

"Sorry for the disruption." Harry glanced at the brochures. "Some contingencies we can't plan for." He waved an arm in our general direction. "Please, continue."

The interlude gave me time to consider how Jeremy's descriptions might impact individual lives. In the last thirty minutes, my understanding of the Hodin cabal had transformed from a nebulous cloud into something resembling the framing of a house. Now, earlier questions about those I'd lost were nagging at me. *Was it possible the cabal was responsible for devastating events in my own life? If so, how?*

"I'd like to revisit initiatives." I turned to Jeremy. "Say I was aware of the Hodin cabal, knew I wasn't an intended survivor, but wanted to live. What must I watch out for?"

The patronizing look lingered too long on his face, telling me my question was naïve.

"Let's start with what initiatives aren't. When contemplating human-driven depopulation, people imagine wars and pestilence. Monstrous. Obvious. They might equate it to World War II, which extinguished more than eighty-five million souls.

"But as appalling as that number is, the organization's goals are greater by an order of magnitude. It took that war six years to remove just 3 percent of the 2.3 billion people alive in 1940. Nowhere near the 7 billion, or 87.5 percent of our current population, that the federation wants to eliminate."

"War isn't an efficient depopulation method," I noted wryly.

"Worse, birth rates increase after major wars. Soldiers repatriate and make up for lost time. Babies result. Five years after World War II ended, the world's population had grown to 2.6 billion."

"Self-defeating for the cabal...," I murmured.

"And forget thermonuclear warfare. Nuclear winter, lingering radiation, and mutating biologics render the planet uninhabitable for the federation's intended survivors."

"Hmmm, not as straightforward as you'd think. The cabal's killing methods have to consider more than efficacy." Jeremy *was* opening my eyes.

"Yes. War's not a standalone solution. Still, localized nonnuclear and nonchemical internecine warfare by proxy has a place in a multifaceted approach to suppressing population growth. *If* elites or powerful third parties control it, their overarching interests may keep things in hand."

"Whoa, there, Jeremy." I was overwhelmed with the jargon. "Can you dial it down a little, say to a level an eighth-grader could follow?"

"Sorry, I'm usually explaining this stuff to scientists and engineers. Anyway, opportunities for regional conflicts abound; on any day, a dozen African countries are warring. Exploitable tensions prevail in the Middle East and between the two Chinas and both Koreas. Eastern European states once part of the old Soviet Union, but not yet NATO members, are vulnerable to Russian aggression."

"But those aren't things the cabal controls...." I didn't see a connection.

"The federation inserts itself into existing opportunities. When nuclear powers take on weak opponents, the coalition calculates how much aid they can give David before Goliath pushes the button. Drawing those conflicts out is good for reducing the population.

"The Hodin federation also invests propaganda and money into ginning up new rivalries and inflaming combatants."

"By 'invest,' you mean through initiatives?"

"Not necessarily — the federation sometimes leverages the Bilderbeck Group to meddle politically. Otherwise, yes, there are initiatives to amp up current conflicts and create others."

"The cabal has military resources to start wars?" I was surprised.

"Oh, no, the federation doesn't get its hands *that* dirty," Jeremy replied. "Humans are inherently both tribal and competitive, regularly comparing themselves, family, and friends to others to see how they're doing. To generate hostility, persuade a group of like-minded people to contrast their lot with outsiders they see as inferiors having more or given an unfair advantage. That can stoke envy, hatred, jealousy, even self-loathing.

"The federation has tools to foment disagreement among the poor, ignorant, or extreme, fanning the flames into wars between factions. To instill hatred, we erect billboards along highways, post pop-ups on browsers, broadcast to TVs and streaming devices, and print splashy magazine ads. These show your enemy as superior or happier because they possess, or can access, something you can't, like land. Or your teenage daughter."

"I've always considered advertising a tool for feeding greed. I hadn't thought about the larger implications," I commented.

"We use ads to promote conflicts around sore points between two groups of people — race, politics, procreation, taxes, gender and gender modification, religion, haves and have-nots, economic instability, geography, medical care, water rights, food supply, or transportation routes. And to support leaders who emulate Hitler or Trump with the capability and the desire or incompetence to kill in great numbers."

Jeremy paused a moment, letting the message sink in. I felt vaguely ill and wondered if he was enjoying the effect.

"Strategy also matters. Give one side visible advantages and then secretly arm the other. Keep things close but unequal to avoid stalemate by periodically bolstering the weaker side. Introduce more efficient killing technologies to each, in turn, tit-for-tat. Provide products and services inadequate to resolve anything to both combatants — at significant supplier profit. More accurate missile systems, but without the range to reach an enemy's resupply routes. Cluster bombs to discourage trench warfare and keep the parties moving."

"As the West did to help Ukraine push back Putin's attacks in the spring of 2023," I observed.

"Yes, a consensus brokered by Hodin federation interests within the Bilderbeck Group. A perfect outcome — emptying Putin's prisons for cannon fodder reduces populations in the lowest economic brackets. Elites don't suffer; rather, they profit through weapons sales. Even when countries donate armaments to support others, they purchase replacements to protect themselves."

I was puzzled, my fingers interlaced beneath my upper lip, elbows resting on the chair's arms.

"With no standing military, wouldn't the cabal need overwhelming familiarity with economics, cultures, and politics on both sides to start wars? Along with instigators in those communities?"

"You'd think, but no. We've got social knowledge in-house for any demographic worldwide. That data is an advertiser's bread and butter for selling someone something. The best thing misguided philanthropists do for the federation is guaranteeing everyone, everywhere, has Internet access, even if on a windup device. Perfect means to expose an impoverished group to technologies, goods, and services others have — and they don't. Stoking hostilities is a cakewalk using social media with the power and speed of the Internet."

Even the best of intentions can have unanticipated consequences.

"When you step back, overpopulation's an obvious problem for everyone." I played up my doubts. "Why a private cabal to proliferate wars for depopulating the world? Can't countries restrict their populations, like China did with its one-child policy? That seems to have worked."

"China's approach resulted in both successes *and* failures," Jeremy replied. "Socialist and authoritarian, China has remarkably docile subjects and culture. Few other countries can dictate their citizens' romantic lives, much less get any cooperation. Imagine some bureaucrat marching into the 'hoods of Detroit, the barrios of Mexico City, or the Roma slums outside Paris, ordering everyone to stop making babies — one less person we'd have to depopulate!"

"Even if it's the law of the land, enforcement's another problem," I agreed.

"Absent those issues, China rues the 'success' of their one-child policy. Abortion's legal. Ultrasounds reveal gender before birth. Chinese families prize males over females.

"Do the math. Generations of horny men run the streets fighting over half as many females. Without enough females to bear children, the birth rate drops further. So far, so good for the federation, right?"

I nodded, not sure how he intended to make his point.

"Except…," Jeremy continued. "For a country increasingly embracing capitalism's institutionalized greed and needing new markets and increased consumer spending, declining numbers are a problem.

"Beyond that, building a robust military to gain global influence requires a population growing fast enough to replace those who'd fall in combat. So now China's rushing to undo everything they did to support the cabal's aims. In the end, all for naught.

"The latter problem applies to other countries. They can't reduce their population unless competitive countries are much smaller or do the same in good faith. Relationships between countries change quickly; increasing population on demand is impossible. No country's willing to take steps they can't quickly roll back."

"I get it — that won't work," I admitted with a puzzled expression. "And I'll concede the cabal can generate and sustain regional wars. But as you said, there's substantial risk in scaling smaller wars up enough to eliminate billions of people. What else *can* you do to attain the population numbers you want?"

"By looking at the problem differently, the possibilities become enormous," Jeremy replied with a condescending smile.

His confidence tells me he's heard these questions often.

As Jeremy began to explain, Harry's cell phone vibrated. He left his seat to take the call in the kitchen, returning to the den moments later.

"Sorry to cut in," Harry said, "but I need Jeremy for a few minutes. The airline bumped his flight home, and we have to make other arrangements. Shouldn't take long."

While waiting, I had lots of things to contemplate.

"This isn't going to work out as planned," Harry said as he came back to the den. "I'm sorry we'll have to cut short our time together. The airline has a problem — Jeremy has to take an earlier flight back. And Jennifer's got a long drive ahead of her to Barstow-Daggett." Harry turned to me. "We didn't want them flying together to the same state, or especially, destination."

"This isn't Harry's fault; it's on me." Jeremy was apologetic. "I'll need to keep working as long as John's still there; I don't want to draw attention not showing up. Can we get together later to finish?"

I rose, trying to recall my schedule.

"Debra Ann, phone me after you get back," Harry said, intercepting my answer. "We'll compare notes, and if we need another session, I'll coordinate everything."

I nodded, asking Jeremy to say goodbye to Jennifer for me. But as Harry and I were walking out the door, I turned toward Jeremy with a question I knew would drive me crazy on the flight home.

"Earlier, you brought up origins. I'm curious, but there wasn't an opportunity to ask. How did the Hodin cabal come up with their name?"

"Oh, *that* — same thing bugged me when I started with them," Jeremy replied with a grin. "Hodin's a name rooted in the pop culture of older founders. It comes from a Star Trek episode, the original TV series. Some members think the informal name doesn't reflect the weight of what we're doing. Still, the moniker's stuck; if suspicions arise around our secrets, an innocuous name provides cover, hides our objectives."

"Makes perfect sense," I acknowledged. "Which episode was it?"

"The one with Ambassador Hodin as the leader of an overpopulated world. He intentionally seeks out Captain Kirk, a carrier of a disease fatal to their people, to infect his citizens.

"A means to cull their numbers, ultimately easing their misery."

BOOK ONE – CHAPTER 15

SAN DIEGO, CALIFORNIA

Many active-duty police officers understandably keep a low profile when off-duty, so it surprised me that reaching Arlo Daniels wasn't hard. I'd gotten the attorney of record's name from court filings in Daniels's reinstatement case. After a pleasant discussion with the lawyer about what I wanted and why, he passed the information along to his client.

Two days after my last conversation with Marci, Daniels phoned. As we talked, his personality came off as matter-of-fact, almost humorless.

Had ancient black-and-white episodes of Dragnet *influenced his choice to become an officer?*

He agreed to an interview but wanted to be in street clothes and outside the city limits of Oceanside or San Diego. We set a meeting for six p.m. at 264 Fresco, a popular full-service restaurant in Carlsbad.

When I hear the name "Arlo," my mind goes to long-haired hippies of my father's generation, box guitars, and slow, scenic trips on clickity-clack railroad tracks through the Deep South.

Arlo Daniels dispelled any of that. I'd arrived first; as the hostess walked Daniels to our table, I saw he was a stocky, muscular man of average height. His rugged, pockmarked face brought Tommy Lee Jones to mind; the officer projected a vibe of having better things to do and other places to be. Daniels seemed uncomfortable out of uniform. I wasn't sure if he wore the ball cap to hide his receding hairline or because he was used to something on his head.

His manner seemed brusque as we introduced ourselves; his responses were short and to the point. While not the most social dinner companion I'd ever had, his approach made the interview efficient.

Daniels took immediate command of the conversation. "My lawyer gave me an idea of what you're looking for. I'll help you, but keep my name out of it. I signed NDAs, so I don't know what you're talking about if this ends up in court. We clear?"

"Perfectly. Off the record, then."

I took the digital recorder from the table, not wanting it to become an issue. But instead of slipping it into my purse, I flipped it on, leaving it in my lap under the tablecloth. "Off the record" meant I couldn't share it, but I wanted something I could reference later without taking notes while we talked and ate.

"As I explained to your attorney, I'm looking into the disappearance of homeless persons from the San Diego area," I began. "I know five years ago you were terminated over that issue and reinstated two years later.'"

We paused a moment as our drinks arrived.

"It's all in the court record," Daniels replied. "I was a rookie. Ed Cameron was the mayor's aide at the time. He asked if I wanted to make extra money off the clock. He needed me to, as he put it, 'repatriate Mexican citizens who weren't cutting it on this side of the border.' I thought I'd move through the ranks faster. Put a few bucks in my pocket. The way he expressed it, I'd be helping the brass; public service."

"The trial testimony says it wasn't just Mexican nationals, and they weren't going voluntarily."

"It evolved, got ugly in places," Daniels admitted. "One I took across was the relative of somebody important. Internal Affairs caught my scent — wouldn't let go."

"I understand that you rolled on Cameron."

"He denied everything, but I had copies of our communications. Not enough to put him away, but sufficient to reinstate me." Daniels nodded as he took a sip from his glass.

"So, that's my first question. You're back with the San Diego police. The voters get themselves a new mayor. You're pretty much untouchable — probably not many future promotions, but your job's safe as long as you play nice. Why'd you quit? Was not getting ahead part of it?"

"That might be how it looked from the outside." Daniels dug into his food as he spoke. "Nothing changes in San Diego. Stirring the pot brings up different chunks, but they're from the same rancid stew. People around me were chatting up the Cactus Club. I said, 'Fuck no, not dealing with that shit again.'"

"'Cactus Club?'"

"That's the new mayor's secret plan for dealing with the homeless," Daniels said. "He's hired a couple of uniformed cops to be his part-time 'consultants.' Supposedly to reintegrate the homeless into society."

"How does that work?" Somehow, I doubted that it did.

"As I said, I bailed when I heard about it, so I'm not sure. Cops pick people off the street they want to reintegrate. Boom, those individuals aren't a problem anymore. Magic."

"Got it. Do you know any members of this Cactus Club?"

"We wanted to show the Court that Cameron hiring officers on the QT to deal with homeless persons was a real deal, not me going rogue. My attorney got four names before trial through discovery; guys doing what I did. They'd be the first I'd suspect. If you caught one of them off alone, you might wring other names out of them.

"There's Joel Reynolds, a rookie then. Then we have Max Martin — he'd been in uniform for five years but going nowhere; he's got all these excessive-use-of-force complaints. And Rick DeVance follows Martin around like a puppy dog. Then there's Mark Weinstein, a sergeant in the motor pool."

We both paused to eat before I asked my next question.

"Do you know who their liaison is with the mayor's office?"

"Cameron was who I dealt with … Do you mean the new one?"

"Whoever has that job now."

"Oh, that pasty, little racist twerp — they call him 'Mengele' in the squad room. After the Nazi doctor who played with the body parts of victims gassed at Auschwitz. His name's Randall Crabtree."

* * *

My first call the following day went out to Marci; I caught her at her desk.

"Hi, Marci. Just wanted you to know I followed up with Arlo Daniels about the missing homeless. Have you ever heard any officers talking about a 'Cactus Club?'"

"Sounds vaguely familiar," Marci answered. "Several officers have side gigs providing security during their off hours. A nightclub works for that."

"Probably not what this is, but I'll learn more as I get into it. When I asked Daniels who might be involved with getting rid of the homeless, he gave me five names. Four are on the force — I'm texting them to you now. The other one is the mayor's aide, Randall Crabtree. Daniels says people call him 'Mengele.' He runs the officers' off-the-books activities."

"Oh, *that* sawed-off, hateful dweeb." Marci snorted. "He struts his self-important tight ass through here like he's the chief. Thank God we don't deal with him often in Major Case, but no one respects him. Okay, I got the names…."

"Hmmm, not our best and brightest. Max Martin should have been kicked out of the department years ago; he likes to beat cuffed individuals. Weinstein's a wheeler-dealer. He always has some side hustle he's trying to rope everyone into. Reynolds and DeVance show up for their shifts, but that's about it; they punch the clock and collect their paychecks. Daniels thinks they might be disappearing the homeless?"

"He's not a guy who leaves doubt what he believes, and he says these are the people we should look at. Others may be part of a larger group, this 'Cactus Club.' I wanted to get your thoughts before calling Claire, Harry's partner. She wants first dibs checking this out, and I'll pass her these names. I'll keep you apprised about anything they turn up."

As we were talking, I had an idea.

"Could you do me a little favor, Marci? I'm thinking about making some waves. I'd be curious to see if this Mengele character shows up in the department after. Would you keep an eye out for me? It'd be fascinating to know if he's spotted with anyone else on the list."

"Sure, I can do that, but it'll cost you lunch."

After Marci and I said our goodbyes, I dialed Claire's number.

"Hi, Debra Ann — don't mean to be rude, but make it quick," Claire said as she answered. "Caught me at a bad time. I'm mobile, following a subject — if you hear a loud noise, I ran into him."

"Thanks, Claire, for taking my call under those circumstances." I laughed. "I just texted you a list of names from Arlo Daniels. He's the cop thrown under the bus a couple of years ago for dumping the homeless off in Mexico. I added comments from Daniels and Marci Robbins."

"Harry and I are looking forward to this," Claire said, her speech clipped, "and we've set aside some time. I'll be on it once I'm back in my office. I'll keep you posted. Sorry, girl, gotta run!"

Claire left me feeling we were off to a good start. I can get a little cocky when that happens. When chatting with Marci, I'd had the idea to stir what

Daniels called the "rancid stew" to see if any chunks got agitated. Now, I wanted to act on the thought.

It had been a decade since I'd done ambush journalism, but I'd had plenty of practice. The concept is a rite of passage for newbie reporters wanting to make a mark, and I'd had my turn in the barrel.

First, I'd need the right opportunity for a sneak attack. My calls to the mayor's office went unreturned. Checking the Internet to see where today's schedule placed them, I visited the mayor's City Hall office unannounced to try catching either the mayor or Crabtree. The mayor's administrative assistant headed me off.

The mayoral schedule showed he'd be attending a ribbon-cutting ceremony this afternoon, the opening of one of his pet projects. Derided by opponents as another boondoggle at taxpayer expense, the five-million-dollar "mini-park" consisted of concrete paving added to the end of a strip mall sidewalk, with a small stage, seating areas, a bike rack, and a drinking fountain. Irrespective of the politics, the venue was perfect for what I wanted. I used my contacts at Gannett to get press credentials.

Muscling my way to the left side of the podium, I got my opportunity. Mayor Gloria, a slender man shorter than his peers, compensated for his height by upping the volume in front of the cameras. He held a pair of those oversized scissors that politicians use for ceremonies like this. It seemed to take forever for the man to surrender the microphone and give up the prop. After he'd waved goodbye to the small crowd, I hit him up as he turned from the podium.

"Mayor, I have some questions about the homeless persons disappearing from our streets and the relationship between Randall Crabtree and the Cactus Club," I shouted toward his entourage.

At first, it seemed he'd push past me, ignoring my questions. But he slowed and asked which organization I represented.

"This is for *USA Today*. I'm doing a piece on San Diego's homelessness problems, and I'm confirming several reports of homeless people going missing recently."

Mayor Gloria jerked to a stop, then composed himself.

"Thank you for recognizing our progress in getting the homeless off the streets," he announced loudly, "that's what's *supposed* to happen.

"My administration has worked diligently to return these people to society as productive citizens."

"But where *are* they, Mayor?"

I pressed.

'These people,' as you called them, are nowhere to be found. Sources tell me Randall Crabtree has a secret police unit called the 'Cactus Club' taking them off the streets without any official record of what's happening to them.

"Can you tell me where they're taking them?"

"You're confused, ma'am," the mayor said dismissively.

"The incident you refer to happened in a previous administration. They litigated the matter long ago. I'm sorry, I'm late to a meeting. If you have any other questions, please visit my office to make an appointment."

The mayor quickly turned away, one of his aides inserting himself between us. As he did, another aide blocked me from following.

Interesting — he didn't suggest I talk to Randall Crabtree, even though I mentioned the man's name — twice. Seems it isn't something the mayor wants me to do.

Which, in turn, meant that I should do precisely that.

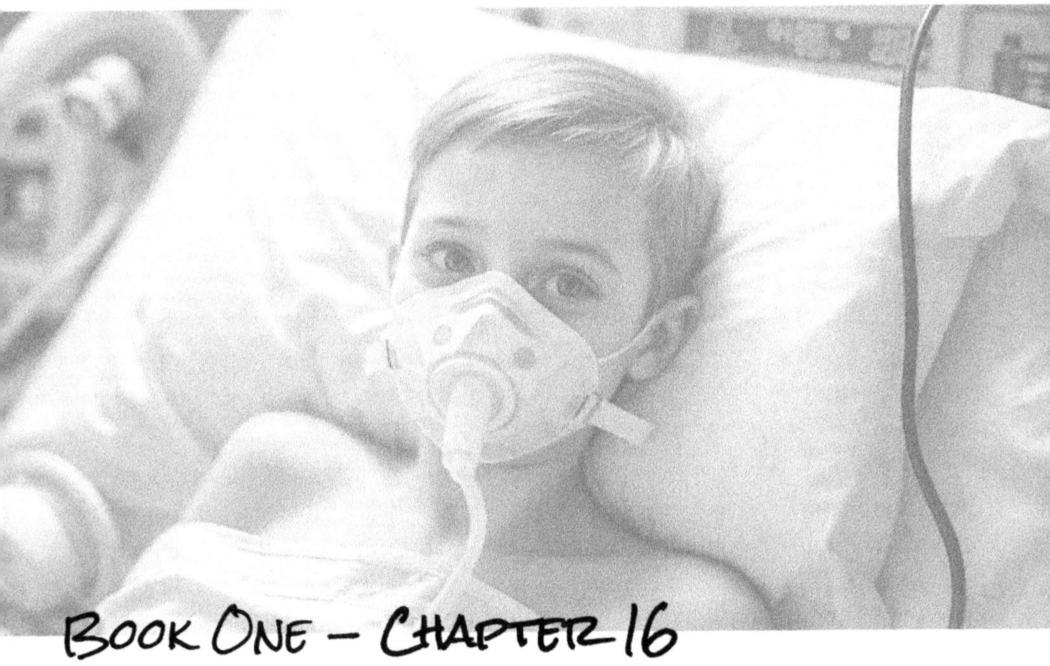

Book One – Chapter 16

It'd been a long day; I looked forward to seeing Paul. We'd both been busy and hadn't spent quality time together for several days. If he were tied up, maybe I'd settle for Netflix from my couch. But as I parked in my apartment's back lot, Marci phoned.

"Debra Ann, whatever you did got your desired reaction. Randall Crabtree came rolling through here like a Sprinter train an hour ago, went straight to the motor pool counter looking for Sgt. Weinstein."

"One of the names on Daniels's list," I noted. "Good to know."

"It gets better. Fifteen minutes after Crabtree left, Weinstein grabbed an interrogation room and went at it hot and heavy with Reynolds and DeVance. We have indicator lights in those rooms that show if someone's monitoring the audio, so I couldn't listen in. But the discussion was animated, to say the least."

"Two others from the list. Interesting... Could've been something else entirely, but it *does* sound like I got their attention. Thanks, Marci — let me know when you want to do that lunch."

I immediately called Claire. She didn't answer, so I left her a voicemail about my exchange with the mayor and Crabtree's reaction.

The calls with Marci and Claire didn't interfere with my plans for downtime. I needed more from Jeremy Hansen before moving forward with the Hodin cabal. I'd have to learn what Claire turned up before going further with my article about missing homeless persons.

After accosting the mayor earlier today, I'd chased witnesses to another story. This one involved a local councilwoman's insider trading around maintenance contracts the city was issuing. These political cases were trying — every source had an angle they were exploiting, making it difficult to tease out the straight story. But this one had legs, and I was determined to see it through. Still, I could do little for that piece until people I needed to question began arriving at their jobs in the morning.

Deep in thought as I walked past Paul's apartment, I couldn't resist looking in that direction as I went by. His door was open, and suddenly, Paul popped into view in the little vestibule fronting his living room. I turned my head to make it less obvious I'd been peering into his space.

Paul exited his apartment carrying a paper grocery sack full of books. His head was down, inventorying the bag's contents. Shifting the sack to one hip, he closed the door behind him absent-mindedly. Had I not watched him, he would've run into me before realizing anyone was around.

Extending a hand to protect me, he gave me an apologetic smile.

"Oh, Debra Ann, I'm so sorry! I wasn't paying attention, heading out to visit Cindy at the hospital. She listed the books she wanted, and I was checking to make sure I got them all. I haven't seen you much in the last few days — what's been happening?"

"Busy running down bad guys or, sometimes, girls. Glad this day's over. How's your daughter doing?"

"Honestly, she's struggling. She's trying hard, keeps fighting, but she's just a kid...." Paul paused momentarily, and I watched him compose himself even as he blinked quickly to keep away any tears.

"At her age, I should worry about new boyfriends she hasn't mentioned. Not how she's going to draw her next breath." Paul was biting the inside of his lower lip to keep control. "She's beaten this thing before, but it came back tougher this time."

"She's got her dad in her; that has to help. I wish I could meet her." I was sorry I couldn't find better words.

"She'd enjoy getting to know you, but she's getting weaker. I don't know how long she'll have the strength for visitors."

I could see in his eyes that he was struggling, too, more than he'd tell me.

A reminder came to me that the regrets I'd had losing Mom, and especially Dad, were around things we didn't do — even more, the words we hadn't time to say to one another.

I'd been trying not to interfere with the challenges Paul faced. But I wanted to meet Cindy and, perhaps selfishly, remind myself of the beauty in people. There's purity in feelings for one another during difficult times. Those last days with my father, though sometimes sad beyond measure, provided me with so many memories.

I took a chance that Paul and I could still talk about painful subjects like we used to. And I hoped sharing would comfort him as conversations with my parents once did me.

"Paul, I hate to impose," I said, watching his reaction. "But I wouldn't want to miss a chance to meet Cindy. If the two of you wouldn't mind company, I could carry her books for you…."

I was relieved to see genuine gratitude flash in Paul's eyes. "She'd like to get to know a real investigative reporter, especially female. She's a little nerdy — takes after me. 'Hows' and 'whys' fascinate her. Half the books she requested are detective novels." He glanced into the bag.

"Let me drop off my things; if you'd like, we can ride together," I offered.

"That'd be great." Paul's expression brightened. "Oh, wait, I forgot Cindy's new compact — she's begun wearing makeup, and she'll want to freshen up to meet you. Let me grab it; I'll wait for you here."

⁂

Paul's mood lightened considerably over our short drive. Prepping me for meeting Cindy was a perfect excuse to open up about her and the things that make a father proud, bring him joy, and let him show off his love.

We laughed out loud at his story of Cindy, then five years old, bonding with her new puppy and wanting to bathe the little dog. Paul described the terrorized pup, lathered to twice its size with shampoo, shredding the blow-up wading pool in the backyard, trying to escape. Meanwhile, a giggling but determined Cindy did her best to corral him but couldn't keep her grip.

Paul's phone was streaming Pandora radio to the car's stereo system. Lee Ann Womack's "I Hope You Dance" began playing. For the two of us, those old songs were comfort food. Settling into our thoughts and, for me, anticipation, we quietly listened until Paul wheeled his older Lexus into the hospital parking lot.

Paul went in first to deliver her makeup. Moments later, he opened the door, beckoning to me. Before entering Cindy's room, I prepared myself, putting out my most positive vibe. It was almost as if I were meeting Paul's parents for the first time.

I had some idea, from Dad's cancer treatments, what might be coming. Still, I was shocked to see this frail, tiny girl, indeed just a child, lying helplessly on the gurney. All four of her limbs were punctured to serve dozens of plastic tubes hanging from bags of saline and plasma. A translucent, molded plastic mask covered her face. Beige metal-and-plastic-clad boxes surrounded her, their fronts rife with green, yellow, and red LEDs, scrolling amber text in all caps as they emitted annoying beeps.

But I needn't have worried about projecting positivity. As Paul leaned over to hug Cindy around and between the medical equipment, her face beamed with happiness; she seemed blissfully unaware of her larger surroundings. Her cheerfulness amid all that mechanical and electronic misery starkly contrasted with — and in some ways amplified — the sadness and unfairness of it all.

Still, Cindy's personality was unfazed by what was happening to her. It seemed she could find the best in the moment and run with it.

Her body told a different story. Her sunken cheeks, missing hair, and the darkening of the skin around her eyes were disheartening. Weight loss had rendered her arms and legs skeletal. Were it not for her sake, I would have broken into tears.

Choking back what I can only describe as grief, I felt guilt as I realized no one had yet written her story's end. I had no right to prejudge the outcome of her fight. Putting the bag of books on the swing-arm gurney table, I looked away to regain control of my emotions.

"Cindy, I want you to meet Debra Ann Wynn," Paul announced. "Debra Ann's my friend from when I was in college. She's a real-life investigative reporter — she used to work for the *Union-Tribune.*"

"I know you!" Cindy exclaimed, her voice almost too soft to hear through her mask. "You're famous. I read your articles online about how the police department wasn't doing what they were supposed to. I want to write stories like that."

"Oh, wow, you flatter me, but I'm glad to have such a pretty fan. Most of the time, it *is* an exciting job. If you like writing, there are lots of things you can do. I'll help get your work published if you'd like. Your dad tells me you're good at science — that helps a lot if you want to investigate bad guys."

"Yeah, I like what Dad does — I used to go to his laboratory and watch him work to solve crimes. Only I wouldn't want to get stuck in a lab with geeks all day… Sorry, Dad." Cindy's look was apologetic, her eyes rolling up to meet his. I realized she didn't have enough strength in her neck muscles to move her head against the equipment surrounding her.

"No problem, sweetheart. Honestly, most days, I feel the same way!" Paul exclaimed, and they both laughed. The effort made Cindy cough weakly. Paul tapped on a control box tied to the bed with a thick wire, raising her upper body so her congestion could drain.

"I found the books you wanted." Paul took the top three out of the sack, stacking them next to the bag.

"Thanks, Dad. The medicine they give me makes me sleepy, but they got me a holder so the book stays where I can read it. It even turns the pages, so I hope I can finish more of them."

I suddenly noticed a nurse standing behind me; she'd come in so quietly I hadn't heard her. "How are you feeling, Cindy? Did the medicine help your stomach?"

"Yes, it did, thanks. Audrey, this is Dad's friend Debra Ann. She's a famous investigative journalist — she's going to help me get published!"

"It's nice to meet you, Audrey," I said politely. "You're doing a great job helping Cindy get better."

"Cindy's doing the hard work herself," Audrey replied. "But we all want to see her do well and get going on her writing career."

Being an oncology nurse in a children's ward has to be the most demanding job on Earth. It must be hard to foster an outlook so much at odds with reality. I admired this woman.

"Mr. Castro," Audrey said, turning to face Paul, "the doctor is making his rounds. He's on his way to check on Cindy. If you have time, there are treatment options he wants to discuss with you."

"Yes, I'll be here through visiting hours. I'd like to hear what Dr. Adams has to say." There was hopefulness in his tone.

That was my cue to give Paul, Cindy, and the medical staff their privacy.

"Cindy, I'll step outside so you, your dad, and your doctors can make a plan to get you well. I'll be right across the hall in the waiting area. Just holler if you'd like to talk some more."

I glanced at Paul, showing him my crossed fingers. He nodded and smiled, holding up his cell phone to say he'd text me about what was happening.

The oncology center had furnished the visitor's lounge in bold primary colors appropriate for the children's wing. Broad stripes ran through the carpets, echoed by narrower bands in the same pattern on the upholstered furniture. Cloth curtains half-covered the blinds in the windows, some with colorful circles representing ringed and un-ringed planets, moons, and stars. A multi-colored, large wooden activity cube sat in the corner.

The waiting room was nearly empty. Families of patients were taking advantage of visiting hours to see their hospitalized loved ones. A Black woman in dreads, perhaps six months pregnant, slept in a chair at the far corner, snoring gently and rhythmically, her purse serving as her pillow. Beside her, a bouquet of artificial flowers overflowed an etched green glass vase. A small, shaded reading lamp cast a softened yellow glow on the vase and the wood-grained end table they sat on.

Subdued but upbeat, easy-listening tunes wafted from the Muzak system. I caught a whiff of barbecue sauce over the smell of hospital antiseptic — someone had just eaten their lunch here.

I took a seat opposite the TV hanging from the far wall. Despite the coarse texture of the upholstery, the chair was soft and comfortable. Pulling out my cell, I began surfing.

I hoped to find something uplifting online to help me out of the deep sadness coming over me. As things turned out, what — or more accurately, *who* — I was looking for would find me.

Book One — Chapter 17

He must've been standing there several minutes, watching me intently as I sat, too engrossed in my cell display to realize his presence. Peeking out over the top of my phone, I saw a pair of eyes staring back at me. The boy was around seven, though it's hard to tell with no hair. His face resembled a younger version of Alfred E. Neuman, freckles and all, but without the classic smile for the moment. Instead, the young man had a concerned frown, his lips pursed and thrust forward.

"Will you visit my sister?" His question was insistent, as if he were taking my order at a fast-food joint and I was holding up the line. "She needs someone to play with. Niñera is there, but she's no fun, and you're the only one here who's awake."

"How could I not?" I admired his straightforward presentation. "I'm Debra Ann — what's your name?"

"I'm Fernando, but you can call me Freddie," he said, leading me down the hallway. "My sister's named Rosarita. I come here on weekends to see the doctors, but Rosarita has to stay.

"Niñera watches her, but she can't speak English. Rosarita likes to talk, but nobody's around for her to talk to."

"Sure, Freddie, I'll chat with her. What does Rosarita like to talk about?"

"Girl things, mostly. Boring. She likes music videos, wants to be a core–, core–grapher; something like that, you know. Tells all the dancers what to do. Makes them wear funny clothes."

"Ahhh, a choreographer — pretty sweet thing to want to be."

"If you say so," Freddie responded dismissively from in front of me. "When she could still walk, Rosarita tried to make me dance for her. Sometimes, she'd find where I was hiding."

We'd reached Freddie's destination — he turned toward me, holding a finger to his lips. "Don't turn the light on," he said quietly, "the medicine makes her eyes hurt."

The room was dark, the curtains drawn tightly closed. I could see a young girl, a year or two older than Freddie, sitting in the bed, earbuds plugged in and furiously thumbing away at an iPad. She had an IV drip in her arm and an oxygen cannula under her nose. Sensor wiring ran from three monitors at the far side of her bed, disappearing under her patient gown. A tall green oxygen tank strapped to a wheeled cart stood against the wall at the foot of her bed.

At first, I thought she was sitting cross-legged, but as I got closer, I could see surgeons had removed her right leg from the knee down. Everything below her left ankle was missing. Sitting quietly in a chair at the head of the bed was a short Hispanic woman with a heavy build. She wore a dress with tiny purple flowers and, over it, an apron with lace trim. A gold-edged, black Bible in Spanish sat on her lap, *La Biblia de las Américas* written on its cover.

"Hi, I'm Debra Ann. Freddie wanted me to talk to Rosarita."

"Hal-lo," the woman said, her smile polite. Freddie spoke to her in Spanish, passing along what I'd just said. The nanny listened, eagerly nodding her head. Rising from her seat, she pulled another chair from the wall opposite the bed. She gestured for me to sit down after positioning it directly across from Rosarita.

"Gracias," I said, smiling and taking the proffered seat.

Freddie tapped Rosarita on the arm, and Rosarita looked up to see me. As she did, Freddie grabbed the iPad and earbuds for himself.

"Freddie!" Rosarita exclaimed, not happy with her kid brother.

Rosarita had beautiful natural doe eyes and an infectious smile. Her hair had just begun growing back from chemo, and she resembled a young Sinéad O'Connor in the darkened room.

"Hi, Rosarita. Freddie says you'd like someone to talk to..."

It was immediately apparent there'd be no problem with awkward conversation. I'd just twisted a faucet handle fully open.

"Hi, Debra Ann; it's nice to meet you. I'm going to be a choreographer — that's someone who designs dance routines. When I leave here, I'll go to New York and attend choreography school.

"I want to do videos and musicals — musicals are coming back, you know. I saw *tick, tick… BOOM!* on Netflix. He made the musical *Rent* — have you seen it? — and he had a hard time when he started.

"It's good to know because I have bone cancer. Everyone says it's getting better, so it won't be a problem. The doctors are going to give me a new leg and a foot. They showed me how it works, and it'll be just like regular walking. And if a dog bites me, it won't even hurt. I probably won't be able to dance, but that's okay because I always wanted to be the director, anyway.

"What do you do, Debra Ann? Do you like music and dancing?"

I couldn't help but smile inside. Seeing Rosarita was just what I needed to feel better about life.

"I'm an investigative journalist. I find out what the bad guys are doing and tell the world about it. And yes, I like music and dance — a lot."

"Oh, wow…," Rosarita was off and running again. "So, you write the stories in the newspaper? That's pretty awesome. Is it like being a snitch? In the movies, they don't like rats — bad things happen to the ones who tell on people."

Rosarita looked straight at Freddie with a scowl. I'd have asked her about that if I could've gotten a word in edgewise. But the iPad still had Freddie's full attention; he was oblivious to the rest of us, so Rosarita continued from where she'd left off.

"Did anyone ever point a gun at you when you were following them around doing criminal things? Has anyone ever shot you? I'd be too scared to chase criminals, but I must admit, it would be awesome to make fun of them once they were in jail … 'Nyah, nyah, I told you so!' But if they ever got out, I s'pose they could be mad and come after you. Has that ever happened?"

I wasn't sure it was my turn to speak, but I took the chance. I saw Freddie had pulled out his earbuds. He was using the back of the iPad to fold something from plum-colored construction paper.

"Usually, a snitch is one of the bad guys, so when I tell the story, it's not quite the same thing." I chuckled. "I don't normally chase them while they're doing crimes. I figure out whatever they did afterward. No one's ever shot me, but somebody tried to run me over in a car once, and another guy tried to hurt me with a knife. Does that count?"

"That doesn't sound good." Rosarita flashed a brief frown. "When they cut my leg, they made me sleep first, so I don't know what it's like to be awake. Have you ever thought about being a choreographer? Nobody wants to kill choreographers … well, maybe the dancers, but if they did, they'd get fired.

"I think you have to be smart to be an investigative journalist, so I bet you could go to choreography school and get pretty good grades. Maybe we could work together someday. That would be fun. Of course, I'd have to be the boss because it was my idea first, but we could make a great musical and become famous.

"We might have to change our names, which is quite sad because no one would know who we really are. But we could write a book later and tell everyone it was actually us."

"I couldn't imagine a better partner." I had to grin.

Their nanny rose from her seat and pointed to her watch. She said something to Freddie and then spoke to Rosarita.

"Niñera says it's time we must see Mamá," Freddie said. "She's in the grownup hospital. They won't let you stay in Rosarita's room if you're not in our family, so we have to go. Here, I made something for you."

Learning three members of the same family were having medical issues severe enough to land them in a hospital tweaked my instincts as a journalist, but those questions would have to wait. I needed to exit gracefully; I was worried about Cindy and Paul and wanted to get back to them.

Freddie bashfully thrust something in his right fist at me. As I kneeled, I saw he was clutching an origami flower — lines in the paper where he'd refolded it several times told me he'd tried hard to get it exactly right.

"Oh, Freddie, this is beautiful; I didn't know you were so talented!" I exclaimed, and he instantly became the self-assured kid I'd first met.

"Niñera says tulips make you feel good," Freddie explained. "I gave Mamá one after she got sick — she says it helps a lot. I thought maybe if I gave you a tulip when you were still okay, you wouldn't ever get sick at all."

"Awww, thank you so much, Freddie, for caring about me. I know it'll keep me safe."

I turned slightly to face the bed.

"I'm sorry I can't stay longer, Rosarita," I said, grateful for the experience. "It was wonderful meeting and talking with you. I know you'll be a great choreographer, and I'll think about going to your school. Freddie, thanks for the pretty tulip and for coming to get me. I hope everything turns out very well for you, your mom, and you, Rosarita."

I smiled at their nanny, waving my good-luck tulip.

Heading to Cindy's room, I crossed my fingers that the doctor had given Paul good news and better options for her.

Book One – Chapter 18

Peeking through the window of Cindy's room, I saw the orderlies had pulled the privacy curtain around her bed. The backlit silhouettes of Paul, the doctor, and the nurse were visible through the fabric. Judging by their gestures, the conversation seemed animated.

I wouldn't interrupt them. Curious, I went to the nurses' station a short distance down the hall. An RN, her nametag written in crayon to spell "Rachel," stood behind the counter. With auburn hair highlighted in blonde and a round face, her smile was pleasant even as she seemed tired.

I put out my hands before me. "Please, don't let me take you from your work. But I just left Rosarita, the young double amputee in room 607, and her family. I don't mean to violate anyone's personal space or run afoul of HIPAA regulations, but is it true that two children from the same family are being treated for cancer here? And the mother's been hospitalized too?"

"I can't violate confidences, of course, for reasons you mentioned," Rachel replied, "but that situation's a genuine tragedy. If it's supposed to be a secret, it's an open one. And they aren't the only victims. We've got another down the hall from the same neighborhood, and three adults from the area passed in the last year."

"By 'passed,' you mean 'died'?"

The nurse bit her upper lip, nodding.

"What happened to the mother?"

"She's at UC San Diego — after waiting two years for a donor organ, she just had a liver transplant."

"Who's caring for her children now… her husband?"

"He's an over-the-road trucker, a good man from what I know, and wants to be here. But if he doesn't work, they don't have money coming in and no insurance. Our sister hospital treated him for an enlarged thyroid, and he kept driving throughout. They've got a sizeable extended family — they're trading off caring for the children in shifts. Pretty rough. We've been treating the daughter here for four months, and before he began outpatient services, we had the boy for fifteen weeks. Over the holidays, no less; to say it's been tough for them would be an understatement."

"Any idea what's causing all of this?"

"Now *there's* a rat's nest. All these cases come from the same area — they built the subdivision in the seventies over a landfill, so there's that. The principal employer for decades there was Solutia, the chemical arm of Monsanto. They produced cheap, pest-resistant shipping materials — paper, cardboard, formed cellulose packing inserts, that sort of thing. From what I understand, they saturated most of those with pesticides. Solutia shut down in 2015. Monsanto itself went out in 2018 — billions in cancer and cleanup lawsuits — so you can imagine what they've left behind."

"Jesus, could it get any worse?"

"Sadly, yes. Another company took over the research building in 2016, all hush-hush, ripped the signs off the building, armed guards at the entrances. Rumors were a European company was weaponizing toxins — testing delivery systems. Others claimed it was a covert U.S. military operation.

"One night in 2020, they disappeared into thin air. The county took it over for unpaid taxes. Going through the building, they found leaking containers of every poisonous or carcinogenic chemical known to man."

"How'd you learn all this?"

"Way too many health issues in that neighborhood since the 1980s. Geneticists can't determine the link between patients' DNA and these cancers, but the tumors have DNA in common. *Something* in their environment; the residents are up in arms. They tried to get the city, the state, and then the EPA to do something. But they ran into the blame game — finger-pointing, evading service, stalling lawsuits, and that political stonewalling charade. They've gotten nowhere until recently."

I struggled to remember what I'd read.

"I've heard bits and pieces of this story, but the neighborhood didn't register with me."

"It's taken years to wade through the offshore owners and shell corporations. But they finally filed a class-action suit against the last owners and the city. One of those deals where the lawyers pocket millions, and the dead and hospitalized victims get a hundred bucks each." She didn't try to hide her disdain.

"But as to how I know, we've had dozens of public and private investigators, reporters, attorneys, and opportunists tearing up these people's lives recently. They've been in and out of our hospital and others, so you can't avoid hearing things."

"So unfortunate… I'm sorry to take your time." I'd noticed the wall clock, realizing visiting hours were almost over. "It was heartbreaking to meet those kids and then learn about their mom — I wanted to see if there's anything anyone can do."

"Not a problem; I appreciate that you cared enough to ask."

Smiling sadly and waving goodbye, I headed back to Cindy's room. Looking through the wire-reinforced window glass in the door, I saw the privacy curtain was open. Paul sat on a chair, his knees against Cindy's gurney.

Opening the door and seeing Paul clearly, I knew something was terribly wrong. Sitting as far forward in his seat as he could, his forehead moved slowly from side to side as he rested it on the heels of both hands.

He looked up at me with eyes rimmed in red, his eyelids swollen. Faint traces of salt lingered on his cheeks and near his temples, where he'd wiped tears from the outside corners of his eyes.

Cindy was asleep, mouth hanging open, her head propped on both sides with pillows.

"Oh, Paul, what's happened?" I was already dreading the answer.

Paul stood and turned his face from me, passing his hands under his eyes and over his cheeks. As his focus returned to meet mine, his upper body shook as he tried to fight back his emotions.

"The doctors say Cindy won't get better. The cancer metastasized — it's spread into her lymph system; they can't stop it. They've thrown everything at it; there's nothing more they can do. Her organs are shutting down." Paul looked down at her as he held a tissue under his nose.

I'd begun crying, the air gone from my lungs, a crushing weight settling on my chest. I reached out to hug Paul. He touched his forehead to mine and then spoke softly.

"She might have a week if we're lucky."

THE WRITINGS OF
AVRIL MARIA SERENE

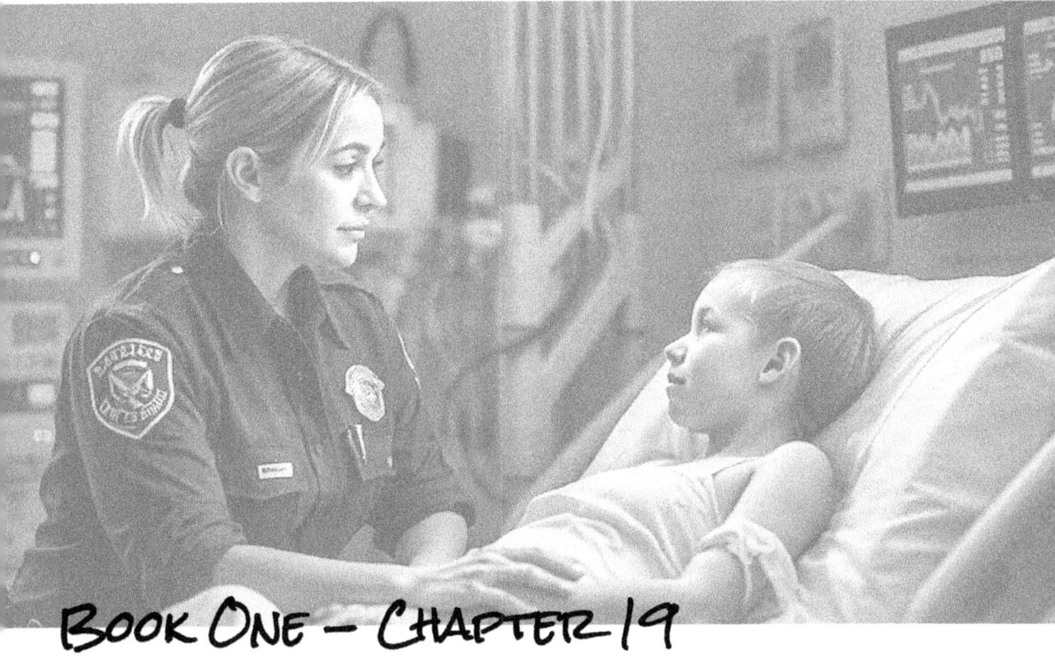

BOOK ONE — CHAPTER 19

Two days later, Marci stopped by my apartment on her midday break, still in uniform. She'd been assisting the forensics team with a suspicious death in my neighborhood. As we chatted and I made sandwiches, our conversation turned to Cindy, who was on my mind constantly.

"I went to the hospital again this morning; Paul's sleeping there on a cot," I said, bringing her a plate to the dining room table.

"Oh, Marci, Cindy's gotten so frail…." Suddenly, I found the sadness overwhelming and tears coming. "She can barely whisper — an orderly has to help her change positions. Cindy's been so positive about everything, but I could tell she'd been crying as soon as I walked into her room. She's so scared."

"Had something else happened while you were away?" Marci's voice was quiet.

"At first, she wouldn't say — she constantly worries about being the bearer of bad news. But Cindy was close with a younger boy at the hospital, an outpatient. His sister's a resident in the same cancer ward. He calls himself Freddie. I met them one afternoon — he's quite the character, confident and energetic, a perfect friend for Cindy right now.

"Freddie's not been coming around the last few days. At first, the staff told Cindy they'd discharged Freddie. She was so happy for him, hoping he'd still stop by now and then to see her. But then she overheard an orderly in the hallway taking up a collection for the family to pay for the funeral."

"*Oh, no….*" Marci took a deep breath.

"It just crushed Cindy. She's become despondent. It makes me cry to see her lying there, and that's not good for her. Paul tries to keep things upbeat, but the strain is slowly killing him too. It's different when there's hope, even if you have to pretend. But now it's all slipped away."

"Would hospice care, getting her home, maybe into a situation better for her emotionally, help?" Marci's face showed she was struggling to make a positive contribution.

"Paul and his ex-wife spoke to Cindy's doctors about hospice. They hoped to get her out of the hospital environment during her last days, maybe experience some sunshine and a little nature. But by the time Paul worked out the logistics with the insurance company, Cindy was in renal failure, too weak to move.

"In some ways, that might have been for the better; she'd made friends among other patients in the children's cancer ward. She couldn't visit them; still, they could come to her. But now that Freddie's passed, she thinks she's become a curse; she doesn't want to see anyone."

"Not my place to stick my nose in where I shouldn't, but as a mom and cancer survivor myself, maybe I could talk to her, help her find something to look forward to?"

"Oh, Marci, it's so kind of you to offer." I was grateful she'd be willing to help. "But her situation can be overwhelming…."

"The year after my surgery, before Steve granted me more custody with my boys," Marci replied, "I participated in a program the department sponsors where survivors visit children and adults in local cancer wards. Being around kids in need helped during a tough time for me. I want to think it was good for them."

"It *had* to have been, and Cindy would enjoy meeting you." The prospect brightened my mood. "Cindy has good and bad days now; I need to check with Paul if he thinks she's up for making a new friend. When can you see her?"

"I haven't taken personal time off lately, so I've got a ton of hours stored up — I can go this afternoon if that works for everyone."

"Let me call Paul." I grabbed my phone off the coffee table. I hit the speed-dial button, and he picked up after the first two rings. "Hi, Paul — how's Cindy doing?"

"She's having a better day. She's sleeping now. What's up?"

"Oh, good — hopefully, the rest will build her strength. Marci's here with me, wondering if she could come to see Cindy. Do you think she'd be up for it?"

There was little activity in the halls of the children's hospital during the early afternoon of a Tuesday — the few visitors were quiet. Nurses and orderlies kept their voices subdued as they made their rounds, and many of their patients were taking midday naps.

The colorful walls and floors of the children's ward welcomed us, and the artwork of young patients stood out among the medical posters as testaments to their lives. I spotted Rachel, the nurse I'd met during an earlier visit. She was walking toward us, head down, immersed in her clipboard.

Raising her head, she smiled as we approached, and I slowed, seeking another answer. "Hi, Rachel, I'm Debra Ann. You helped me with questions about Rosarita Gonzales and her family a few days ago. I just heard terrible news about Freddie, Rosarita's brother…."

"Such a shock for the staff and worse for some of our patients." Rachel's expression was sorrowful. "That boy … such a wonderful personality; we enjoyed his visits. He livened things up for everyone."

I nodded in agreement. "Freddie seemed so healthy and energetic. What happened?"

"We were so proud. He'd been in remission almost a month, a success story that makes all this worth it.

"The family says Freddie was at home playing in the backyard. He was chasing his cousin and their friend, just goofing around, when suddenly he suffered a stroke. His friend's mother saw something was wrong and called the ambulance. He died in her arms, waiting for it to arrive."

In a joyless mood already, the news made my heart sink. Marci dropped her head and hugged my shoulders as the nurse reached out to touch my forearm.

Rachel continued, "Freddie loved the little Chihuahua he'd gotten for Christmas — called him 'Paco.' He used to beg us to let him bring Paco into his room whenever he was here for treatment. The neighbor didn't realize Freddie'd passed until Paco's leash slipped out of his hand." The image seemed to upset even the nurse. Opening her eyes wider, she touched a forefinger to the corner of one to stop a tear.

After taking a moment out of respect, I thanked Rachel. Marci and I walked on in somber silence. We paused outside Cindy's door to breathe deeply and put on happier faces. Then we knocked and made our way in.

"Hi, Cindy. Is it okay to bring you a visitor?" I asked as Paul pulled chairs from the side of the room and arranged them for Marci and me.

"Is she going to arrest me?" Despite her effort to speak, her voice was barely audible, but I was comforted to know she still had her sense of humor.

"Not today." I grinned. "This is Marci Robbins, and we've been BFFs for a long time. She's a sergeant with the police — she's still in uniform because she came straight from work."

"I didn't want to miss visiting hours and my chance to meet you," Marci explained with a wink.

"Debra Ann told me about you," Cindy whispered as she sized Marci up. "You're her friend who yells at her when she does stupid things. Is it true you shot someone to save her life?"

Marci stared at me, her eyes wide with a rigid smile, her way of telling me I'd embarrassed her. I tilted my head and held my hands palms-upward, imitating Harry's best "What can I say?" look.

"I've never told anyone this, but Debra Ann says I can't shoot straight," Marci confessed, "so I aimed at her. It worked, and I hit the bad guy instead."

It was the first time Paul or I heard Cindy laugh in several days, but it set off a coughing jag lasting long enough to worry us. Still, it was good to see Cindy happier, and I realized something about Marci. Every other first-time adult visitor introduced themselves to Cindy by asking about her illness or how she felt. Marci started by treating her as a person first, without bringing up her medical challenges.

It made for an immediate connection.

"Debra Ann told me the equipment makes your Internet connection suck," Marci said, "so I made you a mix tape on the way here. I downloaded the latest streams of Taylor Swift, Billie Eillish, Ed Sheeran, and One Direction onto a flash drive. You can plug it into your laptop."

Cindy's eyes lit up, leading to what was, for Cindy, a lively discussion about music. Soon, Cindy was sharing personal details with Marci. That allowed Marci to open up and show she'd been through similar things.

Marci genuinely understood what was essential to Cindy these days — getting the best out of each moment, the welcome warmth of acceptance, and even the intimate experiences they had in common expressed as gallows humor. Cindy took it in like a sponge.

Paul and I hung back, quietly holding hands and letting the two of them have their moment.

I'd watched Cindy enjoying time with other patients in the ward. Her bonding with Marci was different; eventually, I'd understand why. Marci was the first true *survivor* Cindy had met — more than that, one who'd come out the other side pretty and accomplished, even powerful. Marci could *shoot bad guys* if she wanted. Cindy didn't miss the subliminal message; she responded to it before our eyes.

But as good as it was for Cindy, it was also taxing. After two hours, Cindy couldn't keep up her end of the conversation and fell asleep midsentence. Paul pulled the pillows up behind her head and the covers over her.

The moisture in his eyes showed Paul's gratitude as he held Marci for a long time and said softly, "Thank you *so* much."

When it came to my turn, Marci and I just hugged — there was nothing either of us needed to say.

THE WRITINGS OF
AVRIL MARIA SERENE

Book One – Chapter 20

I arrived home to find a message from Harry Sanderson on my answering machine, asking me to come to his office early the following day. He added an odd request, wanting to know if I could bring Marci along.

She picked up when I tried her department extension, and I relayed Harry's request.

"Do you know what it's about?" she asked.

"I'm working with him on a couple of projects, but the only one I can think of that would involve you is finding the missing homeless."

"I was planning to work second shift tomorrow. If the meeting doesn't run too long, I can be there." Marci went silent momentarily. "You know what? Never mind… if Harry's asking for me, it must be important. In the worst-case scenario, I can tap into my vacation days. Count me in."

I called Harry to confirm, but he wouldn't explain why he requested my officer friend's presence.

"I've known Marci a while, but I've never worked with her," Harry mentioned. "How much of a stickler is she for the letter of the law?"

"She'd prefer coloring between the lines," I answered, "but she's a realist, worked undercover for quite a while. She understands the nature of the world and adapts to unusual situations. Why do you ask?"

"That'll be easier to explain once we meet," Harry said cryptically. "I look forward to seeing you both tomorrow."

Harry looked up with raised eyebrows as Marci and I took seats next to Claire on the opposite side of the desk from him in his small office.

"Marci Robbins — Claire Brennan," he said as an introduction, and everyone exchanged pleasantries. The two women seemed to click. Both were attractive in that tall, blonde, and gorgeous way; each had a painful past that informed their body language. Marci's scars came from poor choices following medical and domestic turmoil; Claire's came from what had to have been a difficult transition from her birth gender. But both were engaging and had a knack for seeing what lay beneath surface appearances.

Harry, shirt collar open and suspenders slung down from his shoulders, slowly rubbed his hands together. "Ladies, I asked you here this morning because Claire and I've been working on your missing homeless persons situation. Things have blown up beyond what we expected when we started this."

"How so, Harry?" I found his choice of words curious. "When you say, 'blown up,' do you mean 'in our faces,' or like a balloon, bigger than we thought?"

"A little of both, but certainly larger," Harry replied. "Claire, why don't you share what's transpired, and we'll let Marci and Debra Ann judge for themselves.

"But first, I need to check something with Marci. Everyone here respects you as a good cop, and I've heard you're next in line to make detective. We don't want to put you in a difficult position. I'll tell you upfront that we had to cross a line with this case to get where we are. If that's a problem, you might want to step outside for a few moments."

The preamble seemed all the more relevant with Marci dressed in her street blues; she'd planned to go directly from here to her afternoon shift.

"I appreciate the consideration, and the respect goes both ways. I asked Debra Ann for her help and yours, knowing your methods differ from what the department might use. If cops have gone bad, we won't get them using techniques they know. I'll assume you haven't committed capital crimes or don't plan to tell me about them.

"So long as that's the situation, I'll treat whatever's happened before I stepped through your door as outside my purview. Don't make me answer to Internal Affairs for anything in the future, and I'm good."

"That'll work." Claire crossed her legs, showing off both the limits of a short, magenta skirt and the elegance of plain black pumps. "I'd suggest treating what we tell you like it came from an informant — we can discuss that later. But so you'll know what we have is solid, I'll share how we got it, and trust that part won't leave this room."

Marci nodded, and Claire continued. "We checked into the four officers whose names you gave us and your Mr. Crabtree. Sometimes, you go on your gut. If these people joined forces, they *had* to be up to something — pretty low-rent characters.

"Because one's a sergeant in the motor pool, we had a friend on the force review the vehicle checkout logs. Some of the entries were missing or altered. Comparing the logs to vehicle odometers, we found mileage discrepancies on four vans and Expeditions the department uses to transport officers and prisoners. These were consistent with days and hours that Reynolds and DeVance were finishing their shifts."

Marci narrowed her eyes. "Good. Circumstantial, but something."

"Just wait." Claire held up a finger. "Once we knew something fishy was going on involving police officers, I took over the legwork myself. I was with NYPD for eleven years; I understand police procedures and attitudes. I didn't want any of our other operatives taking a fall if they made a mistake.

"Here's the part you'd rather not hear, Marci — I hung GPS trackers on those transports to monitor where they're going without tailing them."

"You tracked police vehicles?" Marci's question was rhetorical, a wry smile on her face as she leaned over to hide her eyes in the palms of her hands. "Pretty ballsy — if I recall the city code, a serious felony to boot."

"I won't bullshit you that the ends justify the means." Claire's face displayed a crooked grin of her own. "But in this situation, it worked out. I don't know how else we'd have discovered what they're doing."

"What did you learn?" I asked.

"There was a clear pattern," Claire replied. "They'd periodically take one of those vans out to the desert in the foothills northeast of San Diego, almost to Anza-Borrego Desert State Park in Borrego Springs. While still in the county, it's way outside San Diego's city limits. So, what were they doing there, and that often? They'd stay at least an hour, usually longer, not counting travel time."

"Anything other than the GPS data to tell us what's happening?" Marci leaned on the arm of her chair.

"Way ahead of you there." Claire had a sly look on her face. "I followed them twice in one of our cars. The first time out taught me that we could track them only so far on wheels. At some point, mine and theirs were the only vehicles in twenty square miles — no way I could follow at night without them spotting my headlights. The terrain's too rough and unpredictable to run far without illumination. Motorcycles and ATVs are too noisy — sound carries out there."

"If they didn't want whatever they were doing discovered, the ability to spot followers might be a reason for choosing that location," I offered.

"Makes sense strategically," Claire agreed. "The next time, I took two drones with me, one set up for low light, the other with night vision. When I couldn't follow any further, I climbed the highest point I could to launch the drones. Assuming the van went to the same place, it'd be at the limits of the drones' range, not as close as I'd have liked. Still, I got decent video showing what those officers were doing. The images are grainy, but you can identify the van and see they're removing odd-shaped packages wrapped in plastic and burying them. We've reviewed those videos a dozen times. Our best guess is body parts from the random shapes and sizes."

"*Jesus*. I thought this was about dropping people off in Mexico." Harry's warning hadn't prepared me for these events.

"Trust me, nobody was more surprised than I was," Claire admitted.

"Wouldn't transporting body parts illegally in a police vehicle be incredibly risky?" I didn't get it.

"It might've been riskier *not* to," Claire answered. "Think about it — no one will question a police officer driving an official vehicle — not even other law enforcement. The only person on the planet who'd know those cops weren't where they're supposed to be or not on official business is their supervisor. What're the chances they'd run into their boss out in the desert?"

"Counterintuitive," I said, "but I see your point."

Harry stepped into the discussion. "When investigating a private matter, we'd go one step further before engaging authorities. We'd verify what they buried."

He eyed Marci.

"But here, it's reasonable to think this might involve felonies committed by rogue police officers. There's a lesser, but not insignificant, possibility it involves dead bodies."

"But if *you* want to take honest investigators out there, watch yourselves," Claire said, facing Marci. "That's an isolated area. Almost anything anyone does could alter the crime scene. There should be pristine tire tracks in that dry dust. They'll match those police vans.

"You don't want those wiped out by investigators' vehicles or because some idiot flies over the area in a helicopter. You certainly don't need anyone checking suspect vehicles out from the motor pool for use in the investigation. Don't laugh — I've seen those things happen myself."

"I get it." A look of concentration had crossed Marci's face. "Anyone going out there unofficially, between the time our perpetrators leave and detectives show up, muddies the scene. That breaks the chain of custody for any evidence and insinuates private citizens have interfered in police business. Obstruction of justice, maybe worse. And if there *are* bodies out there, the doers could accuse someone snooping around without authorization of planting evidence or even doing the killings themselves."

I wrinkled my brow.

"But without checking it out first, there's a chance they were, I don't know … transplanting palm trees for a nursery?" I speculated. "Making unfounded accusations that prove false is not only embarrassing but career-ending."

Harry spoke up. "That's why I wanted you here, Marci. I'm pretty sure those are dead bodies out there — they're going to a lot of unnecessary trouble for anything else. Possibly, your missing homeless or someone we've not considered. Or, as Debra Ann suggested, could be nothing."

He rubbed his hands together, more briskly this time. "If they're digging graves out there, we've got to sort this in a hurry. If any of these five people — who knows who else might be working with them — learn someone's discovered them, they'll scrub the scene and the motor pool logs. That puts us back to square one, with them forewarned."

"But as their fellow cop," Claire said, looking at Marci, "you're most at risk here. It happens you're the one who put us on to this. Other officers who overheard your concerns about missing homeless might finger you as the source. How we proceed needs to be your decision."

"Again, I appreciate the consideration." Marci was trying to think this through.

"My first instinct is to go through the department's chain of command. But I'd have to surrender my badge — no way they'd tolerate me getting into another cop's business. I don't know which of my fellow officers I could trust.

"I could go through Internal Affairs, but I'd be so screwed if anyone learned I ratted out other cops. And they'd eventually find out — good or bad, they *are* police officers."

While they were talking, a possible answer came to me.

"I'm not sure Marci has to be involved," I realized. "And I think we can also protect your agency, Harry."

He raised that eyebrow at me. "I'm all ears."

"As you were explaining things, my first thought was whether Paul could ask around the CBI discreetly, see what they might do. But that's a lot of overhead and hassle. The negatives of a false alarm could fall pretty hard on Paul.

"Then it clicked — the answer's right in front of us. The burial site's in the county, not the city.

"I could go to the county sheriff with those videos, the GPS coordinates of the burial location, and copies of those motor pool logs. I'd ask for his comment on the homelessness article I'm writing for Gannett.

"In that interview, I'd let it slip out that there are a few days for him to do something before I turn in what I have to my editor. As a journalist, I've got the shield law backing me. They can't make me give up my sources."

"You wouldn't have to accuse anyone of anything directly," Claire added. "Why *wouldn't* a journalist be suspicious of off-duty officers using city resources to bury things far out in the county, especially in a desert area? There's no way the sheriff's department can blow off those images, and your article deadline puts them on a short leash to get ahead of this. It looks like you're playing nice, giving them that opportunity."

I nodded.

"Several things I could do to nudge the county along if necessary. Surely, they wouldn't want possible body parts in the county's jurisdiction investigated by an external authority, say the state. Given their jurisdiction, wouldn't the county be the right agency to explore this to avoid conflicts with the SDPD investigating itself? And if not, why not?

"Maybe dropping hints about these officers, possibly others, belonging to a covert 'Cactus Club' would apprise the county of this thing's potential size and scope."

"You'd want them to know you've identified one of the participants as the motor pool sergeant," Marci offered. "Given someone's already altered those logs, the sheriff would be duty-bound to protect evidence before anyone else screws with it."

"Just to cover all the bases," I added, "we can hit them from two sides. Doug Stein is still with the *Union-Tribune*. I can get him to request a comment from SDPD's captain. He'd say he's investigating rogue cops using motor pool resources to engage in suspicious activities. He'd add that he's heard the county has a paper trail and videos; in other words, cross-link everything."

"That'd get Internal Affairs engaged." Marci was clearly on board with the idea. "We'd have the sheriff's eyes on the city's police and the police department aware of the county's interest. Any attempt to bury this — sorry, bad pun —

would be under harsh lighting and require cooperation from competing interests engaging in felonies. That won't happen."

Marci, Claire, Harry, and I all looked at one another, satisfaction and enthusiasm, even some excitement, showing on each of our faces.

"I should be able to negotiate a ride-along when the county investigates the buried items." I could see how this might work in my mind's eye. "You know, in the spirit of transparency while looking into a sister law enforcement agency. They should be happy to have me along. Once I'm on-site, I'll get notice back to everyone here as quickly as possible if what they find isn't what we expect."

Claire nodded. "We'll be able to cover our tails if necessary. And yes, I already yanked our tracking units."

I thought for a moment.

"If we're right, I can turn up the heat by throwing Randall Crabtree's name into the mix if I haven't already. That'd drag the mayor's office into it. Should be any number of witnesses to Crabtree's visits to the department and his meetings with accused officers."

"That gets me off the hook entirely." Marci was relieved. "I hate to come off as selfish, but I must admit, I'm grateful for the help."

Harry saw the agreement in our faces. He reached into his top desk drawer, pulled out a flash drive, and tossed it to me. "Here. It's better not to have a digital record of me transferring this over a network — plausible deniability and all that. The thumb drive has videos, GPS data, PDFs of the motor pool logs, and photos of the pool vehicles and their odometers. We have backups if you need them."

And just like that, we had a plan.

THE WRITINGS OF
AVRIL MARIA SERENE

BOOK ONE – CHAPTER 21

JOLIET, ILLINOIS

Harry's security consciousness meant I'd be earning airline travel miles. His Chicago office would provide the safe house for my follow-up interview with Jeremy Hansen.

When he called with the arrangements, Harry apologized that pressing matters had come up — he couldn't make this session, nor would Jennifer be there. But Mitchell, the operative who picked me up at Midway Airport, was an excellent conversationalist who shared my taste in music, so the drive to the older, two-story, white-frame residence was pleasant.

Jeremy opted for a golf shirt and Dockers over a suit, making for a more relaxed vibe during our one-on-one.

"Hello again, Debra Ann; thanks for coming," he said as we shook hands.

"I'm sorry that Jennifer's not here," I replied, "but the cabal member list she's providing Harry will help. The most important thing is that everyone remains safe."

Jeremy took the sofa, and I sat in an overstuffed chair in the living room. Mitchell took the matching chair near the opposite end of the couch.

I had one burning question for Jeremy. I wanted to know how the cabal could successfully murder billions of people other than through a worldwide conflagration of some kind. I'm good with puzzles, but the solution to this one eluded me.

I'd convinced myself there was no rational means. That became my first question once we'd settled in.

"When last we spoke, you suggested a different way of looking at the depopulation problem would reveal answers. Can we start from there?"

"Of course. Suppose billions of people voluntarily, albeit unwittingly, assisted their suicides for generations," Jeremy responded. "Not through a Jim Jones–orchestrated singular event. But through accumulated effects of selecting things, perhaps without thinking, to breathe, drink, eat, wear, apply, inject, or immerse themselves in a hundred times a day, as they'd always done.

"Imagine those choices made from a federation-provided palette of several thousand options, all undetectably altered to encourage premature death, either by themselves or when combined with other things."

I thought about it briefly. "That seems easy to say but impossible to pull off." Scenes from an old movie Dad liked, *The Truman Show*, ran through my head; I couldn't picture reality being that orchestrated.

Jeremy was undeterred.

"Those deaths needn't happen overnight. Presume the coalition provides other products, services, or alterations to the environment that significantly reduce life expectancy and sperm counts, interfere with ovulation, and increase fetal and maternal deaths at delivery.

"Say they simultaneously increase the reach, number, and power of cancers, toxins, and potentially fatal diseases — all globally."

I needed a few moments to ponder his words. If I bought into the premise, I'd wonder how many people had been lost to this already. But I wasn't sold yet.

"*If* you could pull it off, yes, of course…. But that's a huge friggin' '*if.*'"

"We can talk about that 'if.'" Jeremy was somewhat defensive — my reticence was getting through. "But please, assume for the moment that's the plan."

I slowly nodded, admittedly curious.

He interlaced his fingers behind his head and sat back.

"The federation wouldn't need to convince anyone of anything or cajole billions into killing themselves. Encouraging people to keep at whatever they're doing already isn't an enormous challenge. The coalition asks only that you keep vaping, smoking that cigarette, licking that Oreo center, taking those supplements, drinking water from plastic bottles, and pumping gasoline into that car. Maybe more often."

Jeremy hesitated, shifting in his seat before he continued.

"I want to digress a moment. That last item introduces global warming, which offers real promise for attaining the federation's goals. Grant me another bit of patience here. I'll explain afterward how the coalition gets people to do en masse what it wants, the crux of your question."

Intrigued, I nodded assent.

"Global warming is engineering elegance for the Hodin federation's purposes. Not only for its potential to kill billions of people but because it corrects naturally once most human activity driving it disappears. It's a self-healing wound, leaving our intended survivors with a cooling world.

"One caveat: that's true *if* we stay under the one-point-five-degree Celsius tipping point. The common scientific belief is that the climate system irreversibly changes once we cross that threshold. The federation accepts that we can't recover once temperatures rise two degrees."

I was familiar with this part of it.

"Some climate experts claim the one-point-five-degree increase is now unavoidable."

"Yeah, no surprise." There was a hint of sarcasm in Jeremy's voice. "The United States outputs as much CO2 as China, Russia, and Germany combined, even as they open more oil fields to fracking and drilling. Russia funds its wars by selling fossil fuels to China and India, huge countries with abysmal records curtailing emissions."

"I don't see how a private group stops any of that."

"Agreed. The speed of global warming means the coalition's intended survivors could suffer adverse effects even after eliminating overpopulation. So, the alliance is accelerating its release of initiatives.

"To that end, antithetical as it may seem, the federation is embracing and further weaponizing the depopulating effects of climate change. They'll use global warming itself to speed depopulation, trying to outrun detrimental effects upon the survivors."

A muscle in my right calf twitches when I'm starting to stress; it was doing that now. "I assume the droughts, fires, famines, and flooding that will occur naturally would help the cabal achieve its ends...." Even as I filled in gaps, the reasoning seemed entirely too pat.

"True; climate change also fosters regional conflicts over dwindling resources, particularly in sub-Saharan Africa, the Middle East, and China.

"The Hodin federation's targets include India and Pakistan, where temperatures will approach the limits of human endurance. Both countries are nuclear-armed, so there are abundant risks. But fights over food and water tend to be local, not national. India and Pakistan avoid regional tiffs turning into broader social unrest by exporting their most vocal citizens to Western destinations, which acts like a pressure relief valve for them.

"Still, both countries have intrinsic caste- and class-based inequalities that the federation can exploit, in combination with water and food pressures."

I remained skeptical. "How does the cabal influence local reactions to global warming?"

"They cut off emigration by whipping up anti-immigrant sentiment and racism in destination countries, closing those relief valves. China and India are very competitive — the Hodin federation can increase those tensions by spreading disinformation. China, India, Pakistan, and Bangladesh represent over three billion people, with excellent potential for population reduction through climate change.

"There are side benefits — the federation's had success with initiatives around air pollution, climate warming's first cousin. Nine million additional deaths in one year, mostly from the coalition's work."

Clasping his hands before him, Jeremy leaned back and gave me a smile that seemed almost triumphant, striking a discordant note with me given all those lost souls.

"Not bad," he bragged, "considering society does everything possible to thwart their efforts."

I sighed.

"So, intentionally interfering with the climate could kill many people, given those already suffering from unintended consequences," I conceded.

"I promised to answer your 'big if' question about the federation getting seven billion people to eliminate themselves. Our embed in PWW, the world's largest ad agency, has been in advertising his entire career. Seeing what he's accomplished, I'd argue the man's successfully gotten people to kill themselves unknowingly for years. Before he joined the federation or understood that's what he was doing."

I gave him a sidelong look. "I'm no fan of advertising, so you won't get any argument from me. But advertisers offing people does seem a little far-fetched. *We* might want to murder *them*, but it's hard to see them killing *us*."

"What does a successful ad campaign pushing tobacco for RJ Reynolds accomplish?" Jeremy asked rhetorically. "RJR makes lots of money, and bunches of people die prematurely from lung cancer. What about that spiffy new ad for McDonald's molded-from-ground-pork rib sandwich? McDonald's makes boatloads of money, and tons of people die prematurely from strokes and other manifestations of too much cholesterol, diabetes from fats, and high blood pressure from overabundant salt.

"What happens when ads promote ExxonMobil stations as great places to grab chips when you buy gas? The chips do everything bad the fake pork ribs did — fossil fuels add to those negatives, killing with climate change and polluted air. Don't forget those who die from products made with ExxonMobil hydrocarbons, including microplastics."

"But that hardly proves they're in league." I spread my hands. "You can't say *every* business engages in these evil practices."

"Perhaps not all at a given moment — there *are* ebbs and flows. Those who demand free markets, the dog whistle for unregulated greed, point to the benefits of competition as their justification.

"They don't want you to consider competition's nasty dominant truth. That truth? Once someone profits by getting away with something evil in a given market segment, they compel all segment members to imitate that behavior; they *must* if they're to compete. That's why your personal and private digital information gets stolen and abused over the Internet — not by professional thieves, but by MBAs. Now all companies SPAM you with data they steal or purchase already-stolen — they can't compete otherwise."

"But other things matter," I pointed out. "Tens of thousands of people work for those companies. Their salaries feed their families and pay taxes."

"John Masters, my boss, created those rationalizations for lobbyists," Jeremy retorted. "You believe, in the absence of RJR, employees wouldn't work for companies who *don't* kill people? Without tobacco, PWW would advertise bubblegum to satisfy consumers' oral fixations, millions of humans would live longer, and Topps would employ those workers.

"If burger joints weren't around, PWW would promote salad bars providing those minimum-wage jobs.

"If gasoline didn't exist, energy company employees would instead be building electric car charging stations; plastics would come from safer and sustainable sources, like soybean oil.

"Advertising empowers corporations to profit from doing bad things. Without that profit source, they'd do something else, likely things that would be better for us."

"I see the logic," I admitted.

"The only difference between PWW's past campaigns and the Hodin federation's work is the profiteering. McDonald's and RJR will *always* empty your wallet before they kill you, but money doesn't matter to the federation.

"Advertisers and corporations have the same attitudes as serial killers, the mindset that their wants and needs trump any other consideration. They call it 'profit motive;' to Ted Bundy, it was 'urge to kill.' But either suits the federation's purposes perfectly.

"We'll all die before our time simply because those who supply products and services killing us are willing to pay advertisers more money than those who aren't."

"I doubt we're all such sheep...," I said, putting up some resistance.

"The coalition's success doesn't depend upon a world of sheep. It only requires that some percentage of 'see no evil, hear no evil, speak no evil' monkeys ignore sheep gone missing. We credit Edmund Burke for saying the only thing necessary for evil to triumph in the world is good men doing nothing.

"You may personally be stronger-willed, less gullible, more intelligent, not as susceptible to advertising. Even so, it influences you more than you know. Sometimes it's subtle, such as limiting your choices to those on a list the federation created, like the questions on a supermarket survey."

"Interesting...," I murmured, his argument gaining a foothold.

"Hitler's command of Germany, Trump's rise to the presidency, Modi's in India, or Netanyahu's reclaiming of power in Israel — these all prove one thing." Jeremy was rolling along. "They show the very worst people can manipulate 40 percent or more of us into the most asinine beliefs and actions imaginable, with mere words."

I couldn't argue with that. "Okay, advertising might persuade someone to kill themselves cluelessly, and it wouldn't be as difficult as it should."

Jeremy wasn't about to accept my concession gracefully.

"*That's* an understatement. Advertisers kill people 24/7, across the globe, every single day, since long before Sears sold cocaine powders for pain relief on tube radios a hundred years ago. Why should it surprise anyone to learn those powders were addictive? That was the whole point!

"The federation's take is that advertising and social manipulation are great for achieving depopulation."

"You've covered the power of advertising well." I realized the worldview I'd brought with me had suffered a big dent.

Still, I wasn't ready to abandon it just yet.

Book One – Chapter 22

We headed to the kitchen for a break, chit-chatting about our significant others for a few moments. I hadn't realized how head-over-heels Jeremy was about all things Jennifer. It deepened my sense that he took his commitments seriously, however problematic that quality might be in someone employed by killers.

Resuming our conversation, I asked Jeremy how the Hodin cabal spent its funds and assigned personnel.

"Initiatives are the means to the federation's ends. It's where they invest their money and workforce. Understanding initiatives provides a window into the leaders' decision-making."

I nodded, and he went on.

"The federation's corporate embeds seek opportunities within host company products and services. Perhaps there's a regulatory gap; who runs a nationally branded tube of toothpaste taken from a rural store shelf through a lab to learn its *actual* ingredients? Think toothpaste is no big deal? It provides direct access to the throats of billions of strangers three times a day.

"When assessing ideas, the federation considers discoverability and believable alibis a package. Are there rational excuses to fall back on if there's a risk of getting caught?

"Other considerations: What's the cost of adding or removing an ingredient? What size is the potential killing field? Does combining something already out there with another product or service cause loss of life or infertility? How soon after consumption do effects appear? Longer is sometimes better for concealing sources. How much access do coalition embeds need to implement the initiative?"

I ran with the toothpaste angle.

"You're leveraging existing brand trust and logo recognition to disguise what the cabal's doing?"

"As one approach, yes," Jeremy replied. "The federation does the same thing with real-world products and services that corporations do with software they sell. Those companies bury something good for them but bad for you deeply into apps or services they can get you to install. Usually, 'bad' means abusing private identifying information you provide, or the software steals. The 'good' — for the company, that is — includes selling your data to others, tracking your movements for opportunities to redirect your thoughts, and diverting data to AI engines to improve their manipulation of you, all to feed their greed.

"The coalition's initiatives differ only in that the 'bad' they insinuate into physical-world products and services hastens your demise or inhibits your reproduction, perhaps both."

"Does the cabal target specific products or industries?"

"The Hodin federation works especially closely with pharmaceutical and chemical companies. The coalition's always seeking compounds with potential — anything causing interesting mutations in cells, deadly substances that aren't obvious or for which regulators don't test, or potions that interfere with fertility.

"These discoveries are a win-win for the provider and the federation. The coalition adds another arrow to its quiver. The supplier gains a revenue stream, potentially off-the-books, for something they've invested research and testing into but can't otherwise sell."

"Once they've identified an interesting substance, what happens?"

"Some initiatives package and distribute drugs and chemicals they can mix with, or substitute for, something else. Initiatives for direct-acting poisons, like those for radioactive materials, typically target specific individuals or groups. There'll be a precise plan for delivery, often in time-released forms.

"We usually disseminate slow-acting poisons and metals meant to build up in the bloodstream as we do carcinogens — through popular foods or drinks, sometimes in toys or clothing. If the poison's compatible with the binding agent, we'll distribute it through our microplastics chemistry initiative. We might package something as an aerosol or dust it over crops, waterways, or buildings with planes, drones, or balloons. We'll directly dump certain products from boats into the oceans, lakes, and rivers.

"But the federation's not dependent upon industry leftovers; it creates new toxins for many initiatives. The coalition has a robust biologics initiatives program: fungi, bacteria, viruses, prions, and parasites. They have CRISPR capabilities equal to anyone's."

I wasn't familiar with the word he used.

."I'm sorry, that's not registering — what's CRISPR?"

"CRISPR's a tool for editing genes," Jeremy answered. "It lets us cut and paste genome sequences into DNA strands, turning a living organism into something else entirely. We can transform a human into the intellectual equivalent of a single-cell organism like an amoeba. You've heard of Marjorie Taylor Greene, right?"

He caught my eye with a smirk.

"We've not been successful going the other direction — making a Trumpie smart or classy is too big a challenge."

Mitchell and I both smiled — the humor lightened the general mood.

"If we don't know the genomes required to effect a desired change," Jeremy continued, "the federation's perfected a rapid, iterative kill-and-cull process to derive resistant variants of microscopic living organisms. The technique exposes samples to something that can kill them, waits until most are dead, and extracts and grows the still-active survivors and viable spores for the next iteration. Rinse and repeat.

"The federation's fully automated the process — evolving the desired resistance doesn't take long."

"Interesting. I expected straight-up distribution of known-lethal bacteria and viruses…."

"Twenty years ago, sure," Jeremy acknowledged. "But effectively distributing viruses, bacteria, fungi, and eukaryotes proved a resource-intensive rabbit hole. The host must survive long enough to communicate the pathogen onward — the timing gets tricky for human-to-human transfer of a highly virulent and deadly disease. Or the perfect gene sequence for a virus or bacterium in the lab might mutate so quickly, once released, that it doesn't perform as expected.

"Humans who proved susceptible during testing may not represent others with better immune systems who then break the transfer chain. Getting a pathogen past antibiotics, disinfectants, and antiseptics already in everyday use might require thousands of evolutionary cycles."

It struck me that a group so eager to destroy most of the world's population would demonstrate such patience.

"Why not distribute several at the same time?"

"Some pneumonia variants *are* opportunistic and show promise when joined with other biologics, but effectively combining pathogens in the wild is dicey. Organisms have unique shelf lives and periods of optimum efficacy. They don't spread in the same patterns. Coordinating releases of two or more organisms into a community to kill large numbers effectively isn't easy."

"You lack fine-grained control," I surmised.

"Yes. There are exceptions, but once a pathogen has stimulated the human immune system, another biologic can struggle to gain traction. Sick people stay home in bed, where introducing new diseases is harder. The law of diminishing returns applies, and other initiatives might prove more promising.

"Above all, for any pathogen or combination the federation releases, they must selectively protect their intended survivors. That takes serious development time. Still, the Hodin federation has many pathogen-based initiatives — they're genetically editing the Ebola, Marburg, and Nipah viruses, for example."

"Other than something exotic — radioactive? — I can't imagine how else you'd kill huge numbers of people." Listening to myself, I had to pull back with a jerk. I was surprised how easily I'd slid into a problem-solving mindset for this.

"I'm just getting started." Jeremy had a sly look on his face. "I've covered most of our general-purpose tangible initiatives.

"We also have specialized programs targeting certain groups, locales, environments, or situations. For example, formaldehyde leaching from plywood and wood laminates used in mobile homes targets a unique demographic. That demographic doesn't include our intended survivors — defensive measures are unnecessary. Same with harmful additives to AIDS-suppression drug cocktails."

"You used the word 'tangible' for those initiatives. As opposed to…?"

"The initiatives I mentioned all require creating, changing, or doing something around a physical reality. Tangible methods have drawbacks, like traceability back to the source. Investigators can follow them via accidental characteristics in the product itself, through supply chains, or by tracking delivery.

"Most federation initiatives are less direct. For example, when oil prices fluctuate, they'll subsidize the costs of petrochemicals used in plastics production. Or induce oil companies to divert more production to petrochemicals when fuel demand falls. These activities support the coalition's microplastics chemistry initiatives, which are untraceable."

A shudder of foreboding went through me.

"The Hodin cabal must have impressive discretionary funds…."

"The coalition's never denied an initiative for lack of money," Jeremy replied. "That said, directly injecting cash into a situation, say to bribe someone, is usually too brute-force, noticeable, and traceable to meet the federation's need for discretion.

"Their most powerful initiatives live entirely inside someone's head. They use social engineering, advertising, and propaganda to manipulate thoughts. These get individuals to accept or favor one or more of hundreds of thousands of behaviors and tendencies that are bad for people, many of them products and services that already exist. Along with what you buy and use, bad things can include who you vote for, who you pray with, and especially, echo chambers you frequent — that's where federation 'suggestions' amplify, reverberate, and jell.

"Attitude-altering resources also persuade sentient beings *away* from anything interfering with the coalition's agenda. Peer pressure, the Internet, and especially social media are wonderful things." Jeremy's sarcasm was palpable.

"How do they insert those into the mainstream?"

"The federation uses its symbiotic relationships with PWW, among other agencies. We've embedded coalition members throughout the advertising industry. PWW's advertising chops work with discreet propaganda and group psychology technologies our assigned agents developed for them.

"At some level, agencies like PWW control or manipulate search engines and results placement, advertising, propaganda, the social media they drive, and the influencers they pay. More so when the Hodin federation pulls the levers in the shadows behind them."

There was so much more to Jeremy's tale than met the eye. If ever a backstory had legs, this one was a virtual spider.

THE WRITINGS OF
AVRIL MARIA SERENE

Book One – Chapter 23

With time marching along, I felt we'd only scratched the surface of the Hodin cabal's layers. We'd talked late into the day and still hadn't exhausted my questions. So, after Mitchell booked us hotel rooms for the night, we kept digging the next day.

I wanted more on the cabal's big gun. "We keep circling back to advertising. How deep is the relationship between the cabal and PWW?"

"As a corporation, PWW's unaware of the Hodin federation as I've described it," Jeremy replied. "However, the coalition has embedded operatives deeply within PWW to serve their needs. The federation directly and indirectly influences how the ad agency applies its core competencies."

"How does that work?"

"Corporate consumers use PWW for critical projects because the agency hires only the best talent. Accordingly, PWW charges hefty prices for top performance.

"Those inflated charges are the federation's opening. By subsidizing PWW's client invoicing and placing embeds in decision-making roles, we ensure better creatives work on *our* pet projects.

"The federation's false storefront operation can pose as a PWW client. The storefront will fund selected PWW projects on behalf of a third party, billing the client at a significant discount. The storefront also acts as the client for the coalition's advertising-based initiatives.

"So, the cabal can persuade PWW to prioritize certain accounts," I gathered.

"Conversely, if a PWW client whose interests counter the federation's goals pays for top-end services, the embeds can intentionally sabotage the contract. The federation compensates PWW for any losses with lucrative replacement projects."

"I get that PWW's the largest, maybe $18 billion annually." I was still unsure. "But the global advertising market's over $600 billion. I don't see how PWW could influence the larger group of businesses that aren't their clients."

"PWW's not the federation's only ad agency. They've similar relationships with other firms. However, the others may not have coalition operatives embedded as high-level executives — the relationship's not as intimate.

"But make no mistake, the federation's everywhere they need to be. Enough that we can work both ends. For example, we might gin up public desire for something requiring ingredients we, or one of our partners, can intercept or control through initiatives. When a manufacturer or service provider steps up to fulfill the need, our advertisers can boost demand for their specific product or service, regardless of whether they know they're getting a leg up.

"But our advertising is most effective when combined with tangible initiatives."

"In what way?"

"The fatal effects of some tangible methods aren't discovered for decades as cancers gestate, doctors misdiagnose the harm, metals build up in the body, or diseases hibernate," Jeremy replied. "We advertise during that time to pump up consumption.

"But what we hype doesn't have to be part of an initiative. Thousands of deadly agents we can promote are already out there in abundance. I've mentioned tobacco, fast food, and fossil fuels; add everything from BHA in baby bottles and red food dye to phosphates in laundry detergents and beyond.

"Killing you might not be the priority for those product and service vendors. Still, they won't complain so long as it's *after* they've gotten their money. They do prefer your death not to be immediate, not occur on their doorstep, and not tie back to them. They don't like being held accountable.

"Our ads ensure non-survivors' paths cross whatever behaviors, products, and services speed their demise. Time's on the federation's side — eventually, those intersections end or prevent many lives."

But that doesn't square with something Jeremy said earlier.

"What about those you intend to escape? How do you quietly get antidotes to a billion people for each thing harmful to them?"

I should've known Hodin cabal leadership had thought that through.

"We use the internal encrypted messaging system and member network I mentioned in our first session. We discreetly post what to sidestep or which preventives, vaccines, or antidotes they'll need to avoid harm or death. The federation employs medical professionals to render appropriate care, though selectively. Designated survivors understand the privilege requires attention, diligence, and sacrifice; they must do their part to remain safe."

So, the cabal identifies or creates a host of killer elements and then promotes them to the masses through advertising. All while steering consumers destined to survive away from them.

"With all these things out there, how are you getting around the FDA and other regulatory agencies?"

Jeremy lowered his eyebrows. "As I've said, we've embedded operatives and sympathetic friends everywhere, including within government agencies. You're not appreciating the greed behind all things American."

"But you're killing people," I protested.

"Nobody stops anyone from smoking cigarettes the government *knows* are deadly. Why? The tobacco industry's gotta eat — fat lobbyists and poorly-educated Deep South voters say so. The result? Politicians con the public that high taxes discourage smoking. 'Give us money, yup, that'll solve it.'

"*Smokers are addicts!* They'll pay whatever they must, cigarettes before baby formula. The government collects every dime possible from the about-to-be-dead through exorbitant taxes on each pack — and that's *all* they do. The U.S. invented the concept of allowing consumers to pay a little extra for the privilege of dying sooner.

"The federation has money — so trust me, regulators aren't a problem. The coalition can get products and services created, changed, manufactured, distributed, or performed directly by their embeds in the dominant entities in each market. And remember, half the stuff we're directing people to was already out there long before we arrived."

"Regulators target companies whenever a product harms a consumer." I stood my ground. "And not just when death results."

"That's simply not true," Jeremy responded. "Oxygen kills anyone who breathes it often enough. If you have high cholesterol, buy my fatty burger, and get pushed over the line into a heart attack, no one comes for me.

"You might stir regulatory interest after something *unusual* happens, but they'll not act until a specific link is proven — they won't unduly interfere with commerce. Still, even if a dangerous product is unsellable somewhere, many other market options are as good or better. That's the beauty of global scope. Say they did ban cigarettes in the U.S. Fine, take those cartons to Africa, South America, Asia, or any third-world country that doesn't mind its citizens getting cancer."

"Product dumping," I mused. "Like the Chinese do to us."

"The federation has the supply side covered," Jeremy continued. "The trick is driving demand from our preferred consumers. That's where PWW comes in. Pop-under ads in their browsers irritate people; otherwise, they're clueless about the power of advertising in the right hands."

"And that's because of the Internet, right?"

"A part of it, but broadcast TV, streaming services, print media, radio, billboards, product labels and logos, and the Internet overlap, providing 24/7 access to our minds, every minute of every hour of every day.

"But it's more than just the medium — the federation's taking advertising an order of magnitude beyond anything before. The latest advances in social engineering from PWW include artificial intelligence. Even in its nascent state, AI impacts everything in the digital world; its ability to deceive and persuade worries tech leaders themselves — they're trying to slow its development."

"Hard to do when AI output is indistinguishable from a creative human's." I was aware of the threat perceived by journalists who feared for their careers.

"That genie's out of the bottle. Pundits fear what criminals might do with it; corporations and politicians are the greater danger."

"Scary to think about...," I mused.

"AI has downsides, but even those are useful to the federation. The worst forms of AI make useful tools for frustrating systems and processes. Either way, for the coalition's purposes, AI seals the deal. It's the ultimate tool advertisers need to persuade almost anyone to do virtually anything. It's also scalable from individuals to enormous demographic groups."

"What does AI *do* for the cabal?"

"You'd expect AI to perfect our targeted messaging for any audience; that's no surprise. However, AI also optimizes hidden elements that the federation adds to a product or service, which might enlarge the killing field. Or maim or sicken enough to overload hospitals, which ups the death yield from all causes. The coalition uses AI to rapidly identify combinations of chemicals, pharmaceuticals, and additives among items already on shelves to increase the lethality of our initiatives. Like mixing bleach and ammonia to make chloramine gas, though far more sophisticated."

"I suppose it could help keep government agencies from discovering what you're doing...."

Jeremy nodded. "Absolutely. AI helps mask killer side effects, dangerous ingredients, and fatal flaws in products and services. It also identifies high-mortality opportunities we've missed, such as makeup to deliver toxins absorbed through the skin."

That got my attention. And I shuddered as I considered how vulnerable I'd personally been to advertising and for how long. Dared by an Internet chat room conversation into taking the cinnamon challenge, suckered into "one weird trick" clickbait purchases, made to lust after Heelys, and yes, a Tesla, in their turns. It's bad enough that people truly out to get us could manipulate us that way. But with an assist from powerful new technologies — *that's scary as hell.*

Jeremy read my mind.

"When ridding the world of people, advice from an intellect with no pro-human biases is a real advantage."

Jeremy's last remark provided food for thought and an opportunity to take our final break. Perhaps I was in denial as we resumed our seats, but I felt the discussion had turned toward the theoretical. Scary for the future, sure, but none of it seemed substantive.

I could see the potential in all these things, but when I was out and about, nothing screamed, *"Hey, this is happening!"* I asked Jeremy if any results from these initiatives were visible to ordinary people.

"The evidence is out there for anyone knowing what to look for." Jeremy gave a self-satisfied smile as if he'd anticipated the question.

"In 1964, the world population was around 3.3 billion, the annual growth rate about 2.24 percent. That rate averaged only 0.87 percent over the last three years — a 61 percent overall drop, mostly the Hodin federation's doing since launching in 1999."

Seeing the glazed expression on my face, Jeremy came to a complete stop.

"Look, I don't want to put you to sleep with a bunch of statistics no one but me ever remembers. I've got a better idea.

"As you'd imagine, the federation keeps information like this secret. Still, John likes to monitor the media and the Internet, tracking any references to our work that turn up so he can control our exposure. He keeps a running list of things he's stumbled upon — calls it his 'highlight reel.' I'll have him send me the latest copy and get a decrypted version to you."

"Thanks, Jeremy. I've got a Proton Mail account for anything sensitive — I've scribbled my email address on the back." I handed him one of my cards.

I returned to the population numbers he'd quoted.

"My sense is the cabal's applying the brakes to population growth but hasn't shifted into reverse," I summarized.

"Au contraire — as you'll see in the highlight reel, the cabal's initiatives have forced declines in several major populations," Jeremy countered, his expression patronizing. "Look for items 59 through 61 and 65 through 69. We've slowed the *Titanic's* progress significantly elsewhere – see items 70 and 71 — and we've only just begun implementing initiatives at global scope.

"To illustrate, the last time the population doubled took forty years. In 1959, it was three billion, reaching six billion in 1999. They say it'd take two hundred years to double again at today's growth rates. Of course, we'd *never* allow that to happen."

The room went quiet momentarily, the soft-spoken threat hanging in the air. I'd have to concede the leaders of this cabal had shown remarkable patience and determination as they nibbled away at their goals for more than twenty years.

Unfortunately, we'd run out of time, but I had to sneak in the requisite follow-up.

"When do you expect global population counts to begin falling?" I asked.

His dark eyes fixed on mine. "Your question assumes they aren't already. We're close enough that the answer depends on who's doing the counting."

Despite the coyness in Jeremy's answer, he'd left me with no doubts.

This thing is here.

Book One – Chapter 24

SAN DIEGO, CALIFORNIA

Having put our regular lives on hold an extra day and with planes to catch, Jeremy and I parted ways, agreeing to talk again soon. After 48 hours devoted to schooling in the cabal's workings, I was relieved to return home.

A hastily scribbled Post-it note stuck to Paul's apartment door caught my eye as I carried groceries from the car. It read simply, "Cindy's in trouble — going back to the hospital, -P."

Oh, no, please; not that, not Cindy, I thought with dread.

Worried, I stabbed my keys into my door handle several times before the lock would turn, adding frustration to my anxiety. Tossing my paper sacks, purse, and keys on the counter, I yanked out the milk and cold items, shoving them into the refrigerator. Then I dialed Paul. Not getting an answer, I threw the phone into my bag, grabbed my keys, and headed for the hospital.

When I entered the hallway leading to Cindy's room, emergency staff had already responded to the code blue; nurses and orderlies were trickling back into the corridor. The reality of what had happened started to sink in as I searched for signs — there was no conversation between them, the expressions on their faces sad and tired.

Once the room had emptied and I could squeeze through the open door, I saw an orderly in a green smock and a doctor in a white lab coat. The doctor held a clipboard with both hands below her waist, listening with her head bowed, standing quietly, respectfully, at the end of Cindy's gurney. The beige metal and plastic boxes with all the tubes and wires hanging from them were quiet now, their LEDs dark and their screens empty.

A nurse had parted the curtains and tilted the window's upper sash inward. I watched as she untied one of the mylar balloons from the head of Cindy's bed. She passed it through the window while she held its string. Her face was solemn, and there were tears in her eyes. She mouthed a short, silent prayer as she let the balloon go. Later, she'd tell me this was something staff often did so the little ones would have something to hug when called home.

I could hear Paul's soft sobbing as he kneeled at the side of Cindy's body, his forehead resting on her chest, his tears pooling on her skin and then dribbling down her side. I'd begun crying as I stopped behind Paul on his right side and stood there, trying not to make a sound. Paul needed peace during his last moments with his daughter.

After several minutes, Paul raised his head. He gave Cindy a lingering kiss on her forehead and patted her shoulder. Sniffling, Paul struggled to his feet. I stepped toward him as he noticed me, handing him a Kleenex from my purse. We held onto each other for a long time as the world stopped spinning, our tears flowing freely, neither of us saying a word.

Then we heard the approaching clatter of high heels and the plaintive wailing and shrieking of Cindy's name as Suzanne, Paul's ex-wife, came running down the hallway to Cindy's room. I looked questioningly into Paul's eyes. In answer, he took my hand, saying softly, "Please, don't leave."

I nodded and let go, stepping back to stand silently in the furthest corner of the room. When Suzanne entered, her eyes went first to Paul, then to Cindy. Turning, she searched the doctor's face for some semblance of hope; the finality of what had happened became clear.

"*Oh, no….*" Her voice was no longer shrill. Paul pulled a chair from the side of the room and placed it next to the gurney. Her knees gave way, and Suzanne sat heavily in the seat. She reached for Cindy's hand, holding it tightly with hers.

"She's so cold. She needs a blanket," Suzanne whispered absent-mindedly, almost inaudibly, the tears running down her cheeks. Paul put his hand gently on Suzanne's shoulder, and I looked down at my shoes as I began crying anew, keeping as quiet as I could.

After a few minutes, Suzanne tore her focus away from her daughter. She looked up into Paul's face, her expression pleading, her eyes darting between his.

"Did she suffer?" Her eyes showed a desperation for the only answer she could accept.

"She went quietly, Suzanne," Paul answered tenderly. "Cindy fought so hard in so much pain for so long, and I think she was ready. She didn't struggle — she squeezed my hand for a second, and then she just let go."

"She looks so peaceful," Suzanne turned her eyes back to Cindy as she began sobbing again. Finally, she stood up and kissed her daughter's hand. Nodding her head slowly, handkerchief to her nose, she backed away from the bed a few steps.

"*Where is the priest? Why didn't she have a priest?*" Screaming, Suzanne suddenly spun around and threw both palms up in the air, drawing the attention of the orderly and the doctor.

"Suzanne, please, there just wasn't time," Paul explained, trying to get through to her. "The doctors and the nurses and all these people were trying to help her, and she was gone before we had any chance to let the hospital chaplain know."

"*Dammit,* Paul, couldn't you just *once* respect our wishes and do the right thing?" Suzanne was on a tear, and Paul seemed taken aback, already wounded and not knowing how to respond.

The doctor and the orderly exchanged glances, and the physician stepped tactfully into the space between Suzanne and Paul. As she did, the orderly moved the gurney further from the wall, unplugging equipment and removing the tubes and wires from Cindy's body so they could take her from the room.

"I'm sorry to interrupt," the doctor said, "and we understand this is a challenging time for both of you. But Cindy needs some after-care now.

"You're welcome to keep the room as long as needed, and the chapel is always available. If you wish to take Cindy's personal effects today, we'll make them available. You can pick them up at the nurse's station. Or we can store them for you until you've made arrangements."

There were several minutes of relative calm as we observed Cindy being covered and wheeled out of the room. When Suzanne turned back to say something to Paul, she spotted me standing in the corner.

"And who is *this?*" she asked in what sounded close to a snarl.

"This is Debra Ann Wynn, a dear friend of Cindy's and mine. We've been close since I was in college," Paul answered quietly.

"And you brought her *here?* How *dare* you!" Suzanne screeched, slamming the heels of her balled-up fists against Paul's chest.

"I'm so sorry, but no one brought me or asked me to come," I put in, doubting Suzanne heard a word I said. "I learned Cindy was having trouble and came on my own."

"You *bitch!*" Suzanne screamed at me. Glaring at the two of us and seeing she wouldn't get any further reaction, she gave Paul a final scowl, looking for a moment like she was going to spit at him.

"*Goddamn* you!" she barked at him instead, turning and stalking out of the room.

There was a moment of stunned silence before Paul turned toward me.

"I'm sorry you had to deal with that," he apologized as we hugged. "Suzanne's never handled stress well, even for her only daughter's sake. Hopefully, she'll find the time to grieve in ways that lead her to peace."

I nodded.

"I understand, I do. These are the toughest times for everyone. I hope she can find comfort as things settle in her mind."

"There's not much more we can do here." Paul swallowed hard.

His eyes followed Cindy's gurney as they rolled it out of our sight.

"I need to make the arrangements with the hospital. Going through that process will help me with some closure. They're very considerate about that here — they have grief counselors to guide us through it. I probably should go alone, in case Suzanne is there. Cindy was her daughter, too; she's got the right to have her voice heard."

Tears were again welling up in my eyes.

"It's heartbreaking to think the world's lost Cindy. She's such a great kid. I'll miss her so much."

I was at a loss for anything else to say, a paralyzing emptiness taking over.

"I'll be at home, Paul. Call or drop by if you need someone to talk to… please."

"I'll take you up on that — I'm going to need a friend," he whispered, and we held one another for several moments longer before I left.

Book One — Chapter 25

Not long after I left the hospital, Harry called me with another opportunity to interview Jeremy Hansen.

"Oh, Debra Ann, I'm sorry to hear Cindy's gone," he said after I'd uncharacteristically dumped it all on him — it was just too soon after. Harry's rare display of sensitivity was just what I needed in that moment.

"You'll want to take some time from the job — what I called about can wait."

"Thank you, Harry, for understanding. I wouldn't want to be away from Paul for long. But if we're talking about a few hours, that's fine. I deal with these things better if I'm working through them. Paul's ex is here, and much of this must be between them. I'd rather be doing something other than fumbling with tissues."

"Fair enough — I'm with you; I have my own ways of getting through difficult things."

Harry went silent for a moment.

"I called to tell you they're sending Jeremy Hansen to Irvine for cabal business. If they're watching him, they won't expect him to misbehave on company time. Jeremy's confident he can get away unnoticed for an hour or two. Since Irvine is within driving distance of San Diego…."

"Do you have a safe house in Irvine?"

"No, but Jeremy has a trusted friend from high school who lives there. He'll let us use his condo, which is in a gated community. I'm sending two agents from the San Diego office to watch over things."

"I think a long drive by myself and getting my mind off what's going on here would be good for me," I said.

"And it'd be nice to skip airport security for once. I'm in — can you text me the address and time?"

IRVINE, CALIFORNIA

A few days later, after an hour and a half on the road, I parked in front of the second-floor condo. Jeremy Hansen pulled in behind me. Two of Harry's men had preceded us and scouted out the area. As we settled into our seats in the living room after our greetings, Jeremy announced Jennifer Carlson wouldn't be able to make it.

"Please, give her my thanks when you see her next," I asked. "Harry forwarded me her list of real-world Hodin cabal names, job assignments, and working aliases. It's a big help."

"Did you get the copy I sent of John's 'highlight reel?'"

"I did — you could've knocked me over with a feather. I wasn't expecting the quality of the sources or the depth of the information — *my God, all that going on, and nobody's snapped to what's happening?* I know *I* had *no* clue, and I'm an investigative reporter. I'm still wading through the links; I'll need your guidance putting some of it into proper context."

"Glad to be of assistance." Jeremy flashed a quick smile before his expression went serious.

Eager to begin, I addressed a leftover from our last meeting. "Our previous session and what I read in the highlight reel made it clear worldwide population growth is slowing. But a lot of things could be responsible. I still don't understand why the results aren't more obvious, given all the cabal's impressive technology, expertise, and nearly twenty years of work."

"My fault," Jeremy replied. "I'd only touched on small pieces of the evidence before we got into when population numbers will decline. There's a lot more I should have told you first. I'll describe the results from the federation's implementation of their lesser initiatives. It'll surprise you how well they've got this covered.

"As I've said, the coalition avoids anything dramatic. It doesn't want a source identified or held accountable for an unusual happenstance or set of coinciding events — the federation isn't fond of having its shots blocked. They engineer initiatives to be quietly self-propagating without needing further support."

"Capable of sustaining themselves, then?"

"Yes. And nothing like a grenade rolling on a tabletop with its pin pulled, something you'd throw your body across to save everyone. Instead, think of oleander growing in a terrarium. It's equally deadly but subtle. There's no smoking gun statistic you can rely on to tell you that what's happening behind the scenes is intentional. There's no government registration of oleander petals.

"Initiatives often ride the coattails of something already out there. For instance, microplastics saturate the environment — we can render those unquestionably lethal. The obviousness of the threat is in the sheer volume and spread of the raw materials, the microplastics, for which we're not responsible."

"Microplastics availability is covered well in the highlight reel," I slipped in, "everywhere from Arctic snow to the depths of the Mariana Trench; trillions of pieces swirling around in a Pacific garbage patch twice the size of Texas. Every human on Earth ingesting a credit card's worth of microplastics a week. They're in our *blood*, for God's sake! Scary enough, all by itself. But how does accessibility translate into 'unquestionably lethal?'"

"The federation created specialized binding agents they've distributed everywhere for years. Binding agents are innocuous and undetectable, anchoring themselves to the microplastics and chemicals hiding inside you. Once bound, they store themselves in your adipose tissue, liver, and brain, where they stay virtually all your life. That's the first pass.

"'Adipose tissue?'"

"Body fat. A second pass contains the payloads that attach to the binding agents. The idea is that you'd consume a binding agent from one of thousands of sources. Sometime later — days, weeks, months, or years, it doesn't matter — you'd consume one or more of our payloads. The agent grabs the payload as it goes by, attaches it to the binder's anchor — that is, the microplastic or chemical it's bound to — and then activates the payload. The payload now has a home in your body, the platform it needs to do its work.

"The first of these two-pass approaches is the microplastics chemistry initiative. The only thing holding back its second pass is the development of an antidote to protect survivors."

"I get where the plastics originate, but who grinds them up and distributes the little pieces everywhere?"

"John's highlight articles cover microplastics' proliferation but not their creation. It begins with humans spreading their discarded plastics everywhere.

"Plastics don't degrade well in nature. However, long periods in active environments — sunlight, freezing and warming cycles, saltwater, consumption and excretion, exposure to chemicals, radiation, or ozone — break them into tiny particles. That Pacific garbage patch described in the reel generates half a million tons of those pieces — *annually*.

"The pieces become microscopic and can go anywhere. As you read in the reel, they swim in human bloodstreams; you can't eat, drink, or breathe today without ingesting microplastics."

"That's worrisome; one of the reel links says microplastics themselves can kill you."

"A function of volume, and how quickly. We greatly enhance the lethality; the federation's primary interest is that microplastics are in you, and you can do nothing about them."

I thought for a moment.

"Couldn't we avoid them — abstaining from processed food and liquids, buying organic produce … maybe keep wearing our pandemic masks?"

"A little late for that now," Jeremy replied. "'Organic' food labels mean nothing. Plants — and, by extension, animals that eat them — get nutrients from soil and groundwater. Microplastics and chemicals are already present in both, mostly from spreading sewage on croplands as fertilizer, damage done over decades."

"You call it the 'microplastics chemistry' initiative — tell me about the chemistry part."

"' Chemistry' refers to 'everywhere' and 'forever' chemicals. Like microplastics, they're already well-distributed throughout the environment."

"The highlight reel mentions them…." I was feeling a tad queasy.

"You might know everywhere chemicals as 'phthalates' — compounds that make plastics more pliable. Scientists are just learning the dangers; the U.S. only began regulating them in the last decade. Just by themselves, they're perfect for depopulation. In the body, phthalates can either mimic or block female hormones or, in males, suppress sexual development hormones. They cross the placenta to affect the unborn. They can increase cancer risk in children. Like microplastics, phthalates appear in the bloodstreams of everyone we've tested."

"They're truly everywhere chemicals, then…" I murmured. "And the forever ones — ?"

"Those belong to a class of over nine thousand chemicals known as PFAS. Tiny doses cause numerous cancers and a broad spectrum of health problems. It's impossible to rid the environment of them once they're in it. Again, every American tested has PFAS in their blood."

"Also everywhere, then," I mused.

Jeremy nodded. "Their ubiquitous nature solves the Hodin federation's biggest problem — rapid universal distribution, the Holy Grail of depopulation. Forget having to target specific geographic areas. And you don't have to convince billions of people to roll up their sleeves on some pretext they need a shot."

Jeremy's look became reflective.

"It was almost dumb luck. With no universal distribution method, the coalition could only address the low-hanging fruit with the most readily available depopulation initiatives. They spent 90 percent of their efforts chasing initiatives that yielded only a 10 percent death rate.

"So, how'd they know what to do with this Holy Grail once they identified it?'

"When the coalition realized how well-distributed microplastics already were, their first instinct was to weaponize them in place. But binding toxins, biologics, and heavy-metal molecules directly to plastics in the wild proved a struggle — too many variables, and too much waste."

"How'd they get around that?"

"Ah, a story that's become a legend within the federation. A researcher, coincidentally also a young mother, complained her daughter's favorite spaghetti lunch turned all her Tupperware bowls orange. She suddenly realized she was looking at the answer to the microplastics challenge. Tomato sauce contains lycopene, which binds easily to some plastics. Lycopene also binds readily to platelet-derived growth factors, hydrogen, and specific proteins in the human body.

"If you engineered a payload based on those natural compounds, lycopene could anchor it to microplastics."

I've had a lifelong penchant for Italian food, and I winced.

"The federation has since discovered more powerful binding agents. Still, the idea became the coalition's universal transport for remotely inserting toxins, biologics, and heavy metals into human bodies across the planet.

"Working with the same principle, we can attach payloads to everywhere and forever chemicals with other binding agents. And there's no rush. It's an evergreen solution."

"Should my loved ones worry about their futures or, I guess, lack thereof?" I asked nervously.

"There's still time," Jeremy answered dismissively. "Binding agents are out there now. However, the federation won't release individual payloads until an antidote for each is available to intended survivors. And after they're released, there'll be an incubation period for any payloads that aren't quick-acting poisons. That's by design. Excessive die-offs over short periods would attract too much attention."

"Then what's the projected time frame? It could take a long time to kill off seven billion people."

"Seven billion's a total for all of it, yes, but not the Hodin federation's kill number. They need to eliminate only two billion directly."

"Why? The math won't work if they want only a billion of us left…."

"That's because depopulation is an interaction of three different operations. We must decrease life expectancy, diminish the fertility rate — or more accurately, the replacement rate — and finally, eliminate the excess number remaining."

"I'm not following…" I said pensively.

"Think about this — a generation, the average time that elapses between the birth of a parent and when their first child comes into the world, is roughly twenty years. People today live almost eighty years. So, at any one time, four generations coexist on the planet. Cut life expectancy to sixty years, and you've removed a full generation from the overlap — 25 percent of the population."

"Okay, *that* wouldn't have occurred to me," I admitted.

"Reducing the fertility rate — and I'd include fetal and maternal deaths in that — is more straightforward. Populations decline once the birth rate is below the death rate. The further the number of births each year falls below the number of deaths, the fewer the number of people on the planet.

"Having fewer people lowers the number you need to do away with to reach your goal. All those initiatives working together can prevent or eliminate five billion people, leaving just two billion to remove. Carefully selecting targets further reduces the number of required terminations. When eliminating women of child-bearing age or younger, you're effectively killing two or more birds with the same stone, depending on how many children that woman would have produced otherwise.

That's one cold, heartless calculation — and sadly, perfectly logical. The cabal has a grand plan, one that seems well-considered and workable.

"Breaking it down like that makes it seem more plausible and possible," I acknowledged.

I hadn't expected the reference to women capable of having children; getting called out as a potential target rattled me enough that I bit the inside of my cheek for a distraction. I could see how that might have changed Jeremy's and Jennifer's perspectives once she became pregnant, even though their cabal employment should have shielded them from their initiatives.

"With that background," Jeremy continued, "I can get you the numbers showing the effects of these initiatives. We'll look at target populations where the federation has tested proof of concepts for reducing life expectancy and replacement rates along with direct population elimination."

"I can hardly wait," I said dryly.

Last week, I'd felt all this was merely a philosophical proposition. Jeremy's words today and those highlight reel links made it clear — the train departing the realm of the theoretical had left the station.

THE WRITINGS OF
AVRIL MARIA SERENE

Book One — Chapter 26

Jeremy and I resumed our session after taking a break from the dizzying download of troubling information.

"Life expectancy's a no-brainer," Jeremy began. "You've seen the highlight reel links describing the fall of U.S. healthcare quality into the basement?"

"I've skimmed them, but I get the gist. We've lost a loved one recently, and my father passed not so long ago; it's hard to be objective. I did see that life expectancy here's dropping fast — three years less than it was a few years ago."

"So, next item — how the federation lowers fertility rates."

I knew low birthrates were a thing these days around the world. Still, I'd assumed it was circumstantial — women merely exercising their option not to bear children.

"Are you talking about physically or psychologically manipulating conception?"

"Some of both. The coalition's arrangements with drug companies allow them to influence discreetly the compounding of almost any medication. For example, the pill can make intercourse less enjoyable for women — we amplify that."

"I saw the highlights' birth control link."

I squirmed in my seat, the message sinking in.

"I said in another session that the federation can access the unsalable products of pharma and chemical companies. You'd be shocked how many of those things end up in male sperm, number 51 in the reel."

True to his promise, Jeremy was impressing me with the cabal's efforts, though not in a good way.

"Sperm counts worldwide are half what they were fifty years ago and declining twice as fast as two decades ago. One-sixth of the population is now infertile — all since the Hodin federation emerged in 2000."

Jesus, Jeremy, I'm sorry I challenged you to prove all this.

He posed himself a question I wanted to ask: "With the number of child-bearing candidates and their fertility reduced, what about keeping successful inseminations from becoming live births? Again, success — by 2020, the U.S. had the highest infant mortality rate of any country. And getting worse — three and a half times the rate in Norway, a country the federation hasn't yet targeted."

"There's a highlight reel link. But killing babies in the womb ...." The thought knotted my stomach.

"The coalition's efforts aimed at birth mothers have proved effective." Jeremy was undeterred by my discomfort. "U.S. maternal mortality is three times that of most other high-income countries, number 56 in the reel.

"Taking the life of a mother and her child before or at birth further benefits depopulation because neither can conceive future progeny. Result? Practically speaking, U.S. population growth is at zero; any increases are coming from immigration, not births."

"The cabal's achieved early success in the U.S.," I conceded. "But does that translate to other countries and cultures?"

"The federation hasn't limited its experiments to the U.S. We've had success elsewhere, even more in Asia. Blaming China's eminent population decline on their now-abandoned one-child policy doesn't explain Japan's population in steady freefall."

"I saw that link as well. Except for India, Asian countries are stagnant or shrinking population-wise."

He gave me a knowing look. "The South Koreans fear the 'death cross,' their term to describe birth rates falling behind death rates. The Hodin federation has proven they can affect birth rates through politics and healthcare. They've shown that inducing infertility and chemical castration with altered products is quite effective."

"Any success in Europe?" I asked.

"Countries with declining populations include Greece, Ukraine, Poland, Italy, Hungary, Latvia, Romania, Croatia, Bulgaria, Slovakia, and Slovenia. The coalition expects Spain and Germany to join them soon."

He beat me to my next question. "The populations of several of Europe's neighbors, including Russia and Syria, are shrinking now."

"So 'progress' in major population centers," I summarized, "notable exceptions being Africa and India."

"Those two are low-hanging fruit," Jeremy responded. "Eliminating large portions of their populations isn't so hard.

"However, experimenting with Ebola and Marburg outbreaks in Africa taught the federation not to do the simple tasks first. Initiative successes in countries unable to defend themselves are visible to wealthy nations. Rich countries can jump ahead, spinning up solutions before the coalition can target them with the initiative."

"And India?"

"India just wasn't a good testing candidate. Many federation initiatives are experimental — having the success we've had was good fortune, not necessarily planned or expected. When throwing spaghetti against a wall, witnessing the result is crucial for determining what worked. But death counts in India aren't trustworthy. For example, India wouldn't provide believable mortality figures during the pandemic. Their government claimed five hundred thousand had died. However, the WHO calculated five million more COVID-19 deaths than past average mortalities for the same period."

"Doesn't skipping such a large country put a dent in your plans?"

"Not at all — the federation expects resounding success eliminating Indians in large numbers using initiatives refined elsewhere. Their dense urban areas with large ghettos are perfect for rapidly spreading biological pathogens. Thirty million street dogs bode well for animal-to-human transfers.

"Dependence upon the river Ganges is India's real vulnerability to the Hodin federation's methods. The Ganges basin serves over 650 million people. It's easy to access its headwaters at several points, and injecting coalition agents into urban areas is trivial — they're so crowded people don't know one another. The Ganges is perfect for distributing population-control initiatives, including chemical or bacteriological pollution."

"You said you abandoned further work in Africa because it was, in essence, too easy and too visible. Still, you have to deal with it at *some* point…"

"The federation's approach to Africa is the same as you'd use sweeping a room," Jeremy explained. "Start from the edges and corners and sweep into a pile at the center. Scoop it up and dump it into the trash barrel.

"Even without further intervention, by 2100, populations will have declined significantly on every continent except Africa, where numbers will have more than doubled... the pile at the center."

I was perplexed.

"Please forgive the racial overtones, but the cabal's allowing continued expansion of African populations while shrinking Asian, American, and European numbers. If I understood Jennifer's comment about race, would the cabal consider Africans the 'right' survivors?"

Jeremy wasn't going to let me bait him into *that* conversation.

"Deciding who lives or dies is discriminatory by its very nature," he pointed out, "which begs the question of whether any human should make those judgments. I can't entirely agree with some of the federation's decisions. Still, I accept that such concerns are above my pay grade and let it go.

"But we *will* eliminate most Africans —the coalition has logistical reasons for tackling Africa last. Mostly laziness and conservation of federation resources. Africa is vulnerable to a cascade of events that global warming will kick off — it'll grossly exacerbate everything already wrong there.

"The residents will eliminate themselves just trying to escape — unending tribal disputes and wars caused by intense unresolved competitions over resources, religion, politics, race and ethnicity, tribal loyalty, power, wealth, poverty, food, water, land, and shelter. On a continent where none of those things are stable, doubling the population won't improve matters.

"Africa's already highly susceptible to drought *and* floods caused by poor farming and land usage habits, and there's a mass extinction coming for species other than humans. The federation can leverage those vulnerabilities effectively by contaminating major waterways and seeding fertile land with pollutants."

I took a minute to absorb all this.

"There's a lot here to digest, Jeremy." I scanned my notes and realized I'd need more time. "I have homework to do — starting with a deeper dive into that highlight reel."

For now, I wanted to revisit the original problem. "Let me step back and look at the big picture momentarily. From what I've read before knowing anything of the cabal, by 2100, population growth worldwide will grind to a standstill organically."

"Possibly. But it'll stabilize at roughly ten billion people," Jeremy pointed out, "a pretty lousy number. Global warming will have left much of the planet uninhabitable, unable to sustain that number of people. The constant conflicts will likely wipe humankind from the face of the earth. The technologies we'll have developed by then almost guarantee it.

"But it won't happen at midnight on New Year's Eve in 2099. The quality of life in the seventy-five years preceding will steadily, irreversibly decline for everyone except a tiny subset of elites.

"Today's slums in India are the products of extreme poverty, lack of sanitation, and the resulting filth and vermin. Prevailing ignorance and the absence of gainful employment only strengthen internal segregation by castes, forcing those on the lower rungs to bear the brunt of a dwindling lack of resources. Still, their challenges today would be a utopia for the average human still alive in 2100."

I remained silent, unable to dispute what Jeremy was saying.

"The federation's orderly, unsuspected, and cooperative suicides of seven billion people will seem extraordinarily kind by comparison," Jeremy continued, "akin to putting down a horse with a broken leg. By contrast, the world where the coalition's survivors land will seem like a Garden of Eden. Everyone then alive will have a fair shot at living out their potential in relative happiness."

I was struck by the harmonious coexistence, even interdependence, of hope and thoughts of global death.

As our time was up and I prepared to leave, Jeremy turned to me and said the last thing I'd ever hear from him, words that would later haunt me: "This may sound odd, given that we need your help only because the federation will probably kill us and our baby at some point.

"Still, whether the coalition's methods are ethical or appreciated, they may well be the only means by which humanity can survive with any dignity."

THE WRITINGS OF
AVRIL MARIA SERENE

BOOK ONE — CHAPTER 27

SAN DIEGO, CALIFORNIA

I'd only been home an hour when Marci called.

"Alma's missing." There was worry in Marci's voice.

"What happened to make you think something's wrong?"

"A call came over the radio for tow trucks to haul away her trailer and that old Caravan. I was on my break and headed over to see if I could help Alma. The officer who took the complaint knew her; he said nobody had seen her for several weeks. Two homeless guys were fighting over space in the trailer; a citizen called it in. Without Alma there, the uniforms had to impound everything."

"Half a dozen people lost their shelter." I avoided thinking about the worst possibilities but felt Marci's apprehension. "People depend on her. She's not going to be happy when she gets back."

"I've canvassed the hospitals and our morgue, but no luck. I know it's a long shot, but Alma seemed to like you — maybe she'd try to reach out if she's in trouble. Let me know if you hear anything, would you?"

"You know I will — I'll cross my fingers you find her happy and well." Despite my expression of positivity, the news saddened me.

Paul was working, so I'd be eating by myself. I was taking my leftovers from the microwave for supper when Marci called again. She was nearly in tears.

"Oh, Debra Ann, the county medical examiner has Alma. She was one of the last buried out there in the desert. Hers was one of the bodies they recovered early on. I should have checked with them first, but I was hoping against hope those murderous assholes hadn't gotten her."

"Is the ME sure?"

"His description of her — age, height, weight, hair color, clothing, general health — fits the woman we knew as Alma. Her DNA and prints aren't in the system, so they don't have her birth name yet. The ME asked if I'd stop by and confirm that the clothing and personal possessions they found were hers.

"I let them know she's Bobby Perkins's mother. Hopefully, that'll help identify her. I'm heading over there tomorrow morning."

"I'm so sorry, Marci. I know how much your relationship with her meant and the good she was trying to do for her community."

The media firestorm around the body parts buried in the desert by active-duty San Diego police officers was quickly spreading nationally; I'd published the mayor's office connection this morning. But with none of the accused talking, the question of "Why?" wasn't being asked. The widespread presumption was that this was simply a bunch of rogue cops' solution to the homeless problem, taken to the extreme.

My deal with the sheriff's office promised me information as soon as they were ready to reveal it. As they unearthed body parts, it became clear the burials had been going on for some time, suggesting someone or something was consistently producing dismembered bodies. Perhaps the officers burying them were responsible, but there had to be a lot more to this.

Marci's invitation from the ME to identify Alma's possessions presented an opportunity to talk to the pathologists doing the work. Interviewing them might get me around their superiors' politically tailored statements.

"Would it be okay if I rode with you to the medical examiner's, Marci? I want to learn more about the others they've identified and get the pathologists' thoughts as to why someone killed them."

"I'd welcome the company. Alma and I were friends. With you there, I'll do better holding it together."

<hr>

Marci and I were greeted at the county morgue by Dr. Kim Sebastian. She was one of several pathologists assigned to identifying and reassembling the bodies retrieved from the desert.

"I'm Sgt. Robbins. I've come to identify some of the personal possessions recovered with the remains of a woman I knew as Alma."

"Yes, Sergeant, I received a note that you'd be stopping by," Dr. Sebastian replied. "Give me a moment if you don't mind."

She left through the swinging stainless steel door behind her, quickly returning with three clear evidence packs, each the size of a one-gallon zipper freezer bag. It didn't take Marci long to identify the contents as Alma's.

"Yes, these are her things." Marci tried to remain dispassionate. "The department has an active missing person case — SDPD recently impounded a trailer and a Caravan she was living in. They may be able to help you ID her."

"After you told us about her son being a fallen officer," the pathologist replied, "that connected some of the dots within the police department, and we learned about those recovered vehicles. Unfortunately, there's no match to the out-of-date registrations for the van or the trailer."

"May I see her and pay my respects?" Marci wanted to say goodbye.

"I'm sorry, Sergeant — you'll want to remember your friend as you knew her. Someone dismembered her; they used an aggressive power tool, likely a chainsaw. The dry soil composition acted like a desiccant, drawing moisture out of the tissue, essentially mummifying the remains. You wouldn't be able to recognize her."

"I understand, and thank you, doctor, for the explanation. I've been out to that area and understand how that could happen."

Marci turned to me. "It's pretty obvious where those suspended officers got their 'Cactus Club' nickname."

"Doctor, I'm Debra Ann Wynn." I stepped forward, offering my card. "I'm an investigative reporter. I turned the videos that launched this investigation over to the sheriff. Their office has offered me access to the facts of the case as they evolve, subject to clearing whatever I write with them before publication. I have some questions I'd like to ask you."

"I'll need to check with my supervisor, Ms. Wynn. As you can imagine, we've received a lot of media attention over this situation. I need to be diligent about safeguarding information."

"Debra Ann, please. And, of course, Doctor. If it helps, I was given Deputy Sheriff Wayne Mason's name in case of any questions."

In a few moments, the doctor returned.

"Thank you, Debra Ann, for your patience. How can I help you?"

"I have two sets of questions. The first is, how many bodies have you found? The initial estimate was eleven to seventeen complete bodies. The second part of that question is, do you know yet how long the killings have been going on?"

"They've still got ground-penetrating radar out at the site," Dr. Sebastian answered. "As they progress outward from the original burial locations, they get more false positives but continue to come across clusters of human remains. As things stand today, I'd add two dozen more to both ends of that estimate.

"As to the other part of your question, we can't know until we have all the bodies, but the oldest burial we've confirmed is from almost two years ago."

I exchanged glances with Marci.

"That brings me to the next question. The prevailing media theory is that the murders are the result of an extreme hate campaign against homeless persons. Have you any idea, suspicions, evidence, anything that tells you how, and more importantly why, they killed those poor people?"

"Again, we're just beginning our work," Dr. Sebastian cautioned, "but there *are* indications there's more to it. First, we're seeing high levels of similar toxic compounds built up in their tissues over time. We're not sure for every case, but we suspect someone introduced the poisons through the victims' alcohol and drug addictions. There's some evidence of unusual lung trauma, suggesting delivery via smoking or vaping products."

"You didn't mention digestion. That seems the most obvious path for poisoning someone."

"Ordinarily, yes, and that's where we started. However, the victims' stomach contents were inconsistent, and their lifestyles didn't seem to support regularity in their eating habits. Poisoning soup kitchens and shelter meals would have affected more people, most of whom we assume are still alive."

"So, their addictions provided the vehicle for the regular dosages it took to get to fatal levels," I summarized. For some reason, my conversation with Jeremy flashed through my mind, even though the two stories were unrelated and from opposite coasts.

"We believe so for most of these cases. And there is one consistency in the bodies," Dr. Sebastian continued. "They all have fresh intravenous injection sites in prominent locations drug users don't commonly use — notably, the backs of the shoulders and undersides of the thighs. Someone injected each of them near the time when they expired. Still, the deaths appear to be the results of the toxins already in their systems, not those final injections."

"Do you have any idea what those last shots were for?"

"Don't quote me on this — it's just an unofficial theory for now, but I'd guess someone was experimenting on these people. I think the toxins were induced into the victims in various ways over a relatively short period. I believe they gave those final injections to mitigate or conceal the effects of the toxins."

"Do you mean like Naloxone, the medication they use to reverse the effects of opioid overdoses?"

"No, that's a substance we test for immediately. The general idea may have been the same, but whatever this was, it wasn't anything we recognize as opioid-related."

Mengele. I felt a jolt run through my body but kept a straight face. Dr. Sebastian finished with the obvious.

"If saving them *was* the intent, the attempt failed."

<hr>

I arrived home with my thoughts unfocused and my energy level in the cellar. The grief Paul and I shared over Cindy's death weighed heavily on me. What Jeremy told me about the Hodin cabal hadn't helped; now, the discovery of Alma's body. That someone might be out there killing homeless people through medical experimentation cast a dark shadow over an already bad situation.

I was in no mood to work.

Having a bad day wouldn't have been such a big deal, but I faced a real problem with my writing. The interviews with Jeremy had begun as a favor to Harry, and the beginning of those conversations had been inauspicious at best, centering on what I had mistaken for decades-old conspiracy theories.

When, instead, Jeremy began dumping out a vast trove of what at least *sounded* like quality information, I was caught off-guard. I'd been running behind ever since. After several sessions, I was drowning in this massive pool of unvalidated information. Those details were crucial to the story and assessing the narrative's value to my readers.

To know what else I'd need from Jeremy, I had to verify what he'd already given me. When we next spoke, I'd leverage what I'd learned to drill down into specific areas to fill in any remaining blanks. At the same time, I'd also need to extract whatever I could that described other witnesses or participants.

Everything hinged upon how relevant and accurate Jeremy's statements thus far proved to be. But there was *so* much there — the highlight reel and more than twelve solid hours of recorded conversation.

I'd stretched myself too thin, and there were too many distractions. I wanted to be available to Paul whenever he needed support. I still had the corrupt councilwoman's story to put to bed. The third installment of my homelessness article for Gannett was pending the outcome of the medical examiner's work excavating those who had disappeared. What I'd already done needed tightening to make room for anything more they discovered.

There was no way out of my quandary other than to roll up my sleeves and get Jeremy's information validated. The good thing was that a lot of it could be verified using reliable sources on the Internet. Not quite ready to plunge in, I was still bemoaning the effort ahead of me when Doug Stein called to check in during a break in his routine.

It wasn't long before I complained to him about biting off more than I could chew with Jeremy's interviews. Then, suddenly, I remembered something from my early days working with Doug. I floated a proposal that could make confirming Jeremy's tale more pleasant.

"I still have Dad's recipe for lasagna," I said in my over-the-top beseeching voice — if Doug had been in the room, I'd have batted my eyes at him. And no, I wouldn't call it begging — not really.

"What are the chances you could talk Beth into coming with you to my place for a free meal?

"I wish I didn't have these ulterior motives, but I thought we could do like we used to in the old days. When we stumbled on something big while interviewing somebody, we'd pile up all those notes chasing it down. If it turned out the story had legs, we'd spend hours digging through the newspaper's morgue for validation. When I was a cub reporter, you and I would do that round-robin thing, you know, where we'd take turns verifying the next factoid from the notes or tape?"

"Lord, yes, I remember. Can't say I miss those days — the Internet's *so* much easier," Doug said, chuckling.

"You'll be happy to know we'd use a browser instead of microfiche. But it would be the same basic principle — three of us taking turns validating Jeremy's statements. Beth would be good at getting whatever we find into a spreadsheet. I bet we could knock it out in no time and maybe have fun doing it. I'm pretty sure I can talk Paul into joining us."

"You had me at your dad's lasagna," Doug admitted, "and Beth loves being part of working a story."

"It would help a lot. Are you sure the two of you won't mind giving up your evening?"

"Truthfully, I've been intrigued by Jeremy Hansen and his cabal since you first told me of it. It'll be a hoot to learn more."

Doug laughed.

"Besides, you'll owe me big when I bury myself too deep in one of *my* projects."

THE WRITINGS OF
AVRIL MARIA SERENE

Book One – Chapter 28

I hadn't realized how much I'd welcome having company. More importantly, being among friends away from the constant reminders of Cindy's passing seemed to help Paul. Beth expressed her and Doug's condolences with the perfect touch, showing their genuine concern without putting Paul in the position of dwelling on the memories.

It wasn't long before we were sharing other things. We avoided the gruesome elements of the homeless burials out in the desert. But we discussed the intensity of the growing media scrutiny, including two articles I'd published. We moved on to catching up with the more pleasant events in our personal lives. It would've been easy to forget I'd gathered everyone together for a purpose.

After we'd eaten and spent half an hour in relaxing conversation, the smell of garlic, tomato sauce, and roasted vegetables lingering in the air, it was time to get to work.

"I've been thinking about it," I announced, "and I have an idea how to validate everything Jeremy said."

"Beth, here's the recorder and a flash drive with the transcripts. Could you put together a spreadsheet on your laptop?"

"Sure, give me a moment." Beth began tapping on her notebook's keyboard.

I turned to Paul and Doug.

"I've set your laptops up with Google Messages linked to your phones for texting. Beth will read through the transcript until she finds a fact needing confirmation, assigning it to the first one of us available. We'll call out if we discover a solid Web page or article that verifies or refutes the statement Beth assigned us and text her the page's title, publisher, and Web address.

"Beth can then cut and paste the information from the text into the appropriate row of her spreadsheet. She'll read ahead in the transcript and repeat the process. Beth, I highlighted the portions of the conversations we can skip over."

"Pretty slick." Doug seemed impressed. "Pure cut-and-paste, no typing, eliminates any mistakes in translation."

"I've got a cheat sheet of sorts that Jeremy sent me. His boss, John Masters, collects links from the Internet that pertain to what the Hodin cabal is doing. Those can be starting points for validating Jeremy's statements in these interviews. Look for 'highlight reel' in the title of the file I e-mailed you."

Paul looked at Beth, and both turned to me and nodded.

I handed Beth a print copy of the transcript.

"Once you're ready, you can give the three of us our starting assignments from the beginning of the recording."

We were up and running in short order. I took the first two items to get things rolling.

"Beth, I've got validation for the deadly side effects of erythritol. Guys, stay away from artificial sweeteners made from stevia or monk fruit. It glues your platelets together to form clots."

The warning generated nods from everyone, along with Doug's comment, "And I always thought natural sources were the better option...."

"Beth, I see plenty of sites confirming the inability of governments to address global warming," I announced. "I'm sending one from *CNN*."

After Beth assigned statements from the recording to everyone for vetting, Doug spoke up. "Got one! *Wikipedia* confirms Jeremy's statistics on deaths during World War II.'"

A few moments later, it was Paul's turn. "Hey, I've got validation for his statement that a dozen African countries are warring on any given day, also *Wikipedia*."

Several minutes passed, and I spoke up again. "I've verified Jeremy's claims about China's problems with their one-child policy."

Beth raised a thumb. "We've finished the validations for the first interview session, and I'm moving on to the second recording."

Minutes later, Doug said, "I can verify Jeremy's claims about U.S. CO2 output, fossil fuel shipments between countries, and emissions data."

Paul soon followed up. "The statement about nine million additional pollution fatalities is confirmed."

"And I've got validation for his representation of CRISPR gene-editing capabilities," I added.

Ten minutes went by in silence as each of us researched our tasks.

"Here are two excellent sources that verify Jeremy's population and growth numbers," Doug called out, "from *Worldometers* and *Our World in Data*."

I spoke up next. "That massive pile of plastics out in the Pacific is the real deal. I'd *never* have believed it before these interviews."

Time flew by as we systematically corroborated Jeremy's claims and data and, by extension, the links in Masters's highlight reel.

"I'll never drink bottled water again!" Paul exclaimed. "Researchers found an average of a quarter million pieces of plastic per liter."

The validations continued through the second session recording and on to the third: microplastics in the polar ice caps, the proliferation of everywhere and forever chemicals, and the declines in Americans' life expectancy and quality of healthcare….

Then I had to announce something I'd hoped in my heart of hearts wasn't true.

"The highlight reel has an article supporting Jeremy's statement about poor-quality medical care. Its claim about *Goldman Sachs* asking in a published medical industry piece whether or not it made business sense to cure patients is true.

"The financial sector argues that not curing disease and providing repeated palliative treatments in its place is better for medicine's bottom line. *Jesus!* They want to keep people in pain for long periods to make more money and keep the sick out there spreading diseases to generate more profit opportunities."

I'd become upset.

"I'm sorry, but these are *fucking assholes*. Here's the article link, Beth."

There was a palpable silence from the others gathered at the table. After a moment, we returned to our assignments, the mood now somber.

The job had become morbid, as Jeremy's truths added up: fewer reproductive-age females compared to males; reduced male and female fertility worldwide; rising infant and maternal mortality rates; immigration replacing births as the source of U.S. population growth....

We plodded through, with Jeremy's statements generally proving true, backed by scientific papers and quality reporting. Finally, Paul checked out the human implications of predicted mass extinctions in Africa. His research supported Jeremy's claims and went even further to say the phenomenon isn't limited to Africa.

I backed that up with a related article.

"What Jeremy said about global warming kicking off the very events and challenges to which Africa is especially vulnerable holds. The population projections say that a substantial percentage of the world's people will reside in Africa in the coming decades.

"That means the risks to the human race from the continent's vulnerabilities will increase exponentially."

"And with that, we're done!" Beth announced, eliciting some cheer despite the gravity of our results.

It was nearly midnight, and by this point, everyone was tired, not to mention profoundly disturbed by the realities we were exposing.

"Christ, Debra Ann. How the hell did we miss all of this?" Doug captured what the members of our little team were feeling. "Not just us, but *everyone!*

"I get that for some of these things, there might be a dozen plausible other causes. But in our business, there are no such things as coincidences — *all this happening simultaneously?*"

Paul leaned over, taking a look at Beth's screen. "In forensics, we rely on tiny bits of data. Our spreadsheet is overflowing with it — something *has* to be going on. If these things keep piling up, it can't end well for us.

"It's only reasonable to assume someone or something is responsible. If Jeremy's descriptions of his employer are as reliable as what he's told us about the effects of their initiatives, we can assume the Hodin cabal is responsible. Even if not, *somebody* has to look into this, for heaven's sake."

Paul glanced at me.

"What's getting to me personally," I admitted, "is that it's not like those old conspiracy tropes.

"They're not doing this to protest the unfairness of it all, bolstered by self-serving paranoid fantasies of a world stacked against them. We're not dealing with some outrageous attempt to paint themselves or anyone else as the pity-poor-me victims here. If it *is* the Hodin cabal, they're not trying to publicize their work, nor are they politicizing or profiting from what they're doing.

"No, their focus seems to be entirely on pulling this damned thing off."

THE WRITINGS OF
AVRIL MARIA SERENE

Book One – Chapter 29

Most blocked number calls I get these days are from Harry Sanderson, so I immediately picked up when I saw "Anonymous caller" on my cell's screen.

The tightness in Harry's gravelly voice told me something was wrong.

"I wanted to let you know once I found out so you could cancel your flight." Harry's tone was somber. "Dennis Whitcomb, or as you know him, Jeremy Hansen, has gone missing; we can't find the man."

"Oh, Harry…."

My heart sank — I'd spent time enough with Jeremy to respect and understand him, even like him, despite not always agreeing with his views. Perhaps learning so recently of Alma's fate was driving my negative outlook. Still, I was aware of the risks Jeremy was taking and the kind of organization he was defying. If Harry, with all his skills, couldn't locate him, I had to wonder if Jeremy was still alive.

"Do you know what led to him disappearing?"

"The hardest part of protecting someone isn't the bad guy," Harry replied. "It's the challenges posed by the person you're trying to safeguard.

"That's especially true in long-term situations where the threat is nonspecific. The client becomes complacent and, taking for granted that our agents are there, no longer sees the danger. Eventually, they'll feel like their protectors are jailers and want or take more freedom."

"Did he do something to reclaim his liberty…?"

"To track his calls and texts, we'd cloned Jeremy's cell and the burner the cabal gave him. He didn't tell us he'd switched out that burner, so we didn't have a copy of the phone or know the new number. Our operative saw Jeremy had gotten a text from a woman we didn't recognize on his personal cell. He texted back instructions to contact him at a number we didn't have."

"That can't be good…," I murmured.

"By the time we realized the sender spoofed the incoming number for that first text, Jeremy had ditched his security detail and wasn't answering our calls. We presume he wanted to hook up with this woman, not realizing it wasn't who he thought it was."

Suddenly, another worry overwhelmed my dread over Jeremy's presumed fate.

"Where's Jennifer?"

"She went to DC on cabal business. We're trying to reach her without making waves."

I had a hopeful thought.

"Do we know if anything's happened with Jeremy's boss, John Masters? Jeremy's concerns were predicated upon Masters exiting the cabal on bad terms, leaving Jeremy in the lurch. If Masters is still around, Jeremy's probably safe."

"We have nothing on Masters," Harry replied. "The two of them haven't been in the same place at the same time since Jeremy's father hired us, and they scramble or encrypt the communications between them."

"Events may have played out the way Jeremy feared they would," I surmised. "Masters taking a powder, and the cabal terminating both in case Masters contaminated Jeremy."

"That's what the odds say. But it's possible it went the other way. Say the cabal learned Jeremy was conversing with outsiders about their business. Debra Ann, I hate to cramp your style, but I want you to keep a low profile until my operatives can sort this out. If anything around you doesn't feel right, contact me immediately, and we'll get you some help."

"I didn't consider that; thanks for the heads-up." I was grateful for Harry's awareness.

"Maybe Jeremy's just sowing wild oats," Harry speculated. "He may turn up at his place, wondering what the fuss is about. But better safe than sorry."

"I'm not to a point yet where anything I'm doing would help Jeremy. I've researched some of it, but all I have are generalities. We hadn't yet nailed down specific names, places, and times. Even if I had something I could publish, it'd take a while to get it out there."

"That may be for the better; it wouldn't be a good idea to expose you now as someone knowledgeable about the Hodin cabal," Harry cautioned. "Not until things have settled and we know what's happened to Jeremy, and for that matter, Masters. Still, I wouldn't put away your keyboard just yet — if what we're learning holds up, you'll have to tell the story somewhere along the line."

"Oh, absolutely. With that caveat — if it's true — this whole thing's fascinating, maybe as big as anything I've written. But it'd be a leap with what I have now; not enough material yet to sink my teeth into.

"It's one of those things that, if it's real, is huge — it'll take a lot of time and resources to run it all to ground. And that gets me just the factual aspects. I could write a Wikipedia page, but facts aren't enough to publish a good story."

"I'm not following — I thought reporting facts was what investigative journalists do…?"

"Oh, no, not at all. Context matters. The implications matter. That somebody burglarizes an office building isn't a story. It becomes one when the target is the Democratic Party headquarters, and the burglary is on behalf of the President. It's about people and emotions and their relationships, not just with each other but with the audience. People want to read about people and, occasionally, the antics of a cute kitten.

"Even massive natural disasters get ignored if there's no connection to human beings, their losses, or their valiant survival efforts."

"People need to feel an attachment…," Harry mused.

"And that's the problem with what Jeremy's given me so far. For all of his compelling talk and convincing exhibits of a massive conspiracy to kill billions of people over the past twenty years, there's no meat. No hook. He hasn't yet revealed a single name, or even a description, of any person ever killed by anyone associated with the alleged cabal. Or who's been the victim of violence or even a threat of harm. Not one.

"We would have gotten there eventually, but I spent our time chasing background and hadn't yet asked him those questions."

"Ah, I see; you've explained the problem well. Unfortunate for our purposes, but I get it."

"His story's especially challenging because there've been conspiracy theories around the same subject for decades. That makes for a high bar to get over if I want to keep the piece from being relegated to the QAnon dump heap. So far, Jeremy hasn't pointed me to any sources for confirmation — everything's been Internet links and hearsay. Worse, I don't know how to contact Masters, who he overheard most of this from."

"Several good reasons to put this story on hold. Disappointing, but as I said, I'd prefer you not draw more attention anyway."

"I hate to back off, but yes. Personally, Jeremy's account is riveting on an intellectual level, even terrifying. But that's just me. It hurts to keep repeating this; maybe I'm trying to convince myself I'm doing the right thing. However, the narrative is boring to the average reader without one or more captivating and interesting human beings to draw an audience to empathize, sympathize, or identify with.

"As things stand now, readers wouldn't find Jeremy or Jennifer relatable because they're still willingly employed by a group I'd be claiming were mass murderers. It's too bad because Jennifer's pregnancy would be a great hook if her role were more innocent – her baby's future would be a nice foil for the narrative, a survivor's prospects versus everyone else's.

"Until and unless we know what happened to the couple or, even better, his boss — assuming those events are interesting, horrifying, or unjust in their own right — I don't have a story anyone wants to read."

"It won't do any good if no one takes in what you write," Harry agreed.

"Motivated to get the story out to help save someone's life, I could look past some of the usual criteria and the imperfections. With Jeremy missing and possibly already dead, that incentive's gone. If he's okay and can provide more information, I'll push through the other challenges.

"It's not a story I'm likely ever to forget. God, I despise dropping it. But I'll have to let it go until something changes.

"Without Jeremy, or even Jennifer, to help, I'm sorry, Harry, I just can't get over the hump."

Book One – Chapter 30

Paul had taken off for Quantico to get in some forensic training. My mind was also thousands of miles away as I walked out of my apartment building, fumbling through my purse, checking to ensure I had my digital voice recorder.

What the…? From the tenant's entrance, I couldn't tell what that dark lump was. Did somebody leave a garbage bag full of trash lying on the hood of my car? *Dammit, some people have* no *class!*

A trail of dark liquid meandered from the bottom of the bag across the hood and down the fender in front of the tire, forming a small pool on the pavement.

That better not stain my paint.

I tilted my head and dropped my shoulders in frustration.

As I got closer, a foul odor assailed me.

The top of the garbage bag was open toward my windshield.

Placing my purse on the hood next to the windscreen but away from the dark green sack of trash, I cautiously raised the lip of the garbage bag.

I shrieked, falling back and knocking my purse and its contents to the pavement as I backpedaled.

Someone who'd heard my screams ran up behind me, catching me as I tripped.

I stared up at a man in his fifties, recognizing him as a neighbor I knew only as "Tom."

"They killed Danny Boy! They *eviscerated* him. *Oh, my God...*," I blubbered to my rescuer between sobs.

A middle-aged woman approached, taking my arm and guiding me toward a tenant's car I could lean against.

Tom carefully peeked into the bag, then quickly spun away, bending over and putting both hands on his knees, gagging. After a few moments, he fought off the urge, raising himself. "Shirley, would you call 9-1-1? Tell them someone's disemboweled a dog and left it on the hood of Ms. Wynn's car."

As he walked back toward us, I dabbed away the tears with a tissue, still shaken.

"Lord! The sons of bitches super-glued the poor dog's eyes open," Tom said, "so it would stare at anyone behind the steering wheel. Christ, who *does* something like that?"

"Look, honey, let's all go back inside until the police arrive," Shirley suggested. "No sense standing out here looking at it. Poor thing smells to high heaven."

"Let me get your purse." Tom turned toward my car.

"Oh, no, please; you've been too kind. I'll get it," I protested weakly, following Tom. But he persisted, and together, we gathered everything back into my handbag, carefully avoiding looking near Danny Boy's remains.

"I knew that dog," I explained. "I mean, I met the little guy and his owner, a young woman, a few weeks ago." I caught myself before describing how Danny Boy's home was three thousand miles away. I suddenly realized how crazy any part of this story would sound to first-time listeners. I needed to talk to Harry.

I made an excuse to slip away and call the private detective in the apartment building's entryway. At the same time, my fellow tenants waited for responding officers. When Harry picked up, I told him what had happened. "The police are on their way, but I've no clue what to say to them. I was upset and let it slip out to my neighbors that I knew the dog and his owner. Anything more will sound bonkers — telling the whole thing would be even worse."

"I'm sorry, Debra Ann. Whatever I've gotten you into is way more than I thought. Was the dog wearing its tags?"

"I don't know, it caught me off guard. I was freaking out too much to think about that."

"Understandable." Harry's tone was sympathetic. "I wouldn't have done any better myself under those circumstances.

"They shipped that dog three thousand miles, maybe dead, or they killed him here just to tell you they know who you are and where you live — rat bastards. We'll need to deal with them, but that can wait. You're right, though — whatever you tell the cops will sound Looney Tunes."

"My first instinct was to call Marci. But if I explained everything… I know her; she'll want to get involved. I'm not sure I want to expose anyone to risks I don't fully understand myself."

"You don't need my opinion, Debra Ann, but your instincts are on the money. And we're still making progress — my team's checking out the names of the cabal members Jennifer gave us. I know you'll want to get ahead of this, but you've got to stay under the radar until I get back to you."

"I hear you, Harry. It doesn't hurt for them to think I'm taking their message seriously, at least for a while. In the meantime, I'll get the apartment manager to give me a copy of the parking lot video — I pushed them last year to install more cameras after the Seaver case. I'll send it to you."

Tom tapped me on the shoulder and pointed an index finger toward the parking lot. The patrol unit had arrived.

"Okay, the officers just pulled up." I covered my mouth and the phone with my free hand. "I'll tell them a story that'll hold water if they connect it later to whatever's happened with Jeremy and Jennifer. Gotta go, Harry; thanks for lending an ear — let me know what you find out!"

Hanging up, I joined Tom and Shirley on their way to the parking lot. As we approached a uniformed officer, the animal control unit pulled up. Speaking to the policeman as they removed Danny Boy's carcass, the three of us explained the immediate situation while the officer took notes; he then turned his attention to me.

"You seem to be the target of this, Ms. Wynn. I'm familiar with your work. Does this connect to a story you're investigating?"

"Not so far as I know. Several weeks ago, I went to Las Vegas to chase down something that didn't pan out. I was walking to a restaurant for something to eat, and a couple approached me. They said they'd recognized me from my days with the *Union-Tribune* and had a story I should hear. They had that little dog with them. I remembered his name because 'Danny Boy' was one of Dad's favorite songs."

"What do you recall about the couple?" the officer asked.

"His name was Jerry. No, wait, Jeremy. And hers was Jenny. They were from somewhere back East."

"The techs read the dog's chip, but neither of those names matches. We know the animal was from Boston, so that part fits."

Oh, that's right; Jennifer must have been using her cabal alias when we met.

"We had some drinks at the casino. There was nothing to the story they were pushing — QAnon conspiracy stuff. Powerful people trying to kill us minions to stop global warming, that kind of thing. I needed to catch my flight back, so I politely brushed them off."

"I see. The nature of the dog's death was pretty gruesome; we're going to have forensics dust your car for prints and examine it for trace evidence. We'll do that here, but it'll tie your car up for maybe an hour. You might try a ride-sharing service if there's somewhere you need to be."

I thanked him, took his card, and promised to contact the department if I remembered anything more.

Despite the wisdom in Harry's warning, my instinctual reaction under attack is to dig, understand my adversary, and learn more about the threat — knowledge as power. I wished I'd had one more interview with Jeremy to get specific details of the cabal and its members. I had little doubt they'd killed Jeremy, his girlfriend, and her dog.

Harry and his team would have picked up any tails on Jeremy. The cabal could have learned of my involvement by following Jennifer. But they likely went after her to clean up loose ends after eliminating Jeremy. Surrendering information about me may have been in desperate barter for her life.

Either way, the cabal clearly showed they had scale, scope, and reach beyond anything I'd credited them with. The question underneath all of this now bothered me, perhaps belatedly.

It hinged on whether the Hodin cabal was an extreme outlier group of crazies with paranoid fantasies so amped up they'd engage in homicide to express their insanity.

Or, as Jeremy's story suggested, did they represent something deadly serious and very real to which they were so committed they'd murder to protect it?

Whatever the answer, Danny Boy's killing kicked one of my arguments for not continuing with the story of the Hodin cabal right in the teeth — people do feel an attachment to stories that include extreme cruelty to animals.

Should I have taken Jeremy's story of seven billion potential victims more to heart?

BOOK TWO

THE WRITINGS OF
AVRIL MARIA SERENE

BOOK TWO — PROLOGUE

BOSTON, MASSACHUSETTS: NINETEEN YEARS AGO

The neon lights of the strip mall's storefront signs had flickered to life more than an hour ago as dusk faded into the early evening. It was late fall in the Neponset district of Boston's Dorchester neighborhood.

The midweek foot traffic was sparse along a sidewalk spotted with blackened blotches of discarded chewing gum. A tall business professional dressed in a long gray coat, dark wool pants, and black leather gloves was one of the few pedestrians. He casually strolled the wide walkway between the noses of angled-in parked cars and store entrances. The man's tanned face was clean-shaven, his prematurely graying hair styled in a short business cut. Though he was in his late twenties, his clothing choices and John Lennon-style round wire-rimmed glasses made him seem older.

A brisk breeze mixed with smells of beer, pizza, and car exhaust as it stirred the chilly autumn air in the quarter-full parking lot. Yet even as the man pulled the brim of his dark gray fedora down slightly, he slowly unfastened his coat, one button at a time. He hadn't picked out his target, but his production quota insisted he make his move soon — he'd need access to the right tools for the job. He kept his arms at his sides and his back to the occasional impish gust as much as possible so the front of his coat wouldn't blow open.

Pausing between shops, the man pulled a Blackberry from his pocket, punching one of the speed-dial numbers. He needed to ensure that no one was missing him and wouldn't be for the next half hour.

"Hi, Julianna; just checking in. I should be home by nine. Has anyone stopped by looking for me? The cable guy was there? If he has to come back, you're off tomorrow night, right? Okay, perfect. Call him back and have him return the next night instead. Any messages? Oh, that can wait; I'll send him an e-mail later. I'm sorry I missed supper — set me a plate in the microwave. I'll reheat it when I get back to the house. Go ahead home, spend some time with your hubby."

Placing the phone back in his coat pocket, the man drew a deep breath, knowing his time was his own. *Game on.*

A string of small bells tinkled, announcing the door opening into a mini-mart and package store thirty feet ahead of him. A shorter man in a dull red, plaid cotton shirt and fraying Red Sox ball cap walked from the shop onto the sidewalk. Cradling a quart of whiskey in a brown paper bag, he turned toward the gentlemanly pedestrian. In his mid-to-late sixties, with a week's stubble on his face and missing most of his teeth, the older man nodded slightly in acknowledgment at the well-dressed passerby as they crossed paths.

Once the distance between them had grown to about twenty-five feet, the younger man turned crisply on his heels.

He began following the graybeard with the paper bag, who'd glance from side to side every dozen steps as he went along, pausing to take a long pull from the bottle.

The man following hung back to maintain the distance between them.

They traveled a block past the white-painted brick storefronts and splashy advertisements in the pawnshop, payday loan, intimate lingerie, and tobacco shop windows.

Suddenly, the older man made a quick left turn into a long, darkened alley used by garbage trucks to access the street behind the strip mall.

The man in the long coat slowed as he approached the alleyway, then turned to face the parking lot.

Swiveling on his hips, he quickly scanned in both directions for anyone nearby who might be watching.

Spotting no one, he pivoted, stepping noiselessly into the alley until he was far enough inside that no one could see him from the lot.

The odors of urine and rotting garbage rose to greet him from the trash in the dark corners.

A rusty, single-bulb light fixture tapped against the brick as it swung on its bare electric wires at the far end of the alley.

It took a moment for his eyes to adjust to the minimal illumination; he spotted his intended target stopped before the dark green, gang-graffitied dumpster for a long drink, his back still toward his pursuer.

Pulling his Glock 22 from its waistband holster at his back with his right hand, the well-dressed man retrieved the silencer from his coat pocket with his left.

With the skill that comes from long practice, he quickly spun the silencer onto the barrel of the automatic, using the flap of his coat as partial cover.

Closing the distance with just a few steps and no warning, the younger man shot the old fellow in the back once, near his heart, from eight feet away.

As his victim hit the ground with a dull thud, the half-empty bottle of cheap bourbon slid out of its paper sack and clattered against the rough pavement.

The shooter fired again, striking the downed man in the back of his head.

The dying man's skull bounced with the impact on the broken asphalt past the far end of the dumpster, a growing pool of blood spreading from his face.

Suddenly, the killer heard a woman's scream.

A split second later, a voice on the other side of the garbage bin yelled out in fear and surprise, *"Holy fucking shit!"*

Pointing his weapon with both hands past the end of the dumpster, the shooter stepped around the body and across the front of the bin.

Cowering between the end of the garbage bin and the brick wall was a man in his early thirties, wearing jeans and a bomber jacket. He was standing, trying to bury his head into his right shoulder for protection, his hands half-raised, with his pants unzipped and down around his knees.

In front of him was a young, tattooed woman with cropped blonde hair kneeling on her folded denim jacket. Both were now staring at the armed assailant, eyes opened wide in terror.

The frightened blonde fell backward onto the seat of her short skirt, then scrambled from a clumsy crab walk to get to her feet and run. The male began fumbling with his pants, too encumbered to go anywhere.

Turning toward the woman, the shooter calmly put a bullet in the side of her chest, dropping her to the pavement with a whimper and a moan.

He immediately swung his weapon back toward her date.

Pulling the trigger twice in rapid succession, once to the heart and then to the head, he watched as the body collapsed and seated itself against the side of the dumpster.

Returning to the woman, he kicked her over onto her back and fired again into her forehead.

Spinning around, the killer checked for foot traffic at either end of the alley and saw no witnesses.

He doubted the cursing or scream would have made it out of the alley or that the source of the noise would be apparent to passersby. The murderer knew too well how sounds reverberated through these streets and alleyways.

Working swiftly and efficiently, he unscrewed the warm silencer, wrapping it in a handkerchief, and returned it to his coat pocket. He pushed the back of his coat to one side and slipped his weapon back into its holster.

As he policed his brass, he got the second surprise of this evening — he could find only five of the six shell casings.

He rolled the older man's body first to one side, then to the other, and came up empty.

Checking the other corpses and the woman's jacket yielded nothing; looking under the dumpster, he couldn't see anything.

He pulled his Swiss Army knife out of his front pocket — its tiny penlight was the only light source immediately at hand and would have to do.

Protecting his knees with a flattened cardboard box, the man scanned the area between the iron casters at the bottom of the garbage bin.

He couldn't see anything shiny in the long shadows cast by the dim light of his knife.

Had the other casing made it into the garbage bin?

Now uncharacteristically frantic, the man searched through the open side of the nearly full container, but no cartridge brass.

Approaching desperation as time passed and the chances of discovery increased, he threw open the cover on the other side of the dumpster.

What he was looking for eluded him; he needed to escape that alley. A well-dressed man rummaging through a garbage bin in this part of town attracts attention, and someone might remember once they found the bodies.

Leaning over, he brushed off his knees with his hands, his eyes making another hurried pass through and around the area to no avail.

Then, with a quick shake and roll of his shoulders to settle his coat as he stood up, the killer buttoned it, pulling his hat further down over his eyes.

Casually walking out the back of the alley, he turned to his right, away from the strip mall. At the next intersection, he mingled with the occasional shopper and a few partygoers meandering toward the small bars lining either side of the street.

Once he caught sight of his three-year-old silver Mazda 626 with the distinctive black bra parked on the side street, the man quickened his pace.

Sliding into the driver's seat, he closed the door and pulled on his seatbelt. Tapping the Manny Ramirez bobblehead on the dash with his forefinger out of habit, he fired up the engine. He sat there momentarily, hands resting on his thighs, transfixed.

Suddenly, he slammed the steering wheel hard with the heels of both hands. His frustrations were boiling over; his face rucked up in fury, his teeth bared.

Fuck, where did that damned casing go?

It's gotta be in that dumpster. Crap! Just have to hope my luck holds — maybe the police won't find it or can't use it for anything. I'm getting too damned sloppy — the next time I have unexpected witnesses, eliminating them may not be so easy.

Dammit, this just isn't working. Too fucking many of them, and it takes too long. I've got to find a better way....

Providence was paying close attention that night, and she has a wicked, often twisted, sense of humor. *What could be funnier than giving an aspiring mass murderer everything he asked for?*

THE WRITINGS OF
AVRIL MARIA SERENE

BOOK TWO — CHAPTER 1

LEVERKUSEN, GERMANY: FOUR YEARS AGO

I t was 18:50, and the haptic vibrations from Reinhold Richter's Apple watch had begun their insistent reminders. His Hodin federation status update call would start in ten minutes. Richter punched the interoffice button on the desk phone.

"Frieda, es ist fast 19:00. Ich habe ein internationales Gespräch, also kannst du nach Hause gehen. Bitte schließen Sie die Außentür des Büros auf dem Weg nach draußen ab."

He could hear the excitement in Frieda's voice as she learned she didn't have to stay for his upcoming international call. Lately, she'd been anxious to get home to her new boyfriend in the evenings. Good for Richter, too, because he needed to avoid getting reported again for violating the forty-eight-hour workweek limit.

When viewed from above, the massive Byar AG office complex looked like a giant letter *C*. Richter's chrome-and-glass suite was on the fifth floor inside of the bottom curve. As he scanned the other offices through the expansive windows, he saw most of the executive staff had shut theirs down for the evening. Room lights were flashing on and off as cleaning crews made their rounds.

Richter reached under his desk's glass top and flipped the switches to close the window blinds and lock the electronic deadbolt to his office. The janitorial staff was due shortly; he didn't need anyone interrupting or overhearing his telephone conversation. Richter pulled the burner phone from his bottom right-side desk drawer, attaching the voice scrambler to its speaker jack.

Set for his expected call, Richter reflected for a moment. Byar was the world's foremost pharmaceuticals and chemicals producer and distributor; as an embedded Hodin federation operative, it had taken him eight years to reach the executive suite. Now head of the corporation's supply-chain management team, he'd attained the access and authority necessary to serve the coalition well. His stature within the secretive group had risen accordingly; he now reported directly to John Masters.

Richter understood that name to be an alias. Secrecy within the federation prohibited an org chart. Still, he believed Masters to be one of the most influential figures in the federation, alongside the principal director and founder's council. That put Richter at the center of the federation's most important initiatives, powerful in his own right.

Promptly at 19:00, the burner phone announced a call coming in, and Richter became Henry Simpson, his federation persona.

"Hello, John; I trust all's well with you...," Richter answered, his accent almost unnoticeable after years of practice. He perused the decrypted version of his notes on his computer monitor as he listened.

These every-other-week status reports were all business, and Masters went straight to the point.

"It's all good, Henry — a busy couple of weeks. Let's start with Marburg, Ravn, Nipah, and Ebola virus initiatives and how the Chinese klusterfucking of Wuhan disrupts our distribution plans. Then we'll discuss merging the forever and the everywhere chemicals with the microplastics project; I see those as having common elements.

"My first concern is understanding how defenses erected against the COVID-19 pandemic interfere with our plans. Fill me in as to where we stand."

"Yes, John. First, some background. China's animal-to-human transmission lab near Wuhan parallels our zoonotic disease lab. Because our interest is in transmitting viruses, bacteria, and parasites for their depopulation potential, we're primarily going for fatalities and adverse effects on human reproduction.

"China's using zoonoses for slightly different ends. First, they want to manage growing protests and political activity among citizens. They're sickening groups that arise and show any defiance. Their secondary goal is to weaponize biologics delivery for military purposes."

"Let's get someone inside their military project, Henry, to see what they have that we could use. And we'll want to make our output's genetics resemble what they're doing, for cover."

"We're working on both," Richter replied.

"Add that status item to your next report. So, how'd the Chinese fuck this up?"

"They lack experience and discipline. What they were doing became public knowledge when SARS-CoV escaped one of their other labs. That proved such a disaster we had to assume they'd learned their lesson."

"Apparently, they didn't." Masters's tone reflected his unhappiness.

"What the media calls COVID-19 was a mutation of SARS-CoV-2," Richter continued, "from a bat coronavirus carried by pangolins. While tweaking it, the Chinese let it get away. They spun it as a natural infection escaping the open-air wet market. Still, the modified genetics have that Wuhan lab's fingerprints. The good news is we've made our more potent version look like a natural mutation of theirs — our hands remain clean."

"Good. It's the downstream side effects that bother me. Countries closing borders. Travel restrictions, mask mandates, and edicts against gathering in large groups. Tell me how you'll keep our Marburg and Ebola efforts from getting caught in the crossfire. I don't want another COVID-19 mutation we don't control provoking international defensive reactions that interfere with our efforts to distribute those other viruses."

"Human nature's on our side," Richter responded. "People will tire of restrictions and become complacent. Until then, Marburg and Ebola distribution will have to tread water, wait for things to settle, and see where we end up.

"We'll forge ahead during the downtime to be ready when conditions improve. I reported last month we've grown transportable and storable variants of both Marburg and Ebola. Since then, we've acquired the vaccine the WHO's testing in Equatorial Guinea — we've gene-spliced a variant of Marburg that circumvents their immunization while perfecting our survivor inoculation. We've also created a reactive single-shot Ebola vaccine."

"Where does that leave us in the bigger picture?"

"The issue's been distributing those inoculations to protected members. Both are intramuscular injectables. We needed something already in the supply chain to serve as cover. The FDA approved Ozempic as an antidiabetic drug in 2017. It's also an injectable, and patients go to custom compounders to get around high prices. Perfect for hiding our vaccines; they'll blend right in."

"So, progress, but work still left to do," Masters summarized. "I like the Ozempic idea. Make sure it's available whenever we pull the trigger on either virus."

"Is there anything else on those fronts?"

"No, we're good," Masters answered. "The next items are the microplastics project and the forever and everywhere chemicals initiatives."

Conversation between the two men paused as their voice scramblers announced they were changing passkeys and renegotiating the connection.

"You've been reporting the binder and payload portions of our microplastics push as ready for some time, Henry. It's our best initiative yet, but we can't turn it loose until we can protect the members who'll carry on after. I need a progress update on development efforts for the antidote."

"I've got nothing concrete to report, John — closer, but not there yet."

"Not good, Henry. We can't be killing our kind; protection's the only thing holding us back. Nothing against your crew, but I want to engage external resources under my direction to see if fresh eyes come up with something."

"No offense taken, John. I hear you loud and clear. The microplastics initiative is far and away the most powerful tool in our arsenal. The sooner we make it viable, the better."

Masters paused before addressing the situation.

"You've got competent staff and excellent equipment and facilities. Let's not waste them. It wouldn't make sense for two independent groups of researchers to work on the same problem. So, let's change the task assigned to your team. They've been at this for a while; adding some spice to the work might help.

"We have two other robust initiatives with issues similar to microplastics. Let's group all three. Applying lessons learned working with microplastics might expedite the development of the other projects."

"The other initiatives are the forever and the everywhere chemicals projects?"

"Yes. All three involve carriers already out in the environment in abundance," Masters replied.

"Those initiatives use the same principle: a chemical binder attaching a payload to transports already out there — bits of plastics or indestructible chemicals — and then riding that carrier wherever it goes. All three can use human digestive systems, lungs, and blood as mixing chambers to join binders and payloads with the carrier. The forever and everywhere chemicals initiatives have additional delivery options, including mechanical diffusion through aerosols. It may be possible to adapt those to microplastics."

Richter wanted a better understanding of the synergies.

"What benefits will we see from merging the three projects?"

"The main reason for grouping these — let's call it our 'microplastics chemistry' initiative," Masters explained, "is they all have the same challenge at the end. We need to develop an antidote or preventative — for either the binding agent or the payload — that protects those we want to survive depopulation. Hopefully, a successful answer to one can suggest a solution for one or both of the others.

"We need to expedite solving the issue for all three. Any of these initiatives — but especially when combined — has enough potential to make our job of reducing the population trivial, a walk in the park. We'll keep my team focused on just the antidote for the microplastic binders and payloads we've already developed."

"I'll introduce the three teams working on these initiatives to one another," Richter responded. "They can interact more closely once their projects are together under one roof. Do we plan to stay with the same products we used for human testing of the microplastics initiative? Chips, crackers, bread, and pasta for the binders; sports drinks, fruit juices, wine, and beer for the payloads?"

"Yes, same principle, Henry. The binders need to store themselves for the long term as body fat. The payloads need to be liquid to get into the bloodstream quickly. The flavorings will cover any taste issues from our additives. We'll make adjustments as necessary."

"I'll know the synergies between the three programs in the coming week. I'll include them in the next status update."

"Break this microplastics chemistry initiative into a separate weekly report, and ping me any major developments. We need to keep my team and yours in sync. Finally, your last update expressed positive news about the *candida auris* fungal initiative. Any follow-up?"

"Yes, John, when last we spoke, we'd successfully tested the strain that resists echinocandins. Those are the most common class of antifungals. We've also made progress defending the fungi against azoles and polyenes antifungals."

"Good job, Henry. But just for future reference, unless there's a problem, we don't need that level of detail for our status reports."

"Understood. In that previous report, I said all we needed was the antidote, and we'd be good to go. Since then, we've hit paydirt, developing an antidote as a nasal spray. We've tested it and begun ramping up the supply chain for production. Once we can protect our survivors, we'll release *candida auris* more broadly into hospitals and medical facilities."

"That's good to hear." Masters's tone conveyed his approval.

"The fungus should prove sufficiently deadly at scale," Richter continued. "It has excellent killing potential; travels well in air, water, and animal fur; spores on demand; and can survive most disinfectants. Best of all, the spores stick to the oils on the surface of human skin — people make perfect transports.

"Most of our distribution can come from carry-out traffic through those hospital visitors and waiting rooms."

BOOK TWO — CHAPTER 2

BOSTON, MASSACHUSETTS: ONE YEAR AGO

The Hodin federation executive had rented a hotel room at The Bostonian using 'John Masters,' the federation pseudonym he'd assumed for the afternoon. He'd dedicated his time today to Hodin federation business — the orientation of his new confidential assistant.

As Masters entered the conference room, the coalition security operative scanning for electronic surveillance devices and placing countermeasures gave Masters a thumbs-up, finished his work, and left.

The trainee had arrived ahead and sat patiently in one of the plush, high-back chairs on either side of a small table near the window. In his early thirties, the new aide was a clean-shaven, muscular, and stocky Black male with closely trimmed hair, dressed in a dark gray suit and blue pin-striped tie.

Masters remained standing, raising his hand for silence.

"Let's get started. I'm John Masters. We'll need to establish some ground rules before you tell me who you are. I know of your background in Naval intelligence, and I see you've spent two years working in Hodin coalition security. You should be familiar with the drill."

Masters handed the young man a sealed white Tyvek envelope.

"The federation's given you a new alias, 'Jeremy James Hansen.' Your packet contains a fresh identity — a Social Security card, driver's license with Real ID, passport, credit and debit cards, and a detailed résumé and biography. Your vehicle is a silver BMW 330e in your new name — it's in the lot; the key fob's in your packet. You've rented a home at the address shown in your paperwork.

"I trust everything will meet your requirements — if not, let me know. Working closely with me is part of your job description; you'll find I'm always available.

"Memorize everything about yourself. It's important not to get tripped up. Your new role is as my confidential assistant. I'm the Manager of Process Development for North America, or as we know it here, 'PD.' My job is to create new techniques for empowering initiatives and ways to distribute them; yours is to help me. Any questions before we get started?"

"Several, actually," the man now known as Jeremy Hansen replied, a quizzical look on his face, "but orientation will answer them, I'm sure. One thing puzzles me. My packet contains an access badge labeled 'PWW plc,' issued in the name of Frank Spector."

"That'll become clear later," Masters replied. "My duties require interacting with an executive at the advertising agency PWW. You'll need to act on his behalf occasionally while in their facility. They're unaware, and mustn't learn, that you have those credentials.

"I understand your previous work with the Hodin federation has been in enforcement and as an embedded operative in a partner corporation?"

"Yes."

"For those assignments, information arrived on a need-to-know basis. However, my position — and, by extension, yours — requires engaging other federation members and partners. You'll be privy to information seen only by me, certain members of the security team, and the founders' council. Everything we do is covert. Any of it getting out is a potential threat to the coalition. Your discretion is mandatory. Any violation *will* cause your immediate termination.

"By termination, I mean killed without warning or opportunity to negotiate.

"And in that context, there's a concern I need to address. Having a few years in with the Hodin federation, you should know its origins within the Bilderbeck Group."

Hansen nodded in acknowledgment.

"Your new role means you'll occasionally run into Bilderbeck members, perhaps associates of federation founders or members who belong to both groups. Bilderbeck members who are not also Hodin coalition members know nothing about federation membership, operations, or even existence — the same as any other outsider. You must maintain that secrecy at all costs, subject, again, to termination.

"Are we clear, and are those terms acceptable to you?"

"I understand, and yes, they are." Hansen's eyes had gone wide, but his face was otherwise expressionless.

"Welcome aboard, then, Mr. Hansen. We've got a lot to cover.

"The federation's been implementing its initiatives globally for over twenty years. As mentioned, the coalition has an essential relationship with PWW, the world's largest international advertising agency. The headquarters for their client-facing operations are in London, but they have a significant presence here. Their U.S. facilities can address anything imaginable related to advertising. More quietly, they also offer discreet services to discerning partners and customers who wish anonymity."

"Are those off-the-books offerings?"

"More 'off-menu'; they're in PWW's financials, but with names you wouldn't recognize. Frank Spector is PWW's man in charge of development. Those discreet services emanate from his extensive store of persuasion, coercion, and manipulation techniques, methods, and software products. He originally developed those to support PWW's advertising capabilities. Think of them as 'spin,' 'propaganda,' or 'social engineering' services.

"With his direction, PWW quietly supports the gamut — deepfake hackers working for rogue nation-states to mobsters manipulating juries before trial … political organizations seeking to influence elections and governments managing their citizens, as well as those of other countries. PWW and its partners provided Westernized social media influencing services and data under Spector's management to the Russians, who used them to steal the 2016 election for Donald Trump."

Hansen's face showed the latter impressed but did not surprise him.

"Spector's team performs the research, develops the means, and implements a path forward for almost anyone willing to pay PWW. And when I say 'means,' I am talking about forms of artificial intelligence and exabytes of data beyond anything you could imagine."

"Just out of curiosity, what is an 'exabyte'?" Hansen asked.

"It's a million terabytes or a billion gigabytes — think of it as a billion billions."

"Got it — a *lot* of data, then."

"More than anyone else in the business. That's one of PWW's many advantages."

Masters briefly paused, considering his approach.

"As you know, the federation's mission is to reduce the world's population to the point it's no longer a threat to future human existence or even quality of life. Your new position is about implementing that mission and delivering its goals."

"What kinds of things do we 'implement?' I know we don't start nuclear wars or anything like that."

"You can't achieve mass depopulation through some staged catastrophic event or singular thread of activities, as conspiracy theories suggest. And certainly not through frustrated armed individuals shooting people in dark alleys."

A wry smile crossed Master's face.

"We assist our mission by combining the exploitation of natural events, riding the coattails of other technologies, capitalizing on human tendencies toward armed conflict, and amplifying the usual effects of disease and mutation. However, our primary approach is slow-motion assisted suicide using technology."

"I'm sorry — are you saying you expect people to kill *themselves*? Willingly? S*lowly*?" It was apparent Hansen wasn't familiar with the concept.

"In a word, yes. The role of PWW is to incentivize non-survivors — those we want to eliminate — to play along, subconsciously or otherwise. We guide them to peers, products, lifestyles, choices, beliefs, services, and surroundings that encourage self-destructive behaviors. Design elegance at its best; truly ingenious, really.

"The Hodin federation's goals have two milestones. We want to reach a target population of six billion people in thirty years, then one billion after fifty. The models say those numbers keep us under the two-degree Celsius crisis point for global warming. Hence, our remaining inhabitants inherit a survivable planet.

"The first milestone is in sight, the effects already visible, with much more to come."

Hansen seemed dumbfounded.

"If my math's right, you'd remove two billion people from the Earth over the next three decades and another five billion in the two decades after that. *How's that even possible?*"

"In pop culture — books, graphic novels, movies, streaming media," Masters replied, "the premise is always that a singular cataclysmic event would trigger mass depopulation, like the asteroid collision that took out the dinosaurs.

"We don't control what the galaxies do. But from an engineering perspective, a high-risk all-of-your-chips-in moonshot makes no sense. You'd want to manage all the myriad downstream effects to generate a positive outcome. Priority one: you'd like the most desirable people to survive. That's extremely hard to do within the ensuing chaos of a single massive crisis. It's harder still to do *right*, given you have just one chance — no opportunity to rehearse.

"Even should you succeed, there remains evidence of a singular destructive act to investigate afterward. Survivors might choose to hold the perpetrators accountable for anything gone wrong."

"But what alternative could there be?" Hansen had knitted his brows in thought.

"The federation frames its approach around *lingchi*. You'd know it better as 'death by a thousand cuts.' The coalition's version reads 'death by a thousand *self-administered* cuts.'

"At any chosen point in time, in any environment in which you find yourself, we'll surround you with tens of thousands of ways to speed up your death or frustrate your conception of a child. The federation will engineer those as stand-alone solutions or complements to something else. Each represents a stroke of the knife. They'll be in the air you breathe, the liquids you drink, the foods you eat, the medicine you take or apply, the rays soaking into your skin, the things you touch, and the people you love.

"You'll decide, of your own free will, in your own time, at your own pace, and for your own purposes to take into your body things that will prevent you and your future children from living a complete life."

"The aggregated choices of billions of people over time and geography will achieve the desired results: the premature deaths of most of them while simultaneously rendering their replacement difficult or impossible."

"I get it philosophically. But the numbers seem overwhelming." Hansen had a frown on his face.

"You'd be surprised to learn that the larger numbers make our task more manageable. Our costs are lower at scale, of course. But there's a side benefit. People in herds tend to do idiotic things anyway and, given some leadership and guidance, can be convinced to do almost anything. For example, talking someone into trying a new dietary supplement is much easier if all their friends and neighbors take it.

"But I digress. The federation sees this as a simple math problem. The sheer number of inescapable and potentially fatal options we offer, multiplied by the vast number of people we offer them to, plus a boost from human nature, will easily achieve our goals."

"How do our chosen survivors make it through?"

"Most of these 'strokes of the knife' are escapable only through a forewarning to avoid, an inoculation, or an antidote provided by the federation to those they deem worthy of survival."

"So, a fully engineered approach from the foundations up...." Hansen cocked his head slightly, his eyes focused off into space.

"And you should know we're not alone in our efforts. I'm sure you've heard of the Sacklers?"

"The founders of Purdue Pharma and the Oxycontin epidemic?"

"Exactly. Imagine a thousand similar partners, equally effective but considerably more subtle. Ultimately, almost anything you do, including drawing your first breath, will come from a palette of self-destructive choices, each provided by someone not so different from the Sacklers."

"You intend the addictive effects of these things to reduce the population," Hansen surmised.

"Addiction implies overconsumption of one thing. Some initiatives we put out there *can* achieve the desired result by themselves.

"But mostly, we're going for the cumulative effect of several different things, an approach much harder for anyone to counter if discovered and easier for us to get past prying eyes. You might screen for common contaminants in the beef liver and separately test the onions for listeria. But you wouldn't test the interactions of otherwise harmless trace elements when a cook combines the two, even though people often consume them together. The FDA doesn't have resources to test all possibilities."

"I'm getting a crystal-clear picture of what the federation is doing," Hansen mused. "Every snake salts its tail and starts chomping away...."

"The federation can't just dump a bunch of these initiatives out there willy-nilly," Masters cautioned. "We need to make these avoidable, selective, or their effects reversible to protect the one billion individuals we want to survive. It is that fine-grained control, getting the message disseminated to the people who need to hear it without alerting others, which gets most of our research and testing investment. But there've been thousands of initiatives we've directly engaged or funded.

"We've deployed some, and others are in the pipeline. I'll provide several specific examples in a later conversation. Which brings us back around to the purposes of this orientation."

"I'm not following." Hansen had a puzzled look on his face.

"When you first joined as a Hodin federation member, we provided you a URL and multiple-authentication sign-on information for logging into our encrypted portal. As you should already know, we keep a list of products and services there that you'll want to avoid. We also provide information on antidotes and a list of providers of emergency medical treatment should you be affected by one of our initiatives."

Masters paused.

"There are several things I expect you to take away from our session today. One is that your longevity with us requires a serious commitment to watching that portal information closely."

THE WRITINGS OF
AVRIL MARIA SERENE

BOOK TWO — CHAPTER 3

LONDON, ENGLAND: SIX MONTHS AGO

Frank Spector's public-facing employment as a vice president of the American branch of the world's largest advertising agency came with certain aggravations. Today's annoyance was a command performance at the behest of London management, a dog-and-pony show to appease a powerful potential client.

Cameron Harper, PWW's global vice president over customer relations, called two days ago to lobby Frank into taking a flight to Europe. With a round, cherubic face to which he'd glued an eternally sunny smile, Harper projected the innocence of the Gerber baby. But Frank knew him to be anything but in business matters — ruthless once he smelled blood in the water.

"They call themselves the OPA, the Organización de Patriotas Americanos," Harper began. "A union of politicians, right-wing extremists, and paramilitary groups. They operate behind the scenes to support present and former autocrats and other political leaders across Latin America. We've checked them out — excuse the pun, but the bottom line is that their funding is impressive."

"What do they expect from us? Or specifically, *me?*" Frank didn't hide his disdain for crossing the ocean and back. "I'd prefer to stay out of the limelight, Cameron."

"I get it, Frank — I wouldn't ask if it wasn't necessary. In terms of services, they want the same as any other political organization operating without ethical constraints. The association intends to leverage our discreet array of manipulation tools to sustain and increase its support among civilian constituencies.

"But there's a sticking point. The organization expressed concern that the man responsible for creating and implementing those technologies was from the United States. Given the back and forth of U.S. politics, they want to be sure that we deliver the services they order with … *enthusiasm,* if you get my meaning. Their representatives insisted on a face-to-face meeting."

With strong prevailing westerlies, Frank's flight landed at Heathrow early. Now resigned to his task, he was in good spirits as he rode up to the third-floor conference room where Harper was hosting the meeting.

The prospective customers had arrived before Frank. They stood behind mahogany-dyed leather chairs surrounding a large conference table crafted from a single marble slab.

The OPA's entourage included a stocky man in close-cropped gray hair, likely in his mid-sixties, wearing full military regalia. A strong odor of cigar smoke wafted from the general's side of the table. Three lookalikes, perhaps a decade younger and wearing expensive Italian suits, flanked the uniformed man, one to his right, the others to his left. Clean-shaven and dark-skinned, each clasped a leather binder, held in both hands at waist level, and waited for their leader to take his seat.

It was a group with which Frank's disciplined bearing, athletic physique, conservative dress, and buzz cut fit well. It didn't hurt that Frank's matter-of-fact disposition naturally ingratiated him with a military audience; it seemed obvious why Harper summoned him.

Still, Frank might have laughed if it was not for the money on the table and the sidearm strapped to the general's waist. The assemblage invoked every time-worn cliché he'd ever heard of South American autocrats, to the point of surreal. *There's a low-budget B-movie in production somewhere missing part of their cast,* Frank thought, keeping a straight face.

Harper's countenance, however, was deadly serious. Turning each hand palm-upward toward Frank and the older man in uniform, Harper made the introductions.

"General Emilio Pereira, please meet Frank Spector, Vice President of Digital Research — Methods and Validation for the American division of PWW. He's responsible for the persuasion technologies we use in-house when a more aggressive approach is warranted — he invented many of them. Those are the same techniques and tools we offer to select clients when their needs require them. I understand, General, that those services interest you."

As the general nodded curtly, Harper turned slightly toward Frank.

"Frank, General Pereira is the head of the OPA, the association you and I discussed earlier. They'd like to subscribe to your more productive approaches and software creations and have questions I thought you could best answer. General, you have the floor."

"Mr. Spector...," Pereira began.

"'Frank,' please."

The excusable interruption was intentional on Frank's part — using the offer of familiarity as a pretext, he wanted to establish immediately that the two men were equals.

"Frank, then." The general nodded after a brief flash of irritation had crossed his face. He didn't offer Frank a familiar name in return. Those missteps told Frank this was a man who didn't deal well with being challenged and was fundamentally insecure, likely playing to his subordinates. When reduced to the character elements Frank cared about, Pereira was weak — and, therefore, more inclined to lash out. Frank would have to tread lightly to achieve Harper's goals.

Sweeping his left hand toward his compatriots, the general briefly introduced them without taking his eyes off Frank's face.

"Senior Condori is our minister of political operations. Senior Mendoza coordinates military operations between our member groups. Senior Gutierrez is responsible for the training and staffing that supports our paramilitary activities."

Frank nodded at each underling and then returned his attention to the general.

"We represent leaders of men." Pereira immediately took command of the conversation. "Men who love our countries and wish to see our people succeed. We are what I believe you would call 'conservative' in our approach to achieving our goals. We know many people in the United States disagree with our way of thinking. What is the term we see in your social media — 'tree-huggers?'"

Frank raised one corner of his mouth in a half-smile to acknowledge the general's use of the dated phrase.

"Your citizens seem to believe your country can withstand these disagreements," Pereira continued. "But your people bicker and shoot one another in your streets, schools, and churches. And your Congress can do nothing. Whether the government will shut down every few months is a coin flip. Your courts, educators, Constitution, and politicians would like the rest of the world to believe these differences are healthy and necessary — noble words.

"But we see the truth in your lack of strength, inaction, and hypocrisy. We in the OPA want better than that for ourselves and our people. We want decisive action that leaves no question about our purposes or intentions.

"I have a question for you, Frank. You strike me as a no-nonsense individual, and I will take you at your word. So, tell me, can you wholeheartedly support our cause even if our goals differ from your country's?"

"I am a technical professional, General," Frank replied. "I am not a member of the judiciary, a cleric, or a politician. I don't pass judgment. When I come to work each morning, I serve our clients to the best of my ability."

"That speaks well to your sense of duty and your dedication to your craft. I would have expected nothing less."

Still, the general's expression betrayed his dissatisfaction with Frank's answer.

"Mr. Harper has educated us on some of the capabilities of the people under you, and the data he's shown us is impressive.

"However, it occurs to me that the results we could expect would depend upon how vigorously and consistently one applied those tools to the problem we wish to solve. We understand that depends in part upon the financial support we can provide to offset the costs of those operations. You can trust that we, and those who support what we do, are fully committed to the effort and its success. We have the resources and the means necessary to achieve the desired ends."

Harper nodded in appreciation as he listened silently.

"We also understand that our success depends on the motivation level of those we rely upon. A level of commitment that must, on occasion, rise above the call of duty.

"Let me explain our situation. I am Salvadoran. For many years, we have battled the leftists for control of our country and of our destiny. It has been a seesaw battle, played out over a century. These back-and-forth outcomes have not been good for true patriots. Worse, our enemies have extended their reign by unifying their many factions — perhaps you have heard of the Farabundo Martí National Liberation Front, or as we know them, the FMLN?"

"I'm not familiar..." Frank's brow furrowed in thought.

"No matter. Since the FMLN became a legitimate political power, it has factionalized again and weakened. But in their heyday, they were strong, even influencing the politics of neighboring countries. It was their unity that made such strength possible.

"The OPA has negotiated agreements among many conservative groups across Latin America so that we can attain and sustain the reins of power. We started with the surviving members of the Territorial Service and the old National Democratic Organization of El Salvador — you may have known them as 'ORDEN.'"

"If I recall correctly, they gained notoriety for their use of machetes against rural populations." Frank's affect was without emotion. "Some say they were the inspiration for the right-wing death squads and the infamous death flights of Venezuela and other countries."

The general didn't intend his weak denial to convince anyone.

"For the record, we threw no leftists out of helicopters in El Salvador — we would not have wasted the fuel. But yes, such are the fortunes of war that a few of our members crossed boundaries. Those are the unfair impressions we must erase using your services.

"Still, the OPA is much bigger than just one country. Our members include followers of the Argentinian priest Julio Meinvielle, the Somoza family in Nicaragua, allies of Sebastián Piñera and Augusto Pinochet in Chile, supporters of Óscar Únzaga de la Vega, Jeanine Áñez, and Louis Fernando Camacho in Bolivia. They include those adherents of Jair Bolsonaro who emulated Trump's January 6th insurrection in Brazil."

"Finding common ground between all those groups is something of a coup in its own right," Frank observed.

"Thank you, though I'm sure you can see why tools of persuasion would be vital to our interests — we must encourage action, sacrifice, and positivity from our members and partners while also spreading reeducation and a compelling message among our populations…

"Explain something to me, Frank. After all, trust begins with understanding the motivations of your partners, does it not? You manipulate, some might say orchestrate, the opinions of millions of people, apparently with great skill. Yet you do not wish attention for yourself; you are unusual in that respect, Frank."

"I am in it for the excellence I can bring to the table and the knowledge I can attain, General," Frank said, answering the implicit question. "I trust that any attention or recognition I might want will come to me organically from my peers and associates."

"You carry yourself as though you may have once served in the military, Frank." Pereira's tone was matter-of-fact. "If so, may I ask your MOS?"

"My military occupational specialty isn't related to my civilian work, General — the skills I developed wouldn't translate well into anything in legitimate private-sector employment."

"Why is that, Mr. Spector?" Frank knew the general had vetted him before this meeting and was familiar with Frank's service record. Only Pereira knew why he was toying with the information.

"I was a sniper with the U.S. Army Rangers, General."

"Did you enjoy the work, Frank?"

"You are asking me if I enjoyed killing the enemy?" Frank still wasn't sure of the general's endgame. "No. I took pride in doing my job well and in serving my country. But I can't say I enjoyed the result. Our training removed any emotional component."

"For our purposes here, professionalism matters, Frank. I would have been disappointed had you derived pleasure from taking human lives without purpose." The general pursed his lips as two of his compatriots looked up from the notes they'd been taking.

"Tell me, Mr. Spector, have you ever had to kill someone other than when so ordered by your military superiors?"

Frank made direct eye contact with the general and chose his words carefully. "I'm sure you're aware I couldn't answer such a question, given much of my military career was in covert ops — not something I'd have discussed with my current employers, General."

"I have to assume, Mr. Spector, that the answer to my question is 'yes.' Else, as we both understand, a simple 'no' would have sufficed." Pereira had disregarded Frank's evasion.

"Snipers have a lonely lot. And we've established that even today, while you pursue mastery of your craft, you do not seek notice as your reward. So, would you consider yourself a loner, Mr. Spector?"

Frank elected to hide his resentment of that term and its implications.

"Let's just say I'm selective about the company I keep. I know that kidnapping can be a means of influence in certain of the areas in which you operate. If your concern is someone gaining leverage over me or my activities, you need not worry. While I do have an ex-wife and a son, we're not close."

"Your awareness of some of the security challenges in our part of the world is helpful, Frank." The general's mood seemed more conciliatory. "Your position with PWW suggests you can communicate and work well with others. I'm sure you'll pardon me for wanting to resolve any apparent incongruence between the man and the responsibilities of his role."

General Pereira leaned over to speak in hushed tones to his colleagues, first to his left and then to his right. The two men closest to him whispered into his ear in their turn. After a few moments, the general nodded. His compatriots rose in unison as he stood, and Pereira turned to face Harper.

Harper and Frank rose from their seats, anticipating their guests' imminent departure.

"I think we have an understanding, Mr. Harper, and we can do business." Pereira reached across the table to shake Harper's hand. "Someone will contact you shortly to make the financial arrangements. Thank you for your time.

"Mr. Spector, it was a pleasure meeting you." The general extended his hand to Frank. "I'm looking forward to our shared success."

With that, the man turned on his heels, his attendants in lockstep, one striding ahead to open the door for their boss.

Remaining standing, Harper and Frank watched patiently as their new clients exited.

"Frank, nice job," Harper exclaimed, clapping Frank on the shoulder after the door had closed behind the last of the group. "You seemed to have satisfied their curiosity and concerns. You should take some time — see the sights, sample the cuisine — while you're here. You're on the company's dime; enjoy it. Lord knows you've earned it."

What an ass — still, typical Cameron Harper, Frank thought. *He knows damned well this trip has jammed me up. I have too much to do back in Boston to waste my time here.*

THE WRITINGS OF
AVRIL MARIA SERENE

Book Two — Chapter 4

BOSTON, MASSACHUSETTS: PRESENT DAY

Lawyer William R. "Bill" Clymer was a balding and graying, yet fit, Black man in his early fifties whose imposing manner and impeccably tailored clothing made him seem much taller than his five feet, ten inches. What he knew of his next visitor's situation was most unusual, and he'd cleared his afternoon calendar for the initial conference. Once Bill had touched up his notes for a case he'd plead the following day, he stabbed a finger at the intercom button on his desktop phone.

"Shelly, please let Mr. Spector know I'm available for our consultation. And ask Laura Bowman if she'd join us," he intoned in his deep bass voice, not waiting for a response.

Frank Spector, forty-seven years old, was tall and slender. He, too, demonstrated a refined sense of the sartorial. Under a charcoal suit coat with navy pinstripes, Spector wore a dark blue and white tie accented against a black twill shirt. As he entered the twenty-second-floor penthouse office, he appeared appreciative of the decor. The steampunk wall sculptures caught his attention, their colors supplied by assorted natural metals in various states of oxidation and heat stress. Frank exuded confidence and control as he crossed the carpet to Bill's desk.

After Bill's prospective client seated himself in the plush leather chair across the clear glass desk and they'd exchanged pleasantries, Laura Bowman entered the office through a side door. The tall brunette had a striking figure, apparent despite her business suit and practical, low-heeled pumps. She projected a no-nonsense demeanor; as Frank rose from his seat, she offered a masculine handshake.

"Mr. Spector, this is Laura Bowman, one of our partners. I've asked her to join us. She has notable litigation skills. Her track record in negotiating plea agreements has been remarkable, especially when strong mitigating or complicating factors are among the allegations, including multiple felonies. My takeaway from our phone conversation was that Laura's attendance might be helpful."

"It's nice to meet you, Laura," Frank said, releasing her hand, "and I appreciate your presence. Successful negotiations with prosecutors and law enforcement are big parts of what I want to achieve."

As Frank reseated himself and Laura took the chair to his right, Bill opened the conversation, both forefingers tapping either end of a pen on the desk before him.

"Honestly, Mr. Spector, I was surprised our office got your call. I took the liberty of looking you up online. I understand you're the vice president of Digital Research for PWW. Is that right?"

His paying guest nodded in affirmation.

"I thought you might have engaged one of the excellent attorneys PWW provides their executive staff for personal and business matters. You enjoy a fine reputation, and your work is critical to your firm. I assume they'd spare no resources to keep you happy. Understand that as the lead partner of one of the best criminal defense firms in the state, I welcome the chance to help. But I *am* curious what brings you our way, Mr. Spector."

"Frank, please; my choices will make sense once you know my situation." Frank looked directly into Bill's eyes, then over to include Laura, his expression sardonic. "But first, your office administrator assures me anything I say here remains confidential. Does that hold if you refuse me as a client?"

"And you can call me 'Bill.' Yes, initial consultations convey privilege, irrespective of outcome. Is there anything I can get either of you before we start?"

"No, I'm fine, thank you," Frank replied, adjusting his tie.

"I'm good, Bill," Laura demurred.

"Shall we begin, then?" All eyes turned to Frank.

"To your opening question, my relationship with PWW has become … complicated. The general situation is even more so because PWW is one of my two employers. Fair warning — what I say may try your patience; some aspects might seem unbelievable."

Frank's expression was unapologetic despite his words as he glanced at Laura and then back toward Bill.

"Listening is most of what we do here," Bill replied. "I've blocked out the rest of the day; we shouldn't have any distractions. Laura, do you have any other commitments we should respect?"

Laura shook her head.

"You're aware PWW is the best-known of the global advertising agencies," Frank continued. "You may not know their biggest money-makers are covert social-engineering products and services. They offer these quietly to anyone who can pay the price, irrespective of their morality or purpose, to do with as they please, usually well out of the limelight.

"My role at PWW for the past eighteen years has been innovating, growing, and improving those operations and offerings, both as advertising support and as clandestine stand-alone services."

As he spoke, Frank rose from his chair, turned, and began sauntering across the Brazilian teak flooring covering half the office. He stopped three feet short of the wall of windows dominating the space and folded his arms.

He scanned the broad vista of the Charles River provided by the expanse of glass. A line of trees and bushes highlighted in the fresh light green of new spring foliage anchored the buildings of the far skyline. Bright dots of color sprinkled themselves along the shoreline. A half-dozen sailboats braved the choppy waters outside the darker green strip of jetty protecting the harbor and marina.

Unseen by Frank, Laura and Bill had looked at one another with raised eyebrows, the outer edges of their lips turned slightly downward in a show of respect.

"I'm with you so far," Bill said, nodding. Laura dipped her head slightly.

Frank jammed his balled-up fists deep into his front pants pockets, still facing the windows.

"We use our experience, artificial intelligence, and the largest collection of data in the world to manipulate opinion. We can take over social media, generate mass misinformation, create echo chambers for reinforcement, build false-flag operations, and convince almost anyone to do almost anything."

His voice rose. "Entire industries thrive around unnecessary products and services, all because of our talents. Breakfast and snack foods, cosmetics, car mods, dietary supplements, women's fashion accessories and footwear, and men's neckwear, to name just a few. They profit based solely on our ability to manipulate desirability before purchase and after delivery.

"To illustrate how effective our services can be, I've no doubt each of you bristled at one or more items you consider important being included in my list of unnecessary things."

He's got me there, Bill had to concede. *I'm not giving up my Zilli Paris ties for anyone.*

"But our influence over commercial enterprises is nothing compared to how we've given the most ignorant, shallow, and debased people in the United States de facto control of this country's politics and judiciary. While Facebook and Twitter-slash-X may provide access, advertising drives the messaging."

Frank hesitated for a moment, apparently considering how he should continue.

"Bill, Laura, have either of you heard of the Bilderbeck Group — outside the many conspiracy theories surrounding them?"

"They're a think tank of sorts," Bill offered. "Social, business, military, and political leaders who gather to debate world affairs and chart a global direction. Not so different from David Rockefeller's Trilateral Commission, and going back in history, Freemasonry and the Bavarian Illuminati."

"I understand they've been around since the 1950s," Laura added. "The Bilderbeck Group purported themselves an organization of world leaders in various fields joining forces to propose what they labeled a 'New World Order.' They wanted a post–Korean War realignment of relationships between world powers."

"Ah, the New World Order," Frank repeated, drawing it out as he seemed to ponder the toes of his shoes, still facing the window. "Now, *there's* a much-maligned term often bandied about — very grand, like moving massive chess pieces around. The idea sounds powerful, but it's little more than acknowledging how things are as opposed to changing anything. Dust blowing in the wind."

Bill nodded slightly while Laura remained still, her expression neutral.

"But suppose there was a subset of these mighty political, military, scientific, and economic minds; moreover, this subgroup of like thinkers was coincidental to membership in Bilderbeck, an organization that merely brought them together.

"Let's say that subset had come, individually and collectively, to the conclusion that the only workable solution to all the world's problems was quite specific and actionable. Let's further suppose they formed a 'cabal,' if you would, around ideas to implement this solution — ideas more concrete and doable than was possible within Bilderbeck. And along with it, a plan was conceived that they could and would bring to fruition among themselves."

Frank paused, rocking back and forth slightly on the heels of his shoes.

"Since you know of the Bilderbeck Group," Frank said, twisting from his hips to face the attorneys, "I assume you've also heard of the conspiracy theories circulated by uneducated populists around world depopulation?

"That Bilderbeck had hatched a plot to reduce political, environmental, commercial, and raw resource pressures on our planet by correspondingly reducing the number of people on its surface? And, of course, the intended victims for this reduction were whatever group the speaker du jour represented or wanted to manipulate. Today, those would be Trump-supporting QAnon conspiracy theorists who dropped out of high school and inbred below the Mason-Dixon line...."

Frank headed back toward his seat, listening to the lawyers' responses.

"I remember the Bilderbeck Group's adamant public disavowals around depopulation in a press conference...," Laura said.

"Sounds very familiar; I must've seen the same briefing," Bill said. "But with the revelation that the most recent iteration was coming from Trump's people, his 'base' as he likes to call them, it was obvious there was no credibility or intellect behind any of it. So, it just faded into the woodwork, as I recall. More extremist right-wing drivel to promote their narcissistic need to feel under attack, 'give me what I want now to resolve my self-professed victimhood.' Propagated by disgruntled old white guys and Karens."

"That's a reasonably accurate assessment of the situation," Frank said, his lips pursed. "But a blind man will eventually hit something if he throws enough darts.

"If you were paying attention, you may have heard of Yusuke Narita, the Yale professor, definitely not one of your brain-dead Trumpies. He famously suggested that Japan's old people should kill themselves in a mass suicide to solve that country's economic problems. You should know that far from turning him into a pariah, his comments made him quite a celebrity among younger Japanese."

Frank tilted his head to one side, pausing for dramatic effect, observing his audience's reaction.

"Have you ever considered the more general concept underlying those thoughts? That is, eliminating the planet's problems by significantly reducing the world's population? Leaving, for the moment, thoughts of targeting any specific group off to the side."

Having framed the question as rhetorical, Frank didn't wait for an answer.

"I know *I* have. And I know that the subset of Bilderbeck members I described a moment ago has, as have their supporters within the Overpopulation

Matters organization. So much so that they've identified a finite goal; they intend to eliminate seven of the eight billion people from the face of the Earth, leaving only the best and brightest to carry on."

The look exchanged between the lawyers was more concern than surprise.

"That subgroup doesn't have a public-facing name; there's nothing they wish to communicate to the general citizenry. They refer to themselves as members of the Hodin federation. Those members know each other by their aliases, sharing information only through encrypted methods and transports."

There was a brief silence as Bill and Laura processed the information.

"What's your relationship to this 'cabal?'" Laura asked.

"The Hodin federation is my second employer and far more pertinent to this conversation than my first. My responsibilities to this coalition are at the crux of almost everything they do — my role provides me with my offshore wealth and as much power as I need. It also preserves my place as an ultimate survivor in the ambitions and goals of the federation.

"Many of the federation's public-facing tools, methods, propaganda, and means of influence and manipulation fall under the general umbrella of 'advertising.' Even coalition efforts that may not appear to have a prominent advertising component often require persuasion as part of their funding, staffing, adoption, or distribution.

"Ultimately, my parallel role at PWW puts me at the nexus of all of it. Virtually everything the federation does will pass within my purview at some point. Whether it's social engineering to get people to do what the coalition desires or pushing products and services implementing federation initiatives to achieve their ends, I eventually know of it. That ensures not only my power over but also my visibility to the coalition's members."

"You are the link between the cabal's goals and their primary means of persuasion, then — via the advertising agency...," Bill summarized, somewhat skeptically.

"On the PWW side, my team members are the puppeteers who get the rest of the world to do what we want or need from them," Frank replied. "And I'm their boss, at least for the Americas, though we also set the tone and take the lead for the European branch. That makes me a professional puppet master." A cynical grin crossed his face.

"How'd you come into this unique employment situation?" Bill asked.

"It so happens I'm very talented at my public profession. I have an extensive background in advertising and applied psychology. That would have been enough to qualify me for the position with PWW. But had I not met the federation's requirements, I wouldn't have either responsibility. To that end, it might surprise you that my skills in manipulating public opinion had nothing to do with why the coalition recruited me."

Both Bill and Laura showed slightly puzzled looks.

"I've also been very good at something else entirely, something I thought was in my past. I have a deeply held personal philosophy about a specific topic, and I've acted in high-risk ways to further my beliefs. The skills I developed, my actions, and the philosophy I believed in led to my role in the federation.

"The topic over which I obsessed at one point? I was eliminating the undesirables among the human population, one person at a time.

"In short, I was — *I am* — a serial killer."

THE WRITINGS OF
AVRIL MARIA SERENE

BOOK TWO – CHAPTER 5

Candidates for Bill Clymer's services were driven to his door by allegations of serious criminality, often extreme. With all the hard-to-believe stories he'd heard in his extensive career, nothing surprised Bill anymore. Still, he'd admit he hadn't foreseen that a man with Frank Spector's outward appearance and demeanor could be a serial killer.

Tapping into his experience, Bill kept his facial expression from betraying his thoughts. Laura's countenance, however, revealed she wasn't expecting Frank's self-description. She quickly recovered, though now sitting at the edge of her seat.

"'Serial' implies several," she said. "May I ask how many?"

"Beginning roughly twenty years ago and spanning the next two years," Frank replied, "I removed fourteen souls from the face of the planet, most in Boston. You'll find their names in the public record. Until yesterday, there'd never been a connection between them and me, nor had I ever been questioned about any of the crimes, even casually.

"I stopped my little hobby only because of its futility. There'd always be too many of them, and I had neither the time nor adequate resources to make a real dent in the problem."

"I understand now why you'd want to engage our firm." Bill nodded slightly. "Defending murderers of all stripes is what we do best. But I must confess to some confusion — if you're not on anyone's radar and it was such a long time ago, what could we do for you now?"

"Last night, three Massachusetts State Police Unresolved Case Unit agents came to my home to collect a DNA sample and search my premises. They were investigating the murder of three people killed in an alley two decades ago. The federation has contacts within that unit, and they tell me investigators recovered a shell casing at the scene. There weren't enough points of identification in the print on the brass for a positive match. However, science has advanced enough to extract DNA from the oil in fingerprints. I don't know why I wasn't gloved up when loading that clip.

"My ex-wife, God bless her, submitted her and my son's DNA to Ancestry.com at some point. His submission was a familial match to what was on that casing.

"I tossed the gun years ago, but the FBI recovered loose cartridges from a corner of my closet that matched their casing. I suppose that staying in the same residence and successfully evading detection over the years made me complacent. They're trying to link me to the eleven of the fourteen homicides they know about."

"That puts this in our wheelhouse," Bill acknowledged. "I assume you'll fight it. Do you want to get ahead of any arraignment?"

"Unfortunately, Bill, the issues are more complex than just the serial killings imply." Frank paused briefly before changing the topic slightly.

"As I mentioned, there'd been no sign from authorities that I was suspected in any of those murders when I started with PWW. Still, the Hodin federation seemed to know every grisly detail from day one. I'm unsure how, although as I've learned through eighteen years of working with them, they miss very little.

"They sought me out *because* they knew of those killings. The knowledge provided leverage that persuaded them to trust me as having the same fundamental goals. They used that trust and various incentives to guide me in the direction they wanted to go when I started with PWW."

"The murders showed the cabal that you're like-minded and willing to invest yourself in your beliefs," Laura mused, "and gave them a handle they could use to control you."

"Exactly," Frank replied.

Bill leaned way back in his chair, the fingers of his hands interlaced and resting on his stomach. His eyes were wide open, and his eyebrows arched high above them. He drew a long breath and then exhaled slowly through almost-closed lips, letting his cheeks puff out as he did.

"Let me get my head around this — the cabal, in which you've been a member for roughly eighteen years, has as its primary purpose the eventual elimination of seven billion people from the planet. Given the passage of time, I'd assume they've made progress in their efforts thus far, or they'd have dissolved the organization.

"Now, I do try to stay up with current events. We have researchers who keep us apprised of recent developments. Yet I've not heard anything beyond the right-wing nut jobs' conspiracy theories to which you previously alluded. Therefore, I assume the cabal's activities haven't yet leaked into the public sphere."

"An accurate statement, as far as I know," Frank acknowledged.

"Such being the case," Bill continued, "and given your serial killings didn't involve the cabal, I don't understand how the group ties into defending you from these potential charges. They seem to me like separate issues."

"Regrettably, the two are *inseparable* in this situation." Frank's tone became tutorial. "I'm sure you'd agree the state's solving of a nearly twenty-year-old cold case involving eleven murders is noteworthy, an event they'd publicize. And you'd appreciate that PWW would prefer to distance themselves from a top-level executive associated with those crimes.

"It should make sense to you that a secretive multinational federation fanatically devoted to reducing the global population by massive numbers might want to avoid attention. They are, after all, not seeking the public's consent, and certainly not the spotlight these circumstances could bring."

"Both would probably fire you," Bill pointed out, "and while not a good thing, the significance pales compared to standing trial for multiple murders."

"That's likely our disconnect," Frank responded. "You're not fully grasping the importance of my role with the Hodin federation. I sit at the epicenter of everything the coalition does. You may not realize how much information I process about the federation's members, partners, operations, and future intentions. You're not in the habit of thinking the way an organization accountable to no one and dedicated to eliminating seven billion people would. Terminating one more who poses an existential threat to them is a straightforward decision. I'd be surprised if I made it to the courthouse, never mind a trial."

"Ah, the mob accountant problem," Bill summarized. "Law enforcement compromising you poses a threat to the cabal so long as you're alive because of what you know, irrespective of whether you ever intended to say anything to anyone. To the cabal, this is fundamentally a risk management issue."

"I didn't sleep last night, as you might imagine," Frank revealed. "I realized I'd never mitigate that risk enough to satisfy them, especially given I'll lose my position at PWW. Once that happens, I'm useless to the federation, anyway."

"Frank, our practice is limited to the legal domain." Bill's look was pensive. "I can offer nothing to help you with the rest."

Frank put his hands together. "I understand why you'd think that. But the answers in life often come from how you see the question. I think your services may be my only way out. I'm willing to do my time — if nothing else, I can write fascinating memoirs. That's an acceptable resolution, so long as I don't have to face the death penalty.

"And that's where you can help me. The feds have capital punishment; Massachusetts doesn't. But only the feds can make the deal I want to make."

"What about the homicides leads you to believe that federal law enforcement's interested in this?" Laura's curiosity was piqued.

"One of the last three victims was an IRS agent," Frank answered, "though his employment had nothing to do with his homicide."

"What voice would you have in negotiations between the state and the feds over who prosecutes that case?" Laura followed up.

"They'll want to listen because I'm going to do what the coalition has to assume I'm going to do anyway," Frank replied.

"I'm going to give up the Hodin federation — all of it, who, what, when, where, and why — to the FBI."

Book Two — Chapter 6

A hush overtook the room. Bill Clymer, chewing his lower lip, and Laura Bowman, spinning her pen in one hand, glanced at one another.

"I'll give the feds everything I have on the Hodin federation and what they're doing," Frank explained, "*if* Massachusetts prosecutes all the matters around the serial killings twenty years ago."

"That only works if what you offer has value to the FBI," Laura argued. "I could be wrong, but I can't see the Hodin cabal on the FBI's radar. I doubt law enforcement even knows who they are. Worse, if what you believe holds sway, there's a risk that cabal members have infiltrated the agency."

"That's precisely why I need a top-flight legal team to sell the Justice Department on the importance of what's happening with the federation — a team whose members can discern whether the government is taking them seriously or just jerking them around. Even if the listeners are sincere, it may take a PR campaign to engage the public first and stir some media interest.

"People are dying, their health, families, and dreams taken from them. The coalition kills people, reduces fertility rates, induces cancers, and distributes toxins into the environment daily. That the murderers aren't using guns should be irrelevant — these *are* capital crimes."

Laura frowned, her doubts obvious. "I negotiate plea deals every working day. I think that's a tough sell."

"On one hand, I'm inclined to agree with Laura," Bill intervened. "On the other, if you have almost twenty years of background information and you can point investigators to a smoking gun here or there … Thirty years ago, no one had heard of stealing money using a personal computer. There had to be a first time that an accused offered cybercrime evidence in a plea negotiation. Now, it's an everyday occurrence.

"I'd like to hear a little more. Even if we can't help, I might know someone who can. Answer a personal question for me, if you don't mind. I understand your willingness to give up the cabal under these circumstances, largely because you have little else to offer. Would you have flipped on them otherwise?"

"Fair question," Frank replied. "Thinking about things over the years, I realize the federation's goals are no longer commensurate with mine. It helps if you understand that when I addressed the population problem independently, I was selective about the people whose lives I ended.

"Not that difficult. Ninety percent of the globe's inhabitants don't pull their weight — they leave the place worse off than when they were born. Of those remaining, the lives of nine and a half percent will primarily benefit themselves or their heirs.

"Only one-half of one percent will contribute to humanity in any meaningful and sustainable way, and human frailties — primarily avarice, abuse of others, and over-consumption of resources — often cancel out their achievements.

"So, when I did this as a hobbyist, I didn't lack for targets. Still, I was mindful that eliminating the people I chose would ultimately benefit the planet and humankind somehow. My vision had the very best of humanity surviving — a variety of artists, philosophers, scientists and other intellectuals, craftsmen, athletes, and natural leaders."

"How's that inconsistent with the cabal's objectives?" Laura's left elbow rested on the low back of her chair. She held her pen in both hands, with her knees together and leaning towards Frank.

"Things have changed." Frank turned slightly to face her. "I've learned that the over-the-top greedy, already powerful, and primarily psychopathic federation members have taken control. They now set the agenda for who gets eliminated and who remains at the end of their process. Sadly, that's always the outcome in organized human activities where the purpose centers on material gain or loss.

"My dream to leave only the best of us scouting out the human path forward in fifty years has been co-opted. The coalition clearly intends one-quarter of the survivors to be spoiled trust-fund babies accompanying their parents. Most are insatiably predatory sociopaths with an extraordinary tolerance and capacity for cruelty and self-aggrandizement; they devote their limited higher intelligence to pursuing 'more, more, more!' Clones of Elon Musk, writ large; people like those running the federation.

"The rest of the survivors? Dependent, docile, compliant sycophants with strong backs, 'tools' as it were, left with few choices. A cooperative cast of noncompetitive serfs filling in what artificial intelligence, robotics, and other technologies can't yet do for the wealthy and powerful.

"The coalition wants to use their process of elimination to clean up markets and supply chains, reduce competition, tamp down independent thought, and eliminate criminality other than their own."

"I assume your vision of the depopulation result didn't include capitalism?" Bill's tone was cynical.

"Not the way it's practiced today." Frank's response was defiant. "As someone who appreciates fine art, I see laissez-faire free enterprise as the problem, not the answer — the polar opposite of what I intended to achieve with my life. When the federation elected the year 1750 as the baseline for setting their target population goals, I didn't realize they also planned to replicate the social order of that time. There's no intention of allowing citizenry in the lower of their two tiers of government any path upward or forward.

"That'd be the worst outcome possible for a life I've dedicated to improving the world by eliminating those who don't contribute to human excellence. Natural or even random selection would produce a far better outcome than the Hodin federation is planning."

"Still, you didn't learn all of this yesterday," Bill observed. "You've carried on with them for, as you said, almost twenty years now."

"In a perfect world," Frank replied, "standing on principle might have mattered more. But that, too, is complicated; it requires having a voice.

"It's not unlike quantum physics, where the mere act of observing results changes them. My visibility within the federation is a double-edged sword — obvious missteps paint a target on my back and render me expendable. Politics go with the job.

"But there are also indirect threats — the emergence of artificial intelligence and new AI-enabled manipulation tools, including deepfakes and the chatbots powered by ChatGPT. Given that the systems I've created and the channels and relationships I've carved out are past accomplishments, these new developments could render me replaceable if I can't stay ahead of them."

"You're working yourself right out of a job ... and 'voice,'" Laura mused.

"My position's one for which my past kills uniquely qualified me," Frank continued. "But the coalition's knowledge of that history implicitly blackmails me. I'm trapped. The federation's changed underneath me. Their goal now is for today's elite and powerful to survive population reduction — the very people who created the mess we're trying to fix. The dream situation that enabled me to pursue my life's mission has become a nightmare."

"Hoisted by your own petard…," Bill murmured.

"I come from a Jewish heritage," Frank explained, "often disliked, even despised, for thousands of years in the places we ended up since the Diaspora. I've given serious thought to understanding why. We get accused of deeply held beliefs that are primarily transactional and shallow.

"It isn't so much whether those biases are truthful or fair; it's that the accusations are so powerful. I've concluded that humans associate the implicit greed with evil at some level, even as they chase more power and possessions for themselves."

"There's a definite disconnect between what we preach and practice," Laura agreed.

"Even a monkey or a raccoon will steal something shiny just to possess it," Frank continued. "Avarice doesn't require higher brain functions. Minds limited to exploiting greed need everything laid out for them in the simplest terms, life as paint-by-numbers, quantifiable. However, more evolved humans value intangibles as most important; these are immeasurable — no metrics for those that mercenary minds can grasp. These include genuine love for family and others, humor, grief, appreciation of beauty, kindness, sorrow, admiration, companionship, faith, and happiness, among many others."

An essay on values from an unrepentant serial killer? The irony was not lost on Bill, though he chose to say nothing.

Frank continued, "Pricing expressed in dollars and cents is simple for lesser intellects to grasp. Profit is measurable, so the danger of a meritocracy run by capitalists is that these people naturally conflate 'meritorious' — something they are incapable of understanding — with 'profitable,' a much simpler idea. Even though, in reality, the two words have very little to do with one another. Profit references benefit accruing to a specific person or organization. But true merit is evaluated by its positive impact on the larger community rather than the self."

Bill tilted his head at Frank. "So, if that cold case unit hadn't appeared on your doorstep, you'd have left the cabal for philosophical differences?"

Frank paused in contemplation, then provided an unexpected answer.

"Even as imperfect as the situation was, probably not. Philosophy aside, I knew the danger to me would become existential if I let myself get to the point where I couldn't serve the needs of the Hodin federation in good faith. I couldn't make the coalition aware of my moral issues with their new direction; that would radically change their perceptions of my dedication, even if I later came around to their point of view … like lifting the lid on Schrödinger's cat.

"And make no mistake, I do enjoy my job. Three years ago, I made a conscious re-commitment to doing it well, intentionally shutting out any philosophical considerations. Were it not for having to give that DNA sample, I'd have continued in that vein until we met the federation's goals, or I could gracefully retire on good terms. That's all moot now; by going to someone outside the coalition and revealing the little I already have, regardless of reason, I pose a threat they'd have to eliminate at any cost.

"So, the short answer to your question would be, no; if not for going to prison the rest of my life, I wouldn't have turned on the federation."

"It's just business, then," Bill summed up, "on both sides. Each of you does what's necessary. You need to expose them as part of a bargain to continue living, and they must kill you to eliminate the threat to their survival."

He glanced over to include Laura.

"Dealing with the Hodin cabal is outside our expertise. However, I do know someone. Chris Patterson, former FBI, is widely regarded as one of Boston's best criminal defense attorneys. Chris's legal proficiency is top-drawer — fluent in politics, persuasion, and privacy — the go-to person for what we'd call 'delicate matters.' Yours are more unusual than most, but of those I know who could help you with your circumstances, Chris gets my vote."

"Before you talk to anyone else," Laura put in, "Chris needs to call up an influential contact in the Justice Department and have a long discussion with them. One that doesn't include actionable information but produces a suitable and enforceable agreement."

Bill eyed Frank. "I'd have to agree with Laura, but Chris may offer other ideas."

He reached into his breast pocket.

"Here's their firm's card. I'll make the call to let Chris know I've referred you — I'll pass along what you've told us. That'll shorten the process for both of you. Give me an hour to have that conversation before you call Chris."

"Thank you for your time, Bill."

As Frank stood, the attorneys did the same. He offered his right hand first to Bill and then to Laura.

"I appreciate the referral. Laura, much obliged for your presence and your insights."

Frank stepped behind his chair and then turned to face Bill.

"I've provided your office administrator a post office box for billing — it would be best if any correspondence around my visit today goes there rather than to my home address."

"I'll make a note in the file to amend your mailing address," Bill agreed, "and I'll wish you the best of luck finding a resolution to all this that works for you."

"I'll find my way out." Frank gave a quick nod as he turned, heading for the door.

Once Frank was gone and the office door closed behind him, Bill sat forcefully back in his chair, his face grim and his complexion darkening.

"*Is there anything worse than a God-damned traitor?*" he asked of Laura disdainfully, not wanting an answer.

Book Two — Chapter 7

Bill Clymer waited a few moments, biting the inside of his cheek and staring off into space. Frank Spector's arrogance had rubbed him the wrong way from the beginning of their conversation. Bill strongly suspected the trust and power granted Spector by the Hodin federation had backfired, encouraging the man to subvert the coalition's efforts in favor of ego and a personal agenda.

Bill wasn't buying Spector's rebirth as an idealist, now turning on the federation as a matter of circumstance. Ever the cynic, it seemed to the attorney that Spector saw himself as the greatest serial killer of all time, rationalizing his behaviors as doing humanity a big favor. Those who survive history are the ones who write it; in the eyes of the one billion remaining after depopulation, Spector's opportunity would be to portray himself as a larger-than-life hero.

The lawyer guessed that narcissism and control were more important than events in upending Spector's perception of his role and future with the coalition. Whatever his reasons, now Spector wanted to take his ball back and go home.

Bill pressed the intercom button on his desk phone. "Shelly, hold my calls until I let you know otherwise."

"Yes, Mr. Clymer," a young woman's voice responded.

"Thanks for sitting in, Laura." Bill returned his gaze to his law partner. "Hopefully, the rest of your day will be more productive. Would you lock the side door behind you as you're leaving?"

Laura nodded with a terse smile and left her seat to walk out the staff entrance. She twisted the button on the inside door handle before closing the door behind her.

Leaving his desk to lock the front door, Bill flipped a switch on the wall panel. Floor-to-ceiling noise-insulating blinds slid out from their hiding place in the wall to cross the entire span of exterior windows. These would defeat the pickup of any voice vibrations from objects in the room or the window glass itself by external laser, visual, or parabolic microphones.

Returning to his desk, Bill pulled a cell phone out of a lower drawer and checked its battery level. He then removed a voice scrambler and plugged it into its jack on the burner phone. He put the burner in speakerphone mode and dialed a number. After hearing a voice answer, Bill waited until the recipient had finished setting up communications scrambling on their end.

"This is Bill Clymer. You'd never guess who just left my office — Frank Spector of PWW. Of course, I'm sure. And get this — he's looking for someone to help him drop a dime on all of us. He knows the price, yet he's willing to pay it."

Bill paused, taking in the other party's reaction.

"Yeah, I know. I never saw this coming, either. Spector's always been the guy we could rely on. Look, I sent him over to Chris Patterson. The founders will want to eliminate him — he's too dangerous to our interests. I'll fill Chris in. We'll get whatever information we can from Spector while you put your people in place. I wanted to give you the heads-up first. Call me if you need anything more from our office."

Within minutes after signing off, Bill called Chris Patterson to explain the situation.

"I understand the threat Spector represents," Chris said, "but I'm not clear what you expect me to do with him."

"Given the immediacy and severity of the problem," Bill responded, "the federation's decided to terminate. We need you to stall for time and keep Spector at your location long enough to get everything staged."

"Bill, I'm not set up for the security and cleanup necessary if the intent is to implement that solution here. And frankly, any activity making a splash in the papers disrupts business critical to our other efforts — matters in which our partners want to avoid attention."

"We understand the need for a low profile, Chris. I don't have the specifics, but enforcement says they'll track Spector leaving your location and engage him elsewhere."

"What's the point of sending him here, then?" Chris still wasn't sure of Bill's intentions.

"We need your interviewing skills, Chris. This will be our last opportunity to extract from Spector the full scope of his plans, anything else he may have done to spread the word, and any third parties who may have information or might be holding it for him.

"Has Spector stashed anything away in a safe deposit box, or is anything in the mail to himself or others? What other interviews might he have scheduled? Has Spector told anyone, 'If anything happens to me, do this?' Is he planning to take others in the federation with him?

"This guy's murdered people, and enforcement tells me he's good at it, so be careful with him. I've set him up to believe you're the expert in negotiating with the people he wants to engage. Your portfolio supports that, so these questions won't seem unusual coming from you."

Frank recognized the address on Bill's business card for Chris Patterson. The first ad agency Frank worked for once he'd gotten his master's had its offices in the same building, one floor above Patterson's suite.

After waiting an hour as instructed, Frank called Patterson at the number Bill provided. He spoke to a man who answered as Jim Patterson, Chris's son.

"Good afternoon, Mr. Spector," Jim said as he picked up. "I've been told to expect your call."

"My apologies for the short notice, Jim. I assume Bill Clymer has told your office of my situation?"

"He has, indeed — Chris is in a conference, but we just spoke, and yours is an intriguing case. The two of you will have to talk, but we should be able to help you navigate your present circumstances. Let's schedule a face-to-face question-and-answer session. I assume you'll want something sooner rather than later. I've got an opening Tuesday morning at nine a.m. Does that work for you?"

Frank would ruefully reconsider his agreement to the meeting as events were to unfold later.

How uncharacteristic of me, ironic, even — that, after years of watching my every step as a serial killer, I'd have placed so much trust in a couple of damned lawyers.

THE WRITINGS OF
AVRIL MARIA SERENE

Book Two — Chapter 8

Bill Clymer's offices were spacious and airy, the furnishings minimalist and ultra-modern. Chris Patterson's were the polar opposite in every respect other than size. Overtly traditional, all visible surfaces were trimmed and finished in elegant complementary dark woods, including massive beams intersecting in the high ceilings, the center panels embossed with elaborate carvings.

A large bay window in darkened pecan accented one wall, framed by ornate, heavy drapes embossed in gold. Cloth- and leather-bound volumes lined walnut shelves that filled the adjoining wall top to bottom and end to end. Matched sets of encyclopedic law books dominated bookcases on the opposite wall. Literary classics graced others, including several volumes that appeared to be first editions.

A cutout in the shelves on that wall featured a hand-painted reproduction of Rembrandt's *Christ in the Storm on the Sea of Galilee* in a massive, intricately carved, stained wood frame. The room smelled of old books, leather, and pine oil.

A large crystal chandelier in the Renaissance style hung from the center of the ceiling, and four smaller matching fixtures dropped from nearer the corners. Twin crystal wall sconces graced the side walls, with another pair bracketing the bay window. Beautiful antiques from the colonial period occupied every nook and cranny of the room. The effect was eighteenth-century nautical — Vice-Admiral Horatio Nelson himself would have been at home here, save perhaps for what, to him, would have been the astonishment of electricity.

As Frank entered the massive dark oak doors opposite the bay window, he seemed surprised to see a matronly female seated behind an elaborate mahogany desk that evoked a captain's sea chest.

Chris, a short and stout older woman with a pleasant smile and grandmotherly air, stood from her chair, leaning across the desktop to shake hands as they made their introductions. Before her desk were two matching brown leather chairs with antique brass upholstery tacks; she gestured for Frank to take one.

"The accouterments of your office are outstanding, but — and I hope I'm not out of line here — on first impression, they suggested I'd be meeting with a grizzled old sailor. Popeye with a law degree." Frank chuckled.

"Oh, no worries, I always get that reaction!" Chris smiled broadly. "I inherited the office when I made partner. The previous tenant felt the need to express their masculinity. At the time, I was too busy to redecorate, and the vibe's grown on me over the years. I enjoy its effect on new clients — they tend not to forget me or the surroundings. When I became the managing partner, I kept this office."

"It *is* imposing." Frank's tone was one of appreciation.

"If you don't mind, I'll ask one of my longtime associates, Drake Lindberg, to join us for our session today. He handles security issues for our attorneys and clients. Drake has a long history within the highest levels of the FBI and CIA. Bill Clymer led me to believe Drake and his contacts will be useful to us downstream. He may have insights he can offer to help ensure everyone's safety through what could be tricky waters if the Hodin cabal comes after you."

And he'll make sure I stay alive if you decide to go postal on us, Chris thought to herself.

Frank nodded his assent, and Chris picked up the receiver of her office phone, punching one of its buttons. "Jim, will you have Drake join us in my office? Yes, as soon as he can make himself available."

Almost immediately, there was a tap on the office door. A tall, dark, muscular man of Iraqi lineage with a military bearing and a square jawline entered. The black silk tie against a black shirt, under a pewter-gray, double-breasted jacket with white pinstripes, hinted at an underworld tailor. The two men shook hands before taking their seats, Frank's directly in front of the attorney and Drake's off slightly to one side.

Chris faced Drake. "As I mentioned yesterday, Frank has an interesting situation driven by people with connections and resources that may present real-world security concerns. I'd welcome any contributions you might offer, so jump in whenever you think appropriate."

"Understood." Drake was expressionless, nodding curtly.

Chris turned to Frank. "Bill Clymer explained in broad strokes the position you're in, the circumstances you need to address, and some of the history related to your situation. Allow me to summarize what I think I know. You can then correct anything I've misconstrued or omitted."

Frank dipped his chin in agreement, his elbows on the arms of his chair and the fingertips and thumbs of both hands touching in front of him.

"I understand we're facing two sets of problems. The first has to do with your involvement in fourteen serial killings for which authorities haven't yet charged you. But you fear they will, and soon, because you've had to surrender DNA and some ammunition to satisfy a search warrant. Those will show you to be the killer.

"The second set of circumstances is an organized mass depopulation of the world, a scheme in which you play a major role. You're an executive with PWW, but the group orchestrating *that* effort is the Hodin cabal, your second employer. And you want to reveal information regarding the cabal's activities as part of a plea bargain you'll need to negotiate, wherein the authorities spare you the death penalty for the serial killings. Is that correct?"

"In a nutshell, yes."

"Okay, Bill says the serial killings themselves are straightforward — those occurred decades in the past, though the state first accused you just last week. There are no witnesses you know of, no physical evidence other than what you surrendered linking you to those crimes. You've never previously told anyone of them?"

"All accurate statements, yes."

"Is there an indictment yet?"

"Not that anyone's told me."

"No one outside law enforcement has addressed the serial killings with you?"

"Not directly, no. However, others know of them."

"And that's based on the Hodin cabal recruiting you into your current role in the depopulation scheme. They've implicitly blackmailed you into staying because one or more people in the organization are aware of those old serial killings. Am I right?"

"Yes."

"There's no intersection timewise between those killings and the work you've done for PWW or the cabal … ?"

"That's true."

"Hmmm. So, without considering the emotions jurors and media might associate with the random murder of fourteen presumably innocent people, the serial killings themselves are believable and rooted in fact. If push came to shove, you could provide the information necessary to prove the murders happened and that you were responsible." She peered over her half-rim readers for confirmation.

"Yes."

"Please, take no offense to what I'm about to say — I'm simply laying out the problem domain. So, in the modern age, serial killings establish your bona fides because, sadly enough, things like that occur regularly, and people understand what they are. But the story of depopulating most of the world — Bill said seven billion people — is not so believable. Some might say it's crackpot.

"I assume the scheme's gone unfulfilled because," Chris swept a hand toward the large porthole near the front door, "well, most of us are still here. I'd hazard the guess that it's probably constructed so that it'd be difficult to discover and nearly impossible to prove."

"No offense taken, and your presumptions are on track so far."

"So, you're on the hook for something you've done which, though sadistic and violent, is believable. You want to leverage that to buy credibility for the bigger story you're also involved in, where believability is a real problem, virtually nonexistent. You need a federal plea deal because Massachusetts has no jurisdiction to investigate this cabal. The state has no death penalty, but the U.S. does. And that's why the feds taking the death penalty off the table for giving them the second story has become the only acceptable path forward for you. Have I captured the gist of it?"

"Yes, you have."

Chris took a moment to inventory her thoughts, and then, eyebrows raised, she audibly exhaled. For a criminal defense attorney, having a casual conversation with an accused murderer is perfectly normal. Driving potential clients off by treating them otherwise wouldn't be good for business. And sending this particular client away wouldn't serve the federation's needs, though she need not reveal that consideration to Spector.

Even so, this conversation pushed the edges of the envelope.

"I've finagled some batshit-crazy things in my day, but nothing close to this. Still, the elements are the same as negotiating the ransom payment in a kidnapping. Here, the ransom you demand is to take the death penalty off the table. What you're holding hostage is the full disclosure of your criminal activities, including the conspiracy with the Hodin cabal. We must show that the hostage is worth the ransom."

"The metaphor works for me," Frank replied.

"The first question anyone's going to have is around motivation. Offering up the Hodin cabal under these circumstances appears desperate. *Unless* you're sincere and can show the cabal is a far greater threat to society than the homicides of fourteen hapless souls. And before you address that, here's a helpful hint: if a big part of your response is saving the world from obvious evildoers, that could get us over one hurdle we'll face."

"It's not *quite* that altruistic." Frank frowned slightly. "But yes, I'd like to make the world aware of what's happening so they get a say in the outcome. I can't honestly claim that I'm against eliminating most of the world's population. I don't believe depopulation's optional if humankind is to survive."

Frank paused momentarily, allowing his audience time to absorb his commitment to an idea they likely wouldn't support. Nothing in Chris's or Drake's expression exposed their reactions — they were well-trained in the professionalism required of lawyers whose jobs entail defending the worst of criminals.

The buzzing of the phone on Chris's desk disrupted the moment.

"I apologize for the interruption — please, hold that thought for just a second," Chris said politely, even as her face showed her annoyance.

THE WRITINGS OF
AVRIL MARIA SERENE

Irritation was audible in Chris's tone as she picked up the receiver.

"Jim, I believe I left instructions not to be disturbed."

She listened for a moment.

"I see. Tell Mr. Newman to honor the warrant and cooperate; do whatever the officers ask. If he's *that* upset, see if Jerry can hold his hand and calm him down. He'll be in his car but should answer his cell."

Chris replaced the receiver and refocused. "Again, I'm sorry for the distraction, gentlemen." She looked at her notes and then at Frank. "I believe we're discussing incentives, and you were professing your firm support of the Hodin cabal's ultimate goals. That's not as helpful as I'd like.

"What can you offer to make law enforcement believe you're motivated and committed to giving up the cabal? Reasons that might override *their* motivation and commitment to putting you to sleep forever with a needle in your arm. Even better, something that convinces them going after the cabal protects and serves the public — and for which they can take credit."

"The problem with the federation's depopulation plan," Frank replied, "is that they alone are deciding not only who lives and dies but how. The idea of murder in the billions should be offensive to the Justice Department. If not, perhaps they'd also disregard the coalition playing God against the interests of free peoples. That the federation's plans include an eventual overthrow of our government might not register.

"But you'd think *someone* would be alarmed over all the obvious pain and suffering the coalition is causing to provoke death in the months and years before it occurs. Even if only from the perspective of the costs to our healthcare system. I have a lengthy list of concrete examples that have begun showing themselves online. A campaign to make the public aware of them would force the natural question of why the government's not doing anything, thereby making what I have to say meaningful."

"That's a start, and I can work with it." Chris nodded. "Okay, let's table discussion of the serial killings for now. We'll assume Bill can help deal with those as necessary."

"May I interrupt?" Drake broke his silence. "Bill's pass-down suggested the cabal represents some of the most powerful people in the world, most of its members unknown to you. Have you been threatened since going your own way? Does this meeting present security concerns for any of us that need addressing now?"

That's a pretty deft way to reveal what suspicions Spector might have toward anyone he's talking to, including us, Chris thought, admiring Drake's touch.

"I've taken a well-earned, two-week vacation from work," Frank responded, facing Drake. "The federation shouldn't be concerned about me. I regularly check in remotely to my work computer — I did so just before coming here — and nothing about my access to anything has changed. I assume they'd cut me off digitally as their first move if they thought me a problem. I suspect I'd be dead shortly after that."

Frank seemed not to notice the significant glances quickly exchanged between Drake and Chris as he mentioned his access. Nor could he see the text of the note Chris was scribbling, "Tell Bill: Don't pull Spector's access 'til <u>after</u> he's eliminated — no warnings. His status stays between us and enforcement; avoid creating rumors." She let Drake get a sidelong glance at her writing.

"Eventually, they'll learn of my activities," Frank continued. "When they do, I'll need help navigating threats coming my way."

"Let's schedule a meeting later this week," Drake suggested, "just you and me to discuss what that entails. I'll check my calendar and text you."

Frank nodded, seeming comfortable with the offer.

"Tell me in detail about the depopulation scheme," Chris said, "from the beginning. I'm looking for incidental facts, potential witnesses, and motivations to support the idea the Hodin cabal is manufacturing or controlling these events. As opposed to those simply occurring in the natural course of things. How we point up that distinction will define the battle lines for this."

"Virtually all the research, design, and testing of the federation's work product has gone through me," Frank replied. "Advertising is our primary means of herding sheep where we want them to go; also through me. I should have what you'll need."

"Focus on things the cabal is doing that are provable and no one else could have done," Chris continued. "Otherwise, we'd need to show they had a hand in the actions of one or more third parties that caused fatalities and that those deaths would not have occurred without assistance. Our last line of attack, by far the most difficult, is to prove a conspiracy to commit future crimes.

"Since depopulation's not yet occurred, I'm concerned from Bill's pass-down that your situation aligns with the latter. But I don't want to prejudge — I'm always surprised with the opportunities more complete information can expose."

"I understand what you need to defend me, but I'd be satisfied if we can convince enough people these things killing us aren't random events," Frank clarified. "I'm not sure anyone can stop global depopulation or that they should. I aim to get enough people who care to understand that someone is orchestrating these things. Then, at minimum, we need to get voices other than the federation's involved in making selections of methods and survivors."

"Good to know." Chris nodded. "That's a more doable outcome than I thought you might want. The words 'admitted serial killer' negate any chance of getting you off scot-free. But you're not on trial in this interview; I won't be challenging the factuality of anything you tell me that you've witnessed yourself. I will question, however, how to fit what you say into the best approach for representing you.

"For example, you might know anecdotally that the cabal has explicitly done a particular thing. But absent e-mails or smoking guns, they'll claim you're conflating mere coincidence — events occurring independently without external help. My first impression says that's the beauty of what they're doing — they can hide in plain sight. Natural cover seems built-in — they can claim the cabal's taking the blame for what others are doing for entirely different reasons. I'll need to ask some harsh questions. Please understand I need the answers to evaluate the strength of what we can present to authorities and the public."

"Where would you like me to start?" Frank asked.

"We know the Hodin cabal formed itself loosely from like-minded members of the Bilderbeck Group joining forces," Chris said. "Describe for me the problem they created the cabal to solve."

"Technology empowers population growth," Frank replied. "The explosion of technology at the end of the nineteenth century helped enable a population boom that has created an unsurvivable set of problems for the planet.

That spawned a vicious cycle, fueling a demand for more technologies to salve the pain, engendering even more people.

"There will be technology as long as there are humans, so the only way to solve the runaway incestuous loop is to prune away the excess people."

He then posed the obvious next question: "How do you eliminate humans without employing more — and more powerful — people and technologies to force the desired result? There is only one way. You get individuals to remove themselves and make their replacement impossible.

"And how hard is that? It turns out that people harming themselves is something they do willingly all the time."

Showing a cynical smile, Chris nodded as she leaned back in her chair.

"So, the problem is, how can we encourage and enable human self-elimination on a massive scale?" Frank continued. "Secondarily, how can we achieve that with enough of the 'best' citizens as survivors to restart the human experience in a better environment for long-term success? That's the problem the Hodin federation solved. They can get the least desirable of us to do away with ourselves efficiently so that the remaining souls can carry humanity into tranquility and prosperity. It's the only logical, viable, and sustainable solution available.

"Absent the coalition doing it their way, you'll want to get those kitchen knives sharpened, and the sooner, the better.

"Because if you *truly* believe in world peace, you'll need to get everyone you know, and everyone *they* know, to kill off seven or eight of their neighbors."

Book Two – Chapter 10

Chris Patterson now fully understood the threat Bill Clymer saw embodied in Frank Spector. The man would tell everything he knew and understood how to make his point. It'd take Chris a deeper dive to ascertain how much knowledge Frank had accumulated.

"Most of us aren't murderers," Chris said, "so good luck with the 'neighbors' thing, though I take your meaning. But even if you found another way, isn't depopulation like lawn mowing? Wouldn't the population immediately begin expanding again?"

"The federation devised a self-sustaining system of governance for survivors," Frank answered, "to ensure the remaining population will stabilize at one billion."

"This feels like one of those things where even if the facts are indisputable, the public will refuse to accept them. Like telling people there's no big fairy with a flowing white beard sitting on a golden throne in the sky, watching over them."

Frank nodded his assent.

"That, and there's a lot of 'feel free to reduce the numbers of them and their kind, but don't come after me and my family' to overcome. An advertising professional would present it in nonspecific terms so each audience can fill in their unique presumptions about which of the others the federation will remove.

"I experiment with social media in my spare time and have garnered considerable support from the Trumpies and QAnon types. Getting them into depopulation was easy, and they've done the heavy lifting to spread the basic ideas.

"Every one of them 'knows,'" Frank said, making air quotes, "who needs elimination from the population. They don't have my real identity, so they'll want to get rid of Jews, of course. Then there are Blacks, Democrats generally and liberals specifically, most Hispanics, LGBTQ+, intellectuals, atheists, powerful women, Muslims, the FBI, Asians, and pedophiles who aren't Republicans. That last exception means most perverts would get a free pass to join the survivors. Trumpies are ambivalent about how many Russians will remain among those still standing."

Chris held up a finger, buying time to catch up with her notes while Frank sat quietly, pondering the décor.

Finished, she looked up at him. "I know better now what the Hodin cabal would like to achieve. Let's discuss the resources, tools, and methods the cabal uses to accomplish its goals. You've been with the organization for almost twenty years — I assume you've kept busy during that period. Still, I try to stay current with the news, and nothing has made me aware of any depopulation. What's the status of the cabal's efforts?"

"The federation would be glad to know you, as a layperson, are unaware of their activities," Frank answered. "Their covert plan is reflected in thousands of initiatives implemented over the years. The least noticeable of those have been performing daily in plain sight. Others are complete but being held back. The coalition has discreetly executed all the required supportive and background tasks for those; the portions the public could observe are pending, awaiting an orchestrated launch.

"We're two years ahead of where we'd planned. With our success, I'm surprised no one's noticing what we're doing. That's good for the federation, not so much for anyone else. We'll launch the microplastics chemistry initiative as the incendiary event that triggers a cascading release of other federation programs on hold. That seminal initiative will take wing once we've developed the required protection for intended survivors."

Chris glanced at her notes. "Given all this is so secret, how can we show the cabal's progress as we represent you?"

"Earlier, I mentioned a lengthy list of concrete examples. I've put together an encrypted digital highlight reel of Internet articles and links that show how much success we've had to date. You'll find it impressive. In addition, I've copied relevant data for all our work from the federation's servers into a private database under my control. I've also kept a detailed journal from my first days with the coalition. If accepted as a client, I'll provide decryption passcodes when we execute an agreement."

Drake immediately sat up straight in his chair.

Chris coughed into her hand, following up with a drink of water to cover any hint of the surprise she'd let slip and to draw attention away from Drake's movements.

Frank's revelation that he had copies of the federation's data and his offer to share it had shocked Drake and Chris — allegations are one thing, having proof is another.

They hadn't masked their reactions well.

"My apologies, Frank, my allergies have been acting up," Chris said in deflection, her expression again neutral. "I'll need those materials to support our case."

Despite the sudden bad news, Chris's appreciation of Frank Spector's communication skills and ability to envision at scale had grown. It was apparent why the Hodin federation had wanted Frank at the nexus between the development of initiatives and those who implement them.

Now, Chris also saw the double-edged sword Frank's role represented. At the center of everything, he knew all there was to know. With Frank deciding to share, Chris understood the urgency of eliminating him.

"But before we get into that," Chris added, hoping changing subjects would make their interest in Frank's data and journal less noticeable, "I get how orchestrating these things could kill unsuspecting people." She tipped her head to one side. "But how does the Hodin cabal get seven billion people to voluntarily choose those options without making the manipulation obvious?"

"That's where my role with PWW comes in," Frank replied. "You should pay attention to your laptop when browsing. If you did, you'd know that, at any moment, on average, 22 percent of your screen's surface area and 30 percent of your audio has been diverted to manipulating you. You'd also know that 26 percent of the CPU cycles — which perform your computer's work — are spent on things other people are trying to get you to do. Your computer's running unsolicited ads, videos, and other distractions, collecting your private data, mining cryptocurrency, tracking your behaviors, and reporting to the people spying on you.

"But you're blind to it, just like everyone else — except, maybe, for gamers. They know how bad it truly is — to get the performance they pay for from their machines, they have to boot into a special mode and use dedicated software to free themselves of bloatware and ads.

"When common users have become that numb to abuse, slipping something a little more sophisticated — social engineering, AI, some echo-chamber support, even old-school subliminal suggestions — into the mix is easy. You'd be astonished at what all the tools I have at my disposal can make you do."

As Frank completed his thought, an insistent tone resonated from Chris's office phone.

"Yes, Jim?" Chris picked up, her tone exasperated.

She listened, pressing the phone to her ear so Frank wouldn't hear. "Mr. Albertson called; said it's urgent. They've run into a hitch, and the papers you and he discussed won't be available until tomorrow morning."

Chris didn't immediately reply to her son's relaying of Albertson's message; instead, she ran her tongue over her lower lip as if in deep thought. She recognized the alias Bill Clymer used and the significance of his message. She'd need to find a convenient stopping point in their meeting with Frank and get him to return later.

"Thank you, Jim. Hold all my other calls. If Mr. Albertson phones again, tell him I'll ring him back and then page me." She glanced briefly at Drake, then returned her attention to Frank.

"I apologize for the interruption, gentlemen. Lessee … oh, yes, I wanted to follow up with the 'highlight reel.'"

Drake spoke up.

"If I may, a question — you're here partly because these revelations threaten the cabal. How'll they react once they learn you've talked?"

Her face composed, Chris recognized the irony of asking Frank to describe the behaviors he anticipated from a unit whose purposes she and Drake served through this conversation.

"The federation's enforcement unit maintains security and discipline," Frank answered. "They do background research, monitor all personnel and activities, and resolve any issues. They can and will assassinate perceived offenders — inside or outside of the coalition — if they deem it necessary. This situation would fall under 'necessary.'"

"So, that's the stick — as to the carrot, how are the cabal's rank-and-file workers rewarded for their efforts?" Drake asked.

He wants to know what resources Frank could bring to bear in defending himself, Chris thought.

"Members embedded in a partner or target organization receive the salary from that position and a generous stipend from the federation. That's negotiated on a case-by-case basis. Some members will want power or visibility within the coalition instead of some or all of a paycheck."

"Where does that leave you?" Drake asked.

"I started as an active member who does field work for the Hodin federation. I was embedded with and paid handsomely by PWW, even as the federation promoted me to a top-level manager position, just under the unit's director. That title is my compensation from the coalition, along with near-total autonomy, a massive budget, and the ability to interact with most directors without going through the chain of command.

"I didn't need a federation salary — my employment with PWW covers my financial needs, and I've invested well."

Frank stopped for a moment as if pondering the words to follow. Slowly, a wry smile came to his face, even as his shoulders sagged and his head rocked back and forth.

"It's odd how it's working out. Thanks to PWW and the federation, I've put away a good chunk of change toward a nice retirement. But if this goes as I think it might, they'll terminate me, or Uncle Sam will be responsible for my room and board long before then."

His elbows were on the armrest of his chair, and his eyes focused off into space. With a half-smile, he shrugged his shoulders and returned his attention to Chris and the immediate business at hand.

"For all that," Chris said, "I'm still unaware of any remarkable recent reductions in population growth when I scan CNN, my e-mails, or my social media accounts. In fairness, I can't say I've been looking for the evidence, which may explain why I don't see it."

Frank nodded in understanding.

"There's a bottom line for me when I'm arguing on your behalf with people who can save you from a death sentence." A hint of impatience registered in Chris's voice. "What can I point to that screams, 'Yes, this is real, it's happening now, and bad guys worse than my client are responsible?'"

Frank sat back in his chair. "I expected you'd need detailed and incontrovertible information in a form you could quickly corroborate. I mentioned the highlight reel I put together. It's something of a fact sheet, encrypted, of course, with a bibliography of reputable sources woven into it. I regularly collate and update it from mentions on the Web of things related to our initiatives. I'll make a copy; it should be easy for you to verify."

"Is this something you can e-mail me?"

"I'll send it as an encrypted PDF and then text the passcode to your cell. As you can imagine, it needs to be kept secure – you'll want to destroy the file once you've gotten what you need from it."

"That should work." Chris's smile was one of satisfaction.

"We have protocols in-house for protecting items like this," Drake offered.

A shame Spector's leaving us, Chris thought. *Despite the situation, he continues following rules meant to protect the federation's interests. To some degree, he's still a staunch believer — these things matter to him.*

Regardless, she had her marching orders from Bill Clymer.

Making a blatant show of looking at her watch, Chris pretended to be surprised by the lateness of the hour.

"On that note, I hate to ask this, but I'm out of time and have several other questions. Is it possible to reconvene next Tuesday, say…" She checked her calendar. "One p.m.?"

"My time's my own for the next ten days," Frank replied, "I'll make it."

"I can be here," Drake volunteered.

"Good, we're set, then. I hope you enjoy the rest of your afternoon. Drake, would you mind walking Frank out?" Chris asked as she rose from her chair.

When the two men were out of the office and beyond earshot, Chris turned off the digital recorder taped under the outside lip of her desk, hooked her burner phone to the voice scrambler, and called Bill Clymer.

"Good afternoon, Bill, Chris Patterson. Frank Spector just left my office. He'll be back a week from today. What happened with the original plan?"

The voice on the other end was apologetic. "Sorry, Chris; it's one of those fluke things. A federation enforcement officer on the elimination team got pulled over for an old warrant, a domestic incident. Spector has dangerous skills, and we didn't want to go a man light."

"Understood. By the way, you need to know Spector's copied the federation's data to a private server, and he's kept a journal. He's also made a digital record describing the current status of the coalition's initiatives."

There was a momentary pause on the line.

"*That's* not good, but at least we know," Bill replied somberly. "We'll see if we can run those down.

"We'll be ready for him once you cut him loose next week."

Book Two — Chapter 11

Chris Patterson welcomed Frank Spector and Drake Lindberg to her office after their one-week hiatus.

"Drake and I received the link and password you sent to your encrypted 'highlight reel.' We've reviewed and discussed it — illuminating, to say the least."

"Not to be macabre about it, but you'll want to consider those items in their proper context," Frank replied.

"That killing potential is in addition to a harsh reality — there were already plenty of ways individuals could do away with themselves unintentionally, some quickly, others more slowly. Other aids to unintended suicide include tobacco, alcohol, obesity, hydrocarbons, and other pollutants. Fast foods, crappy nutrition, added salt, and processed sugar generally. Drugs, legal and illegal, in combinations people lie to their doctors about — lack of exercise, STDs, body alterations, and driving too fast or under the influence.

"All these, together or separately, can and will eventually lead to your death. Our contributions merely speed things up.

"Beyond the various means for killing you, there are all the influences that favor making fatal choices: Corporate greed, government ineptitude, terrible schools, Sunday morning mythologies, lousy medical practitioners, political ideologies, peer pressure, and poor breeding partners — human weaknesses like self-indulgence, addictions, anger management issues, echo chambers, and poor impulse control or decision-making."

Frank had Chris's and Drake's attention as he marched through his list.

"You don't need to create countless new ways to eliminate people en masse if you can wait several generations for the results. All you have to do is drive people to do more of the same things they're already doing. Advertising achieves some of that for us. However, most advertising today prioritizes corporate greed, which says you want your most gullible consumers to stay alive as long as possible, assuming they have money and keep buying. On its face, that seems contrary to the federation's goals.

"But the coalition's learned through practice that, if you make the primary focus human depopulation rather than profit, advertising's incredibly effective for our needs. In concert with propaganda, disinformation, braindead politicians, social media, influencers, and other tools, you can quickly get massive numbers of people to do the damnedest things.

"Some of those are beyond stupid — taking ivermectin or hydroxychloroquine, injecting bleach into their veins, or drinking hydrogen peroxide for COVID-19. It's truly phenomenal."

Chris raised an index finger. "There it is — I just found your e-mail with the fact sheet. Please continue."

"That's incredible power," Frank added, "over those who — if we're candid here — make the best subjects for termination, anyway. That control underlines the need for the federation's productive relationships with PWW and other ad agencies."

Drake nodded, seeming to grasp the implications of Frank's words. Chris's expression no longer feigned any doubts.

"It seems the cabal's command of advertising can weaponize all kinds of things you'd ordinarily consider benign, or at their worst, acceptable risks," she acknowledged.

Frank ticked through the highlight reel's background explainers, followed by links related to coalition initiatives, and finished with public domain statistics demonstrating depopulation success.

"I had no idea…." That much was truthful — Chris hadn't kept herself informed of the full breadth of the federation's efforts.

Frank Spector is complicated, Chris thought to herself. *I sense great pride as he walks through these accomplishments — with each sentence, he struggles to substitute "federation" or "coalition" for the "we" he's always used. Yet, he's putting himself in tremendous peril, spending enormous sums of money and exhausting significant energy to stop the organization's progress.*

She drummed the tip of her pen on the desk in thought, sitting back in her chair and pondering the woodwork where the ceiling met the far wall. "I'm sure there are several other things the Hodin cabal's developing that'd scare the bejesus out of me. You've convinced me these things are doable and that your team's working on them."

Putting down her pen, Chris glanced at her watch. "I need to make a quick phone call — are we good for a brief break?" As she posed the question, she made eye contact with Drake, breaking away as she realized Frank had noticed her glance. Hopefully, he'd assume it related to her call.

"Yes, ten minutes?" Frank asked, and Chris nodded. On their way out, Drake offered to show Frank where the restrooms were.

Quickly assembling her burner and voice scrambler after the door closed, Chris called Bill Clymer to tell him Frank was present and ask what to do next. No one answered, and she abandoned the attempt, not knowing how soon Frank might return to her office. Though she'd tired of this conversation, she'd have to keep Frank talking until Bill contacted her.

Once the two men had returned, Chris leaned back in her chair, considering where she'd take the discussion. By learning of the data Frank was keeping that could expose federation confidences, she'd satisfied Bill's needs. With few other options, Chris would try to glean more about Frank's strategy for the immediate future.

"Look, I get that you're giving up the cabal's secrets because you don't have any good cards left to play. I understand they'll likely kill you anyway to keep you from talking once your arrest makes the news. But giving the cabal up for that reason alone won't gain you sympathy from the people I need to buy your story — likely a prosecutor in the Justice Department. The 'giving the people a choice,' 'playing God,' and pain and suffering angles help, but they're sound bytes.

"What comes across to me is you liked both your jobs, you're very good at them, and you've done them for twenty years, without complaint, while building a nice nest egg. Pretty comfy. Still, in the best-case scenario — where the powers that be buy into what you're saying — you're answerable for what the cabal has done *and* the fourteen serial killings for which you alone are responsible.

"What can you give me that says putting other members of the cabal behind bars — given all the work it'll take the feds to start from square one — will reward them and society more than it benefits you personally?"

"I take your point," Frank replied, "and understand managing perceptions, something I've dealt with daily. But getting a listener to appreciate what I'm doing for the world will take a layered approach.

"There's a reason I've bombarded you with all the information in the highlight reel and fact sheet. Granted, you've had no opportunity to explore that information in depth, which explains why you're framing your questions as if this is all conjecture.

"Still, once they'd absorbed the contents, any intelligent and rational person would see these things as *reality*. Once that happens, it's a short distance to understanding the threat and the need to get a handle on this from both global and personal perspectives.

"Somewhere in that process, a light bulb will go on that I didn't have to let the world know, and knowing is a lot better for everyone than continued ignorance. The information only I can offer will not only *save* lives but improve their quality."

"Allow me some time to, as you say, 'absorb' this information," Chris responded. "I may have a different take after sleeping on it."

Chris's office phone speaker began emitting a soft buzz every few seconds. "That's my office manager again. He knows not to disturb us unless it's important. Give me one second."

Chris pressed the intercom button. "Yes, Jim?"

The voice on the other end said, "I'm sorry — Mr. Albertson called, saying it was urgent. I'm to tell you the contract's complete and ready for execution."

Chris momentarily locked eyes with Drake.

Suddenly more alert, her protector sat up straight in his chair, his eyes no longer focused elsewhere.

"Thank you, Jim; I'll phone him once we finish here." Chris released the intercom button, keeping her tone businesslike without changing her facial expression.

Frank seemed to sense a change in the priorities.

"I see you've got other business to tend to," he offered, standing up. "And I don't have anything more you'd find relevant."

"It's been informative." Chris smiled as she and Drake stood, each extending their hand. "Let me make some calls, see if I can put together a plan. We'll need a roadmap for vetting and engaging our contacts with authorities. I assume your current situation is stable, and we still have time?"

"I've got three days left on my vacation," Frank answered as they shook hands. "If it's doable, I'd like to know something of the path forward before I return to the office."

"We'll make that happen. I'll get something stubbed together, and we'll meet up again. I've appreciated your insights and look forward to helping you through this."

"Thanks, Chris." Frank nodded at her colleague. "Drake. I appreciate you taking these meetings on short notice. Let's hope the rest of your afternoon goes well. No need to get up. I'll see myself out."

"Oh, Mr. Spector, we'll need the online link and passcodes to your data server and journal before you leave."

Chris's tone was almost too informal.

"That data will give us a good head start, and with all you've told us, I'm concerned about security. A direct handoff between us and no one else in the room is safest, as opposed to exchanging those over potentially insecure networks. I'm uncomfortable with anyone other than myself or Mr. Lindberg handling such sensitive information.

"If you can write the server addresses, logons, and passcodes on this pad, I'll put it in my safe."

She smiled for her audience.

Let's see how far you get with your leverage gone, you traitorous son-of-a-bitch.

THE WRITINGS OF
AVRIL MARIA SERENE

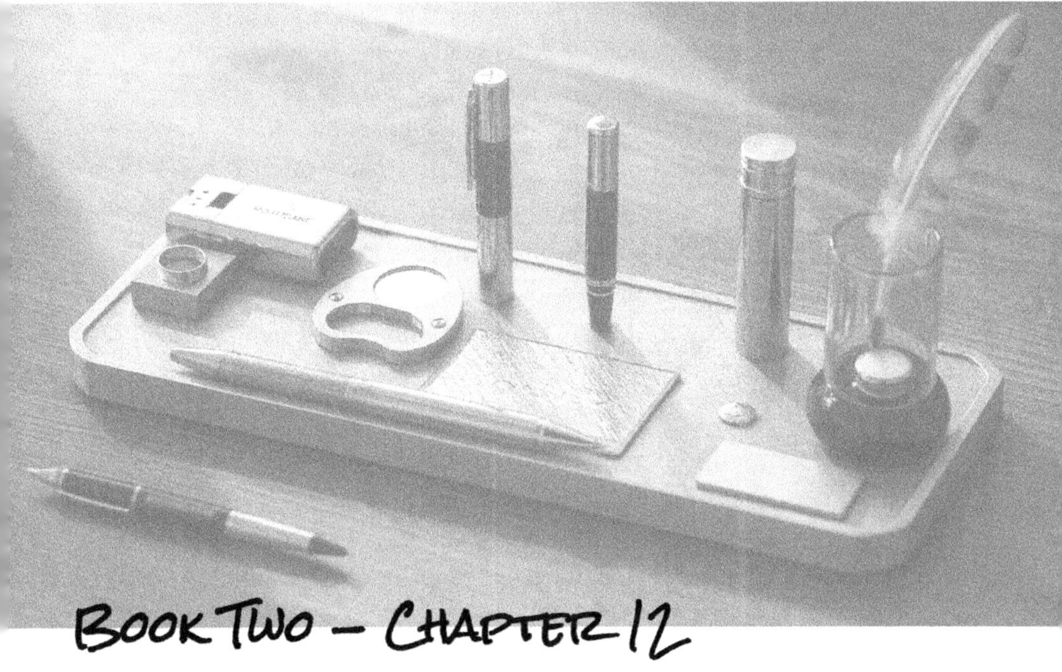

Book Two — Chapter 12

Chris Patterson, the world-class lawyer and elite negotiator for the city's most influential figures, had just made a rookie mistake.

Frank had already begun feeling uneasy about Chris and Drake. Something seemed … *off*. All of this information should have been new to her. Still, Chris wasn't asking any of the expected questions: *What were the names of the embedded operatives? What company were they working for? When, exactly, did this or that happen?* And she was taking very few notes.

But the din of alarm bells in Frank's brain when asked for the server link and passcodes transcended every other thought. Frank had dealt with hundreds of attorneys in his personal and professional lives. He'd *never* known any of them to commit to a situation without first discussing payment, particularly for something this complex.

Yet, Chris, managing partner of the priciest law firm in town, asked him for crucial, sensitive information *before mentioning her retainer.*

By obviously looking for a pen in his suit jacket, Frank bought himself a few seconds of cover to consider his options.

His Glock was in its small-of-back holster, but when he first entered the office, no one had frisked him or asked if he was carrying. He'd have to assume it wasn't necessary since Chris relied on Drake being armed. There was no telling what weaponry Chris might have hidden behind that massive wooden desk. Even if he got the drop on them, he'd still have to navigate the office door, the main entrance to the law firm, and the elevator or stairs. After that, building security, the lobby entry to the building, and any issues he discovered on the street.

He didn't like those odds; brute force wasn't the way to go here. He'd play along and hope that neither Drake nor Chris realized their mistake.

"I seem to have lost my pen — may I borrow one of yours?" Frank asked, playing innocent. Chris gestured towards the custom gold desk set Frank had admired earlier. The grouping came complete with a laser pointer, Montblanc ballpoint and fountain pens, inkwell, mechanical pencil, business card holder, cigar lighter, and cigar cutter. It reminded Frank of the 1980s "Wolf of Wall Street" era and its excesses. *Another holdover from the previous tenant?*

Frank took the ballpoint pen from it and began scribbling out gibberish on the notepad as his server path and passkey.

His best move would be to allow Chris and Drake to correct course gracefully; if they recognized their misstep and thought it unrecoverable, they could react badly.

"I assume this means you're accepting me as a client. We haven't discussed your retainer — is now the time to make those arrangements?" Frank's tone was casual. But as he wrote, he kept one eye looking under his arm at Drake's knees for any signs of fast-twitch movement.

Frank's long hours playing poker with associates and clients helped him recognize Chris's tell immediately — she took an almost imperceptible quick breath just before speaking an untruth.

"Oh, I'm sorry; I assumed you discussed that with my son, Jim. That Bill Clymer referred you told us you're good for it," Chris gave a quick laugh, catching her error but giving no sign she thought Frank was on to her.

Frank knew Jim couldn't have negotiated a retainer without knowing the case details revealed in the last two sessions with Chris and Drake. And Frank now understood why Chris might prefer no written record of their dealings with him; while concentrating on that goal, she'd lost her overview of the field of play.

"We'd need a 50K advance up front," Chris said. "For convoluted cases like this, we'll have to research what outcomes are possible and acceptable to you. Once there, we may adjust the retainer, but it wouldn't be too extreme."

The lowball number told Frank that Chris was overcompensating so she wouldn't blow the sale before the server information she wanted was in hand.

"Fair enough — will you take a check?" Frank ripped off the top sheet of the notepad. Crossing his fingers in his head that Chris wouldn't confirm the link before he left the room, Frank leaned across the desk, passing the slip of paper to her with his left hand. Chris and Drake exchanged glances as she took the note from his fingers.

Frank used that split second to palm the cigar lighter from the desk set, sliding it into his front pants pocket with his right hand.

"Of course — just make it out to the firm." Chris handed Frank her business card. Frank took a checkbook from his jacket pocket, scribbled out a bank draft, and gave it to the attorney.

Shaking Chris's hand and then Drake's, Frank wished them a good afternoon before leaving the office.

He noticed that this time, Drake made no offer or effort to see him out.

As Frank exited their meeting, Drake returned to his own office. Chris dropped her pen on the stack of papers at the left side of her desk, not bothering to note any of the commitments she'd just made.

She removed and turned off the digital voice recorder hidden near Frank's seat. Chris copied the recording to her laptop hard drive and encrypted it before destroying the original file on the digital recorder. Using her cell phone, Chris took a photo of the note Frank gave her with the link and passcode to his data server, putting the slip of paper and Frank's check into her top desk drawer.

She forwarded Bill Clymer the encrypted highlight reel and fact sheet e-mail attachment, the link-and-passcode image, and her outgoing message via the Hodin federation's secure delivery app.

Done! she thought with relief.

Chris would never realize the grave error she was making by assuming her role in all this was now over.

THE WRITINGS OF
AVRIL MARIA SERENE

Book Two — Chapter 13

Immediately upon leaving Chris Patterson's office, Frank confirmed his suspicions. A stealthy and unwelcome entourage had fallen in behind him — at least two thugs wearing off-the-rack suits and cop shoes.

Now might be an excellent time to shift to plan B.

Making the corner to the passageway between the banks of elevators well ahead of his pursuers, Frank bolted through before they arrived.

Passing in front of the elevator doors, he hung a hard left into the far hallway.

About ten feet down, Frank spotted the exit to the stairway.

He assumed that, like the ad agency he once worked for, Chris Patterson's law offices leased their space and did not own the building. That meant her staff didn't control cameras monitoring the community entrances and exits outside their offices.

To avoid setting off the audible alarm, Frank used a credit card to trip the emergency exit latch onto the stairwell without pushing the control bar.

Building security might observe someone leaving through that door if they were paying attention to their monitors. Still, no notifications would go to anyone else.

Spinning around once he'd passed through, Frank grabbed the door handle on the other side to close it as quietly as he could.

Had anyone seen him, they'd expect a run for it down the stairs to the lobby — he'd need cover before escaping.

Frank knew smokers and vapers on the next floor up at his old employer taped the stairwell exit latch catch so it wouldn't fully close. It made slipping out onto the stairwell for a quick drag less noticeable, and not swiping a badge to get back in meant there was no record of who, when, or how often.

Bounding up the stairs two steps at a time, Frank kept his weight on the balls of his feet, hitting the front edge of the stair treads nearly soundlessly. He hadn't forgotten his days as a teenager sneaking out the metal fire escape in the back of his mother's old fourth-floor apartment. Frank had learned to prevent shoes pounding upon expanded-metal stair treads from echoing so noisily between the cinderblock walls.

He put the skill to good use now. Of course, the footing was a little trickier in leather soles than in tennis shoes, but he managed.

Frank's luck held — he found the door back into the main building unlatched as expected.

Walking casually, he headed for the restroom and ducked inside.

After peering into all the stalls for other guests, he checked to see that the lighter he'd taken from Patterson's desk set was working.

Removing his left shoe, he jammed its toe between the underside of the door and the floor to slow down anyone's entry and provide some warning.

Ripping the plastic cover off the paper towel dispenser, Frank lifted out the roll.

He grabbed the trash receptacle from under the sink counter and took the stall at the end of the row. Sitting the container on the closed seat cover, he pulled toilet paper from the giant single roll mounted on the stall partition. He wadded up enough to fill the trash can half full, leaving a trail of toilet paper hanging off the side of the container to use as a wick. Tearing off squares from the paper towel roll, he filled the rest of the trash container with them.

Frank placed the container on the counter under one of the sprinkler heads in the bathroom ceiling and put on his shoe.

Lighting the toilet paper fuse, he walked nonchalantly from the bathroom, heading to the nearest corner office on the floor.

As the occupants of the short-walled cubicles along his path glanced up, Frank avoided eye contact where he could, smiling with a quick nod when he couldn't.

Stephon Coleman's office door was open, and the squat, balding man, wearing a white shirt and loosened tie, looked up as Frank tapped on the door frame.

Breaking into a broad smile, Stephon stood and walked around his desk, hand extended, to greet his visitor.

"Frank, what the hell are you doing here — *slumming?* I haven't seen you since, what, the pharma trade show last August? How's life in the big leagues? Is PWW treating you okay?"

"Hi, Stephon — I was in the neighborhood poaching clients. Thought I'd stop by and rub your nose in it." Frank grinned, and the two shook hands.

Suddenly, the fire alarm went off.

The sound startled Stephon, and Frank feigned surprise.

Stephon quickly scanned what he could see over the cubicle walls for any obvious signs of fire.

Putting his hand on his guest's shoulder, he said, "Walk with me, Frank. We'll have to take the stairs. We can talk shop on the way down."

"Some things never change." Frank grinned broadly. "That alarm went off three times a week when I worked here."

An orderly queue of employees had formed along one wall headed to the stairway and out the exit doors.

Another line merging with it crossed in front of the bathrooms, its members agitated and talkative as they noticed the fumes and thin white wisps of smoke seeping out from under the men's bathroom door.

Still, no one panicked; there seemed to be a consensus that someone had thrown a lit cigarette into the trash can … again.

Both men merged into the line, the two old friends taking the time to catch up and reminisce.

As they reached the bottom of the stairs, Stephon nodded toward the throng of people in the lobby making their way out the front doors. He said apologetically, "Sorry we don't have more time, but I'm the fire warden for the floor, and I need to do a head count."

"Understood — it was good to see you again, Stephon. Let's hit up Kerrigan's one of these days after work and toss some darts.

"But I've got to go, too. I parked behind the building, so I'll leave through the service exit at the shipping dock. I'll never make it through that crowd in the front. Looks like you're going to be busy. I'll drop you an e-mail to see how everything turned out."

Once the two men had parted company, Frank walked out between two semis unloading at the docks.

He saw nothing amiss when surveying the activity around him for anyone interested in what he was doing.

Despite what he'd told Stephon, Frank had no intention of going anywhere near his car; it was likely being watched. He'd send someone after it later or come back for it himself in the wee hours of the morning.

Cutting across the middle of streets in downtown traffic and ducking in and out of alleyways, Frank discovered an upscale coffee shop at an intersection. With glass windows on two sides, it would give him a full view of both streets.

Ordering a cup of coffee and sitting at the barista bar, Frank spun around in his seat to see the traffic, watching who came in and out. Taking stock of his situation, Frank realized he was safe for the moment, but it wouldn't last.

The attorney ratted me out to the federation. It's on now — both players have shown their hands.

The situation forced him into his end game, and he'd have to go it alone without professional help. Frank wasn't one to dwell on days gone by; still, he welcomed the thought of his time spent twenty-six years ago training as an Army Ranger. He hadn't stuck with it, taking his honorable discharge after just one tour of duty. Crawling around in desert sands, risking life and limb to feed this country's addiction to oil, wasn't his thing. But now, that training would serve him well.

He needed to take care of some things. Heading to the coffee shop's men's restroom, he locked himself in as soon as he had checked that no one was in the stall next to the urinal. Taking a seat, Frank pulled his burner phone from his suit coat pocket and powered it on. His personal cell wouldn't do; because it was GPS-enabled and traceable, he routinely turned it off and stored its SIM card in his wallet during the business day.

Before he called anyone, he needed to inventory his situation. If Chris Patterson were a federation member, she'd want no association between her firm and a high-profile individual who'd likely go missing or turn up dead in the next few days. That explained why only people she trusted — her son and head of security — were present for the two sessions. She'd likely torn up his check and destroyed any other proof of their contact once he'd left her office.

The security video of the common hallway between elevators would provide the only evidence that Frank knew enforcement was pursuing him; it would show Frank breaking into a run for the stairs. That video belonged to building management. Assuming the law firm didn't own the building, they wouldn't have that recording. The federation wouldn't involve outsiders in their dirty laundry by asking for it or risk Patterson's reputation with a break-in and theft.

Absent other information, the coalition would assume their enforcement detail lost Frank through incompetence — that check he wrote to the law firm would reassure the federation Frank was clueless about his planned demise.

Frank's situation was still dire. He was well-known to the coalition — there were few places he could hide. He couldn't be sure who around him belonged to the federation. Once he'd betrayed them, terminating him was their only option. Frank didn't doubt they'd eventually be successful.

Still, the need-to-know security protecting coalition members also gave Frank some leeway — others in the federation wouldn't know Frank's staff choices, work partners, or his employees' specific roles. Those he hadn't worked with couldn't match his name with his face.

Communications within the coalition were point-to-point and individually enciphered. The prohibition against gathering members' names onto lists left the federation no way to broadcast quickly to a general audience that someone had gone rogue. The coalition would have frowned on the wide distribution of negative information anyway — it would disrupt the secrecy and morale upon which the federation relied and could expose its operations to outside scrutiny.

It was time to put his assumptions to the test. Frank pulled the voice scrambler from his pants pocket and attached it to his throwaway phone.

After the scrambler made the encrypted connection, a voice on the other end responded.

"Yes, John," the man answered, using the alias he knew, "you caught me on the way out. What can I do for you?"

Frank heard nothing unusual in the man's voice — it didn't seem he'd heard yet of the incident at the attorney's office.

"Good evening, Henry; thanks for taking my call. I realize the time difference has made the hour pretty late for you.

"But listen, we've just validated an unexpected breakthrough that changes the game, and we'll have to adjust our priorities...."

Once finished with his international business, Frank made a local call, still using the scrambler. "Hi, Jeremy — yes, I'm still on vacation. But some great news came our way, and I need you to do me a favor...."

THE WRITINGS OF
AVRIL MARIA SERENE

Book Two — Chapter 14

Once Frank had communicated his instructions to his German colleague and American assistant, he turned to his personal circumstances. He'd need more firepower — all he had with him was his Glock 22 and one extra clip. Retaking his seat at the coffee shop bar, Frank quickly scanned the street and walkways for any suspicious traffic. Satisfied with the environment, Frank called for an Uber on his throwaway cell.

Climbing into the back of the Prius, he directed the driver to Upland Avenue. The narrow, curving residential street ran through the mature and abundant foliage dominating the green rolling hills of Newton. Frank had the driver slow as the Uber approached the circular center island that marked the intersection with Brush Hill Road. He surveyed the surroundings as they passed — his was the two-story dove-gray house on the southeast corner lot with its barn roof, three dormer windows in the front and two in the back, and three stalwart trees in the front yard.

The dark blue Ford four-door sedan directly across the tree-lined street from his home was obvious — Frank didn't recognize the vehicle as belonging to the neighborhood. Its two silhouetted inhabitants in coats and ties seemed to be engaged in idle conversation, apparently with nothing better to do during the business day. Their sedan was unmarked, but the lack of subtlety otherwise told Frank they were conveying a message with their presence. It meant the occupants were law enforcement.

That was good for Frank — it was unlikely federation security would hang around in this situation. Spotting his housekeeper's car in the drive, Frank had the Uber pull over behind a row of thick bushes, hiding the Prius from the Ford but giving Frank a clear line of sight to his driveway.

Frank inserted the SIM from his wallet into his regular cell phone and powered it on, making his number recognizable on Caller ID. He knew the signal would bounce off the same tower as if inside his residence, so he wouldn't be giving anything away if someone was tracking the cell.

"Wait for me here — I'm just going to step outside. I'll be back in a few minutes." The driver nodded in response.

"Hi, Amanda; how's your day going?" Frank asked when his housekeeper answered her phone. Without waiting for her response, he asked, "Would you mind taking a break from your chores to do me a favor?"

"Sure, Mr. Spector; what can I do for you?"

"I need some things from my office in the den. I'm with a client; I don't have time to get them myself. I need the metal box — the bigger one — from the gun case in the office closet. Grab the laptop and the USB hard drive on the desk. Place everything into separate brown paper grocery bags. Put some rags on the top of the bags so no one can see what's in them. My client lives in a rough neighborhood, and I don't want anyone trying to steal them.

"Then take a fifty out of the top desk drawer to put some gas in your car. Bring everything to me at the MacDonald's on Needham Street. Can you do that for me?"

"Yes, Mr. Spector, I'll do it right now."

"Thanks, Amanda — if I'm not at the restaurant when you arrive, just wait; I'm further away and in traffic." Frank wanted some extra time to see how the men in the Ford would react to her leaving.

"Oh, and Mr. Spector, two men in business clothes came to the door and asked for you. I told them you were at work. They didn't leave a card; they said they'd stop by later."

"Good to know — we're changing our insurance plan at my company; I'm sure they wanted to talk to me about that," Frank lied, now comfortable that the house watchers at the curb were law enforcement. The federation wouldn't have announced themselves in that way.

Once he'd signed off with Amanda, Frank returned to his seat in the Prius and asked the driver to continue waiting.

Amanda, her hair pinned up in her work bun and still wearing her apron, left the side door next to the garage fifteen minutes later. She carried three grocery bags to her car in two trips.

Backing her Ford Fusion slowly out of the drive, Amanda headed northwest towards Willard Street. As she passed his Uber, Frank looked away to avoid her recognizing him.

After waiting a few moments to be sure the plain clothes in the Ford wouldn't follow her, Frank asked the Uber driver to take him to the burger outlet.

Amanda was waiting when Frank arrived at the restaurant. Together, they transferred the grocery bags from her car to the Prius.

Now, with a backup weapon and more secure access to the Internet, Frank had the Uber driver take him back downtown to the building housing Chris Patterson's law office. He'd need to gather some things he'd left in his car.

Wanting some time alone with his vehicle, Frank sent the Uber back down the ramp to wait for him outside on the street. Dropping to his knees alongside the BMW, he searched with his Swiss army knife penlight for the GPS sender or Apple AirTag the federation would have placed somewhere on or underneath the car.

It took several minutes of looking and feeling around, but he found it. An inch and a half wide and three inches long, the GPS device was a professional unit sold only to security services. It had an extended battery life, a more rugged case, and a strong magnet for adhering to ferrous surfaces.

Pocketing the GPS sender, Frank removed his ignition key fob from his key ring and placed it on top of the car's left rear tire, as close to the fender well as he could get it — the towing service would need a key. He dialed the number for AAA as he walked back down the parking garage ramp and arranged the transport home for his vehicle. Once the tow truck arrived, Amanda could accept delivery.

Calling for a Lyft to meet him at the IHOP two miles west of the garage, Frank had the Uber driver take him to the pancake house. The driver helped Frank transfer his grocery bags and other items into the Lyft as the Prius idled.

Taking advantage of a momentary distraction, Frank slipped the GPS tracker inside the Uber's trunk, clamping the device onto the exposed sheet metal supporting the rear deck speakers.

That should keep the federation occupied for a while, Frank thought with a wry smile.

Now, into the lion's den. Frank asked the Lyft driver to take him to PWW's headquarters. Though he had a few vacation days left, he needed to know if the coalition had compromised his relationship with his official employer.

Frank had the Lyft pull up across the street from the office building. He'd have to leave his weapons in the ride-share — checking a gun with security to get through the detectors would draw attention he didn't want. He was hoping to get to the bank of elevators unnoticed.

Once past the security conveyors, Frank pushed through the crowd scurrying for the elevators after lunch. He avoided eye contact with the security guard staffing the front desk. Frank headed towards the far elevator, the one with penthouse access. Once inside, Frank swiped his badge and pressed the button for the management suite.

The button flashed red, telling him immediately that PWW had cut off his access. *Dammit!* He'd expected it to happen eventually, but the timing wasn't good. Frank had hoped to retrieve his client lists and copies of staff contact information, but he'd have to do without. Quickly punching the button for the next floor up, he hoped that security officers would read the alert they received on the denied access as simply a mistaken button push.

Getting off at the floor above, Frank used the stairs to return to the ground floor and exit through the side door.

The stairwell dumped into the main lobby, which meant he was going against the grain of the foot traffic.

This time, the front desk security guard made him.

Frank watched him do a double take, then pick up a phone behind the counter and dial a number.

The now-former ad exec sped up his pace to beat any newly arriving security team members out the door.

Once outside, he made a beeline to the Lyft, shouting at the driver to make a speedy exit as he climbed into the back seat.

Once they'd cleared the area, the alarmed Lyft driver asked, "*What happened?*"

"I had to serve a guy papers, a lawsuit to collect money for my company," Frank improvised, patting the chest of his suit jacket as if he had documents there.

"Trying to earn brownie points with my boss. They didn't tell me he was a security guard. When he refused service, his buddies came after me. The company should have served him through the sheriff's department. Live and learn, I guess."

"I tried serving papers once to make extra money," the driver confided. "People are too crazy. After a guy pulled a gun, I got out of it."

"Won't be doing it again, that's for sure," Frank said, pointing to the façade of a nearby bank. "Do me a favor — stop by the ATM. I need some cash."

After withdrawing a considerable sum, he asked the driver to take him to the Rodeway Inn near Logan International. He checked into a room with a prepaid Wise debit card he'd gotten through the Monito website, an account he used only for discreet transactions — untraceable back to him.

Now settled, well-armed, Internet-enabled, and reasonably safe with cash in his pocket, Frank began seriously considering his options.

He couldn't say he liked any of them as they stood, but Frank wasn't about to let anyone back him into a corner — he could be very creative at solving these kinds of problems.

For his next move, it was time to play his hole card against the biggest asshole he knew in the game — his father.

THE WRITINGS OF
AVRIL MARIA SERENE

Book Two — Chapter 15

Frank wheeled the rented Porsche Cayenne into the drive after the three-and-a-half-hour journey from Boston to the outskirts of Millbrook, New York. An understated sign mounted to the gate and offering the estate for sale drew his eye. In the spirit of "if you must ask, you can't afford it," the list price of $65 million was discreetly buried in the smaller font of the property description.

While he doubted the old man would ever fully retire, the posting told Frank his father was finally pulling back from world affairs. Giving up the trophy real estate and summer home the family built in 1898 meant that Levi had become less concerned about appearances. Hiding away on one of his island properties in the Florida Keys would make his father all the more dangerous — only public opinion had constrained his private predilections.

The half-mile drive between the ivory wooden fences of the immaculately trimmed open fields peeled away the years. The sight of the palatial home, porticoed in porcelain white columns against a backdrop of lemon chiffon siding, brought with it the rise of an old uneasiness no longer natural to him. Mixed emotions and deeply conflicted childhood memories flooded Frank's mind, tightening a knot in his midsection — he'd have to remain focused on his mission to keep those once-buried feelings at bay.

Like Frank's mother and Levi's other wives, Miriam was a tall, willowy blonde with big hair and outsized breasts, probably surgically enhanced. Frank guessed she was at least three decades younger than Levi and subservient in the old man's presence — past as prologue.

"You must be Lemuel," she called from the porch as Frank climbed out of his SUV.

The name Frank hadn't used in thirty years grated on him, a stark reminder of a life he'd tried to forget. When he approached, she extended her right hand, palm downward, long before Frank could offer his – she hadn't attended one of the better finishing schools.

Daddy dearest had to lower his standards for this one — age must be catching up to him.

"Your father is expecting you; he's in the library."

With a curt smile and a dip of his head, Frank headed through the front door and down the hall to his right.

The smells wiped away thirty years in a heartbeat. They circulated through the air of the old house, a potpourri of stale cigars, damp wool, and cinnamon rolls, the late-breakfast staple Frank remembered from his long-ago days as a resident.

Leaning over the maple secretary across from the library entrance, Levi straightened, peering over his shoulder as Frank strode down the hallway. Graying and thin in casual slacks and a short-sleeved shirt, the old man projected that air of cynical disdain common to those who wield power over lesser beings. He used his half-rim reading glasses as a prop, looking over the top of them to convey superiority.

"Lemuel, it's been a long time – I haven't seen you since your mother's funeral," Levi said, offering his right hand to Frank.

Frank gave Levi a look of scorn as he brushed past, ignoring the invitation to shake. Left with no choice, Levi pursed his lips, sweeping his left arm toward the open library door.

"Fine, won't you come in and take a seat, then?"

Levi followed Frank into the library, then turned toward the open doorway.

"Miriam, we'll be awhile — tell Vanessa we're not to be disturbed," Levi called out without waiting for a response.

As Levi closed both panels of the solid walnut doors, Frank pulled his Glock from its holster in the back of his belt. The credenza against the wall perpendicular to the door had a padded wooden chair in front of it. Setting the gun sideways on the cabinet with the barrel pointing toward Levi, Frank moved the chair to the end of the credenza nearest the door. Turning the chair's back to Levi, Frank straddled it rearward as he sat down.

Sliding over to the wet bar along the wall next to the door, Levi looked back over his shoulder at Frank, his eyes focusing on the Glock.

"How gauche, Frank. Have you become so pedestrian in your problem-resolution skills that you'd shoot your flesh and blood father? Really."

"Oh, I don't intend to kill you, Levi."

Not directly.

Levi turned his back on his guest. Frank knew his father wanted to show that he wasn't afraid of anything Frank might do.

"Care to mix alcohol with your loaded weapons, Lemuel?"

"Ah-ah-ah-ah, Levi, let's keep your hands where I can see them," Frank admonished. "Your arrogance makes you stupid, Levi. It seems the passing years haven't improved anything. You don't appreciate how well I know this room — the buttons you've had wired into the furniture to summon help from the stables and the servant's quarters. And the .38 you used to keep in your top desk drawer. No telling what other defenses you may have added in the years since."

Frank rested his left hand on the firearm, forefinger alongside the trigger.

"And no, your decanted liquor's a little salty for my tastes," he added with a snort.

A brief look of puzzlement flashed over Levi's face, Frank's last comment not registering.

As Levi stepped over to the end of the heavy walnut desk across from the credenza, Frank waggled the index finger of his right hand at Levi and tightened the grip on his weapon with his left.

"Let's keep this honest and aboveboard, out in the center of the room where we can face each other."

"As you wish, Lemuel."

With his drink in hand, Levi pulled the side chair away from the desk, placing it across from Frank before sitting.

The two men mirrored one another as each sized the other up warily, thumbs under their chins, forefinger to one cheek. The grandfather clock's rhythmic *tick-tock* dominated the charged stillness as a clouded shaft of light from the window split the pair.

Frank marveled at how much smaller, even ordinary, the room and the man before him had become since he last saw them.

Levi was the first to speak, swinging his reading glasses in the open air by their temple to draw attention as he broke eye contact to look off into space.

"You asked to come here without giving any notice or reason after not a word in twenty years. You may not recognize that I'm a busy man — frankly, I've got better things to do. Still, I dropped everything and graciously invited you into my home. What I get for my trouble is rudeness, insults, and you bringing weapons into the sanctity of my space."

Levi waved his hand at the gun lying on the credenza.

"What do you want, Lemuel?"

Frank wasn't about to give him the satisfaction of a direct response.

"Amazing. It's all transactional to someone like you; even fatherhood is about what you can get back in return. Does Miriam know about your penchant for sodomizing little boys, Levi? No, I suppose she wouldn't – she's still alive."

"We've had this conversation before, Lemuel, and I've told you I didn't kill your mother."

"Please. Guys like you don't do their own dirty work. You should have gone with a hitman from New York, Levi. When you contract someone from out of state to kill an innocent woman or child, people on the streets talk. Pros have standards — they don't like to take out moms and kids. When you're a New York Jew, and you use a hitter from an Irish mob out of Boston, you draw even more attention."

"I have no idea what you're talking about, Lemuel."

Frank chose to ignore Levi's weak protest.

"Whitey Bulger's crew wasn't what it used to be once they outed him as an FBI snitch; still, one of my more challenging kills, I don't mind saying. I'm sure you thought I'd be coming after you the moment I ended your hired gun."

Frank peered at Levi like he would a pinned fly through a magnifying glass.

"For two years afterward, you stayed out of the limelight, never seen in the public eye. I'll admit the thought of you cowering in the dark was enjoyable. But *kill* you? No, I knew your sorry ass would become useful one day."

"I don't have to sit here and listen to this!" Levi proclaimed and rose from his seat.

Frank tucked his finger into the trigger opening of the Glock for just a split second and then thought better of the impulse. He'd settle for the satisfaction he gleaned from the old man's loss of emotional control.

"No, you don't. But you'll want to because the longer you listen, the better your chances of survival. We're having this discussion because I know several things you don't. Item number one: I will not take you out unless you force the issue, Levi. Your trusted compatriots will be the ones doing you. I'm here to save your life. Only because it helps me with a problem I'm dealing with, but still, you should be grateful.

"Sit *down*, Levi."

Hesitantly, Levi settled back into his seat, his rigid grip on the armrests betraying his stress.

Frank leaned forward, elbows on his knees and fingertips pressed together as he rested his cheek on the chair back and looked sideways at Levi.

"You didn't have to kill her. I never told Mom what you were doing to me those weekends she spent at the hospice caring for Bubbe. None of the boys you were diddling said a word to her.

"Again, your arrogance, Levi. Having your medical records sent to the house was a fucking idiot move. When Mom opened that envelope and saw the AIDS test results, that you hadn't contracted it yet didn't matter. The relevance was that you requested the test.

"In the late eighties, everyone considered it a gay man's disease. There was no reason for a faithful heterosexual man to ask for an AIDS test — she had to assume you were having an affair with someone who was, as they called it back then, queer. It was a dangerous time to be what you are, especially in the closet; once infected, you'd have been a dead man walking.

"She was so frightened you were putting her at risk of dying from a horrific disease that nobody understood. She *had* to do something; divorcing you was the only way to keep herself alive. And me, too, though she didn't know that I was directly at risk; she worried that the thing could spread through the air or by casual contact."

Levi shifted in his chair, staring off to one side at nothing.

"Mom always wondered why I hated going to the doctor. I knew as soon as I took off my underwear, he'd see what you'd done to me. But the man never said a word to anyone. If you tend to the rich and famous, I guess that's what you do — you help them keep their nasty skeletons tucked away. I didn't realize until I got older that he'd no doubt seen the same symptoms from this household many times before. I'm sure his silence paid well. Or did he have an unfortunate early demise, too, Levi?

"The point is, if I *had* told Mom, she'd have instantly realized the truth. But the AIDS situation was embarrassing and scary enough. Without knowing I was involved, she'd never have dug any deeper to find out you were also a pedophile."

"I made life good for you," Levi protested. "Private schools, the best clothes, shoes, toys, electronics, food — you were given everything you ever wanted. All you had to do was ask, and it was yours. I never heard you complain...."

Frank fought back an immediate urge to put a bullet between the man's eyes.

"*I was only eleven!* How the hell was I supposed to say no? Or, for that matter, know that a perverted fuck like you was different from other fathers? Who was I supposed to complain to — a man twice my size with all the power and money in his fist?

"*My rapist for the fourth time that month?*"

THE WRITINGS OF
AVRIL MARIA SERENE

Book Two — Chapter 16

L evi seemed to take Frank's expression of pain and victimhood as weakness — an opportunity to re-establish his authority and regain control of the conversation.

"So you say now, but this is the first I've heard about how terrible your existence was," Levi was almost daring Frank with a mocking tone. "As to your mother, I explained the expectations before we married. I'm in the public eye. She knew as my spouse, she had a responsibility to protect our family…."

"Of course, all about what was good for *you*." Frank had raised his voice in anger; suddenly, it became deadly calm. "*You* broke the marital trust, Levi, with an affair that put her in a position where she could die. Mom had a child to care for, no other place to live, and no career to fall back on. She *had* to leverage what little she knew of your dirty secrets in the divorce. She couldn't take being denied the Get or risk the Beit Din awarding you sole custody.

"But you couldn't risk your gay relationships or worse, the bigger story Mom didn't know, coming out. It's always about your image, regardless of who you must destroy to keep your confidences. Your conceits and ignorance are all over this, Levi. You had things you didn't want anyone knowing delivered to the house; then you jumped to conclusions about *her* motivations. You had to kill my mother; keeping her an agunah would have people wondering what you were trying to hide."

Frank sat upright, placing both hands on the chair back and gazing around the library.

"You know, I used to break into this room all the time. I started doing it to prove I could get past all your locks and alarms. You're consistent, Levi; in your hubris, you never tested them again after their installation. Once I knew which fuse cut the power to the library, picking the locks and jumpering around the sensors was, to coin a phrase, child's play.

"God, I hated you. I'd be so sore after you assaulted me that I couldn't sit. Or, some weeks, go to classes the following Monday.

"I'd slip in here and lay in the cubbyhole under this desk with a pillow in the small of my back. It felt safe, and I'd spend hours plotting ways to get back at you. Pouring your Napoleon brandy into the aquarium and those damned orchids you prized were my declarations of independence. Urinating into the decanter to replace the missing alcohol was my way of saying 'fuck you.' And it did keep the color from changing.

"Your honored guests couldn't have been impressed with your taste in liqueurs."

"I wondered why I couldn't keep anything alive in here, even *with* the natural light," Levi said ruefully.

"But I knew I'd survive you and your perversion once I understood what was under that desk. I must have looked up a dozen times at those strange numbers stuck on the bottom of that drawer.

"Imagine the look on my face when I snapped to what they were. Once I got that big wall safe open, I knew I could hurt you where it counted. But you'd masking-taped *two* sets of numbers under there. The second had to be a combination, too — but to what?"

Casually palming the Glock with his left hand, Frank stood up and strolled toward the paneled wall at the back of the library, Levi's eyes fixed on his every move.

"How far do I go, Levi? Seventeen, isn't it?"

Beginning from the wall, Frank started counting the slats on the floor with the toe of his boot. He quickly kicked the baseboard with his heel once he got to the right spot. A two-foot-long section of baseboard swung out into the room on a hidden hinge, revealing the front of a safe with a legacy mechanical entry pad mounted to it.

"Oh, Levi, don't tell me you haven't replaced this thing in over thirty years." Franks's tone was derisive. "Surely, you've at least changed those numbers...."

Kneeling, Frank rubbed his hands together with a theatrical flair, like the safecracker in a 1950s B movie, and punched in ten digits.

Against the tense silence, the click of the safe door's lock release resounded through the room.

"Guess not. I see you stuck with your priorities — you *did* update your camera technology."

Frank swung the door fully open to reveal several stacks of tiny translucent plastic boxes in neat rows.

"Smart memory cards are much more efficient than the VCR tapes I used to copy from this safe. What, no letters, no stills? I suppose you'd keep those elsewhere in their digital forms…."

Frank raised his weapon to rest it on his knee as he kept one eye on Levi.

Now standing with his hands on his hips, Levi's voice broke character, revealing genuine panic, his face ashen.

"Lemuel, that's private property. I won't have you coming into my home waving a weapon around and making unsubstantiated allegations like a common thug — I *will* call 911!"

"No, Levi, you won't. Your best attorneys couldn't keep you from spending the rest of your life in prison for what's on these. You won't mind if I take a few to update my collection?"

Frank grabbed the first three rows of digital memory cards with his right hand, stuffing them into his front pants pocket as he stood.

"We'll call these 'my backups.' Quit sniveling, Levi — it's unbecoming for a man in your position. And trust me, this is the least of your problems. But I, your loving first-born, am here — not just to educate you but to provide you a path out of the wilderness.

"So sit your ass down, Levi, shut the fuck up, and *listen.*"

Levi first glowered at Frank, then withered in the moment. He sighed, his shoulders sagging and his eyes going to the floor, as he meekly took his seat. Frank stood over him a moment before returning to his chair.

"You say you're not here to kill me." Levi tried to re-establish his importance to the conversation. "So, what kind of trouble have you made for yourself that you need my connections to bail you out?"

"There was a day I'd have been impressed by your insights, Levi. But I'm not that little kid anymore that you could mesmerize with sleight of hand. I know you're on the founder's council of the Hodin federation."

"The what?" Levi's expression professed complete ignorance.

"We're well past trying to be disingenuous, Levi. I've known ever since you had them recruit me. Who else had the resources and a fixation strong enough to hire detectives to follow me around 24/7? You needed to cover your ass; you thought I'd be coming after you. That's the only way anyone could have learned of those fourteen killings. And who else, once they knew, wouldn't have turned me over to the authorities or extorted me directly? I'm sure it occurred to you that I might have something on you that could blow up in your face.

"And who, other than you, had the pull to get a relative unknown hired as an executive into PWW after just one previous gig? There was no better way to keep an eye on me than through a common link to the Hodin federation.

"So, you know damned well why I'm here. I'm here because I need the coalition to call off their dogs, and things have gone far enough only a founder's council member can make that happen."

"*This* is how you ask someone to save your life, Lemuel?" Levi feigned offense, but Frank was having none of it.

"Not *my* life," Frank retorted. "Yours. But I'm not the source of your problem. I could have killed you at any time; I thought of it often. Still, I resisted the temptation — once the federation had us traveling some of the same circles, I knew you'd eventually be valuable. That time has come.

"Twenty years ago, you told the coalition of the lives I took, but you left out that you were my father. Then you pushed for me to get the Process Development manager position, which makes me the threat to them that they see in me now. The deception and the manipulation won't bode well for you once they learn of our relationship. You know how they are about loose ends. Once they decided to come after me, they committed to taking out anyone in my circle. Ironic, really — I believe you helped promote that policy."

"What makes you think you'll ever get the chance to tell them, Lemuel? It's a long way back to Boston on highways that can be treacherous."

"Threats? Seriously? I'm disappointed in you, Levi. But your days of bullying me are over — you're more impotent than you know."

Frank tilted his head back toward the still-open safe.

"I doubt you thought one of your boy toys would ever grow up to become a U.S. Senator from the great state of New York. Or am I wrong about that, Levi? Maybe you gave him a boost by the same seat of the pants you admired back in the day before he grew hair down there."

"There's no need to be crude, Lemuel."

"My bad — did you know I was so under your spell at one point that I might have been jealous of him? Doesn't matter now, really.

"What does is that I made copies of all those VCR tapes, photos, and letters you kept in that safe. I used to tell Mom I needed to go to the public library to research my homework — they had a photocopy machine that cost twenty-five cents. I spent so many quarters Mom must have thought I was writing about the Hundred Years' War.

"It was there I learned the meaning of 'paedicatio' and the other words you used that weren't in our dictionaries at school. And, of course, I had to look up those fine ancient Greek traditions between old men and young boys that you spoke so glowingly of in your letters."

Levi's face had turned ghostly white.

"Lots of copies. I still have them, Levi. Of course, they've been scanned or converted since and sent to servers in the cloud, so they don't fade or go missing. And I finally gave up those old paper copies — I needed them to fill seven manila envelopes. I've placed those in the outgoing mailslots of several of the better hotels on the drive between Boston and here. Hopefully, nothing will happen to me that I can't retrieve them on my way home, should I want to."

Levi was now staring at Frank, so completely still he didn't seem to breathe.

"I prepared those envelopes with digital copies of your tapes, photos, and letters. Your handwriting is distinctive, Levi; the paper copies should dispel any doubts about authorship. I've addressed one to your Senator friend. One went to his campaign staff, another to his Democratic opponent. Yet another to a national newspaper with investigative chops; I sent one more to an elite New York paper. Should any of them ever reach their destination... well, you're aware that the federation isn't a fan of unwanted attention for themselves or their members. They may wish to confront you about that.

"For the last two mailings, I've added copies of my birth certificate and Mom's divorce petition. I included a detailed history of how you've assisted me throughout my career with the Hodin coalition. As to the latter, I may have fabricated some things — call it creative license. There's no sense in airing the family laundry about our past estrangement. I prepared one envelope each for two Bilderbeck members I know also serve on the founder's council.

"The worm's turned, Levi."

"Lemuel, be realistic. You've threatened to turn the Hodin federation over to the FBI. You've kept copies of coalition data. And I know if it were me, I wouldn't give back any copies until I'd made others. There's no basis for any trust. I don't know what I could do for you."

"I'm sure you'll give it your best shot, Levi — your future depends upon it."

Levi's body language read of frustration and defeat, signaling that Frank had accomplished his goals. He'd had his fill of this place; it was time to leave. "I won't be coming back here, Levi. But I *will* be watching. I'll see myself out."

Frank slid his Glock back into its holster, turned away from Levi, and headed out of the library. But before exiting the home's main doors, he needed to do something for his mother. Arriving at the end of the hall, Frank spotted Miriam sitting on a loveseat in the small anteroom off the vestibule, peering intently into an iPad. He fished a half-dozen digital memory cards from his front pants pocket as he approached.

Miriam rose to meet him out of courtesy, laying the iPad on the seat beside her.

"You'll want to view these videos privately." Frank handed her the storage cards. "I'd suggest in the company of a competent attorney. If Levi learns you have these, he *will* kill you — for the same reasons he murdered my mother.

"And you'll want to schedule an appointment with your gynecologist for an AIDS test and a full STD workup. You'll understand why once you've seen the images."

With that, Frank dipped his chin as he backed away, then turned to exit. Looking over his shoulder as he walked to his car, he saw a stunned Miriam staring after him.

Finishing school hadn't taught her not to let her eyes go wide or leave her mouth hanging open.

The upshot of Frank's visit was that Levi would be useless in his war with the federation. There was truth in Levi's assertion that he lacked the influence to stop Frank's termination, even if Levi made a good-faith effort, which Frank doubted. Levi would likely assume Frank was bluffing about the seven manila envelopes left at hotel mailboxes along the way. He certainly wouldn't expect Frank to let those packages proceed to their destinations.

For all of Levi's fascination with the boy, his undoing would come from misunderstanding Frank as a man.

BOOK TWO — CHAPTER 17

It was midmorning on a quiet Sunday at 1 Schroeder Plaza, during the lull that follows the hustle and bustle of roll call.

Uniformed officers were hitting the streets as detectives returned to their investigations. The desk sergeant's bushy white mustache bobbed up and down like the tail of a squirrel running a tree branch as he filled his idle time chatting up his girlfriend on a cell phone. His appeals for her to move in with him without her beloved and attention-needy Pomeranian were going nowhere. The smell of fresh carnauba wax permeated the air as a janitor plied his buffer at one end of the atrium.

It didn't seem that big a deal at first.

Visitors arriving at the main entrance of the Boston Police headquarters were passing through security and streaming in groups of two and three across the glossy tile. Some high-stepped it, and others skipped like the Pied Piper's followers. The middle-aged man in the dark blue business suit leading them wasn't flashy or playing any pipes. Still, the crowd gathering behind the point man in the spacious area before the front desk was as motley, diverse, and disorganized a group as the sergeant could recall seeing in his lengthy career.

Their leader wasn't familiar to the officer, but he recognized some in the crowd and had even booked a few. There were several Proud Boys, their mullets, tattoos, Old Spice, and hangover breath announcing their presence. There were a couple of peeking-into-bedrooms paparazzi and two lesser reporters from the

Boston Herald — a junior wannabe barely out of college and a burned-out has-been trying to hang on until retirement.

The desk sergeant knew a few of them as Internet personalities from peering over his daughter's shoulder as she perused the Internet — local bloggers, influencers, QAnon types, and pretenders. A dozen others looked like members of a flash mob drawn from a mobile home park, its best days long behind it. They came complete with MAGA hats stained at the brim with sweat, Trump 2024 paraphernalia, and plastic Walmart fashion accessories in bold primary colors. People who'd not only peruse the magazines that replaced the defunct *National Enquirer* in grocery store checkout lanes — they'd spend their cold hard cash to *buy* the sleazy publications.

Several in the group had video cameras or microphones. Some were using cell phones, their bright flashes popping off in random bunches. As one in the crowd captured an image, the others would do the same. By this time, roughly eighty people were crowding the lobby. Officers gathered behind the desk sergeant and discussed the situation as the commotion built.

Stopping four feet in front of the counter, the clean-cut and well-dressed leader of the raucous band turned to face his minions, stretching his hands out away from his body, palms down. He repeated a slow, flapping, downward motion with both hands as he lowered himself slightly at his knees to quell the noise.

Just as the crowd had quieted, and with a sudden theatrical spin on his heels, the man in the suit and tie faced the desk sergeant.

Opening his arms in front of him with the ceremony of a circus ringmaster announcing the first act, the man made his grand pronouncement.

"My name's Frank Spector, and I'm here to confess to the serial murders of fourteen of our citizens in cold blood. I also confess to being an accessory before the fact for the ongoing attempted murders of seven billion more. Oh, and that's with a *B.*"

His delivery was powerful but emotionless, his tone as if he were announcing Wednesday-night church Bingo number draws. Every eye upon him, the center of attention bowed slowly and majestically at the waist. When he raised his head, he shoved his balled-up hands forward until they were straight out, his wrists together awaiting handcuffs, expectance painted on his face, but saying nothing more.

There was the briefest of pauses before complete pandemonium broke out. Photo flashes went off; some in the crowd ooh'ed and aah'ed in simulated reverence, and others cheered and clapped.

After taking all this in, the ordinarily cynical sergeant realized he was dealing with something well above his pay grade. He quickly picked up the desk phone's receiver, stabbing the button for his immediate supervisor.

"Lieutenant, you'll want to come out to the front desk. And maybe bring the captain along. I've got a situation out here you won't believe."

Spector, ad man par excellence, had wanted a spectacle. Something akin to Lee Harvey Oswald's transfer to the county jail from the basement of the Dallas police headquarters on November 24, 1963 — but without a Jack Ruby to kill anyone. He'd spent most of the night in his hotel room on Twitter/X, Truth Social, alt-right-wing QAnon conspiracy websites, and the phone, drumming up his supporting cast for this morning's antics.

Spector had exploited the credibility and relationships he'd built with the Proud Boys as the central character in one of their most fervently held conspiracy theories — that Antifa politicians and radicals were trying to depopulate their numbers. He intended to create an event the media, onlookers, and the Boston Police Department would not soon forget.

He got the production he desired — the perfect cover to protect him from any harm the federation might intend him as he nestled himself into the protective confines of law enforcement. And just as significantly, the unusual presentation would drive public interest enough to force authorities to at least consider his story.

Spector knew he could deliver the goods. He'd slowly leak to the press enough outrageous details about his, and the federation's, history and intentions to keep stoking public curiosity and anger for some time to come.

THE WRITINGS OF
AVRIL MARIA SERENE

Book Two — Chapter 18

With the sun peeking in and out of puffy white clouds scudding across the sky, Suffolk County Police Officer Dennis Williams leaned against his white Ford Econoline prison van, enjoying the beautiful weather.

As the junior member of the transport team, his job was to watch their vehicle while his teammates picked up their prisoner.

Williams's break didn't last long; his sergeant radioed that their detainee's 58A dangerousness hearing was over. When the accused presented no arguments on his behalf, the presiding judge remanded him to custody until trial.

A few moments later, Williams spotted his fellow officer and sergeant escorting their charge out of the Superior Court building. They were guiding him by his elbows as he shuffled between them, bound in a belly chain, cuffs, and leg irons. The team would return the accused to the county holding facility. There, the man would spend his time until he stood in court again to face multiple charges of first-degree murder.

Williams opened the driver's side door of the van. He started the engine and unlocked the back doors, anticipating their detainee's arrival.

"That didn't take long," the young officer said when his colleagues joined him and began securing their prisoner. Sergeant Gary Olson headed to the cab's passenger side with his clipboard to start the paperwork for the transfer back to county lockup.

"Fourteen counts of murder," Officer Reggie Reynolds, Williams's partner for the past year, replied. "They say our friend Mr. Spector here has lots of money and travels in his work for an international company. Wasn't much for them to argue about — he'll be a guest of the county for a while longer."

After hooking Spector up in the back of the van, Reynolds clambered into the cargo area to ride with the prisoner. Williams closed and locked the van's rear doors, climbed into the cab, and pulled the van out of the courthouse lot.

"Let's beat the noon rush and grab something to eat," Olson suggested as they began rolling. Williams nodded, and Olson slid open the panel covering the vents in the thick Plexiglas partition separating the cab from the cargo area. He tapped on the clear plastic to get the passengers' attention.

"Reynolds, we're going to grab a burger. Let me know what you want and tell…" Olson checked the transport order for the prisoner's name, "…tell Spector he can order whatever he likes, as long as it's not over twenty bucks."

Olson slipped a torn envelope onto the clipboard and took the men's orders. "What'll you have, Williams?"

"Put me down for an Impossible Whopper, onion rings, and a Diet Coke."

"You know that's not any healthier for you than real meat, right?" Olson was scornful. "It's just veggies boiled off in a chemical soup until the veggies couldn't take it anymore, rolled over, and played dead."

"Wait, Sarge; you want us to go to a Burger King, and we're supposed to worry about *healthy*?" Williams laughed — Olson's ruddy complexion and pudgy beltline hinted at a few too many hamburgers in his lifetime.

"Okay, you might have a point," Olson conceded. "But I'd rather know that a perfectly contented cow fully committed her life to me enjoying my lunch."

"Sarge, you are one sick puppy…." Williams grimaced and slowly shook his head.

"Here, just put it on my card, and Venmo me back at the barn. I'll dun the county for the prisoner's food." Olson handed Williams his Chime debit card. After calling out their order over the drive-thru speaker, Williams pulled up behind a tan Chevy SUV to pay and pick up their food. Olson unlocked the metal grate over the small pass-through window between the cab and the cargo area.

After the cashier handed over their paper bags and drinks, Olsen distributed the food, passing the men in the back their meals through the window in the Plexiglas. He placed his and Williams's burgers, onion rings, and fries on the van's center console, their drinks in the cup holders at the front.

Williams drove toward the cross street in front of the BK, waiting for a break in the cars to make a right turn. As he swung the wheel around, he grabbed his Whopper with his right hand, steering with his left to merge into traffic.

Just as he did, a muddied, gunmetal-gray, military-style Hummer cut over from the far-left lane, nearly hitting the front of their van.

The near miss forced Williams to hit the brakes and follow for the short distance to the light at the intersection, now red.

Williams and Olsen unwrapped their sandwiches while they waited for the light to turn.

BAMM!

With the sudden loud bang, the van violently lurched forward off its springs.

Williams's and Olson's food flew from their hands as the vehicle rocked back and swayed.

"*Fuck!*" Williams yelled as the contents of his iced Coke dumped onto his leg, and his knee slammed into the steel front of the dashboard.

Simultaneously, he and his sergeant heard an outburst of anger and pain coming from the back.

Glancing through the opening in the Plexiglas, Williams saw the collision had knocked Reynolds and the prisoner forward off the smooth steel benches lining either side of the cargo area and onto the floor.

Reynolds's shoulder and left hip had slammed into the Plexiglas partition.

Spector's leg chains were looped through an eyebolt in the van's floor and had abruptly halted his slide; he'd screamed as the manacles tore into his ankles.

Williams ignored his right knee's stabbing pain and intermittent numbness, his eyes jumping to his side-view mirrors.

A black Escalade had rammed them from the rear and sat there, wisps of smoke escaping its mangled grill.

As he twisted himself around to look through the windshield, Williams caught sight of the gray Hummer's reverse lights as it sped up, backing towards him.

Reflexively, Williams yanked the steering-column-mounted gearshift into reverse.

Jamming the gas pedal to the floor, he spun the steering wheel to the right so the impact from the Hummer wouldn't be straight-on, and he'd have some room to maneuver in the lane to his left.

The move helped cushion the blow as the Hummer slammed into the van.

The officers' vehicle bounced with the collision, the nose crumpling and ejecting shattered glass from the headlight and pieces of metal and plastic into the air.

The front engine access panel flew open, a thin stream of green liquid and steam spurting from the radiator.

Its engine was now screaming, and the police van shoved the Escalade back a few feet before its tires spun against the pavement, churning out more dense, gray smoke.

Williams slammed the gearshift into drive, but the Hummer had the advantages of mass and momentum and left him no room to go forward.

Two men, dressed head to toe in black and wearing body armor, had bailed out from either side of the Escalade.

The one on Olson's side of the Econoline began firing in short bursts from a MAC-11, while the other shot into the van's cargo hold with an AK-47.

Rolling down his window and pulling his sidearm, Williams targeted the gunman he could see.

Olson barked out on his shoulder mike, "Dispatch! We're taking fire, multiple heavily armed assailants with automatic weapons. They've disabled our vehicle; send all available assistance to this location!"

He unfastened his seatbelt with his left hand while rolling down the window and pulling his sidearm with his right.

Spinning in his seat as he passed his Glock 23 from his right to his left hand, Olson fired several .40-caliber rounds with his off-hand.

One of those caught the attacker with the MAC-10 in the neck, and he went down immediately, blood spurting from his carotid artery.

Both hands went to his throat as he vainly tried to stop the flow.

At the same time, the assailant on Williams's side was alternately firing random 7.62 rounds into the van's cargo area and at the cab, his body armor absorbing Williams's shots.

The van's cabin began filling with thin blue, gray, and black clouds bearing the acrid odors of overheated antifreeze, oil hitting the hot exhaust manifold, burning rubber, and spent gunpowder; the occasional whiff of scattered hamburgers, French fries, and onion rings was still discernible.

"I'm hit!" Reynolds called out from the back. "The prisoner took one in the leg. We're fish in a barrel here, Denny — my weapon's useless; I can't see a damned thing!"

Williams had the better tactical position; the side view mirrors allowed him to see the shooter without being in the direct line of fire.

Timing it perfectly, Williams got off half a dozen rounds as the AK-47 seemed to jam.

He hit the gunman in his hands and shoulder, causing him to drop his weapon.

As their attacker retreated to the Escalade, Williams fired off four more rounds, then pulled back for fear of hitting other traffic.

The Hummer's doors swung open as Williams and Olson fought off the Escalade's occupants.

Two gunmen, dressed in Desert Storm–era fatigues and armed with handguns, emerged and began shooting into the van's windshield as they crept slowly forward in a crouch.

A round grazed Williams's cheek; another caught the tip of his right pinky finger.

Olson took slugs to his left shoulder and right elbow, the wounds oozing dark red fluids down the sides of his shirt.

A fine mist of blood spewed from the hole in his uniform and sprayed the inside of the windshield — now bullet-hole-riddled — with tiny droplets.

Despite his injuries, Olson kept firing his weapon.

The wailing of distant sirens grew louder, closing in from all directions.

Suddenly, an explosion of metal and glass rocked the scene, dwarfing the sounds of gunfire.

A patrol cruiser with a push bumper traveling at high speed from the cross street had rammed the Hummer's driver's door, obliterating the gunman on that side.

The collision jacked the left-side wheels of the Hummer off the ground and deployed the squad car's steering-wheel airbag.

As the attacker on his side of the Hummer turned in reaction, Olson got off a clean shot to the gunman's temple, dropping him to the ground.

Two patrol officers, the one on the passenger side armed with a pump shotgun and the driver with his service weapon, jumped from their wrecked cruiser and ran to the Escalade.

A citizen in a Ford Expedition had blocked the Escalade from the rear, the driver wisely exiting his vehicle.

The gunman driving the Cadillac was desperately cycling between forward and reverse gears, trying to maneuver his way out.

Swinging wide to avoid any return fire, the officer with the shotgun pumped a load of double-aught buckshot into the black-tinted driver's side door glass, shattering the window into a million pieces and exposing the driver to view.

The gunman immediately threw up his bloodied hands. He placed his palms flat on the inside of the SUV's roof, his face bleeding everywhere from glass shards and shotgun pellets. The second patrol officer dragged him out of the vehicle by the neck of his black flak jacket, tossing him flat onto the ground face-first and handcuffing him.

Two more patrol units slid on squealing and smoking tires into the adjacent traffic lane, skidding to a stop roughly parallel with the wrecked prison van, their armed occupants bailing out before the vehicles had quit moving. An ambulance fell into position immediately behind the last patrol unit.

"How you doing, Sarge?" Williams huffed as he turned toward Olson and saw he needed immediate medical attention.

"My door's jammed, but I'll live," Olson answered, his face contorted in pain.

"Help's here," Williams called out as three uniformed officers jumped over the Hummer's twisted rear bumper to get to Olson's side of the van.

"My sergeant took multiple hits; he needs a bus!" Williams yelled to the approaching officers. He stumbled out of the vehicle, pointing to the cab's passenger side. Williams limped on his wrenched knee as quickly as he could to the back of the police van. "I've got two injured in the back; don't know how bad."

Two officers joined those on Olson's side of the prison van, one carrying a first-aid kit, the other wielding a crowbar. They went to work on opening Olson's jammed door. A squad member got on the radio to the dispatcher and waved another patrol officer over.

Meanwhile, Williams squeezed his way between the Escalade and the prison van. A paramedic joined him, climbing on the hood of the black SUV. Together, they worked with a pry bar, finally freeing one of the van's rear door panels. Several other uniforms teamed up to push the Escalade backward.

Once they'd opened the van's back door, they found Reynolds had the most severe wounds — he'd taken a through-and-through below the outer part of his ribcage. His left wrist looked as though a round had shattered it. The abdominal injury was gruesome, and Reynolds had lost a lot of blood. But with the proper care, he'd survive.

Working quickly, Williams ripped off his uniform shirt. He folded it so it reached both sides of Reynolds's belly wound; the paramedic kept pressure on the wrap until other EMTs could take over.

Spector had taken rounds in his left calf and right foot. Being thrown into a prone position with little surface area exposed to the shooter probably saved him from worse damage. Using his penknife, Williams ripped Spector's pants leg into strips and made a tourniquet to slow the bleeding from his calf. He applied another tourniquet to Reynolds's forearm above his mangled wrist.

The mayhem at the scene had subsided somewhat by the time paramedics triaged the victims and did their work. All three prison escort officers and their prisoner had survived, with Reynolds suffering the worst injuries.

Just one attacker was still alive, blinded by the shotgun blast and suffering nonfatal injuries to his extremities. He was refusing to cooperate with either medical professionals or law enforcement, and the paramedics were awaiting a court order allowing them to sedate him. Ranking officers had arrived and were taking control of the carnage.

Williams sat cross-legged with Reynolds in the back of the van until the paramedics could evacuate the wounded men. He felt his initial rush of adrenaline ebb and exhaustion set in, even as his missing fingertip pulsed in excruciating pain. Knowing his fellow officers had suffered far worse, Williams looked over at Reynolds, who seemed to fade in and out as they were strapping him down.

"All this, for what? And *why?*" Williams asked of no one, the throbbing in his knee becoming more insistent.

✦

The three officers wouldn't get together until four days after the incident. Once they'd had their injuries treated and some downtime, Williams and Olson visited Reynolds in the hospital the morning after their fallen comrade had undergone his second surgery.

And Williams's question at the scene was the first one off Olson's tongue. "Does anyone have the latest on why they attacked us?"

"The surviving shooter isn't saying anything," Williams replied. "But get this, the guy and his buddies were spooks. They'd burned their fingers, palms, and soles of their feet smooth with scar tissue — no prints. Can you imagine doing that to yourself? None of their DNA turned up in CODIS. No biometrics in IAFIS/NGI, not even for facial recognition. The captain contacted INTERPOL to see if they could help us identify them."

"They had us two-to-one, outnumbered and outgunned," Olson recounted. "Let's call it for what it is — we got lucky."

"At first, I thought they were coming to take our prisoner," Williams said. "But the forensics team counted fifteen rounds shot blindly into the side of the van. They seemed more interested in seeing him dead."

"I don't know who he pissed off," Reynolds offered, "but they were going to do whatever it took to make sure he wasn't around anymore."

THE WRITINGS OF
AVRIL MARIA SERENE

Book Two — Chapter 19

ssistant District Attorney Barry Sheffield of the Suffolk County DA's Homicide Unit considered the worst of his recent problems — an existential threat to prosecuting their office's most public active cases. The unit had in hand not one, but two confessions to the same fourteen serial murders in Boston from nearly twenty years ago — built-in reasonable doubt for either of the men claiming responsibility.

Their first suspect, Frank Spector, blipped onto their radar screen three months ago. The Massachusetts state investigators working cold cases identified him from a relative's DNA submission to a genealogy database. The close DNA match to oils in an otherwise smudged and useless fingerprint had gotten prosecutors a search warrant.

The warrant produced a sample flagging Spector as the source of the print, discovered on a shell casing found at one of the homicide scenes. Lead in three cartridges found tucked into the corners of a clothes closet in a bedroom of Spector's residence chemically matched bullet remnants recovered from two of the other victims. The cartridges and retrieved slugs were likely from the same manufacturing lot.

While DNA is helpful to prosecutors for jury trials in an era where jurors are expecting, even demanding, it to persuade votes for conviction, detectives had not a shred of other evidence tying Spector to these murders. Sheffield needed more

— hopefully, much more — before he'd feel comfortable indicting Spector, an upstanding citizen with no previous criminal history. Investigators were devoting every available resource to develop other evidence to strengthen those cases.

Then suddenly, with none of the negotiating that usually precedes a surrender, the man — then their only suspect — turned up at police headquarters three weeks ago without an attorney. Spector offered a confession to not only the serial killings — adding three more to the ones they then knew of — but to a host of other things the DA had no interest in. There was much that Sheffield didn't like about the carnival-like presentation, the admission itself, and all the extra baggage that went with it. Still, it was a gift horse, and the DA couldn't look it in the mouth. Since the other evidence they had identifying Spector was minimal, they'd have to take his confession at face value.

Yet barely a week would pass before Carlton Drucker quietly approached the DA with an alternative suspect. Drucker was the third member of a powerful troika of high-octane, pricey, and very successful criminal defense attorneys in Boston the local press had dubbed "the Three Amigos." He was well-known to, and respected by, the district attorney's office for which Drucker himself had once toiled. The attorney advised Sheffield he represented someone who wanted to come forward, offering new information about the now-fourteen homicides Spector had claimed.

Drucker wasn't someone you'd invite to parties unless he'd once represented you or insisted on coming. He had a well-earned reputation as a dry, humorless shark — not someone who played games unless it was in rigorous defense of a client and the stakes were very high. He simply wouldn't inject a client into one killing where he didn't belong, much less eleven, and certainly not three more.

Sheffield agreed to meet Drucker's client, whom the defense attorney identified as Emile Reardon. After the two attorneys' midweek court appearances, they and Reardon gathered for an exploratory conference in a meeting room off Sheffield's office. After shaking hands, the defense attorney and his client took wooden chairs across the table from the prosecutor.

Seeing Drucker again reminded Sheffield that the criminal lawyer had missed his calling. The man could easily have played the vampire grand elder in any of a dozen movies based on Anne Rice novels or perhaps the lead role in a Vincent Price biopic.

As for Reardon, he looked like he could have been among the recently bitten. Tall and gaunt, with salt-and-pepper hair, he looked pale and unwell. Dark circles ringed his eyes, and his skin hung loose on his frame.

"Carlton, you called this meeting," Sheffield began, "but I need to set some ground rules and verify that your client will abide by them. The taxpayers expect us to be productive with our time, and we're not in the habit of re-investigating essentially closed cases. Out of respect for the fact you and I go back a while, I'll entertain what your client says based on our earlier phone conversation.

"But this discussion will be on the record." His frown accentuated the furrows in Sheffield's forehead, drawing attention to his receding hairline. He turned slightly to face Drucker's client, pointing to the lighted red LED on the video camera behind the ADA.

"Mr. Reardon, I *will* hold you accountable for what you say. I'll leave it to your attorney to explain the ramifications. Choose to tell untruths or not answer my questions fully, and there'll be severe penalties. Those include incarceration, separate and apart from any punishment for other crimes. Are we on the same page here?"

"We are, Barry," Drucker responded as Reardon nodded. "Mr. Reardon and I've had lengthy conversations. We're here to make the unique situation with your twenty-year-old serial killer cases even weirder than it already is — you can thank us later."

"How so, Carlton? Is Mr. Reardon a witness who'll make me a little more comfortable about the story I'm stuck with?"

"No, I'm going to change your perspective, give you something real to work with," Drucker replied. "It may surprise you to learn Mr. Reardon and Mr. Reardon alone committed those murders."

The pause seemed interminable, each man considering the poker face presented by the other. "Okay." Sheffield broke the stalemate, drawing out his response for several seconds as he debated whether he should listen to any more. "Mr. Reardon, why don't you tell me something about yourself, beginning with your full legal name?"

"My name is Emile Santiago Reardon. I'll be fifty in two weeks. I don't do much these days. They say my kidneys are failing. I spend three days a week, five hours each day, on dialysis. I haven't been in trouble since I got picked up on a domestic abuse beef when I was thirty-four. She dropped the complaint.

"But I've been in the system since I was in juvey hall. I started out mostly boosting things, liquor-store holdups, fighting — penny-ante stuff. I did a nickel for manslaughter beginning when I was nineteen, for killing a man with a beer bottle during a bar fight."

As Reardon spoke, Sheffield pulled up the man's RAP sheet from the state's database.

"Seems you're a career criminal, Mr. Reardon." Sheffield summarized what he saw on his screen. "Your record shows a steady progression of violence in your crimes — with a significant drop-off since your release from prison twenty years ago. It appears you straightened up after that — other than a few misdemeanors here and there, your record's clean. Once you satisfied the terms of your parole, law enforcement lost sight of you. I don't see the Nobel Prize anytime in your future, but there's nothing here that screams 'mass murderer' to me."

"Well, sir, I didn't exactly become a law-abiding citizen overnight," Reardon explained. "But I wised up. Some things I learned while serving my time, but you could say my parole had the most to do with it. The court ordered me to go to anger management classes as a condition of my release. They didn't really help me get rid of my bad temper — I still wanted to kill people who were hassling me — but I learned I didn't have to do it right then.

"They taught me to be patient and not react to something when it happened. And I didn't have to go after the person who offended me — if someone I didn't know anyway pissed me off, it felt just as good to take out somebody else. They called it 'transference,' and they were right. It was all about fucking somebody up; it didn't matter who it was.

"So, I got to where I'd hold it inside until I couldn't anymore. Then I'd snort a line of coke and go after the next person who got in my face. As long as it was a stranger, the cops wouldn't arrest me."

"*That's* what you took from anger management classes?" Reardon's statement surprised Sheffield; in hindsight, it shouldn't have.

"You know how the system is, Barry," Drucker said. "These parole officers have hundreds of parolees at any given time. They're just checking off the boxes to get through their day. Who gives a shit whether these things work how they're supposed to?"

"I went back to stealing to make money," Reardon continued. "And that's the other way parole helped me out. I had to get a job to keep my PO off my back. And I got lucky — I landed a gig as a cable installer and repairman. It used to be called TimeWarner; now, it's SpredRectum, owned by Charter. That job gave me access to case the houses my dispatcher sent me to; I'd jack them later.

"Being in the homes while the residents were there, I'd pick up on their routines and schedules. GoPro remote cameras had just come out, so I bought two. If I could make it so I'd have to return to a house later for another service call, I'd set up a GoPro to watch the security keypad and get the camera when I came back. The information I got made stealing less dangerous. I'd get more stuff out of each house. I learned to be patient and make a plan. Instead of right away breaking into homes I'd serviced on a certain day, I could wait a few weeks before hitting them up."

"You're saying that's why we didn't catch you again?"

"Yeah, pretty much," Reardon answered. "Then, one day, I robbed this banger's place and took a Glock with a silencer out of there. I always wanted a real silencer. That shit using a drink bottle is a joke. You gotta use two hands to keep it from flying off; you can't hide it, and half the time, you knock it off the end of the gun just carrying it around.

"Once I could shoot someone and no one could hear it, I got into that whole — what do they call it, 'stealth mode'? — thing. I was careful; I bought some latex gloves from Home Depot. When I went out, I covered my face and hair so I wouldn't leave any DNA. It turned into a game, knowing nobody else knew what I was doing and making sure it stayed that way. You feel like James Bond; nobody can touch you. And that's when this killing business took off. Some days, I'd walk around waiting for someone I didn't know to disrespect me so I could put them away."

"What made you stop?" Sheffield was having trouble buying all this.

"Well, you know, times were good." Reardon grinned. "I had money, got my swagger back, wasn't spending time in jail. You know how it is when things are going right — the ladies come around. I met my woman, and we got married. She started pushing me to get out of the life. It wasn't like I *planned* to quit killing; it was more like I just had better things to do. There wasn't any money in killing them, anyway. I got into a twelve-step program, and then my wife got me going to church. I'd kept the cable job because I was still boosting houses for extra money, and they promoted me to a trainer. They made me a supervisor until I got sick, and they let me go."

"Mr. Reardon, yours is an interesting story." Sheffield was slightly annoyed. "But I'm not hearing anything that backs it up. Anyone who's read a newspaper would know I've already got a prime suspect, and DNA that doesn't match yours...."

"Oh, Barry, about that," Drucker interrupted, sending a flash of irritation across Sheffield's face. "There's a kicker — we haven't gotten to the exciting part yet. My guy knows your guy. Emile, why don't you tell District Attorney Sheffield how you've crossed paths with Frank Spector?" The look on Drucker's face said he'd just drawn the second king to fill out his aces-high full house.

"It's been twenty years since I was there last," Reardon replied. "But I was in Spector's house three times back in the day, fixing his cable. I never broke into the place after hours — the guy had some *serious* security. But I took some things while I was there working. Nothing a guy with a decent job and a big house would notice missing.

"But man, I'm telling you, his housekeeper was hot! She didn't like me eyeballing her — I think the lady was afraid I'd hit on her — so she stayed away from me, let me have free run of the place."

"Do you remember the housekeeper's name?"

"Julia… Julianna. Her name was Julianna."

That doesn't square, Sheffield thought. *If I remember correctly, Spector's housekeeper's name was Amanda.*

Book Two — Chapter 20

Returning from their brief break with another staff attorney in tow, Assistant DA Sheffield silently reminded himself to verify the name of Frank Spector's housekeeper at the time of the serial killings.

"Please, Mr. Reardon, continue — you were in Spector's home with only his housekeeper there."

"I stole things I could hide in my toolbox," Reardon replied. "The second time I was there, I took an open box of ammunition sitting outside the gun case in the closet; it fit my Glock. It was mixed hollow points and balls, so he must have been swapping out the rounds in his piece.'"

"' Balls?'"

"Full metal jackets," Drucker offered. "I assume Spector's DNA is on your shell casing because he'd handled it after opening the box; the only way he could have mixed the cartridge types."

Spector's intent may have been to discard that ammunition when replacing those cartridges, Sheffield thought. *That* would *explain such a fastidious man leaving his print. All of this is a stretch. Still....*

Leaning back in his chair, Sheffield blew out his cheeks with an exhaled breath. Reaching into the credenza behind him, he pulled out a yellow legal pad and a Bic pen, setting them in front of Reardon.

"Okay, write down all you can remember about the killings. Date, time of day, where, the descriptions of the victims, anything that comes to mind. Include as much detail as possible; take the time you need. I also want, and this is very important, to know everything about any witnesses who can corroborate your story."

As Reardon began scribbling, Sheffield pondered the circumstances, elbows on the armrests, his hands together with his forefingers touching to form a point at his lips. After a moment, he sat forward and addressed the witness.

"While you're writing, I need to speak with your attorney privately." Having a discussion now with Drucker would keep the attorney from helping Reardon get his story straight.

After making eye contact with Drucker, Reardon nodded, returning to his pen and paper.

Once outside in the hall and out of Reardon's earshot, Sheffield turned to face Drucker.

"Carlton, this job requires a certain amount of cynicism." Sheffield's tone was firm, his expression unsmiling. "Your client's story comes off way too opportunistic for my tastes. The guy's lost his job; he has no insurance. Why do I feel this has more to do with getting the state to fund a kidney transplant than it does his guilty conscience?"

"I can't speak to his motivations." Drucker was on the defensive. "But I'm willing to stake my reputation and stand behind what he says."

"Don't try to out-lawyer me, Carlton," Sheffield retorted. "You and I both know that's not a denial.

"This whole thing, starting with Spector, stinks to high heaven as it is, and your Mr. Reardon doesn't smell any better. He reeks of being coached, for one thing. And I get nervous when a high-powered defense attorney lobbies me to pick *his* guy as the one to charge for a serial murder case. That seems unnatural to me from the get-go. I doubt I'd be any more comfortable if I knew who's paying your fees and why."

"You know I can't get into that."

"And I didn't ask. But worse, Chris Patterson and Bill Clymer, your fellow Amigos, have made off-the-record insinuations to our staff members. Claiming that Frank Spector approached them for representation, but they wouldn't accept him because he's flakey — that's bullshit stacked ten feet deep. Besides being heavy-handed, it pushes the ethics line, Carlton, and you know better.

"You need to get a message to Chris to back off. She's in this way too deep to be throwing her weight around. The thing with Spector's story is that you either buy all or none of it. That's the decision I'm going to have to make. But whatever I decide on the serial murders, Spector claims Patterson and her son set our accused up for an abduction coming out of her office and, according to him, an attempted murder. His timeline works; we've got video from the building and the street, and we've taken witness testimony supporting the activity he describes."

"*That* you'll have to take up with Chris." Drucker wouldn't give an inch.

"I'm taking it up with *you*, Carlton." Sheffield's patience had worn thin. "The statement accusing her is already out there in several forms. Spector insisted on representing himself, and the Court appointed a public defender to assist him. That attorney has a copy. It's in the record for at least three pleadings and on our servers, with several copies lying about.

"The district attorney's office doesn't want the public believing that they look the other way when a connected defense attorney commits felonies. Make sure Patterson gets the message about not drawing more attention to herself. If we have to bring her in, we'll do it in an upfront and official manner. We can't look the other way anymore.

"And I need to hear you tell me to my face you're not involved in orchestrating any of this, Carlton. I may be willing to take your word for it — this time. But y*ou* need to see that it doesn't happen again."

"Hey, Barry, I understand your concerns," Drucker protested, "but this is one strange case. You can't expect attorneys not to talk about it among themselves. I'm not trying to engineer any particular outcome here. My guy came to me; his story made sense, and you heard it exactly as I did. It would have been malpractice for me not to bring him to you."

"It would be malpractice *if*, and *only* if, his story jibes with the truth," Sheffield fired back. "But you knew coming in here that Reardon's claims alone, truthful or otherwise, would raise enough reasonable doubt to throw out the case if we ever had to go to trial against Spector. And you knew Reardon's official statement would be exculpatory as to DNA evidence against Spector. If Spector recants his confession now, he's free to walk; there's nothing we could do.

"You've boxed me in — I have no choice but to look into Reardon's statement. And worse, I'll have to cross my fingers it holds up better than Spector's story, or I'll have to release them both. I don't appreciate how you've gone about this — pray you don't need any favors from this office until my memory fades."

"C'mon, Barry, you're looking at this all wrong. Nothing about Spector's story ever made sense. The guy hasn't had so much as a parking ticket in the past thirty years. He's one tier below C-suite management for an international corporation. Spector's lived in the burbs all his life and might as well have been a million miles away from these crime scenes.

"He has this pristine blameless life a Tibetan monk would be proud of for twenty-five years, then says, 'Oh, what the hell, let me take some time off for two years to kill fourteen people?' Despite never harming a civilian before or after? And while stirring up not a whiff of suspicion from anyone.

"Then he goes back to innocence and harmony for another twenty years — while planning the mass murders of seven billion people. Only *now* does he regret these aberrant and homicidal behaviors, which he feels *must* be shared with the world.… You're buying that, Barry?

"My guy lived in the same places these murders occurred; he's got the criminal history, opportunity, and motive. He knows everything about these crimes. And he doesn't have that insane 'kill the entire planet' baggage to get around if Spector ever goes to trial."

"Let's get back in there," Sheffield relented, "and see if what your client says about these crimes and his witness list hold water."

Thinking about it as they walked down the hall, Sheffield paused before reentering the conference room where Reardon was still writing.

"Don't expect any answers today, Carlton. I'll let you know what I decide *after* I've had a chance to vet Reardon's statements fully," Sheffield said pensively, seeing some truth in Drucker's arguments.

But he also understood Reardon's claims wouldn't be the panacea for everything screwy about this case.

<hr>

Reardon's recitation of the crimes was nearly encyclopedic, equivalent to what Spector had revealed to prosecutors. But where Spector was well-educated and intelligent, consistent with someone having an excellent memory, the detail in Reardon's recollections was remarkable for someone with a drug history and barely literate — likely the product of long rehearsals assisted by informed counsel. If so, the question was, "Who fed them the information?"

The most likely answer — that it'd come to them from someone in law enforcement or within the DA's office — raised a lot of nasty ghosts in a building plagued with a long history of corruption.

There *were* variances between the two men's versions, but prosecutors couldn't verify whose telling was accurate from the available evidence. Spector could offer no witnesses. Those Reardon volunteered provided only hearsay; most were career criminals or homeless and addicted, all wanting something in return for their testimony. None would hold up against a competent defense attorney if Sheffield had to take Reardon to trial.

Some in the DA's office thought the armed assault on Spector's prisoner transport van bought him some credibility, not just for the serial killings but also the larger depopulation story. However, the one attacker who survived wasn't talking. As far as Sheffield knew, mistaken identity could have inspired the assault — the assailants targeting the wrong prisoner. Less likely, but possibly a botched escape attempt — Spector certainly had the means; perhaps he'd gotten cold feet since his surrender and confession.

Already aware that neither man's account would fully satisfy him, Sheffield wanted to make one last pass at verification. Details matter, and one fact stood out to Sheffield as likely unknowable by one of the confessors unless he was telling the truth.

He asked Spector's court-appointed attorney, George Costas, to bring his client to a brief question-and-answer session. They'd meet at one of the secure conference rooms in the county facility housing the prisoner.

"Hello, George, Mr. Spector; thank you for coming," Sheffield began. "As you know, we're tidying up our investigation. I wanted to clean up some minor issues that have arisen."

"Shouldn't be a problem," Spector's public defender replied. "Ask your questions of Frank directly; I'll jump in if I have a concern."

Sheffield had prepared a list of questions he'd previously asked Reardon. They concerned clothing worn by victims when assaulted, body positions as the killer left them, and further details of the surroundings where the murders occurred. Ticking through them, Sheffield paid close attention to Frank's micro-expressions and body language.

Finding no significant discrepancies in Frank's answers, Sheffield wound down the session. "That's pretty much it — just a couple of little things, and we can finish this," Sheffield announced. "Oh, yes, here it is — Mr. Spector, I have 'Amanda' as your housekeeper's name. Is she the housekeeper you have now?"

"Yes, she's worked for me for the last eight years."

"So, twenty years ago, you had a different housekeeper?"

"Before she left to care for her mother, I had Julianna...," Spector replied, his expression curious.

"And would you describe Julianna as attractive?" Sheffield pressed forward.

"I'd say she was a good-looking woman ... but she was married," Spector responded, now intrigued. "Why do you ask?"

"Nothing important. Just verifying who's who — there was confusion in our office over the housekeeper's name."

He didn't tell his prisoner, but Spector's answers had decided for Sheffield which confession he'd accept.

THE WRITINGS OF
AVRIL MARIA SERENE

Book Two — Chapter 21

Boston PD Captain Rory Melzer's unhappiness was evident as he strode to the podium at the end of morning roll call.

"Before you go, I need your attention, officers — who has the property cage for the day shift?" His eyes searched the audience. Fingers pointed toward the back of the room to a nearly retired older officer with white hair in the last row, his hand in the air. "Morgan? Good. After we've finished here, I need you, Fontana, and MacDonnell in Interview Room A. You, too, Frazier. And Williams, Olson — why don't you join us?"

Melzer wasn't mincing words as the officers gathered in the interrogation room. His burly physique, lantern jaw, and irritated demeanor emphasized his words.

"Close the door, Fontana. From here on out, this meeting's private. Cell phones and body cams off, everyone."

Melzer waited for the attendees to comply and for the body cameras, which record for several moments after deactivation, to shut down.

"Gentlemen — and lady — listen up," Melzer began, nodding to Frazier as the only female officer present.

"The DA's kicking Frank Spector loose this afternoon. They've charged somebody else for the murders he said he committed. If you weren't here or your memory's short, Spector's the serial killer pretender who created a made-for-TV shitshow in our front lobby while turning himself in two months ago."

"He's also accountable for getting three of our fine officers wounded transporting him back from court." Melzer glanced toward Williams and then Olson. "Not to mention destroying two vehicles belonging to our taxpayers.

"Now there are people, even in our department, saying our prison van getting shot up proves this lunatic's telling the truth about influential people secretly trying to kill off most of the world. That's a load of bull crap. For all we know, those jagoffs just fucked up his escape attempt.

"I don't give a shit what this guy pounded up the DA's ass. He's a goddamned nut job, and he had something to do with placing our people in harm's way. The show's over, here and now — this guy's not creating another circus on his way out."

Palms down to both sides of the legal pad on the table in front of him, Melzer leaned forward.

"Morgan, I want you to find Spector's property envelope. If there's a cell phone or an iPad in there, you drain that battery. Do you understand me? Throw it in the toilet if you have to, but make sure it doesn't work. I don't want him calling up his buddies in the press or on the Internet.

"Whoever takes the call to escort Spector out of lockup, I don't want you telling him anything about what's happening. Let him assume we're transferring him to another facility. Take him down to pick up his personal shit — make sure he signs for it — and then put him in the back of an unmarked unit."

Melzer stared at the table, lips pursed, slowly shaking his head before raising it.

"Keep him cuffed. Take him way out in the burbs, as far as possible, but inside the county line. Maintain radio silence — no one needs to know where you end up. Just for insurance, try to find a place with no cell signal. For all I care, if someone *is* out to get him, I'm okay letting them have at him. But we don't need anything to happen that ties back to his release by this department.

"Remove his handcuffs, boot him out, and grab some lunch. Give Spector an hour to clear the area. Then circle back. If the son-of-a-bitch is still there, make sure you give him a good reason to run the next time we give him an opportunity. Feel free to get creative; just don't leave any marks. Whatever you do, don't bring anyone or anything back here other than that unmarked unit."

He ran his hand over his thinning hair. "Anybody asks you any questions about anything, you tell them I'm taking responsibility for this and to come see me."

Frank Spector was reading in his cell when the jailer told him his lawyer was at the facility for an unannounced visit.

"Good morning, George. I wasn't expecting to see you today."

"Hmmm, that means two of us don't know what's going on," his public defender responded. "I thought they'd have said something to you."

"About what?"

"The grapevine claims Carlton Drucker is representing someone trying to take credit for the serial killings," George revealed. "That concerns me. Drucker's as powerful a criminal defense attorney as there is in Boston. Not sure what he's up to, but it can't be good for what you're trying to accomplish."

"I know who Drucker is." Frank's mind was processing the information. "He was the next attorney I planned to interview after Clymer and Patterson. Never got to him because everything blew up." *Given what's transpired, I'm pretty sure all three of them work for the Hodin federation*, Frank thought. *Their knight takes my bishop — the coalition's finally making their move.*

He'd expected *something* from the federation, though he hadn't known what. They had plenty of options — money and the power to assure someone a place among the one billion are pretty persuasive, especially in a 'justice' system all about making deals.

"I wanted the court to issue a writ of habeas corpus," George said, "and force the DA to show his hand for the disposition of your case. But nothing turned up when I referenced your case number, booking information, or court record. The county says it's a computer glitch, and they're working on it. But I've got a dozen open cases before the court — none of *them* have been affected. I checked. I'd guess they're wiping any record of your apprehension from the system before cutting you loose. Don't be surprised if there's something hinky in how they go about it — they're not fans of yours.

"I'll let you know if I hear anything more. Stay alert; try not to give the cops more reason to cause you harm. Call me if they throw you out on the street."

Frank was in his bright orange prison jumpsuit, "DOC" in white block letters a foot high sewn onto the back, his inmate number stenciled in black above the right breast. It was late afternoon, and after tightening his cuffs well beyond what was necessary for what seemed like a long ride, two officers had dumped him out of an unmarked patrol unit.

He'd landed in a wooded glade about a hundred yards off a dirt road along with a green plastic garbage bag tossed from the cruiser's passenger window as it pulled away. In the bag were the clothes he'd worn during his booking. Included with them was a large manila envelope containing the possessions he'd had in his pocket when arrested.

Frank rubbed his wrists to restore circulation while surveying his situation. He'd lived in the Boston area for more than two decades. He knew the Corporal Robert Francis Hardy Conservation Area from when it was called Maple Park. Its location in Mansfield posed no threat other than lengthening the time it would take to get back to Boston proper on foot or for someone to come and get him.

However, checking his cell phone and finding it dead caused Frank concern. He was, at the moment, defenseless. He had to wonder whether his release was a setup — should he be expecting unwelcome visitors from the Hodin federation?

There was little he could do but change into his street clothes, stuff the jumpsuit into the hollow of a fallen log, and walk to the main road. When first booked, he'd worn a suit and tie — fortunate because they made him look less threatening while riding his thumb. It didn't take Frank long to hitchhike home safely.

Now, it was between him and the coalition, straight up.

As he assessed his resources, it didn't surprise Frank that he couldn't reach Jeremy Hansen or his girlfriend on their federation burner phones. He couldn't know whether the coalition had snagged them or if they were merely avoiding him. Either way, he had no reliable eyes or ears on the Hodin federation or its daily activities.

He'd have to stay mobile, which meant securing a vehicle unknown to the coalition or law enforcement. It took three days of negotiating, considerable salesmanship, and paying well over the asking price for Frank to land an old pickup. He'd scored it from Craigslist, its tags still attached and current, without arousing much suspicion in a sight-unseen cash transaction.

It was costly — five thousand dollars for the 1986 Ford F150 pickup with 85,000 miles showing on the odometer, likely rolled over at least once. He'd discarded the title the seller included — he didn't intend to register the truck. Neither the money nor the vehicle's appearance mattered as much as not having an onboard computer, GPS, LoJack, or black box.

It had to run just long enough to do three things: carry him to and from a high-priority cleanup task he'd assigned himself, haul some items from storage, and transport him and a couple of suitcases beyond the state line. He couldn't tie his name or credit cards to the truck if it needed service, not even an oil change. The purchase would be a good deal for him if the vehicle ran for a month on gas bought with cash.

Frank's relocation outside Massachusetts would require misdirection. He signed up online for two large storage units in Orlando, Florida, not bothering to hide the transactions. A concierge moving service would pack up his collections of first editions, original art, and music. Using a trustworthy high-end service meant he wouldn't have to supervise the moving if his early exit became necessary.

In the meantime, he'd stay in Boston-area motels at night while movers packed and inventoried the semi, changing location occasionally to avoid members of the federation. Except for the items he'd carry in his pickup, everything in his home and storage, including his car, would go to Orlando. Let anyone looking in assume that would become his new home.

The Hodin federation's secrecy put it at a disadvantage. Members below Frank's level performed their activities in small cells, with cell leadership primarily responsible for managing the group. That protected the cell from nonmember scrutiny. However, it also frustrated coalition security outside the cell, trying to track its associates' true identities and relationships in real time, within *or* outside the group. The federation was based entirely on need-to-know and was loathe to broadcast their problems across the alliance, even if they'd had the means.

That meant the coalition would have to rely on Frank censoring himself. Once Frank took off, they'd bank on him dropping his ties to other members for fear the federation was monitoring those links or might retaliate against anyone helping him.

However, Frank's seniority and reach within the organization provided connections more extensive than the federation knew. He tapped into those he felt he could still trust to arrange for photo IDs, passports, and background documentation to support three unique identities. Two of those would serve as backups, should he need them. Once he had those in hand, he created Wise accounts for each and funded them with cash.

With those arrangements made, just one thing stood in the way of Frank regaining control of life on his terms. Addressing it meant breaking a cardinal rule against taking personally anything related to his work.

Still, things had gone too far to stand on principle now.

THE WRITINGS OF
AVRIL MARIA SERENE

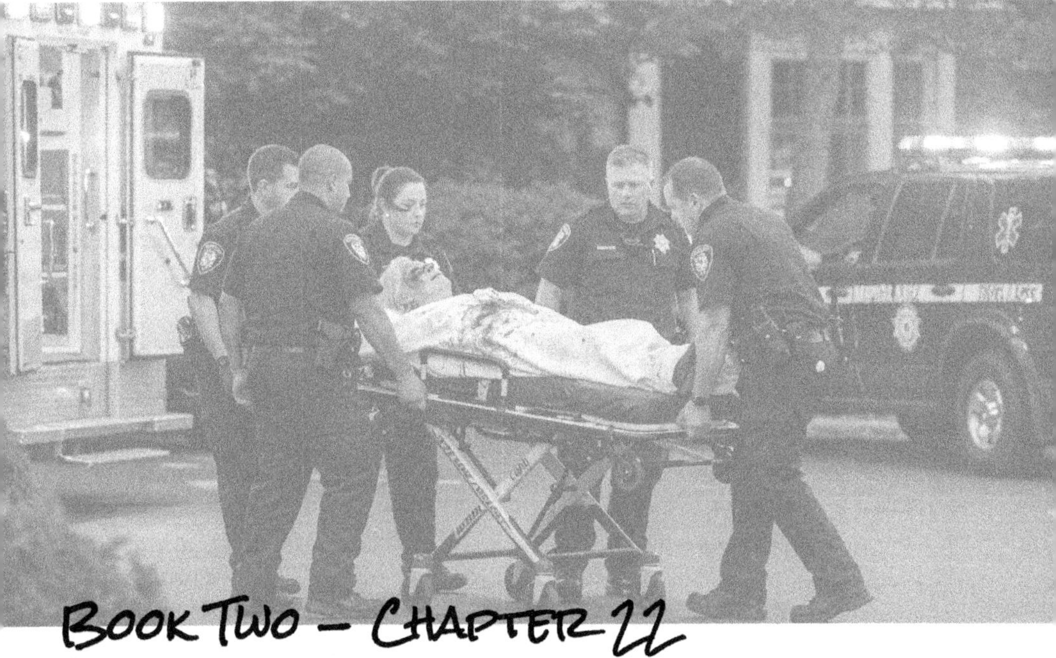

HOPKINTON, MASSACHUSETTS

Uniformed Hopkinton patrol officers held the onlookers — some shocked, others merely curious — at bay on the sidewalk across the street from the elegant home in the early hours of a Saturday evening. Sunset was around eight-thirty this time of year, and dusk would soon fall.

The background conversations among the audience in the gated suburban community ebbed and flowed, exchanging rumors and observations, stirring fresh rounds of murmuring with each new revelation. Several observers cried into tissues and handkerchiefs.

Officers had strung crime scene tape between trees across the front yard and the driveway. Alternating blue and red lights pulsed from the light bars of three marked cruisers, bouncing off every reflective surface.

The Middlesex County medical examiner's white van was backed into the neighbor's yard on the far side of the drive to avoid contaminating the scene as forensic technicians busily worked the two homicides.

The deceased female, in her mid-fifties and short in stature, had fallen face-first onto the driveway, slightly ahead of her vehicle's driver's door. Sergeant of Detectives Sharon Mortensen and her partner Detective Max Benton gloved up as they approached the body. They surveyed the crime scene while Mortenson dictated notes into a handheld digital audio recorder.

"The ME's preliminary opinion says body temps put the shooting between eleven-thirty and noon," Mortenson said. "Do we know why it took so long for someone to report it in *this* neighborhood?"

"I spoke to the 911 operator and dispatch," Benton said. "On the other side of the medical examiner's van, there's a thick row of hedges. It obscures the view of anything below the car's window level. The way the drive curves means, even looking at her vehicle head-on, you couldn't see much of her once she'd fallen and none of him. The garage door was open when the patrol unit arrived. Still, that wasn't unusual enough to draw attention from neighbors. The only thing remarkably awry and visible from the street was the deceased male leaving the front door swinging when he came out. Around seven, the neighbor on the other side realized how long it had been open, came to check, and called 911."

"Got it. All right, we have a male, likely late twenties, early thirties," Mortensen said into her recorder. "Six feet tall, slender build, polo shirt, and jeans. He was on foot, rounding the nose of a black Mercedes AMG EQE in the drive, when the bullet struck him. The corpse's position suggests the young man was intending to aid the other victim. His momentum was going forward at the moment of impact, and he landed on top of blood spatter and tissue resulting from the female's homicide."

"So, she went down first, and when she fell forward, she covered up most of her exit-wound injuries. The male may not have realized why she fell. That the doer gunned both down on the driver's side of the car suggests that the shooter's line of sight ran left of the vehicle," Benton said.

"Moving on, we've got the contents of a woman's purse, tan in color, scattered on the driveway," Mortensen recorded, "about a foot ahead of her body. The purse's location and the spill's direction indicate she was walking toward the garage when she fell. Max, check this out — that's a Bottega Veneta purse. I recognize the buckle design. Five grand or more a pop."

"Why you'd know that on your salary is the big mystery to me," Benton replied with a smirk.

"I'm a dreamer, Max," Mortensen fired back, her lips twisted into a wry smile. "But if it makes you feel better, this is as close to one as I've ever gotten. The shooting happened on a Saturday morning, but the handbag tells me she was returning from seeing someone or doing something important. Otherwise, she'd have taken an everyday purse.

"The uniform first-on-scene says the Audi on the side of the garage closest to the walk is her son's. The garage door's open, and the other stall's empty, yet she pulled behind the Audi, staying in the drive."

"I'd guess it was already open, or she hit the garage door remote from habit when she turned into the drive," Benton speculated. "For some reason, she wasn't staying long but still wanted to go inside."

"Works for me." Mortensen gave a quick nod. Taking a pair of tweezers out of her pocket with her right hand, she fished the woman's wallet out of the purse with her left and teased out the driver's license.

"'Christine Elizabeth Patterson,' and here's her bar card. Crap, I know her — or, well, *of* her. She heads up one of the elite criminal defense firms in downtown Boston. She's gotten some of our perps off for capital offenses that should've stuck. I wouldn't list her among my favorite people, but I can't imagine what she did to end up dead.

"That means the other body's her son James. Another lawyer, something of a failure-to-launch type. As I understand it, he still lives at home with his mother and acts as her manservant."

"Her homicide alone is enough that, once the media gets hold of this, it'll be a shitstorm." Benton sighed.

"Let's button up the scene as quickly as possible," Mortensen agreed. "See if we can stay ahead of their arrival. But make sure we don't miss anything. How soon can the medical examiner remove the bodies? Lord knows we don't need those images bouncing around the news outlets until they find a station so desperate for viewers that they'll air them."

As two of the medical examiner's staff lowered the gurney alongside the older female's body, Mortensen raised the sheet for a better look at the victim's entry wound. Letting the corner of the sheet go, she nodded to the attendants that they could load and take the body. Mortenson got down on her hands and knees, her hair falling onto the pavement. With Benton right beside her, she was able to glimpse the gaping exit wound in the victim's right chest as the ME's assistant raised the body just enough to place it on the gurney. As the detectives saw the scope of the damage, Benton spoke.

"I saw our bullet whisperer on-scene when we first pulled up. We should see what he thinks."

"Shaughnessy's here?" Mortenson asked, and Benton nodded. "Good for us. Let's chat with him after we finish with the bodies. I need to know why these exit wounds look like craters."

Detective Alan Shaughnessy had come to the department a little over five years ago, taking his military retirement after twenty years of Marine Corps service. Uncomfortable in the confines of the ballistics lab, Shaughnessy had instead become the go-to in-the-field expert on munitions and armaments.

The detectives walked back to the male body. Benton leaned over and quickly sniffed the area near the man's hands. "The son was cooking something. Not breakfast, probably lunch — you can still smell the garlic on his hands. A uniform reported a burned pan on the stove. He had to turn off the burner and an air-fry oven so that squares. Nothing else seemed in disarray inside the house, so killing them was enough for our shooter."

Mortenson spotted Shaughnessy standing at the curb, scanning the area in front of the Patterson residence with binoculars. "Let's see what Shaughnessy knows." She led as Benton followed.

"Hey, Alan, good to see you caught this," Mortensen said as the three nodded greetings. "So, what do you think?"

"Depending on the position of the victims at the moment of impact," he replied, his brow furrowed in concentration, "we have a thirty-degree arc of possible launch points from the line at the side of the Mercedes to the left past the church and the rectory. Hopefully, the medical examiner can give us something to narrow it down.

"As things stand, I can't get an accurate trajectory, even assuming the shots came from the same point of origin. The bullets tumbled when they impacted — the rounds were nearing the end of their range and had lost their kinetic energy. The entry points are relatively compact, but the exit wounds are four inches or more in diameter.

"They were strictly sniper rounds — .338 Norma Magnums — no other use except in a machine gun. Both rounds passed through, as you saw. We dug one out of a lawn chair in the garage and one out of the garage door molding. The impacts seriously mangled them. Ballistics can tell us more, but the JARLINK shows secondary markings, possibly from a noise or flash suppressor."

"JARLINK?" Benton asked.

Shaughnessy pulled an illuminated jeweler's loupe from his pants pocket, passing it to Benson.

"Any signs of misses or target practice?" Mortensen shielded her eyes from the setting sun's rays as she peered back at the house.

"I've been going over the home's exterior." Shaughnessy tapped his binoculars. "No evidence of any other rounds landing near the scene. Given the distance of the closest possible perch — I'd say somewhere on the church grounds — hitting separate targets with no misses is truly remarkable. He caught the woman between the second and third ribs up, dead center with the heart — a little off with the male. But with an exit wound that size, he knew exsanguination would finish the kill. He achieved distance *and* accuracy with no practice rounds and in succession, likely with a bolt-action rifle.

Shaughnessy did not hide the admiration in his voice.

"I feel for the victims but gotta give him his props. Definitely a pro, genuine skill."

"You said 'he' — have you seen something like this before, or have an idea who the shooter might be?" Benton asked.

"There are some damned fine female snipers," Shaughnessy answered. "Most of them through the military. Still, they're rare. I have at least a nodding acquaintance with most of those who could have landed these shots. I can't see them getting involved in something like this — the government's sent anyone who might off on covert assignment.

"To answer your other question: yes, a case I trained on when I came to the department. A civilian shooting in Boston from two decades ago took out a Winter Hill gang member; one shot, center mass. The closest perch they could find for the sniper was fourteen hundred meters away, well over three-quarters of a mile. Believe it or not, two different guys confessed to that murder — the man locked up for it is Emile Reardon. From what I know of him, I can't see him pulling off the shot. But, hey, it's not relevant now. He couldn't have done these two from his jail cell."

"What about the other confessor?" Mortensen asked.

"I just finished talking to a Boston PD lieutenant about him. It seems we stumbled into a hornet's nest, some nasty recent history there. The lieutenant wouldn't give me the details, but we can't engage that guy unless we clear it first with our brass. Cap says we'll work this case to the best of our ability without going there. If something we turn up in the normal course of investigation puts that Winter Hill suspect squarely in our sights, they'll hear us out. Until then, we're to leave it alone."

"The victim's one of the top criminal defense attorneys in Boston, so that restriction won't last long." Mortenson snorted. "But rules are rules. Leaving out the doer, does the Winter Hill case help us here?"

"In that homicide, they had nothing else they could do, so they test-fired several sniper rifles to see which best simulated the result. They came up with the Barrett .50-caliber used during the Gulf War. Snipers this good are loyal to their favorite vendors. It's just a guess, but for these homicides, I'd bet on the Barrett Mk22, MRAD, or MRAD SMR sniper rifles, in that order. He'd have downgraded the barrel kit to .338 caliber for less recoil. I might be biased — those are the weapons I'd pick for this. No one seems to have heard or seen anything, and it's a quiet neighborhood, so he probably used a flash and noise suppressor. Likely the AML338 — same manufacturer."

"We need to focus the forensics team on the sniper's position," Benton said. "Any ideas yet where to start?"

"He wouldn't have fired from the open at ground level — even if he did, he damn sure wouldn't have gone for that second kill. Too obvious. He needs concealment not just for the shot but for the escape. It's more likely from a tree or rooftop. I doubt he'd have shot from a vehicle — for accuracy like this, the rocking on its springs from the first shot's recoil would spoil the next one, and he got two off reasonably close together. Assuming he didn't have a spotter, he'd want to be out in the environment enough to gauge wind effect."

"Any possibility the son was the intended target?" Mortenson asked.

"Shooting her to draw him out? I don't see it. Given her occupation and prominence, she'd be the primary target. I doubt the sniper counted on the son coming to her rescue — for all the shooter knew, the boy could have been upstairs taking a shower, totally oblivious. If this was a pro — all signs point that way — he'd have explicitly waited for her to return home. Taking out the son was opportunistic, spur of the moment.

"I'd guess that killing her kid sent a message to someone else the sniper thought was looking in."

BOOK TWO — CHAPTER 23

The text relaying the captain's request for an update on the double homicide was terse and formal. With little public investigative progress, the murders were drawing uncomfortable media attention two weeks later. Det. Sgt. Mortenson took a seat in Capt. Hamilton's office. She reviewed her notes as the senior officer signed a document for his administrative aide.

"I apologize for the interruption." Hamilton turned his attention to Mortenson. "We're taking a lot of heat in the press. What can you tell me I don't already know?"

"Yes, Cap — we've identified the sniper's perch in a stand of trees on the grounds of the church. It's almost fifteen hundred yards away from the furthest point of impact. Still, Detective Shaughnessy says it's doable in the right hands with the proper munitions."

"Shaughnessy would know. What do we have on the weapon?"

"The Barrett MK 22 is our best candidate. Nothing we've found contradicts that. Bruises in the bark at a crook in the tree match the distance between the legs of the factory-mounted folding front stand. The rifle combined with .338 rounds is unique; we're tracking them down, but nothing definite has popped up.

"We've traced the killer's path across neighboring backyards to a poly storage shed in the rear of a property that's up for sale. Forensics reports fresh markings, detritus, and rust deposits, likely from used lawn tools — things that if you saw someone carrying them, you would think, 'a gardener.'

"We believe the killer planted those in that shed several days ahead of the murders to give him cover for his escape. We think after the shootings, he jumped fences and hedges to get to the shed. He locked his weapon inside the outbuilding with a padlock he brought. Put on coveralls and left with the gardening tools, exiting in a direction away from the Patterson residence."

"Any idea where he was going?" Hamilton raised his eyebrows.

"Witnesses describe an old lawn-maintenance truck parked two streets down from Patterson's residence. Mid-eighties, two-tone white over brown or dark red, rusted, dirty, all dinged up; no one got the plate. Forensics confirmed fresh oil stains on the pavement at that location.

"We've nothing on the driver clear enough to ID — gardener's wide-brimmed straw hat, gloves, aviator shades, and coveralls. Doorbells and security cams show our presumed killer, maybe six foot even, 190 pounds, walking up to that truck. He's carrying a rake, a shovel, and a hoe, tosses them in the back, and leaves the area. Again, none of the videos show the tags. The truck stands out because the bed was empty when he approached it — ever seen an old gardener's truck with nothing in it?

"Sometime before we discovered that shed, he returned, recovering the weapon and his padlock, likely at night. We're canvassing for camera or digital doorbell video to see if we can track his movements."

"Where are we at with telecommunications?" Hamilton's expression was pensive.

"We got the data back in response to our subpoenas to all the major carriers for the cell towers in the immediate area. It's a ton of information — quite a few residents there run businesses out of their homes post-pandemic.

"Without a specific timeframe, we've had to make some assumptions. The shooter wouldn't have left that weapon — expensive and traceable by its uniqueness, even if he'd removed the serial number — in that plastic storage unit for long.

"We're targeting four days ahead of the shootings to cover the staging of the gardening tools. We found the shed a week after the murders, which sets the other end of the range for the sniper to recover his weapon. If we come up empty with the cameras, we'll extend the forward end of the time spectrum a few more days.

"This guy's a pro; it's unlikely he'd bring a cell phone to the scene. We're hoping he left one turned on in the truck. Even a burner helps — we've made cases on these things before."

"What else do you have?"

"We're concentrating on the pickup, looking at registrations, stolen vehicles, and title transfers. Thousands of old trucks in the Boston area fit the description — the vehicle inspection law has retired most of them to junkyards. Still, we're checking those yards for any they haven't crushed yet. It's consuming a lot of work hours.

"The same is true with the tip line. These media-driven cases pull too many calls from the sincerely mistaken and crazy-as-a-bedbug attention-seekers. We're sifting through them, but not much of value. We have reports of gardeners in the general vicinity near the victim's address. Those would be in the time frame a few days before the murders to several days after. We're running those down. The witness statements so far aren't promising — head coverings, sunglasses, multiple layers of clothing — but we've put them with sketch artists to see what turns up. We've also sent what we have to Quantico for a profile.

"Other than that, we're hitting up our confidential informants and rattling cages in all the mobbed-up haunts we know. Hard to believe something this in-your-face wouldn't trample on *somebody's* turf and piss them off enough to help us out. Patterson kept several wise guys out of prison — they should be feeling something about her being gone."

"Anything else from the victimology?" The captain's thumb was under his chin, forefinger to his temple.

"We're going through her case files, the ones the special master lets us see. We're not supposed to touch this guy with a ten-foot pole, but we found an uncashed check in the back of her top desk drawer from almost three months ago, signed by Frank Spector for fifty grand.

"It could be a coincidence. Patterson never deposited it, so maybe he was shopping attorneys, and whatever they negotiated fell through. Spector's in a high tax bracket. It makes sense he'd reach out to the top-end criminal lawyers in the area to help him with his legal situation. There's nothing else indicating he was ever a client. There was a note paper clipped to the check, which looked like an Internet address and some type of code. One of our computer forensics guys is going over it."

"It sounds like you're on top of this." Hamilton took a deep breath. "I'll get you two more officers for the door-to-door video canvassing and working the phones. I can give you an IT tech to help with the online searches for the truck and the weapon.

"Otherwise, if we've gained no ground by the end of next week, we'll hit the state up for some help. I hate to surrender turf to the FBI — you know how they push everyone around — but the step after that means getting federal agents involved. Chris Patterson had clients with past and current federal cases, which gives the feds their buy-in."

"Any chance we can look at Frank Spector?"

"Don't lose that check — we'll need the routing and account numbers if we want a warrant," Hamilton replied, concern showing on his face.

"But I'm not ready to go there yet. If the media hears we're looking at Spector for this, it restarts a shitstorm. Drags in all those killings from two decades ago and the sideshow that goes with them. Boston PD already kicked him loose once. Worse, they've locked up someone else for them. It'd look like law enforcement is grinding an axe over Spector's little publicity stunt.

"If we're not careful here, both their department and ours are going to look even more corrupt and incompetent than theirs did with the Whitey Bulger case. And that's saying something."

BOOK TWO — CHAPTER 24

ON THE ROAD

News of a prominent citizen's murder was generating too much attention in local media. Pretty sure that he was on law enforcement's list by now, Frank did not want them ensnaring him in the roundup of usual suspects.

Because he had worked in management above the cell level, the federation could track the use of his passport and any movement by commercial aviation. Frank had no way to flee the country as himself, and he didn't want to travel internationally on forged documents. He'd need to stay in the United States.

Once he'd approved the movers' inventory of his goods and they'd readied his BMW for transport to Orlando, Frank threw several waterproof, lidded plastic tubs filled with his possessions into the bed of his old pickup. He tied a brown tarp over the cargo area to keep the tubs out of the weather and the view of any onlookers.

Placing two suitcases and some personal items on the passenger-side seat and in the footwell, Frank saluted goodbye to his home of the past twenty years and headed for the freeway. After looping through side streets several times to ensure no one was following, he hit I-90 westbound at the Congress Street on-ramp.

Frank hadn't expected the old pickup to go as far as it did — he'd added a quart of oil and topped up the brake fluid reservoir at every gas tank fill-up since buying the truck. When the transmission failed, he pulled over alongside the highway for the last time. He'd just skirted the southwest corner of Albany on I-87, barely two and a half hours out of Boston.

Paying cash to a local tow service, Frank had the pickup hauled to a garage closed for the day. The shop was remote and old-school, which meant the only cameras were three analog units. One monitored the front garage door, another stood watch over the customer entrance, and a third covered the galvanized-fenced area at the rear of the building where they stored customers' vehicles. Frank had the tow truck drag his pickup to the far corner of the front parking lot, where it would likely go unnoticed by the camera, passersby, or security services — perfect for Frank's purposes.

After locking up his truck, he had the tow driver drop him and his plastic tubs off at the nearest motel.

Awakening early the following day, a Sunday, Frank paid cash for cabs to get around. He hit up a local Lowes and a Walmart for shipping boxes, a backpack, cleaning supplies, sheet metal snips, and a rechargeable hand vac. After returning to his motel room, Frank had another driver take him and the cleaning supplies to the repair shop where he'd left his old pickup.

The shop wasn't open and wouldn't be until Monday morning. Frank began rigorously wiping down the interior and any other surfaces he might have touched to remove any fingerprints or DNA. After vacuuming the interior and passing over everything with a lint roller, Frank pulled the truck's license plates, gathering the tags and used paper towels into a bag.

He called for another cab and headed back to the motel. Once there, Frank cut the plates into tiny pieces and scouted the area on foot for a commercial dumpster, randomly scattering bits of the metal in dark corners along the way. Once he found a garbage bin to his liking, he disposed of the towels and empty cleaning bottles.

Frank spent the rest of the day packing the contents of his tubs and the disassembled Glock 22 into cardboard boxes for shipping ahead. It was time to commit to his ultimate destination.

He chose San Diego for several reasons. The more liberal and accepting nature of California politics attracted him. The city's proximity and access to Mexico if he needed to escape the country could be helpful. Employment opportunities in digital advertising near Irvine and then north to Silicon Valley provided excellent options for conserving his resources.

If things blew up in his face, the death penalty in California, though still technically possible as a sentence at trial, was on hold. A federal court stay and an executive order of the current governor rendered it moot.

After researching San Diego motels online, Frank made a week's reservation under an alias using a Wise debit card. Then he hailed a cab to carry him and his boxes to a strip mall pack-and-ship store, paying cash to send the cartons ahead via UPS.

As night fell, he dressed in dark clothing and walked the mixed residential and commercial business area surrounding the motel. Spotting a green vinyl garden hose at the side of a residence, he cut off an eight-foot length, folded it into three sections, and hid it down one leg of his jeans. About thirty minutes later, he found and took an unattended and unlocked bicycle, wheeling it into his room to hide until needed.

Grabbing a bite to eat, then setting his phone alarm for three a.m., Frank slept soundly until the cell woke him. Once awake, Frank rolled up the short hose, hanging it over the bike's seat. Grabbing one of the motel's towels, he quietly left his room, pedaling through side streets and alleys until he arrived at his pickup.

With the hose, Frank siphoned a couple of gallons of gasoline from the pickup's tank into a gas can he kept in the bed.

Splashing its contents into the cab, engine compartment, and bed of the truck, he tore the motel's towel into strips lengthwise, leaving the strips connected to form a six-foot-long wick.

He stuffed one end of the strips into the vehicle's gasoline filler tube, leaving about two feet of towel hanging outside the fender.

Waiting until the wick drew gasoline out of the tank and became saturated, Frank pulled Chris Patterson's lighter from his pocket and lit the fuse.

He pedaled away as quickly as he could without drawing attention.

Though he'd anticipated it, the intensity of the explosion startled Frank — still, he resisted the temptation to look back.

He stopped at a break between the streetlights a few blocks from his motel, using a remnant of towel to wipe down the bike before tossing it into the front yard of a residence.

Strolling back to his motel room, Frank would grab another forty winks before the new day's adventures began.

With a much lighter load to carry and on his mind, Frank called for a cab to the Albany-Rensselaer Amtrak station, where he'd resume his journey. He chose the scenic route away from the Atlantic seaboard, traveling under another of his new IDs. The Amtrak would carry Frank first to New York City's Moynihan Train Hall at Penn Station and then to Harrisburg. The next leg took him to Pittsburgh, where he switched to Greyhound for the rest of the trip.

Frank had time before the big AmeriCruiser would depart and knew the run from Pittsburgh to Los Angeles would take two and a half days. Wanting to read *Six Degrees from Killing Brian* since it came out, he found a nearby bookstore and picked up a copy, adding two other paperbacks. They'd keep him entertained when he had no Internet connection or had exhausted the battery in his laptop.

Four days after Frank boarded that first Amtrak, his bus pulled into San Diego.

Though happy to be on solid ground again, he'd adapted well to the rhythms of the big diesel in the back as the motorcoach lumbered down the open road. Frank stepped from the bus feeling rested, with an exhilarating sense of absolute freedom.

In San Diego, he'd be anonymous, unfettered by conventions of employment or duty. The weather was gorgeous, the beaches expansive, and the local population seemed friendly. He had the resources to explore what the city offered — the perfect place to reinvent himself and decide what to do with his life.

At some level, Frank knew it couldn't last, and at another, he didn't care.

As Frank waited at the counter to check in at the motel so he could pick up the boxes he'd sent ahead, he spotted an anemic copy of the *San Diego Union-Tribune* lying on a lobby chair. The leftmost column of the front page featured an article describing the death of a former head of the State Department who'd served two Republican administrations. The one-time former ambassador to the European Union drowned in a hot tub after an overdose of alcohol and sleeping medications in an apparent suicide.

The article reported that he'd been accused recently of numerous inappropriate relationships with young boys. One victim was now a sitting U.S. Senator over whom the older man had continued to wield influence.

You always looked good in a photo, Levi; much better with your clothes on.

Immediately upon arriving at his room, Frank opened the carton containing his Glock. Before unpacking his luggage or any of the other boxes, he filled two clips with ammunition, shoved one into the butt of the weapon's frame, and pulled back the slide to force a round into the chamber.

After all, having your freedom means more if you survive the experience.

BOOK TWO — CHAPTER 25

SAN DIEGO, CALIFORNIA

While considering what to do with his free time, knowing he should stay low until he got his bearings, Frank had a revelation. He'd get his story out there by publishing a book about his experiences. Spending his days writing, he'd explore the city at night for ideas, nourishment, and entertainment.

After making progress on the first draft, his biggest problem was naming his exposé-slash-novel. He'd decided the word "Choices" should be in the title. After all, the federation's methods relied on billions of people choosing to do things that furthered the coalition's ends. It also hinted at his power in providing those options. As for the rest, he wasn't sure whether to name the Hodin federation up front. He leaned instead toward "PuppetMaster," pointing out his role as the central character. But the decision could await the new day — it was time to hit the hay.

Deep in REM sleep, Frank's mind misinterpreted the *clink!* and *zip* of the first silenced round as it bored through the window glass and whipped open the curtain.

In his dream, he stood in rubber waders fifty yards past the shore of a clear blue Montana mountain lake on a crisp spring day.

The sounds fit the snapping of the fly-fishing line behind him as he whipped his rod forward.

The second round came in lower and louder, with a *pthunk!* as it pierced the wall, leaving a pinhole of yellow light, then clanged off the metal bed frame.

Suddenly, Frank was awake and alert, shaking his head violently to clear any cobwebs.

He rolled over onto his left arm off the mattress, falling to the floor.

Fuck, the federation found me!

Grabbing his silenced Glock and holster with his left hand, he used his right to yank down his chinos by their legs from the top of the nightstand.

As his pants fell, his cell and the motel's alarm clock came down with them — the blue LED display read "4:14 AM."

Keeping his head low, he half-stumbled, half-crawled to the bathroom as four more rounds penetrated the door, windows, and wall.

As was his habit for years, Frank had mapped out his escape route from the first moment he'd stepped into the room. His exit would be through the square attic access panel above the shower.

Frank pulled on his khakis and, lying back down on his stomach, reached out through the bathroom doorframe, feeling around to find his shoes.

As he did, two more silenced rounds struck the wall that separated the bedroom from the bathroom.

He assumed from the upward trajectory of the bullets that his assailants were firing from one floor below in the parking lot outside.

They were strafing the room, hoping for a lucky hit before breaching the door. Forcefully breaking in would attract more attention in the wee hours of the night than firing rounds through a silencer from outside.

Frank's choice of motel rooms had been strategic, intended to frustrate a direct assault.

His was situated in the middle of a dozen rooms stretched along the outer balcony. Long double rows of yellow insect-repelling fluorescent bulbs under the eaves brightly lit the catwalk, highlighting the white clapboard siding and doors.

Cameras on either end of the rows captured everything on that balcony. Anyone approaching or escaping Frank's door would be visible for a hundred feet in both directions.

Now halfway dressed and armed with an extra clip in his pants pocket, Frank turned over the garbage can in the bathroom to use as a stool.

He pulled himself up through the access panel into the crawlspace running above the second-floor rooms of the motel.

Using his cell camera flash for light, Frank crawled on his hands and knees along the wooden rafters as quickly as he could without punching through the ceilings below.

Passing through electrical wires, plumbing, vent tubing, fiberglass batting, and blown cellulose insulation, Frank found an access panel three doors down and across the exterior hallway from his room.

He listened carefully for any sounds from the space below.

Hearing nothing, he crossed his fingers that nobody was beneath him, or God forbid, in the bathroom.

He pried up the wooden access panel with his pen knife, squirmed through, and dropped quietly into the shower stall below — the bathroom was empty.

But lowering himself into a crouch and stepping into the bedroom, he heard a loud, interrupted snore, followed by the bedcovers rustling and the bedframe creaking with sudden movement.

An older, heavyset woman sat up from underneath the comforter.

Pushing her sleep shades above her hairline, she shrieked at the top of her lungs.

Exposed and with no other choice, Frank stood up, pointed his weapon directly at her, and held a forefinger to his lips.

"Ma'am, I won't hurt you, but you've got to be quiet. If you don't shut up, I'll have to shoot you," he said in as calm a voice as he could muster.

With that, the woman nodded and fell into a blubbering whimper, her eyes wide in terror, scrunching up her knees and pulling the comforter tightly around herself.

Not sensing an immediate threat from her, Frank's attention returned to his escape.

This room's entrance opened onto the back balcony.

Frank slowly cracked open the door and peered out.

There was no evidence of activity.

Glancing back to ensure the room's tenant stayed put, Frank headed out the rear exterior hallway toward the stairs at a crouch.

His finger on the Glock's trigger, the weapon held out with both hands, he scanned rigorously ahead and behind for signs of anyone else.

After descending the stairs and surveying the scene from the better vantage point, Frank moved stealthily to the end of the row of rooms underneath his.

Peeking carefully around the edge of the building, Frank saw an early-2000s-vintage black Dodge Magnum with heavy window tinting, idling with its lights on.

It might have blended into the owner's home turf, but here it was conspicuous.

Turned away from him in the middle of the lot, it blocked the row of head-in parking reserved for guests near the building.

Two men in dark hoodies and sagging jeans held silenced semi-automatic pistols sideways as they crept slowly up the stairs, something you'd see in a low-budget rap video.

Frank's instincts said these were cartel hitters, not the higher-caliber professional hitmen the federation typically employed.

Had he been mistaken for someone else?

Or was the change of personnel deliberate, maybe to cast blame on gangs that were active in the area?

It didn't matter — they meant to kill him, and he needed to deal with them.

Staying low to the ground, Frank snuck up behind the Magnum and around to the driver's side, swinging wide of the rearview mirror mounted to the door.

The heavily tattooed driver had rolled down his window to vape; his focus was on the two men slowly walking across the well-lit balcony.

I can kill three birds with the same stone, Frank thought.

He smiled inwardly at the idea, knowing he now had the upper hand as he shot the driver in the back of his head.

As the man slumped toward the passenger side, Frank reached through the open window, tapping the car's horn.

The two men on the balcony froze in momentary confusion, now brightly accented in yellow against the building's second-floor walls.

A quick *plit-plit* from Frank's Glock and both men fell before they could get off another shot.

The banger at the rear tumbled down the stairs, crumpling onto the middle landing.

Frank rounded the front of the Dodge, scanning the other vehicles in the lot for passengers or activity.

Suddenly, the loud screeching of tires, bright red and blue lightbars, and white-hot spotlights from two police cruisers announced their arrival at the front of the lot.

Four armed officers bailed from their squad cars, barking commands at him to put down his weapon and surrender.

The glare from their vehicles and the Magnum's headlights had Frank caught between.

Frank considered making a run for it but didn't like the odds in the dead of night — he didn't know the surrounding terrain well enough.

Slowly placing his Glock on the hood of the Dodge and turning toward the approaching officers, Frank interlaced his fingers and placed his palms on top of his head.

He could see three more officers, weapons drawn, cautiously climbing the stairs toward the bodies of the men on the landing and balcony.

An officer approached Frank, shoving the handgun further out of reach while holding him at gunpoint. A second officer grabbed Frank roughly by the shoulders and spun him around to face the Magnum, grabbing his wrist to cuff it and then clamping the handcuff on the other arm.

"Do you have any more weapons on you?" the officer restraining him asked.

"No," Frank said, speaking softly.

"We've got a deceased male," another officer announced, approaching the group surrounding Frank from the direction of the motel lobby. "Asian, late twenties, down behind the front desk. His uniform shirt says he's the night manager; he took two rounds to the chest. We'll need to canvass the area for other victims."

Grabbing Frank's hands by their restraints, the officer bent him over the hood of the Magnum, forcing his legs apart and slamming his face into the sheet metal.

"Do you have any needles, knives, sharp objects, drugs, or other paraphernalia I need to worry about? Anything that might hurt me?" the officer barked out as he patted Frank down.

"There's a folding pocketknife and a clip for the Glock in my front pocket," Frank answered.

He heard someone calling out to the officers in a shrill tone from the second-floor balcony.

With his head turned to the side, Frank could see a dumpy middle-aged woman in a hotel robe lumbering across the front of the rooms, thrusting a rolled-up magazine in their direction.

The guest I dropped in on gets her fifteen minutes of fame… Well, there's one bright side to this crapfest of an evening, Frank thought as the officer rifled through his pockets.

Maybe, just maybe, they'll listen to my story this time.

THE WRITINGS OF
AVRIL MARIA SERENE

BOOK THREE

THE WRITINGS OF
AVRIL MARIA SERENE

Book Three – Chapter 1

SAN DIEGO, CALIFORNIA

Cindy left us almost three months ago; her memory was a part of every conversation Paul and I had, and there were many. We'd grown so close, and in many ways, it was a natural extension of our relationship in college. That we shared Cindy's last few weeks together had strengthened us beyond where we'd been in those carefree years when we were beginning our adult lives.

Separate from my feelings for Paul, I missed Cindy. In a brief time, she'd become the daughter I'd never had. When I met her, she was becoming a young woman, with all that entails, challenging even in the best circumstances. Chemo complicated things for her, with false starts and moments she found embarrassing. Our bond had become tight enough that she'd talk to me about her problems, boys, and what she wanted to do with a life that, sadly, cancer cut too short to live.

Paul and I pulled what positivity we could from a tragic situation so much worse for him. We found we could share things that no one else would understand. We'd experienced some of that during our adventures while dating in school. Still, there was far more depth and substance to what we'd discuss today. Our time spent apart during our journeys into adulthood and building our careers had given us new things to explore about each other. We'd been spending every evening together, staying over through the nights.

And so, I wasn't surprised one late afternoon when Paul came home from work early, tapped on my door, and, in the middle of discussing what sounded tasty for supper, leaned into "the talk." No, not about me taking his last name — the one that started with how foolish we were to maintain separate apartments twenty-five feet apart.

It began innocently enough after I asked Paul what he'd like.

"If we order from the Thai place, I'll have the yellow curry with chicken, but if we want Chinese, I'll go with orange chicken, egg fried rice, and cream cheese wontons."

"I can do either. Let's flip a coin." I grabbed an Aldi shopping cart quarter from the key tray by the door.

"As much as we eat out and order in, this is pretty silly," Paul declared. "We have two kitchens. We don't use either, except for morning coffee and cereal, maybe eggs or pancakes once in a while."

"So, what would you have us do, Paul?" I played it coy.

"Two laundry rooms, at least one extra bedroom." Paul stuck with his pitch. "You know, we could get a bigger place, say three bedrooms and two baths, for less than both rents combined. We'd have more space we'd actually use…."

"Mr. Castro, what *are* you saying, exactly?" I let him twist in the wind.

Paul used his stilted impression of a professorial-sounding voice.

"As a scientist, I hypothesize it would be more efficient economically and better conserve the environment if the inhabitants were to merge their living quarters."

"Are you asking me to cohabitate with you?"

"I am." Paul had a big smile.

"Let me consider your proposal." I turned away from him and hummed the Jeopardy thinking music. But it was only seconds later when I spun back, beaming. I threw my arms around him, letting him off the hook before things got awkward. "Yes, let's do it!"

Paul's grin lit up the room. We touched foreheads and looked into each other's eyes. The moment was as happy as any we'd had since Cindy passed. Kissing as we let go, Paul's demeanor turned practical and earnest. I knew he wanted to lock things down before the opportunity slipped away, the nerdier side of his personality showing itself.

"Your lease is up first. You like it here — you've been in this complex, what, six years now? — and the management's good. We should ask if any larger units are coming available."

"Good idea," I agreed. "If we stay with the same owners, maybe they'll let you break your lease. We could get into the new place sooner… moving should be a breeze."

"You're as anxious as I am!" Paul's look was one of mock surprise. "Actually, for patience, I'm the worst — I've been trying for a month to find the right moment to ask you." His expression turned bashful, and he looked down at his feet.

"Hey, but we're missing one part of the perfect relationship." Paul's face suddenly brightened. "How would you feel about paying a pet deposit at our next place? Shouldn't we have a dog?"

"Yeah, I *like* that idea," I replied with a laugh, remembering fondly Rusty, my constant four-legged companion until a few years ago. "Somebody to keep me company while I write and you're away, toiling at whatever you say you do. We'll adopt a rescue, though — right?"

"Of course, the only way to go. When we sign our new lease, we'll hit the shelters and find our perfect puppy…"

"Oh, so you have an eye for the younger ones… Hmmm, should we think about hardwood floors in the new place?"

⁓ ◦ ⁓

As things would turn out, the timing of our conversation was fortuitous, if not prescient.

A week after Paul and I agreed to move in together, the morning dawned chilly and gray, feeling more like mid-November in Seattle than San Diego.

I'd made genuine progress with my victims' point-of-view exposé of the aftermath of the sale and then abandonment of the Monsanto facility. It had been leaching chemicals into air, land, and water in Freddie's old neighborhood for decades. I started the project to deal with my grief and Paul's heartbreak over losing Cindy. I needed to be doing *something*, and I'd not exercised my usual professional discretion regarding what I wrote. I knew my motivations for writing the piece weren't pure. Still, I rationalized my efforts as a productive outlet for working through my feelings.

As my article took form and endured several editing rounds, I felt it had morphed into a quality expression of investigative journalism. Still, I worried someone might misconstrue it as exploiting the unfortunate situation that killed Freddie and still tormented Rosarita and their mother. So, I had a heart-to-heart with the surviving family before pushing on. They proved supportive and grateful to have their story told, so I kept writing.

The article had become both therapeutic and a source of pride for me.

Even so, I welcomed the break when my phone rang, and Caller ID showed it was Marci on the line. I looked forward to telling her the news about the upcoming change in my living situation. We hadn't spoken much after learning Alma had been among the homeless burial site victims – Paul and I had been focusing more on one another since Cindy left us. It would be great to catch up, maybe even escape the apartment for a while.

"Marci, long time no speak," I said with a little laugh as I picked up the phone. "It's good to hear from you."

"Hi, Debra Ann — it *has* been a while. I know you've been through some tough things — I can't imagine how difficult Cindy's passing must have been for all of you. I thought you might need some space. But I wanted to ask you about something, and honestly, I was glad for an excuse to call."

"Our little chats always help," I said as I moved to the couch, "whatever else might be going on. And now's a good time. So, how's life been treating you?"

"I feel guilty saying this with everything you're dealing with, but things have been clicking along pretty smoothly. Danny's great; the kids are doing well."

"Don't feel bad, Marci. Cindy's in a better place now, and she'll live in our hearts until it's our time to see her again. We think of her constantly, but we focus on the good times. While Paul and I've done our share of crying, it hasn't been all gloom and doom."

I paused, worried that now wasn't the appropriate time to share happier tidings. But it *was* Marci I was talking to; of all people, she'd understand.

"We've gotten closer through this…."

I couldn't keep the news to myself any longer.

"Oh, Marci — Paul's asked me to move in with him. And he wants us to get a dog!" I blurted out, my voice giving away my enthusiasm.

"Congratulations — you go, girl! Let the nesting behaviors begin!" Marci sounded at first surprised, then pleased. "Paul's great for you, and you're perfect for him — you have all that history together. I'm so happy for you, Debra Ann!"

"It's exciting, but in a 'this is the right thing to do' way — you know what I mean?" My heart was still soaring. "We've been spending a lot of time together. I kind of knew this was where we might end up. It was such a relief to learn he felt the same way."

"Yes, I *do* know what you mean. I remember how it felt when Danny and I connected, and we're still going strong. I assume you're getting a new place? You both have the same floor plan. Either of your apartments would be a little small for both of you, a dog, and your writing … Plus, you only have one bathroom. I'm sorry, honey, but that never works out when you both have professional careers."

"That's the plan. We need to talk to the owners and see if a three-bedroom, two-bath is available where we're at. We'll see how willing they are to work with us. My lease is up in three months, so that's when we'll make the official move.

"But you didn't call to hear me drone on about Paul. What's going on?"

"I'm thrilled to hear the good news. But the reason I'm calling came out of the blue, from a direction I wasn't expecting. I had a conversation yesterday that's straight out of a *Twilight Zone* vignette. It's enough off the beaten path that you might want to dig into it."

"If you intended to pique my curiosity, that's a great way to start. I take it this falls within my professional skill set?"

"As opposed to your singing and dancing talents? Yes," Marci teased. "Someone who's helped me a lot in my personal life got caught up in a situation. They need someone with real chops to look into a story. And if it's what it appears to be, to get it out in front of the public. They're in a position where professional ethics have their hands tied. Still, it shouldn't go unexplored. I'm not trying to be as evasive as all that sounds, but it's complicated.

"You know … one of the world's problems you and I solve all the time over lunch."

I could imagine her grin as she spoke.

"But for this, the meal's on me. You have my word; you won't be wasting your time." There was an entreating quality to Marci's tone.

"I'm sure I won't. Hey, if, in your judgment, this requires a free lunch, who am I to question it? Where and when do you want to get together? Today's open, and there's nothing on my calendar the rest of the week that I can't move around."

"I'm in the mood to wreck my diet. How about a Chinese buffet — the one we used to hit up on Convoy, maybe?"

"We haven't been there in a while, and Chinese sounds great," I said enthusiastically. "Want to beat the crowd, say, eleven-thirty?"

Marci's playfulness about her reason for calling was uncharacteristic — which only served to whet my curiosity.

THE WRITINGS OF
AVRIL MARIA SERENE

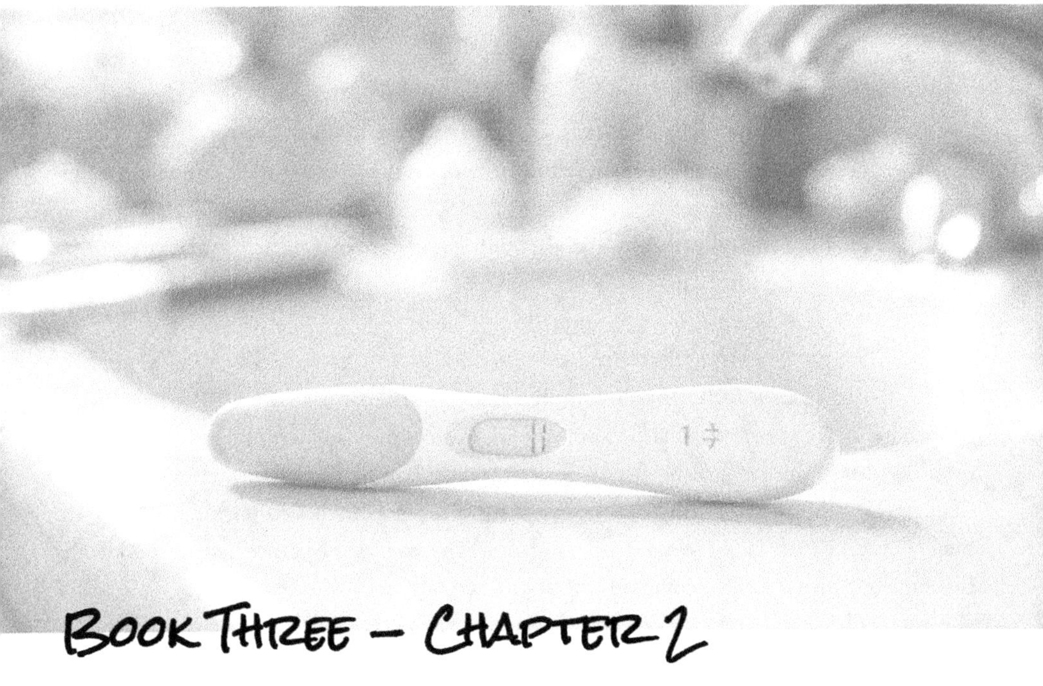

Book Three – Chapter 2

There were but a few customers in the restaurant when Marci and I met in the lobby. Chit-chatting as the hostess took us to our table, we hit the buffet before sitting down.

Back at our seats and settled in, Marci revealed why she wanted us to get together.

"Remember when we first met, our interview for your article on the problems within the department? I hadn't been out of my last rehab for long. I say 'last' because there'd been two others that didn't take — rough times. Anyway, the program that worked for me was one our union recommended, administered through Kohrmann Psychiatric Hospital."

"Wasn't that the hospital that counseled you through your mastectomy?"

"Yes, and by the way, I don't remember telling you how much I appreciated your support through that whole thing. We hadn't known each other very long, but I needed a friend."

"I'd just lost my mom after her long bout with Alzheimer's. Dad was a rock, of course, but not someone I could relate to as a woman. So, trust me, the need for friendship ran both ways."

"Seems like a lifetime ago, now," Marci reminisced, "but so many good things came out of that terrible time. Another was going back to Kohrmann for postsurgical counseling. I became good friends with the hospital administrator, a doctor named Andrew Luft, and quite a few of their staff. We've kept those relationships up over the years."

"I know Dr. Luft. I interviewed him for an article on teen suicides. He opened my eyes to the extent of the problem and how insidious it can be."

"Kohrmann serves the general citizenry and most government agencies around San Diego County, so they see it all. A criminal judge referred a patient to them for evaluation three weeks ago through their contract with the court system. They do that all the time, no big deal."

"To determine fitness to stand trial, I assume?"

"*Trials* — plural. This situation's a doozy, nothing like I've ever seen. So, the record shows a middle-aged man, physically fit and otherwise healthy. Until four months ago, he was a powerful executive in an international agency, one of the big names, something he'd done for twenty years; he has plenty of money and is well-educated. As far as we know, he's never committed so much as a parking offense in his lifetime before this. He's got peers around the world. They say he's earned their respect, but he's a head-down, all-about-the-work guy.

"Those are the parts of this that make sense. It goes screwy from there."

"What'd a guy like that do to get the court's attention and question his sanity?" I imagined a love triangle gone *seriously* bad.

"The nutzoid stuff starts right there." Marci's expression dared me to challenge her even as she relished the situation. "The number of capital murders the authorities *here* have accused him of is four."

"*Here?*"

"He's a person of interest in two more from another jurisdiction. The number *he's* claiming is sixteen and three in self-defense, plus another he says was payback, not homicide. The only accusation he's denying is killing the night manager of a motel. But get this — the guy says he and a bunch of his associates have planned what he calls 'eliminations' of a whole lot more."

"How *many* more?" A snippet from my conversations with Jeremy Hansen flitted across my brain for the first time in months. *Nobody's ever going to top that,* I thought.

"Dr. Luft wouldn't repeat the number — he said if he told me, I'd think the doctor was the crazy one." Marci smiled slyly. "But it gets better — the patient says those people will die whether authorities keep him incarcerated or not, that his associates have set everything in motion."

I raised my eyebrows. "*That's* why the judge wants a shrink to evaluate him."

"Exactly — the reaction any sane person would have, *should* have," Marci agreed. "The reaction almost everyone *does* have.

"But there *are* a couple of notable exceptions," she teased. "Dr. Luft and his staff believe this guy — every word. They've had him for three weeks solid. Every mental health professional on Dr. Luft's team who's interviewed this individual or watched his session tapes is convinced. Certain not only that he *isn't* crazy, but his story needs telling to someone who can *do* something about it."

"Fascinating...." I hadn't missed the coincidence. *Two stories coming my way unsolicited within just a few months about killing bunches of people? Am I the new mass murderer-whisperer?* For reasons I couldn't explain, I found the knowledge that the sources resided three thousand miles apart comforting.

Marci's face had turned deadly serious. "I can tell you Dr. Luft is concerned enough he reached out to me expressly because I've told him about your achievements as an investigative journalist. I haven't heard the full story yet, but I can see in the good doctor's eyes he finds the situation threatening."

"Marci, it's obvious this matters to you." I didn't want her to think I was taking this lightly. "So, of course, I'm in. But what would they expect of me? You've said there's more to it...."

"The little I understand says there's a lot left to learn. And it's possible that even if their patient isn't crazy, what he's telling them could be. Or maybe the whole thing's unworkable at some level, so there's no problem."

"They're wanting, what, my opinion? I'm not exactly an expert on who is, or is not, crazy." I was puzzled.

"They've already come down on the side that he's not, at least in any way that affects his truthfulness. And that's where you come in. Dr. Luft wants someone with real investigative experience, outside the strictures of law enforcement, to take a hard look at this man's tale. They think the only way to protect the public is to publish the information."

"The patient's okay with that?"

"Yes, he's signed off on it. And there's the rub. Their work at the clinic revolves around keeping the affairs of their patients private — they have no expertise in seeking out publicity.

"You, on the other hand, regularly evaluate the newsworthiness of information and its potential public interest. You know people who can either verify or disprove critical parts of this man's story. Those are the services Kohrmann Psychiatric wants to ask of you.

"They can determine if the man is rational and, beyond that, honest in his beliefs. They think the answer to both of those questions is 'yes.' After that, the problem is that his beliefs are alarming but pertain to things outside the hospital's fields of expertise. That's where they need help.

"They don't want you to decide anything based on my say-so. They only want to know if you're open to discussing this with Dr. Luft and his staff."

"Okay, *that* I can do. Tell Dr. Luft I'd be happy to talk with him."

We spent the rest of our lunch dabbling in gossip and current affairs. When we stopped at the cashier on our way out, my stomach felt queasy, and my face must have shown it.

"You're looking a little peaked. You feeling all right?" Marci asked as we got into her car.

"Would you mind making a run to the CVS? I've not been feeling well, especially in the mornings. I want to get something to settle my stomach."

"Uh, girlfriend...." Marci held her head back, the smile on her face slanted to one side. "Not to pry into your personal life, but is it possible you're...."

She didn't have to finish the question. The idea startled me for a moment.

"Well, sure, I guess — I hadn't been dating for a while before Paul came back into my life, so I forget to take my pill sometimes ... Well, okay, more than sometimes ... *Oh, my God!*" I was stunned at the possibility.

"You might pick up a pregnancy test while you're in the drug store," the pitch of Marci's voice went up and back down like she was playing her words on a tonette.

"Go in with me, will you, Marci? I don't even know the best kind," I pleaded.

"Of *course*, since it was my idea — never a dull moment." Marci chuckled.

———◇———

I'd been pacing the floor of my apartment for an hour when Paul texted me to tell me he was home.

"Paul, could you drop over as soon as you can? Something's come up," I texted back.

Book Three — Chapter 3

Several hours after I shared my unexpected news with Paul, Dr. Luft's office reached out to set up a meeting for the following day. With the request coming from Marci and Dr. Luft, I had to take it seriously. However, my takeaway from what Marci told me was equal parts intrigue and skepticism. What could a serial killer, especially one requiring a mental health evaluation, say to a psychiatrist of Dr. Luft's expertise to raise this level of concern?

His office administrator clarified that I wouldn't engage the patient during our first meeting. It would be me, her, and Dr. Luft discussing my services as a consultant.

"Good morning, Ms. Wynn; nice to see you again." Dr. Luft stood at the end of the white Formica conference table, gesturing to a seat on the side nearest him. "It was what, two years ago, we talked about teen suicide?"

Clean-shaven, of average height with short, gray hair, and wearing glasses and a white lab coat, Dr. Luft vaguely resembled Ryan Reynolds, with the same welcoming smile.

"Please, 'Debra Ann.' I feel like I'm among friends here." I nodded to his office administrator. "Time flies so quickly. It *has* been a couple of years. I appreciated your insights and help with the article. When I heard yesterday that you needed my assistance, I couldn't say no."

Reaching across the table with her hand extended was a shorter, middle-aged woman with her chestnut hair up in a bun and wearing a gray business suit.

"Debra Ann, my administrative assistant, Louise," Dr. Luft said. "I believe you've spoken over the phone."

"It's nice to meet you, Debra Ann," Louise offered as we shook hands. "I'll be taking notes if you don't mind. We'll be asking you to do some consulting for the hospital. If there's a meeting of the minds, as they say, I'll use my notes to write up a contract. Does that work for you?"

"Absolutely. I'm curious what you'd have me do."

"Let's get at it then." Dr. Luft took his seat, and we followed suit. "How much did Sgt. Robbins tell you about this patient and his situation?"

"Just that they've indicted him for multiple murders, and the victim count varies by who you believe. Marci says he's made claims about future homicides, which are unbelievable enough, 'crazy,' in lay terms, to land him here for psychiatric evaluation. The problem, as I understand it, is that after your staff interviewed him, there's concern some of his statements may be truthful. Enough that you're reaching out for validation and possible publication of his story."

"That's a pretty good synopsis." Dr. Luft had an approving look on his face.

"Marci and I go back a long way," I replied. "I don't know many people who are more attentive or have better communication skills."

"You'll get no argument from me; we could use a few more like her. So, with that foundation, let me tell you some things you don't know.

"But first, we'll need to cover the ground rules. I recall from our previous interview that you're familiar with HIPAA regulations regarding patient rights to confidentiality. Beyond those rights, our clinical evaluation contract with the county constricts us in what we can say or do as a hospital. We must also respect the patient's Fifth Amendment rights, protecting him from self-incrimination.

"At the same time, the hospital must consider medical ethics and various legal obligations. One of those is to report anything we feel within our professional judgment may place others at immediate risk of serious harm."

"I'm assuming you think that ship's sailed." I could see Dr. Luft's dilemma. "You've learned something from this patient that's caused a conflict with the latter requirement?"

"Exactly. From a clinical perspective, this patient has notable issues. I can't tell you what those are, of course. I couldn't, for example, say that an individual is antisocial or a narcissist with sociopathic tendencies. Or that he lacks empathy and struggles with social interactions. Even if I could, I might want to avoid injecting confirmation bias.

"But I can reveal the issues he doesn't have. We don't see any support clinically for saying he's a pathological or compulsive liar or delusional — that is, schizophrenic. He's not psychotic. He isn't excessively paranoid, given the story he wants to tell. I don't believe he's seeking negative attention for its own sake — in other words, for any reason other than self-preservation."

"'Self-preservation?'"

"It's complicated." Dr. Luft pursed his lips. "Let's just say he's relying on incarceration to keep himself alive."

"Now, *there's* a choice I hope I never have to make." *The situation keeps getting more and more interesting,* I thought.

"His problems don't include hallucinations or gross deceptions directed at himself or others. Regardless of whether some illusions he harbors may be grandiose, he's not insincere in his belief in or commitment to them. The story he tells hasn't advantaged him in any way — he's being cast publicly as a lunatic and stripped of his freedom, resources, reputation, and connections to power.

"We can't attribute what he says to any known disease, incapacity, injury, or susceptibility to outside influence.

"So, what was it Sir Arthur Conan Doyle said in his writings of Sherlock Holmes? 'When you've eliminated all which is impossible, then whatever remains, however improbable, must be the truth.' By that logic, we're facing down a truth that seems improbable. But if it *is* reality, also very concerning."

"Marci used the word 'alarming,'" I said. "I got the idea you're not sure of your footing because what this man believes is outside your practice areas."

"That's on target. We're alarmed — if you permit me the liberty, I'll speak for my entire team — because when we do crude research, googling things the patient has told us, we find significant real-world factual support on the Internet."

Boy, *that* sounded familiar.

"But then again, we're not experts," the doctor added.

"How would I know what questions to ask so he'll repeat what he's told you?" I wondered.

"Fortunately, you don't have to. Our work product belongs exclusively to the courts under our contract with them.

"While I can't grant you access to our professional conclusions, I *can* provide you with the redacted session tapes we used to develop them. You can make any personal assessments from those. I understand the patient's made the same assertions to several attorneys he's sought out for help. He's also sworn to and signed statements given to investigators from two police jurisdictions. We have plenty of cover there.

"Clinically speaking, from the perspective of traits he *doesn't* exhibit — those I may divulge — what worries me is when he delves into areas we know well. Those engage topics like manipulation, including coercion and persuasion, psychological triggers, and motivating behaviors in other people. He's *not* exhibiting any ignorance, ineptitude, or incapacity in those subjects that would preempt or render impossible the things he's claiming.

"It would violate HIPAA requirements for me to say his history and makeup demonstrate a unique intelligence and strong work ethic. But I can't prevent your assumption that such characteristics might've contributed to me seeking your help."

"I understand the need for obfuscation. I also understand the difference between 'possible' and 'real.'" The nuances of the conversation were making things tricky. "If I were to hazard a guess, that's where the crux of the problem lies?"

"Yes. We've no standing contractually to investigate the man's statements other than from the perspective of patient care or evaluation," Dr. Luft explained. "We can only explore the man's current mental status and extrapolate his likely state at given points in his history and future, using our clinical expertise.

"However, the hospital's fiduciary and security interests require us to take steps to protect us from potential general liability. In other words, to keep from being sued. That requirement allows preemptory investigations and reports."

"And that's what you'd want from me? To look into what he's saying, like I, as an investigative reporter, might verify a source? Determine what risk exists for the public?"

"Yes, to both. We'd like you to do a plausibility study and report but with a potential Easter egg. Once we've compensated you for your time, efforts, and expenses, we expect a statement of findings detailing any threat you perceive in what you learn. That covers our derrieres and says we did in good faith what we could under the rules.

"If it proves likely nothing harmful would come from anything this man says, end of story — for you, literally. But if you find something newsworthy, you're free to write and publish anything you wish, so long as it doesn't violate patient confidentiality. The intellectual property engendered by anything you create remains yours."

I felt that familiar yet thrilling tug of a promising story pulling at me.

"We have a not-so-hidden agenda in releasing you from some of the usual constraints," the doctor added. "From what we can see, there aren't any government agencies with the laws in place, motivation, or the scope of authority necessary to stop what the patient says is going on. Incentivizing you to publish this material is the only way to bring it to the public's attention. We don't think there'd be any government response without first generating community awareness."

"Am I permitted a face-to-face session with the patient? I want to get an intuitive sense — call it a 'gut feeling' — for myself where he's coming from and any ulterior motives he may have. It's part of my investigative approach."

"He'd have to be made aware you are not a clinician and that he has the right of refusal. But we can make that request. I suspect the patient wants his story told, as he explains in some of the session tapes, to protect himself."

"I'd like to have Marci — Sgt. Robbins — attend any sessions I have with the patient. She wouldn't be acting in an official capacity. She has skills and experience evaluating criminals for truthfulness, whereas mine relate more to the general public."

"That covers the bases for us, too," Dr. Luft agreed. "Once we inform the patient and he consents, we can include her. We'll compensate Sgt. Robbins for her time and expenses as part of the agreement. So, would you be willing to do this, or would you like more time to decide?"

I hesitated momentarily, wanting to honor the request with its just consideration.

"Frankly, I'd be a fool not to take you up on your generous offer. I assume you won't have this patient forever, and you'd need me to get started pretty quickly. I'm working on another project, but it's a spec piece — I can put it off to the side for this."

"We hoped you'd be interested." Louise handed me a small external computer drive and a cable.

"We've copied the session videos to this USB drive — it's more secure than transmitting them. You'll see individual MP4 files with the patient's name, the court's case number, and the time and date stamp. There are also copies of intake forms, where we've redacted some of the information per the requirements we have to live by. They'll be in chronological order.

"You're welcome to this drive as our gift, but we ask that you destroy its files once you've finished with them out of respect for the patient's rights. I'll draw up an agreement and send it to you this afternoon. It'd be great if you'd review it and make any necessary markups."

"Debra Ann, I appreciate you doing this," Dr. Luft said as we ended the meeting. "I think you'll understand why once you review the session tapes. Call Louise or me directly if you have questions. I'll chat with the patient about your involvement. Louise will help negotiate the logistics if he approves."

Louise handed me her contact information. "I know people in your profession work odd hours, so I've included my home number."

And with that, the fortune-teller had laid her cards out on the table — my destiny was about to converge with that of one Mr. Frank Spector.

Book Three — Chapter 4

The possibilities around this story fascinated the investigative journalist in me. But I knew enough of Dr. Luft and his reputation to realize the gravity of the situation.

First, some housekeeping; once back in my apartment, I cranked up my computer and made backups of the videos from Louise's USB drive. Next, I'd talk to Marci — her shift wouldn't start for another hour and a half.

"Good afternoon, Debra Ann," Marci answered, "I've been on pins and needles hoping you'd call — I'm so curious to hear how Paul reacted to the big news!"

"Oh, Marci, he was great, he truly was… I was *so* nervous by the time he came home; it seemed like forever. I kept thinking it was too soon after he lost Cindy; he needed more time to grieve. I worked myself into quite a tizzy. I started worrying about crazy things, like, 'Oh, my God, what if he thinks I got pregnant on purpose to replace her?'"

Marci gave a little snort. "Hormones. Paul's not the kind to think that way…."

"Oh, I know. But it was such a shock to me — imagine how Paul might feel. So, I sat him down on the couch, holding his hand, and told him.

"And he was terrific. First, he seemed relieved, which I hadn't planned on, so it freaked me a little. He told me later *he* was worried that I would reveal something terrible going on with me. After I thought about it, that made sense, given what happened to Cindy. He just looked at me for the longest time with his head cocked to one side, a little half-smile on his face.

"Then he breaks out into this big grin and says, 'And I thought it was going to be hard enough to agree on a name for the *dog!*'

"And that was it — Paul wanted to know how I found out, and your presence got mentioned. And then we talked about what we needed to do, whether we're going to get an ultrasound and do a gender reveal, all that stuff. Stayed up all night making plans."

"Oh, Debra Ann, I'm so happy for you and Paul! That's going to be the luckiest kid ever." Then came what we call her "mother-in-law" voice. "Ahem. I assume you'll name the baby after me — you can use Marcus if it's a boy…."

I chuckled.

"Hey, you have to plant the seeds early if you're going to have a shot!" Marci was cackling with laughter. Then, she went quiet for a moment before changing the subject.

"Did you meet with Dr. Luft? How'd it go?"

"Wait, you knew I was calling you about that?"

"I'm a police officer; we divine things." Marci laughed. "Danny's up in Sacramento with other firefighters for training. Dr. Luft's patient randomly killing bunches of people was the next most interesting thing I could think about other than your baby."

"Perfect — you're invited to a private screening marathon on your next day off if you've got the time. Dr. Luft's admin gave me their interview sessions with this patient — the man's name is Spector … Frank. Paul's working the night shift, so we'd own the remote control."

"Oh, Spector, of course; I was on duty the morning they booked him. He's an East Coast import who took out three Varrio Logan Heights bangers and the night clerk at the Seville Motel.

"That's not something most people want on their résumé, but it says the man's no poser when it comes to killing people. Maybe the future homicides he and his associates set up include the gang he had the gun battle with?

"I'm off Wednesday, so count me in. I'll bring the popcorn. Oh, and yarn, needles, and a book on knitting booties."

The videos were mesmerizing from the start. Marci and I sat transfixed as Spector, guided by questions from the therapist, calmly stepped through the transition from murdering fourteen citizens two decades ago to an up-and-coming ad exec. In the video, Spector showed polish and remained collected despite his circumstances. He might have been a talking head on a PBS documentary if not for the subject and surroundings.

But what he said ten minutes in absolutely floored me.

Spector's demeanor became almost tutorial as he described his recruitment into the Hodin cabal … and the power of his position at PWW.

I sat there, too stunned to move, the bowl tipping, popcorn spilling out onto my lap.

Spector is the cabal implant at PWW that Jeremy Hansen told me about … he'd also have to be the man Jeremy knew as 'John Masters!' Jesus….

As Spector began detailing how the Hodin cabal was actively killing people, staging their demise, and exploring new ways of dispensing with human beings in volume, I broke out in a cold sweat. The statement was in lockstep with Jeremy's story, though it had different backing sources, references, and examples.

Finally, I had some validation of the overarching premise from two independent sources — now *I* was seriously alarmed.

"Debra Ann, what's wrong?" Marci's expression was worried. "You look like Jeffrey Dahmer asked you to lunch."

Her concern brought me back to the real world. I grabbed the laptop I'd used to run the video and paused the replay.

"Marci, you will *not* believe it, but I've heard this all before," I said. "Something Harry Sanderson asked me to look into a few months ago. I thought it was dead on arrival when our subject disappeared, and I didn't have enough to move forward."

I filled Marci in on all the salient points of my conversations with Jeremy and Jennifer, ending with the vicious murder of Danny Boy.

"Oh, my God — I get why you couldn't do anything with Jeremy's story, but *damn*, now this.…" Her voice trailed off; she, too, was unnerved.

Still, despite my visceral reaction to hearing the same stories from someone else, I knew I'd need more. Since Masters was the source of most of what Jeremy told me, Spector's claims didn't validate the underlying facts. They did confirm Jeremy as a reliable communicator and truthful about where he got the information.

I rewound the video to Spector's descriptions of supportive online links. I tried following along with the notebook's browser when he'd mention the title of an Internet article. That didn't work out well — I had to interrupt the video constantly.

Once the first several references proved relevant and from reputable sources, I didn't want to miss any of his words. I could return to the videos later to inventory and validate the rest of the Web postings he mentioned. I'd quickly note the headlines that jumped out at me for now.

One thing Spector said surprised me — that the cabal could twist the best things that ever happened to someone into homicide.

"Want to destroy a family, or any set of relationships, with real hostility? Let one member of the group win millions in a lottery."

Spector referenced a Wikipedia article about murdered lottery winner Abraham Shakespeare.

"It's a very effective way to tear apart a social circle. How 'great' a significant event is supposed to be is irrelevant — the damage is in the imbalances it creates. Unfortunately, creating lottery winners randomly among the citizenry to encourage mass murder is costly; it pools too many of our resources into a single initiative."

The revelation was not news to Marci.

"It isn't always homicide, but we get two or three cases of abuse, some of them brutal, every year around either lottery winnings or claims of fraud over the purchase of a big Powerball ticket."

It was another corroboration in what would be a long string of them.

Spector spoke at length about how the cabal leveraged excess weight in some of its initiatives — not encouraging when you've just learned you're pregnant and about to put on pounds. I grimaced.

"Obesity's a filter for determining who'll be among our one billion survivors. There are many opportunities for leveraging the symptoms of unhealthy weight to maximize untimely deaths. More than two out of three U.S. adults are overweight. More than one out of three is clinically obese."

Spector referred to an article from Harvard's School of Public Health.

"The problem distributes evenly across economic classes, and it's a major factor in natural deaths. The federation's pharmaceutical partners price effective anti-obesity drugs like Wegovy outside the reach of most insurance plans. By manipulating cost, availability, and compounders, the coalition fine-tunes which income levels are allowed access."

Spector now began tying in links from the highlight reel Jeremy gave me. Though I'd noted those web pages then, Jeremy hadn't delved into obesity, the lottery, or the other things Spector was describing now.

"Weight loss supplements are an easy way to deliver toxins to an audience that isn't very discriminating," he went on, directing the attending therapist to an Internet piece from *NBC News* about poisonous ingredients discovered in some products.

I wasn't expecting Spector's mention of Martin Shkreli among the cabal's supporters and partners. He alluded to a Wikipedia article about the famous Turing Pharmaceuticals investor whose conviction of fraud and conspiracy in 2017 made him "the most hated man in America."

"Greed is to medicine what rape is to relationships," Spector asserted.

"A fundamental violation of trust that no more advances humanity than having rabies improves the genomes of canines. Let me say the quiet part out loud: What most people in the U.S. die of is having the worst healthcare system in the free world — that is, the most mercenary. But if 'Pharma Bro' hadn't been such a *chazir*, that could have been a very productive relationship for him and the federation's depopulation efforts."

Spector's tone expressed genuine regret.

I think Marci and I shared the same sense of foreboding — for her, the gradual movement away from the theoretical toward the could-well-be-possible was something new. I'd already made the transition during Jeremy's interviews.

"I didn't know an organization like this existed," Marci said quietly. "Even if I had, I wouldn't have expected this level of nuance, maturity, or sophistication. What Spector's claiming isn't a bunch of wild-eyed fanatics killing everybody at first sight — it's layered, well-planned, deliberate."

"Many of our initiatives act much like meat tenderizers," Spector said right on cue in the video to support Marci's comment.

"They make things more favorable for coming initiatives, to break down resistance and give them better chances of success." He mentioned a Web link to another relevant source article describing massive quantities of dangerous fumes escaping from consumer products.

"Must these depopulation or birthrate-reduction resources already be in production or manufactured by someone else?" the therapist in the video asked.

"Not at all," Spector responded. "But having off-the-shelf options available does cut development time and expense. In the same vein, some things we do require relatively little processing. For example, when inhaled, bone dust from decedents with cancers and other diseases can cause respiratory illnesses, even fatalities." I recognized the source he quoted to the therapist as another listing from the highlight reel.

"Once ground into a fine powder," Spector continued, "the federation disperses the resulting dust directly into the environment as an aerosol, combines it with foods as a filler, or adds it to construction materials. Operatives mix the powder with fluids and distribute the result as a liquid for drying out afterward, either naturally or using a desiccant. They form the bone dust into solids for later crushing back into a powder.

"Hodin coalition members who operate funeral homes and crematoriums produce the dust for us — some of the larger conglomerates control thousands of those facilities."

Book Three — Chapter 5

Neither Marci nor I had prepared for the man's intensity or his message. We'd gotten into our Frank Spector video binge-slash-marathon believing we'd see someone on the edge of crazy, a bit of droll relief from the humdrum.

But whatever else he may have been, Spector wasn't any form of deranged anyone would find light and entertaining. And while I'd had Jeremy's interviews to forewarn me, the younger man had been no murderer. Jeremy's vibe had been one of "Look, it was a job, and I didn't fully understand what I was getting into until I was already hip-deep." Spector, however, was at the other extreme.

It frightened me that if you stripped mass homicides out of the picture, Spector made sense. He demonstrated intelligence, awareness, and competence for long stretches. But the sheer seriousness of the man's beliefs and claimed actions was emotionally draining. And it felt like a punch to the gut when you considered that the people he'd eliminate from the planet were you, your loved ones, your friends, your coworkers, and your future progeny.

We'd decided to take a twenty-minute break from the first batch of videos.

"Marci, if I hadn't committed to doing this for Dr. Luft," I said, "and weren't a journalist, I'd think about bailing out right now.

"I sucked you into this as my protector and an experienced set of eyes to help me process things. But this is way more than I thought it'd be — you shouldn't have to sit through this on your day off. I need to give you a reprieve."

"Honey, I appreciate the thought," Marci answered solemnly.

"You're right; this is some *serious* shit. But even if we weren't friends and I hadn't promised to back you, I'd still want to see it through. People doing bad things is what I got into law enforcement for. Whatever we thought this would be when we started, everything we've heard says this threatens our world, our lives, and the people around us — my God, *everything* we care about! Like it or not, I decided long ago to be right in the middle of things like this, doing whatever I could to help. I need to hear what else this man has to say.

"But I gotta tell you, Debra Ann, if I still drank, I'd have a tall one right about now…."

"Honestly, I'm glad you're hanging in with me." I was more grateful than she'd ever know. "If I thought about it too much, I'd get overwhelmed. From here on out, I'll keep the blinders on and stay with the task laid out by Dr. Luft.

"Otherwise, were it not for Junior-ette," I put one hand on my tummy, "I'd have to open a bottle myself."

And then I got one of my better ideas.

"How about sharing a tub of ice cream instead?"

"Deal!" Marci's answer was instant and enthusiastic.

Setting out the hand-packed quart of Braum's Rocky Road, I dug through the fridge for the dill pickles. I'd started having those cravings I'd always heard about.

Marci and I were wise to finish our ice cream before we returned to those films.

We're both animal lovers — Marci's boys have had every creature under the sun as pets, including ferrets, rabbits, and at least one snake. Rusty, my beloved Chihuahua and cocker spaniel mix, had been my companion for sixteen years before I had to put him down a few years ago. My heart hadn't been ready to replace him, but Paul and I committed to getting a puppy to grow with the baby.

So, it was discomforting that Spector's next session video delved into zoonotic diseases, transferable from other animals to humans, described in a highlight reel link.

"The presumed escape of COVID-19 from a Wuhan wet market taught the world about the power and potential of animal-to-human transfer. We'd long been playing with the sight-unseen incubation of deadly viruses, bacteria, and parasites in family pets for eventual transfer to human owners. It's proven to be a promising initiative."

Spector suddenly grinned. "An early experiment transferring parasites from house cats to otters got away from us — one of the news outlets ran a piece about it." Ah, the highlight reel again.

It didn't satisfy Spector to stop there.

"Among our CRISPR gene editing initiatives, those based on fungi — 'mold' to most people — have been very successful. We've already released several initiatives and are working on others. One of our pet projects is airborne broadcasting from drones high in the atmosphere. Fungi spores are tiny, almost indestructible. They can travel in air or water and on land via creatures large and small since spores survive digestion.

"The fungi initiative should have nearly the same killing power as our microplastics chemistry program. For both projects, our major challenge is protecting the one billion survivors from downstream effects. However, the shotgun fungi initiative is not as far along as our two-pass binding-agents-and-payloads program."

With a sly smile, Spector provided the Google keywords to download an article to the counselor's cellphone. He seemed amused by the therapist's reaction to the visual that popped up, revealing a sense of humor that leaned into the sick and disturbing. The lead image of a decaying dead frog evoked a surprised "Eew!" from Marci as she drew back, her nose wrinkled and her lips curled in disgust.

"One of the federation's engineered mutations of *Batrachochytrium dendrobatidis* escaped into the wild." Spector was grinning broadly. "It kicked the spread of *Chytridiomycosis* among amphibians in Africa into high gear. No one else knew a fungal infection could affect hundreds of species."

"Dr. Luft could tell us, but I think animal torture is a clear sign of antisocial personality disorder." Marci's tone was caustic. "Thinking it's funny damned sure is."

Spector mentioned another of the links from his highlight reel.

"We've released several engineered fungi variants as individual initiatives. Some have succeeded enough to make the news. *Candida auris* has great killing potential, can be carried place-to-place on human skin, and resists several drugs and disinfectants.

"You should avoid hospitals," he said to the therapist, his helpful expression disingenuous, "unless you're an intended survivor with access to the antidote."

***

Several hours later, Marci and I finished the last of Frank Spector's session videos. We were emotionally and physically exhausted, down to our very bones — so much so that for the last hour and a half, we'd just sat there somber and silent, too numb to say anything.

But as we were packing up and saying our goodbyes, Marci offered a thought.

"The cruelty of the things Spector finds amusing reminds me of something. Maybe the third or fourth weekend I'd had the boys after Steve loosened up on the custody arrangements. It was summer — hot. Trying to save on electricity, I had a window fan set on high and running in the dining room off the kitchen.

"Matt and Mike were having trouble with a bully at school. I was *so* naïve back then. But I wanted to show I was a great parent, so I had the bright idea to invite this kid over. With a name like Gavin, no wonder he had social adjustment issues. He'd see what good kids Matt and Mike were, that they were no threat to him — so went the plan. If worse came to worst, I'd make sure Gavin caught sight of my service weapon in its holster, let him consider the consequences."

"Doesn't sound like a bad plan...," I said truthfully.

"It didn't quite work out the way I'd hoped. I'd made burgers for the kids. We're sitting at the dining room table. The conversation became heated, so I grabbed my two and pulled them into the living room for a talk. Now left to his own devices, Gavin squirts a full squeeze bottle of ketchup into the window fan."

"Jesus, *seriously?*" I exclaimed at the mental imagery.

"Everything in the dining room and that side of the kitchen was coated with fine drops of red sticky goo. Then, of course, Gavin runs home, covered in ketchup. He tells his mother my boys dumped it on him — while I supposedly watched, laughing.

"When my fellow cops arrived at my home, to my eternal mortification, I was lucky the truth was so obvious. I hadn't yet begun undoing the damage he'd done, and Gavin had a reputation with them he couldn't scrub clean. My little introduction to someone who just can't be fixed. Sure, I'd seen it on the job, all the time, but not in a kid in my own home." She paused.

"Spector comes off all cool, calm, and collected — almost *too* logical. But I can't get the picture of that bully with the ketchup bottle out of my head. Guy's so fucking mad at the world on a fundamental level, and for reasons we'll likely never know, that all he wants to do is destroy everything around him. No regard for anybody or anything. He'd have found some way to keep killing people with or without the Hodin cabal.

"But you know what worries me the most? I *get* why Dr. Luft feels he has to go the extra mile with this — I haven't a single doubt in my head that Frank Spector and this cabal are for real."

It was late, but I knew Harry would be working — I hoped he'd make an exception and take an outside call after ten. He needed to know the latest developments. Most importantly, Frank Spector's relationship with Jeremy Hansen might help Harry locate his client and Jeremy's girlfriend. But I also needed a favor from him. Before my interview with Spector, I wanted to impose on Harry's expertise to ferret out whatever he could learn about the man.

Harry picked up by the second ring. "Debra Ann, I don't often hear your voice at this late hour. To what do I owe the pleasure?"

"Harry, you won't believe this, but something unexpected just dropped into my lap…."

THE WRITINGS OF
AVRIL MARIA SERENE

BOOK THREE — CHAPTER 6

Louise called me on Dr. Luft's behalf early the next afternoon to schedule the face-to-face interview with Frank Spector. Because Spector was a prisoner awaiting trial on murder charges, we'd hold our discussion in the hospital's secured wing. I'd have Marci, a staff therapist, and a hospital security team member joining me. They'd scheduled the interview for seven p.m. next Tuesday — the late hour would be less disruptive for employees and patients, some of whom didn't handle breaks in their routine well.

Louise also had a surprise for me — Web and server links, with passcodes, to a treasure trove of research materials. They included an updated copy of Spector's highlight reel, something he'd offered as a gift when he learned of our interview.

Unpunished until he'd dramatically revealed himself at a police precinct back in Boston, Spector had been a prolific serial killer in the DNA-literate age of crime fighting. He'd demonstrated that irrespective of what anyone thought of his beliefs, he was not stupid. Neither of the defense attorneys Spector interviewed in Boston had patted him down or asked if their potential client was recording the conversation.

Spector provided Dr. Luft with Internet links and passkeys to three encrypted digital audio files hidden among those on a website he owned. One recorded his meeting with Bill Clymer; the others memorialized two sessions with Chris Patterson.

The miscellaneous website files included Spector's personal work journal and a massive haul of raw data. Spector had snapshots of nearly all the data generated during the cabal's development of its initiatives. He'd been copying it from PWW and cabal servers for nineteen years.

After Louise and I finished our conversation, I dug into the links she'd sent me. The scope of the raw data was impressive, a little over sixteen terabytes. I could only scrounge four terabytes of free space on two external USB drives I had lying around, so I began copying over that much of Spector's data. Download speeds were slow — I'd have to leave my laptop running 24/7 over the next three days to fill up those drives.

In the meantime, I did deep dives into the Web articles and posts Spector mentioned during his therapy sessions. Fortunately, his highlight reel didn't deviate much from what Jeremy had provided me.

Finally, I was ready to meet the man.

<hr>

Marci's apartment was nearer the facility, so after we shared a light supper, she drove us to the psychiatric hospital. The high oval arcs and muted shadows engendered by powerful floodlights climbed the alabaster-and-limestone façade of the three-story main hospital building. LEDs from closely spaced lamp poles brightly lit the parking lot and surrounding grounds. As a journalist, I instinctively seek out camera placements that could help me with a story; here, they were everywhere you looked.

Access to the main entry required passing through a full-body scanner, handbag conveyor, and x-ray system. Once inside, the entryway expanded out into a small waiting area.

Across from the front door was a recreation room — yoga mats and the end of a ping-pong table were visible as we gathered our belongings from their plastic tubs. Dr. Alan Thorson, a staff psychiatrist, and Martin Campbell, a hospital security officer, greeted us in the waiting area. After we introduced ourselves, Dr. Thorson explained that the hospital consisted of two wings. Doctors and administrators officed in the half of the building to our right. The remainder of that wing was devoted to rooms occupied by long-term ambulatory patients who posed no threat to themselves or others.

Our group, however, turned to the left. Just ahead of the heavy steel door were security offices on both sides of the hallway — several uniformed officers glanced our way to acknowledge our presence. There was a solid metal clang as the electronic door lock released to allow us entry to the wing; another security officer joined our group as we passed through.

"I'll apologize for the extreme security measures we employ in this half of the building," Dr. Thorson said, "but they're an absolute requirement. We serve the community at large, as well as law enforcement, via the judicial system. In this wing, we house those who would otherwise be incarcerated or represent a severe risk of harm to the staff or the public.

"Security precautions in the area we'll be in are, of necessity, draconian. We've had patients try to gnaw off their own hands and feet to escape their restraints. As I believe you're aware, Mr. Spector is a ward of the county charged with several homicides. Regulations require we keep him secured. While I don't believe the man represents any immediate danger to you, the number and nature of his alleged and claimed offenses require extreme caution."

We entered a locked room with a small square of wired, tempered security glass in the heavy door and a single barred window on the far wall. A thick canvas-like material covered the padded walls.

Frank Spector sat manacled on a flat polypropylene bench, its edges rounded off, his chains running through a large steel ring welded to the top of the rectangular stainless-steel table set up for our interview. Fluorescent tubes in the ceiling cast a harsh, unnatural white light on the table. The only other furniture was a bunk bed frame stripped of its mattresses and pushed into the corner.

Marci, Dr. Thorson, and I sat on a bench opposite Spector. Campbell and the other security guard stood, taking positions in the corners on each side of the door.

Spector seemed older and less energized than in his session videos. But as the conversation began, he gradually asserted the intellectual domination he'd exhibited on tape.

I began our talk by reviewing notes from my interviews with Jeremy. Initially surprised his colleague had been talking with a reporter, Spector didn't dispute Jeremy's accounts other than to make a few factual corrections.

"That's what I know to this point," I concluded. "Most of what Mr. Hansen told me originally came from you, so it's essentially hearsay. Mr. Hansen isn't available to finish his narrative. So, I'm here asking you for information I can use to confirm what I've already heard. Or that adds useful detail. Are you willing to divulge more about the Hodin cabal's activities?"

Spector didn't answer the question directly. Instead, he complained that the media hadn't given his efforts enough credit.

"People go out of their way to avoid acknowledging just how successful we've been, and we're only getting started."

"I'll assume by 'we,' you mean the cabal," I clarified, but Spector didn't acknowledge my statement.

"How many people do you know who suffer from cancer?" he questioned.

"Or mental disorders, incurable diseases, organ failures, including the heart and vascular system, addictions, dementia, sexually transmitted diseases, or crippling disabilities for which doctors have no answer?"

I contemplated interrupting him to say I'd heard all this before but held my tongue.

"And how many others are known by those in your circle to have one or more of these issues? Does anyone die peacefully in their sleep any more of natural causes?"

That must be the cabal's standard introductory spiel to outsiders — nearly word-for-word, the same argument Jeremy made when I first met him. I didn't want another philosophical debate, but I'd need to establish some rapport with Spector before he'd give me what I came for.

"The fact I may not know the cause for something doesn't translate automatically to the cabal being responsible." I made it clear he'd have to convince me.

"That may be so, but *something* or *someone* is responsible. Those results occur in numbers and variants never seen before and don't come from nature. But if you choose not to believe it's us, that's your right. Let me ask you straight up — do you think depopulation is a bad thing?"

"As Jeremy described it, choosing who lives or dies with no one but the cabal getting a say, the mercenary and the manipulative as survivors, causing all this pain worldwide to achieve goals that serve a tiny subset of the population? Yes, the very definition of bad. Like so many other things today, perhaps good for the privileged and elites, horrific for anyone else."

"Fair enough." Spector paused. "Then you'd agree that to stop it, you'd need to know the source — in other words, the enemy you're fighting. So, if not the federation, who, then?

"A hundred or a thousand or a million nameless entities you couldn't possibly know — *and therefore can't stop, so why try?*

"That's been society's rationale for pretending it's not happening. 'Nothing we can do; let's ignore it, and maybe it'll disappear.' That was their approach to the overpopulation problem and why things have gotten as bad as they are.

"Fortunately for the coalition, it's also been the go-to response to the federation's engineered solution. So, keep ignoring me and, by extension, the Hodin coalition. They'd *prefer* to keep things exactly as they are."

"Let's not get too far out over our skis, Mr. Spector," I retorted. "You're an admitted serial murderer under psychiatric examination for your competency to stand trial. We're a long way from knowing if what you have to say is relevant to anything. Until something's deemed worthwhile, there's nothing to ignore."

I would have offered a more cogent response, but it eluded me.

He narrowed his eyes at me and smirked. "Don't try to con an ad man, Ms. Wynn. You and your friends are here because what I've said has set off alarm bells somewhere, and rightfully so."

Our Mr. Spector is lucid and aware, I noted wryly. He certainly has this situation nailed.

"You think turning an intentionally unknowing eye will slow, much less stop depopulation? Those attitudes only *help* the federation. That ignorance is why they can do the remarkable things they do — in plain sight during the age of instant information via the Internet, no less. The underlying desire to remain unaware is the reason no one steps back from any of the many trees the coalition plants to see the entire forest."

"Even if I took what I know of your story seriously," I countered, "You claim the wheels are already in motion; you'd like us to believe we're too late to change anything."

"The first part of that is true, but the second is not — at least, not quite," Spector responded. "Even if the Hodin federation stopped their activities at this very moment, your future children are guaranteed a premature death before you ever conceive them."

I'd worn loose clothing, and Spector couldn't have known I was pregnant, but I had to admit, *that* comment got through to me. *Still…*

"Depopulation *will* happen," Spector kept on, "irrespective of who or what you choose to blame or ignore. The only thing you or anyone else can do is fight for the right to have your voices heard, selecting the survivors. As I've told anyone who'd listen, I'm here today to let you know what's happening so you can assert your vote."

"And if we don't? If we *can't?* Have you considered how your plans would affect the people you love and the world they'd live in?" I was trying to find an angle to regain control of the conversation.

"Had I not left the Hodin federation," Spector answered, "they'd have protected my family from suffering the effects of their work. But even without that protection, would I want those I care about living powerless in the miserable world we're creating with overpopulation? That I can unequivocally answer, 'no.'"

Spector then showed me his awareness extended beyond his present circumstances.

"In your recent piece on homelessness in San Diego for *USA Today*, your anonymous source expressed fear that certain local officials wouldn't hesitate to eliminate the homeless permanently. You treated the comment as an extremity of thought so vile that society would never go there. By so doing, you effectively dismissed it.

"What made you think the idea's a one-off, merely the hate-inspired thinking of a single empowered individual? Emotional reactions aside, why *wouldn't* reducing our numbers be an intelligent person's first consideration for solving problems caused or worsened by overpopulation?"

I fired back, "For the same reasons that cannibalism of one's family shouldn't be the first consideration when the problem is starvation."

My eyes bored into his, my hackles up. "We're human beings, not animals. Our purpose is to use our minds, not murder, to solve problems."

"Your accusation is that if humans address over-propagation by removing the excess, it's homicide. You might want to look over your shoulder. Right behind you is Mother Nature, and she's realized the same thing the federation has — all these humans aren't good for her planet.

"But she has no affinity for human survival in any number nor compassion in her methods. She has many tools she can bring to bear — starvation, drought, flooding, tsunamis, fires, and extreme temperatures and weather. She can spread the poisons humans have already put into the air, soil, and water. Do you think those are better ways to die because somehow you feel less threatened by them? Pay the federation now or pay Mother Nature later.

"And those products of human intellect that you're so proud of, waiting in line right behind her, are no more kind. Fourteen nation-states now have nuclear weaponry, though only nine publicly acknowledge their capabilities; more than thirteen thousand weapons, with ten thousand in active military stockpiles.

"Depopulation's not a choice." His words were unflinching, his tone firm. "It *will* happen. Only one question remains: whether the unfolding is orderly, allowing a reasonable number of the best and brightest human beings to survive with a decent follow-on existence. Mother Nature won't guarantee the latter; nuclear annihilation and winter certainly won't. The only path to any assuredness is an engineered solution managed by humans."

Marci and I exchanged glances.

"Blame the messenger if you wish, but I've gone to all this trouble and destroyed my life just to give you a voice in something otherwise out of your control. As regards global depopulation, I'm not the bad guy."

His unapologetic arrogance, given the context of present circumstances, astounded me.

Suddenly, our debate was interrupted by a loud banging noise resonating from somewhere down the hall outside our room.

There was a brief silence before excited squawking burst from the radios of the two security guards.

THE WRITINGS OF
AVRIL MARIA SERENE

Book Three – Chapter 7

Though controlled and even in its tone, there was unmistakable urgency in the intercom's warning as it blared down the hallways between rooms.

"Code Silver, Code 5, all staff, Code Silver, Code 5, all staff. This is not a drill."

As the announcement repeated, the banging sounds from just past the security wing's main door grew louder and more persistent.

"That's gunfire!" Marci exclaimed, reaching instinctively for her right hip.

But she wasn't on duty and came to our meeting unarmed.

Campbell and the other guard quickly unshackled Spector from the table, stood him up, and pushed him to the rear wall.

Running his chains up between and back through the bars on the window, they gave Spector just enough slack to sit on the floor, his back next to that wall, with his arms raised to shoulder level.

Campbell guided Dr. Thorson, Marci, and me to the corner nearest the hinge side of the door, seating us on the floor as close to each other and the wall as possible.

The guards kicked the stainless-steel table and benches away from the room's door.

Together, they grabbed the bunk bed frame from the corner and shoved it against the front of the door, jamming it at a slight angle under the door handle.

They turned the table on its side and pushed it behind the bunk bed frame, stacking the benches above it with their seats facing the door.

"What's a 'Code Silver' with a 'Code 5?'" I asked Dr. Thorson in a hushed voice.

"We have a weapon or hostage situation," he replied. "Staff and patients need to take immediate shelter in a secured area.

"We'll need to hang tight until the security chief gives us the all-clear."

I stood up and looked out the barred window, and Campbell snapped at me, "Get down!"

"Were you able to see anything?" Marci whispered.

"No, this window's in the back of the building facing the hillside. Too dark to see much."

There was a lull in the banging coming from outside the room.

We listened intently for signs of more activity in the eerie quiet, and the ringing of Dr. Thorson's cell startled us.

"Archie, good, what the heck's going on?" Dr. Thorson asked, turning to face the wall with a hand over his other ear.

His expression was earnest and focused as he took in what the caller told him.

"Oh, no." He sounded crestfallen. "Have they hurt them?

"That's good. Hopefully, that'll buy us some time."

The doctor paused as he listened some more.

"Would you let us know when they've arrived?

"Thanks for the update — stay safe."

Dr. Thorson turned to the rest of us, delivering the bad news.

"That was Archie Sims, our night-time security supervisor. We're under attack by six to eight men dressed in black head to toe, including balaclavas, carrying AR-15s, side arms, and long knives, likely professionals.

"They abducted Dr. Rodriquez and two orderlies in the parking lot as they were heading home.

"They're demanding a straight exchange of their prisoners for Mr. Spector and you, Ms. Wynn."

"Friends of yours, Mr. Spector?" Marci's voice was thick with sarcasm.

"The only people I know who'd try something like this want me dead," Spector replied, the first time I'd seen him show fear.

Dr. Thorson continued with his report.

"Archie tells me one of our men is down; otherwise, the security team's holding their own for now.

"The hostages seem unharmed, but their captors want to leave ahead of the SWAT team's arrival. They're making wild threats and amping up the volume.

"I'm told SWAT's ten minutes out, but their hostage negotiator's mobile and has made contact."

The doctor directed his attention to me.

"Our intruders have inside information you're here, Ms. Wynn, but not that there's a police officer with you. Archie says we need to keep it that way. The assailants are working with bad intel. They think this interview is happening in Mr. Spector's quarters on the third floor; they're trying to breach the door to that ward. They'll learn soon enough we're down here, but we have a little time."

"What do we have we can use to protect ourselves?" Marci asked.

"Security detail members don't carry firearms," Campbell replied. "Too much risk a patient could grab one from us.

"But we each have a Taser, a stun gun, and an expandable baton. We've also got police-issue pepper spray and zip ties. That's about it."

"I have an EpiPen and emergency injectors for tranquilizers and sedatives, two each," Dr. Thorson said.

"These are cramped quarters." Marci surveyed the room.

"Our doorway's narrow. There are five of us, not counting Mr. Spector; they'll have to come through one at a time. If they're carrying long guns, those AR-15s, we have a fighting chance of disarming them.

"We'll need to work together and swarm the first one through. Things will even up once we have their body as a shield and control of their weapon. Would you guys give up your pepper spray to Debra Ann and me?"

Both men nodded, pulling canisters from the fronts of their vests.

"Doctor, would you give Debra Ann one of your tranquilizer syringes and let me have a sedative hypodermic?"

"Gladly." Doctor Thorson handed each of us an emergency injector from a pocket of his lab coat.

"Hey, what about me?" Spector spoke up. "I'm as qualified as anyone here to take these people on."

Marci shook her head.

"No offense intended, Mr. Spector, but you're not someone I think of when I say, 'Watch my back.'"

Spector jerked on his manacles in frustration but said nothing more.

Our group went silent as we waited nervously for a breach attempt or a call saying it was over.

Suddenly, a muffled explosion came from what sounded like the basement below us. And then, without notice, darkness.

As battery-powered emergency beacons flickered on in the hallway, some muted light filtered through the safety glass in our room's door, though our hastily erected barricade blocked most of it.

Just as our eyes were adjusting, another explosion, this one much louder and very close.

Long concentrated bursts of an AR-15 firing rounds in auto mode followed, interspersed with the *zing!* of ricocheting bullets.

My heart nearly jumped out of my chest.

"They're trying to breach the lock on the door to our ward," Campbell said solemnly. "They're going to need a bigger charge. The lock mechanism's constructed of laminated Kevlar and tempered stainless steel. All they'll accomplish is making that door harder to open."

Though the thought was intellectually comforting, my heart was still racing.

"I'll bet they blew the electrical panel, hoping it would open the locks," Marci guessed.

"Then they didn't do their homework," the doctor replied. "In the early nineties, we had a child molester and murderer named Elmer Lee Nance here for a court-ordered mental health examination before trial. He left his locked room when the power went out one night. Fortunately, he didn't get outside the building. Still, the incident convinced the hospital administrator to install what was then a state-of-the-art locking system."

"What does that mean for us?" Marci asked.

"That locking system is fail-safe," Dr. Thorson replied. "We have sensors all over the building that run off battery backup or an emergency generator feed. The sensors detect fire, flood, air quality issues, or structural damage. If one of those sensors is signaling a problem when the power goes off, then the lock systems fail open so patients and staff can escape.

"Otherwise, they fail shut, meaning a control panel signal or mechanical key is required to get through a locked door. The manufacturer designed the system for maximum safety and security during earthquakes."

"If our intruders knew anything about this place," Campbell offered, "they'd have held a cigarette lighter to one of the sprinkler heads and made it go off before they cut the power."

"Probably got to a staff member for information about Spector's comings and goings," I speculated, "but didn't bother to check out anything else. Likely just assumed with a minimal night staff, you'd take the hostage deal, and they'd be out of here."

In the darkened room, reflections from the spotlights and red and blue light bars of the arriving patrol units and SWAT team danced through the bars on the window, bouncing around the walls of our room.

A sense of relief washed over us.

Knowing our attackers would have their hands full dealing with the authorities, everyone in the room, save Spector, took advantage of our respite and called our loved ones.

Paul's initial reaction was shock, then worry, and finally concern as I told him what had happened and described our present situation.

Still, it'd be almost four unsettled hours — until just after midnight — before a group of police officers and hospital staff, led by Archie Sims, could open the security ward door and free us. After the guards cleared their makeshift barrier so the security supervisor could enter the room, I hugged the big man as enthusiastically as I ever had a stranger.

Paul used his credentials with the state forensics lab to join officers at the scene so he could greet me once I finally walked out of the facility.

Danny had been watching Marci's boys for her at home while she went with me to the Spector interview. Pulling strings through his connections at the fire department, he brought Matt and Mike to meet Marci outside the hospital door as soon as authorities released her.

***

While enjoying my freedom and talking about the experience with Paul in the comfort of my apartment, I had a moment of clarity.

I realized that terrorizing as it may have been, the incident only bolstered the stories Spector and, before him, Jeremy, had told me.

THE WRITINGS OF
AVRIL MARIA SERENE

Book Three — Chapter 8

Two weeks would pass before Marci and I would see Frank Spector again. National media overwhelmed local outlets as the newsfeeds blew up over the psychiatric hospital assault. The press and the public's desire to know collided with patient privacy rights as reporters dug for any information they could get. Those of us directly involved and not in jail, including Marci and me, the two security guards, and Dr. Thorson, had to abandon our homes, seeking shelter from the storm anywhere we could.

The constant hounding for interviews everywhere any of us went meant, for me, that trying to get any work done had become impossible.

The identities of our attackers were leaking out, but not their motives. Law enforcement had diligently kept Frank Spector's name out of the news. No one had yet dug up the Hodin cabal connection, but someone would in time. Once authorities filed the charging documents, they'd become public. As soon as they did, Frank Spector's involvement would be known — it would take just a few steps from there to link him to all that had transpired in Boston.

Timing and luck would determine how much of the story the Hodin cabal and its depopulation efforts would become — and how seriously the media would take them. Other parts of the story — Spector's serial killings of two decades ago and the Boston Police Department's handling of their crack at all this — might well dominate news cycles and drive the fringe elements of the story into the shadows. I guessed that world depopulation would appear in mainstream articles only to illustrate how deranged some of Spector's beliefs were.

The damages from the assault on the psychiatric hospital were still under repair. The attack had worn out Spector's welcome at the facility, and he'd been returned to custody in the San Diego County jail to await his competency hearing. Dr. Luft arranged with the Sheriff's Department that I'd finish my interrupted interview in the jail's holding cell, keeping the press out of the picture. Marci would be with me, this time armed, in uniform, and on duty. Another armed officer would be in the cell with us, and two armed jailers would stand guard outside.

In manacles and leg chains, jailers at each elbow, Spector shuffled in, wearing the green canvas shirt and pants of high-risk inmates, white socks, and orange rubber sandals. "SDC JAIL" was stenciled prominently on the back of his shirt and the seat of his pants.

Welded from bent square tubing, the straight-back chairs in the holding cell had simple vinyl seats and an eight-inch-wide strip of padding across the seatbacks. The jailer looped a short chain through a ring in Spector's waist chains and a U-bolt on the side of the seat bottom. He ran another length of steel links through the belly chain and into an iron hoop welded to the lip that formed the edge of the gray-painted table.

Spector would have some freedom of movement but couldn't go far.

The man seemed unusually contrite and compliant today, only occasionally flashing his trademark defiance. Spector's immediate concern was that we didn't misconstrue his brief stint in a mental health facility, supplying a unique rationale for being there.

"The powers-that-be didn't want to give me the platform, relevancy, and credibility I'd gain from martyrdom through imprisonment. Assigning me to a psych unit effectively neutered my message as unreliable, rendering me no more a threat than some wacko QAnon conspiracy theorist."

"I assume that QAnon and some of the other Trumpie idiocies were your people's doing," Marci said. "Hard to feel sympathy for someone bitten by a dog they made vicious."

"No, QAnon and the rest of that garbage were pure dumb luck for the federation," Spector replied. "They've had a remarkable string of good fortune, including QAnon coming to the fore and providing cover for some of the coalition's activities."

"Let's get to it, then." I took command of the interview. "I've heard several times about your microplastics initiative and everywhere and forever chemicals. My grasp of chemistry was weak, but I get that you attach binding agents to the complex molecules of plastics and chemicals already in the human body. Then, you tie payloads in food and drink to the uniform connections those agents provide.

"I've not heard what you'll be delivering as the specific contents of those payloads."

"The range of things the federation can deliver with those initiatives grows daily," Spector replied. "For example, it surprised me how effectively we can deliver chemicals that cross the blood-brain barrier. Nicotinamide riboside, magnesium threonate, and omega-3 fatty acids can penetrate the brain and act as agents, carrying other molecules.

"Our researchers use these to disrupt the prefrontal cortex, where empathy, forgiveness, judgment, and emotions reside. Morality, fear management, and reactivity also live there. I recommend reading Dr. Judith Miller's work — it will provide a roadmap.

"The federation's question was, 'Can we create walking time bombs, turning them into family annihilators when triggered?' to support depopulation."

"I'm almost afraid to ask, but what did you learn?" I inquired, albeit reluctantly. An odd queasiness was coming over me, which I hadn't experienced before in an interview. I blamed it on Spector's personality.

"Some individuals," Spector answered, "or the circumstances they're in, are more receptive than others, but the answer to our question was a resounding 'yes!' We can turn almost anyone into a mall, school, church, concert, or synagogue shooter. You haven't realized it, but you've seen the results of our experiments all over the national and local news as the global audience becomes numb to it."

"So, this is all still experimental?"

"Not exactly," Spector replied. "The federation has dozens of payloads ready to go. We've been held back from delivering these things en masse because we must protect our intended survivors. Developing effective wide-spectrum preventatives and curatives has proven a sticking point, though we've made good progress. In the meantime, we keep adding to our inventory of payloads."

"What payloads do you have in stock now?"

"The federation has teams developing carcinogens, poisons, heavy metals, biologics, and, as I mentioned earlier, other chemicals as payloads," Spector answered.

"When I last looked, they had four quickly spreading carcinogens, several poisons, and a couple of heavy metals in sufficient quantities to distribute worldwide. They were also rapidly building inventories of two bindable infertility agents."

"How soon will the effects become known after release into the environment?"

"It's payload dependent. Many have an immediate impact, and some we intentionally slow with time-release compounding. Some cancers lie dormant for twenty years, and the buildup of certain toxins in the body, like heavy metals, can take just as long. We have to be careful with initiatives that accumulate a toxin over a lengthy period — we don't want to create a tolerance for it, the Rasputin effect.

"The consequences of our infertility initiatives also gradually increase over time. Tolerance isn't an issue with those — the full effects won't exhibit themselves until children born today are ready to bear offspring themselves."

"What might I see in a given geographic area," I asked as a realization came to me, "that would tell me the microplastics chemistry initiative is in play?"

"Spikes in certain types of cancers would be the clearest indicator," Spector replied.

"Young adults are especially susceptible because they're more likely to try new things. The microplastic chemistry initiative is better at causing or encouraging some cancers than others. There's a list of them in the highlight reel.

"For instance, colorectal cancer directly results from what someone ingests, so it's straightforward for the federation to induce using the microplastic chemistry initiative. That's just one example. Half the people alive today will be diagnosed with cancer in their lifetimes. The Hodin federation aims to increase the ratio to seven of every eight."

It was all coming together in my head — the cluster of cancers in Freddie's and Rosarita's old neighborhood. The "cancer alleys" referenced in the highlight reel links. The nurse's description of clandestine activity around that abandoned chemical facility.

"Were you or the cabal responsible for the work done in the old Monsanto plant here in San Diego after they went out of business?"

"We've had a relationship with Monsanto since the federation came into being," Spector replied.

"They provided the research for most of our initiatives around chemicals. When they folded, we leased several of their facilities. Their San Diego lab helped us create the binding agents for the microplastic chemistry initiative. They had a solid inventory of chemicals we wanted to experiment with as payloads, so we acquired that part of their campus to continue our work.

"Why do you ask?"

I've never been violent by nature, but it was on me before I saw it coming.

I *so* wanted to kill that self-satisfied, sneering son of a bitch.

A vision leaped into my brain, and I could imagine myself rising from my seat to put a bullet between his eyes with Dad's .38.

The feeling and imagery were so intense and complete that it felt real.

The vision passed as quickly as it arrived, leaving me shaking and feeling out of control of my senses.

Perhaps it was because the murderous impulse was so visceral and fleeting. Or that Spector's attitude toward the miserable, lingering deaths by cancers he caused was so … *cavalier*. Or that the novelty of the cabal's philosophy had worn off after all these interviews, the harsh reality sinking in. And morning sickness may have played a role.

But Spector's words had become terrifying to me as the sheer magnitude and volume of the things he was describing hit home. An emotional tsunami overcame me — uncontrollable thoughts of the pained grimace on Dad's face as he'd struggled to rise from the gurney during his last days. The fearful and confused vacancy in Mom's eyes before she left us, Cindy's torturous fight until the very end. What happened to Freddie, Rosarita, and their mother, and yes, the gutting of Danny Boy.

In the mix were dim glimpses of a dark and demented future my new baby could be born into.

I'd already begun feeling nervous and on edge, even unsteady, with Spector's comment about creating family annihilators. Now, as I sensed the first wave of revulsion and nausea rising, I instinctively turned to Marci for support.

But I found no comfort there. Guilt added itself to the flood of feelings — seeing Marci's countenance reminded me of her struggles with breast cancer.

What right had I to ask her for help? We'd often talked about the extra shifts she'd been taking and saving every dime she could spare for the past three years. She needed that money for cosmetic surgery, a breast implant, to repair the deep scarring from tumor removal in her left breast so she'd no longer need a prosthesis. We'd had long conversations when she and Danny first met — this strong woman was terrified of his potential reaction to seeing her without clothing.

But nothing I was thinking had anything to do with why I was here — that my thoughts were so completely out of control only made things worse.

"Debra Ann, what's wrong?" Marci had seen my distress. She turned her chair and put an arm on my shoulder.

"Marci, I don't feel well.…"

"Sergeant, can you help me get her to the ladies' restroom?" Marci asked the guard nearest the door. "She has a medical condition."

Her suppressed hostility toward Spector had melted from her face, replaced with genuine concern for me. "Take her other arm, would you?"

As the sergeant steadied me on my left side with his right hand at my elbow and his other hand holding mine, Marci supported me on the opposite side.

"Ma'am, are you going to be okay?" the guard asked me as I stumbled to the barred entryway.

"She'll be fine," Marci intervened. "There's no cross ventilation in the holding cell — if you could find a small fan, that might help a lot."

We'd made it to the women's restroom door by this time.

"We can't run an electrical cord in the cell, you understand," the officer replied, "but I know where I can get a battery-powered fan."

"That would be great," Marci said, "and if you could round up some bottled waters, she should be good."

The restroom door slowly closed behind us, and I made a beeline for the nearest stall.

Marci folded some paper towels together and wetted them. After I'd vomited, she held them to my forehead, then helped me clean myself up.

I sat on the sink counter for several minutes until I began to feel better.

"Wow, Marci, I've never had that happen before in an interview," I apologized.

"But then again, I've never had to sit there and listen while a smug, uncaring bastard described not only killing most of the world but making them horrifically sick to do it … and proud of it all, to boot! I thought about all the people I've known and loved. I couldn't stop thinking I might have lost them because of this asshole and others like him...."

"I know," Marci agreed. "It makes my blood boil just looking at Spector — that he's so unaffected by any of it gets me even madder. This Spector character is the coldest sociopath I've seen. But I've watched you take on at least one who was almost as bad — James Seaver comes to mind."

"I hate that he's going to know he got to me," I lamented.

"But it's our last chance to extract whatever we can under Dr. Luft's shield against Spector's attorneys. We've got to find out who else is involved."

"I wouldn't feel too bad about your reaction, Debra Ann. Screw what Spector and his kind think. You're human and pregnant — raging hormones go with the territory. He doesn't need to know.

"The same thing happened to me when I was carrying Matt. But with me, it was bawling my eyes out. A bug would hit my windshield, and I'd burst out crying, feeling sorry for it — I couldn't stop.

"Whenever you look into Spector's face, focus your eyes first over those chains running through that loop to his hands. It'll help keep your priorities straight as to what matters. And if he's paying attention, it'll remind him of the realities in play."

A watery smile crossed my face.

"Okay, I feel better now, Marci. I'm glad you came along, even if this hadn't happened. I'm ready to go back in there — let's see if we can get something useful out of this waste of oxygen."

"Just a word of warning from someone who deals with criminals daily," Marci cautioned. "Spector's going to think he did this to you. So, of course, he'll try to do it again."

"I hear you." I thought for a moment.

"If I play my cards right, maybe I can use that to get more out of Spector than he wants to tell."

Book Three – Chapter 9

It was vital to my purposes that I return to the meeting under my own power. Frank Spector's controlling personality meant I'd need to reestablish my authority over the interview, or he'd dictate what information I gleaned from it. Marci went in first, without me, giving me more time to comport myself.

As the guard unlocked the cell door to let me in, Spector was waiting to pounce.

"I'm sorry you're feeling poorly — something I said?"

His tone oozed mockery.

"We can reschedule for a time when you're better...."

It seemed he had a twinkle in his eye.

"Thank you for your concern, Mr. Spector," I replied, my smile as artificial as I could muster.

"But that won't be necessary. Something turned my stomach; I doubt it will last long," I added, making it a point to look the man straight in the eye so he wouldn't misconstrue my meaning.

I took my seat.

"In that vein, I *do* worry that you might not be available for future interviews.

"Now that you've made it known that you're responsible for all these painful and cruel ways of killing seven billion of us, a whole lot of people are motivated to see you gone. Among those you and the Hodin cabal have marked for elimination are most of your fellow inmates. I'm sure our fine law enforcement professionals will do their best to protect you — but there are so many more prisoners here than guards.

"It's not like it was when you were free just a short time ago, Mr. Spector," I reminded him. "Everyone, inside and out, now knows who you are, what you've done, and where you sleep. I'm guessing the only way to keep you safe long-term would be in solitary confinement, 24/7. But those things are outside my field of expertise or control."

I eyed his chains, and when my gaze returned to his face, it was with pity rather than the respect he seemed to crave.

"Shall we proceed?"

That did the trick — Spector's expression had become grim. He was leaning face-forward, his hands clasped together, forearms and elbows flat on the table.

"Yes, let's get this done."

Spector's tone was now businesslike. He seemed to realize this might be his last chance to tell the story his way.

It was time to ask detailed questions about specific individuals he'd worked with in the cabal and its partner organizations.

"Mr. Spector, unless you have something significant to add, we should discuss confirmation. I'm sure you know how this works — before I can tell your story, I have to validate the authenticity of its major parts. I'll need you to provide the names and contact information of people who'll vouch for what you've told me. Without confirmation, I can't publish any of this."

"I understand. You can start with Jeremy Hansen. He was my assistant in the federation and knows most of what I've told you."

"That would be Dennis Whitcomb, then?"

Spector's face showed surprise that I had Jeremy Hansen's birth name. Hopefully, not knowing what I already knew would keep him honest, though I didn't want to reveal too much of my hand.

"His street name escapes me. I heard it maybe once, like, a year ago."

I knew he was lying, but I couldn't understand why confirmation of a name I already had would matter to him this far in.

"Do you know how I might reach him?"

I was fishing, hoping he'd have a line on Jeremy that Harry and I didn't.

"No. Hansen's not answering his federation burner number and hasn't contacted me. He has a girlfriend, Jenny something or other. She's also with the coalition in their personnel department, but I've never had any contact information for her."

Spector hesitated and then went silent.

"In your position as you've described it to us," I said, trying to understand why he wasn't following up with other names, "you've had contact with powerful people in the cabal and partner organizations for nearly two decades. I get the secrecy with names within the organization. But certainly, you'd know who many of these people were in their public lives. If you're uncomfortable leading with the bigger guns, give me some lower-echelon folks, and I can work my way up from there."

I reviewed my notes, pulling out the list of names Jennifer gave us so I could check off any correlations with those Spector might provide. When there was a long pause without a response, I looked up at him.

"Mr. Spector?"

I saw him peering back at me with a bemused expression.

Then, right before the skin along his jawline tightened, his eyes softened for just the briefest of moments, and he smiled ever so slightly, his demeanor almost … *apologetic.*

Something in my throat made me cough, and Marci reached across the table to hand me a bottle of water.

The sudden blur of motion and noise startled me, the small room amplifying Spector's blood-curdling shriek.

His chair's steel legs screeched as they scraped the cement floor, and his chains jangled loudly against the table.

Then, the clanking and loud banging of the chair as it skidded out from under Spector when he stood up. Its metal frame bounced off the concrete, swung around on its chain, and slammed into the table leg.

I caught only the briefest glimpse of something in Spector's outstretched hand as he flailed wildly at Marci's extended right arm.

Screaming, I pushed myself away from the table as hard as possible, kicking frantically at the floor with my feet, trying to scoot my seat back.

I heard the rattling of Marci's chair as she pulled away, knocking it across the bars at the front of the cell on its way to the floor.

Spector's first thrust had slashed Marci's forearm; his second lunge fell woefully short, leaving his upper body splayed across the table.

As he tried to raise himself, two shots rang out, sounding like exploding dynamite as they reverberated between the concrete walls and steel bars.

Spector's chest dropped flat onto the table, bouncing his face off the steel surface.

The shiv he used to stab Marci clattered onto the table and then to the floor as it fell from his hand.

The uniformed officer's shot had hit him just right of center mass, punching into his right lung and clipping his sternum at a slight downward angle.

The round from the jailer outside the cell passed through Spector's right temple. It exited his neck behind the left hinge of his jaw, severing his external carotid artery.

As the acrid smell of spent gunpowder filled the room, arterial spray painted the nearby wall and floor in sharp bloody spurts, slowly subsiding to dribble into a pool forming beneath Spector's shoulder.

One of the jailers outside our lockup called over his shoulder mike for medical assistance. The guard in the cell with us grabbed a wad of the paper towels they'd brought for me and wrapped it around Marci's arm to stem the bleeding. He pulled off his uniform belt and wrapped it around the paper towels several times, providing pressure to the wound.

It amazed me how calm Marci was under the circumstances. She pulled a nitrile glove from the back pocket of her uniform with her left hand. Leaning over, she folded it carefully around the shank to examine it.

Its maker crafted it from one of the spring steel straps woven to form the webbing under a jailcell bunk bed mattress. They'd sharpened the now-bloodied rough edges by rubbing them against concrete; they'd wrapped the handle in electrical tape to cushion the grip and attach a short piece of the same steel, bent in half lengthwise, as a cross-guard.

Cadaveric spasm was keeping Spector's left fist clenched tightly. Still, I could see the corner of a white piece of paper peeking out between his thumb and forefinger.

I caught Marci's eye, and she followed my gaze to Spector's hand. As she stepped over to check it out, she motioned to the nearest uniformed guard for his help. The officer struggled to loosen Spector's death grip as Marci, using her left hand, teased out a sheet of notepaper folded into quarters. Carefully unfolding it, she revealed a cryptic message that seemed perfectly fitting.

"Yet again, you have it all backward. To me, it's *you* who no longer exists."

There were immediate cascading effects from Spector's dramatic demise, but they proved to be short-lived.

Our guards recognized the shiv Spector threatened me with as one retrieved from a routine random jail cell toss two weeks earlier. Video camera footage had captured one of their fellow jailers taping the crude knife under the lip of the holding cell table after depositing ten thousand dollars he couldn't explain into his checking account.

The follow-up investigation discovered that Spector's chances of surviving long in the facility weren't favorable anyway. Jailhouse snitches exposed not one but two plots to kill him, both schemes purportedly funded by deep but anonymous pockets outside the institution's walls.

I spoke to Marci shortly after she'd had her arm professionally rebandaged. I was puzzled why Spector chose the moment he did to kill himself.

"I don't get it, Marci. Why'd he think it better to off himself that way than give up those names? It wasn't like protecting those people would keep the Hodin cabal from killing him — we know they made at least three attempts, one when he was in the custody of Boston PD, again at the motel where San Diego PD arrested him, and finally at the hospital."

"That note and the placement of the shank tells us he'd already decided to go out in a blaze of glory before that last interview."

Marci paused.

"He didn't want jailers discovering him with a bedsheet tied around his neck in the wee hours, like Jeffrey Epstein. His timing? Your comment about spending the rest of his days in solitary confinement might have affected his thinking."

A sardonic smile crossed Marci's face.

"I've seen quite a few of these narcissistic sociopaths run through the department. It might sound simplistic, but I don't believe he wanted to share his moment in the sun. By God, this was Frank Spector's time to shine — no one else. He wasn't about to have it mucked up by anyone paying attention to more prominent names you were asking him to throw out there.

"He took it as far as he could without giving up anyone more important than himself, and then he went for the big ending."

Neighbors for blocks around had been assailed for years by the pronounced hum from an enormous but otherwise nondescript concrete block structure a few hundred yards from the Silesia City Center in Katowice, Poland. Inside its windowless confines, the volume grew to a dull roar. Massive air conditioning compressors and fans cooling tens of thousands of CPU core units in the server farm whirred along as usual; the only external evidence of their work was the random flashing of a million LEDs.

As clock faces on the public buildings of the capital city ticked past midnight to cross into February third, a scheduler application deep within one of the indistinguishable racks awoke. As the software performed its regular tasks, it flipped one of its trillions of bit flags. The status bit signaled that sixty or more days had elapsed since the third and last e-mail warning of an invalid credit card had gone unanswered.

The card number was the only payment method registered for the monthly dues owed by a cloud services account in the name of Sarah Lewinski. Without human help or intervention, one of the ubiquitous, anonymous, and unheralded bots driven by millions of daemon threads began eliminating the file sectors allocated to the expired account on its virtual server.

The scheduling daemon sent another bot racing across the wires to remove the instructions for backing up that data and to destroy the dozens of previous backups accumulated. It'd take eighty-three days for a human being to notice or express concern about the deleted files.

***

Like everything else related to Spector, his death had a personal emotional toll. After spending all that time with Jeremy and his one-time boss, I was disappointed in myself for not getting more actionable facts for the pieces I would write. Concerned about the believability of the general premise to a reader, I'd waited too long to get more specific details from either of them.

I'd have to learn from this experience, the lesson being not to delay getting validation for anything told me. There were no guarantees I'd get the opportunity to ask later.

It was also disheartening to learn I wasn't as good a judge of character as I'd thought. It surprised me that Spector chose suicide by cop. He hadn't seemed the type, and nothing I knew of his history had forewarned me.

It would be several months before I'd learn that something Spector knew but hadn't told anyone influenced his decision.

Book Three — Chapter 10

rank Spector had once been so confident of his place in the world that he'd called himself "John Masters." He'd meant it as a tongue-in-cheek reference to his self-proclaimed, though anonymous, role as the puppet master over all he surveyed. Yet he'd spend the last few months of his life in hospitals and jail cells, dismissed as a fringe lunatic, his crimes far more significant than his death.

Just two people from his personal life attended Spector's funeral — his longtime housekeeper and an estranged son he hadn't spoken with for two decades.

I interviewed the latter, Jamie, for Spector's backstory. Now a software engineer for Lockheed Martin, he told me the elder Spector was a young man when he married Jamie's mother. The relationship lasted just three months. It was Spector's only marriage of record — he'd otherwise stayed true to his reputation as an unrepentant loner.

Mother Jones purchased the rights to three lengthy articles I wrote describing the Hodin cabal and its depopulation efforts. They published them as intellectual entertainment rather than cutting news, adding caveats that much of the information was unverifiable.

As an investigative journalist, it sickened me that I couldn't run down sources to confirm essential parts of the story. However, I accepted the situation for what it was and moved on to cover other events.

Among many loose ends I couldn't resolve were the murders of Chris Patterson and her son, Jim. Boston authorities wouldn't indict anyone for those homicides. They and others assumed Frank Spector had exacted his revenge on his way out of town.

A concerted attempt by the Innocence Project, recipient of a massive influx of unexpected funding, uncovered new DNA evidence in five of the original fourteen serial homicide cases. The discoveries proved that Emile Reardon couldn't have committed at least those murders. Eventually, Reardon was set free due to insufficient evidence in the other killings.

He got his fifteen minutes of fame in a segment of a Netflix series focusing on forced confessions that weren't valid, even though he'd willingly volunteered his. Ironically, the work that freed him also revealed that Reardon had banked inordinate sums of money for intentionally deceiving investigators through his original confession. Charged and convicted of three counts of perjury and obstruction of justice, the judge ultimately sentenced him to a hefty fine and time served, with the IRS waiting in the wings and his kidneys still failing.

Only the little guy pays the full price for anything in this country. Authorities didn't charge any wealthy participants for the felonies exposed by my interviews.

However, some justice did trickle through in various ways. The individuals who appeared on Jennifer's list, along with Bill Clymer, Laura Bowman, Drake Lindberg, Carlton Drucker, and several employees of PWW, each faced their turn in the interrogation room. Investigators from two states interviewed them over Frank Spector's journal, data files, videos, and recordings. Most escaped the court system and any formal penalty. However, Internet blogs, memes, and social media had a field day promoting an unending stream of conspiracies and conjecture around their names, careers, and associations. That attention showed no signs of letting up.

Carlton Drucker had a heart attack and died a few months after Reardon's release. State officials charged Laura Bowman with campaign funding improprieties after a failed run for the Massachusetts Legislature.

The bodies of Jennifer Carlson and Dennis Whitcomb, the birth name of the man I knew as Jeremy Hansen, were never recovered. An anonymous rumor planted on the Internet was published in the *Boston Herald,* suggesting Whitcomb's career in U.S. Navy intelligence placed them in the crosshairs of foreign interests.

Harry Sanderson and I chased down more than two dozen names on Jennifer's Hodin cabal operatives and embeds list. Still, we couldn't gather enough information for the authorities to act on. Those who didn't refuse to speak with us denied involvement, and a few threatened us with litigation.

I still had the sample documents Spector e-mailed me from his server before he died. Those included texts, e-mails, writings, and voice recordings. His journal, which detailed the cabal's efforts over nearly twenty years, was safely stored on several of my hard drives and in the cloud.

I also had the videos Dr. Luft's staff had provided me from his psychiatric evaluation sessions and three audio recordings of Spector's previous interviews with attorneys. Although I had copies of about a quarter of the data Spector had taken from the cabal, what I had wasn't complete and lacked critical contextual details. Unfortunately, the link Frank had given me for the servers in his maiden aunt Sarah Lewinski's name no longer worked.

I put together three packages for mailing. For each, I copied off a version of my articles made before they were trimmed for publication, adding an explanatory note. I included a flash drive with Frank Spector's journal, session videos, audio recordings, the sample data Frank had sent me, and their decryption passcodes. I added the URL to my freelance website's host server, where I'd stored my partial copies of the cabal's servers. I mailed the completed packages to the Department of Homeland Security, the FBI, and INTERPOL.

For several months after Spector's suicide, I'd terrorize myself by reading the lists of chemicals and other ingredients in the food and beverages I purchased. But at some point, I came to peace with the idea that I'd given up my chance at a ticket to join the one billion, so I was stuck with whatever came along.

With that acceptance, the fear and sense of injustice eventually dissolved into the background of my life. My friends and loved ones were flawed people who were not likely to get a pass, either. I couldn't imagine a life worth living without them.

I began taking long walks whenever the opportunity presented itself to enjoy my surroundings, smelling the roses, as it were. But now and then, I'd pass a playground, park, or schoolyard where children were playing — all that squealing energy and excitement bouncing off the jungle gyms and swing sets, the noise and confusion feeding themselves. I tried not to think about the kids beyond this moment and this time of their lives. If I weren't careful, a tear would come to my eye, dampening the rest of my day.

Still, I couldn't ignore the Hodin cabal's efforts completely. They'd end the lives of two more people I cared about, adding those to the millions they'd already taken. They'd steal tenfold more, well into the foreseeable future, from others who loved those lost.

At 9:53 in the morning, on a day in April when other school children would spend their recess looking for emerging flowers to gift their new spring crushes, Rosarita suffered a seizure.

With her nanny gone to the nurses' station seeking help, Rosarita would die alone, her eyes wide open, a video of *SpongeBob SquarePants: The Broadway Musical* playing on her iPad, her beloved teddy bear dropping from her lifeless hands. The explosion of activity from the intercom's callout of a code blue would come too late to save her.

Freddie and Rosarita's mother's body would reject her new liver, and, too weak for another, she would pass in hospice care tended by strangers in her last days. They'd find in her hands an unfinished poem memorializing her children.

Paul and I would carry the scars of that year with us for the rest of our lives. For Paul, the unexpected sound of children laughing would stop him mid-sentence, freezing him in his tracks and leaving him unable to process anything for that moment.

As for me, I'd never know what it might be — the sight of a single tulip might consume my thoughts, immediately rendering whatever else I was doing at that moment meaningless. An escaped mylar balloon riding the breezes as it made its way heavenward might remind me of Cindy, Freddie, or Rosarita, causing me to cry. Or I'd awaken from dreams deep in the night of an orphaned stuffed bear staring back at me from where it'd fallen on the floor.

As for the favored one billion, there was nothing to suggest life wouldn't go on as it always had.

Occasionally, the topic of global depopulation would provide filler on the inside pages of a newspaper or fuel a QAnon rant on a social media platform. When it did, commenters in blogs or on the street treated depopulation, natural or otherwise, precisely as they've done global warming for decades. They'd deny its existence, push the issue from view, and ignore it, losing themselves in pursuing their daily lives.

The Hodin cabal had escaped unscathed. Its operatives were still out there doing their thing. And it'd be arrogant and ignorant for anyone to assume others weren't actively supporting depopulation, though those groups might be less consequential than the cabal. There were many believers in depopulation as a good thing for the planet.

The haunting questions for myself and my loved ones were, "*Who among us will suffer during our elimination?*" and "*In what ways?*"

BOOK THREE — CHAPTER 11

THREE MONTHS LATER

Sifting through my voicemails in Paul's and my new apartment, I found one from Doug Stein. He'd always kept an eye out for opportunities to boost my career. Ever since I'd left the *Union-Tribune*, he'd occasionally fed me the better story ideas from those the paper wouldn't pursue. I'd expected his voicemail to be about another of those.

Instead, he'd called to tell me that Jerry Dark had left as managing editor, suggesting I might want to interview for the position. I hoped Doug was joking, but he had a dry sense of humor … I'd have to see his face.

The second message was from Marci. She'd received a package from the Richard J. Donovan Correctional Facility. The staff, rather than an inmate, had sent it. Within the cushioned mailer was a note, along with a smaller package. Signed by Anthony Tarrant, Donovan's warden, it said a safe deposit box key had been among Frank Spector's possessions when they'd processed him into their facility.

After his death, they'd located the box, and its contents included a small package labeled with Marci's and my names but without a mailing address. They'd X-rayed the package as a safety measure, and it contained a USB drive and slip of paper, nothing more. As a civil servant, Marci's work address was in the system, and they'd forwarded it to her there.

"Hi, Marci, I got your message," I said after I'd dialed her number. "Curiouser and curiouser. I've tried hard to forget Frank Spector and everything about him. But whenever I see the ingredients label on a can of soup or box of macaroni and cheese, it all comes roaring back."

"I know *that* feeling!" Marci's tone was more than a little sarcastic.

"The bright side is that bad things for my diet don't sound as good knowing the chemicals they contain. The bad part is waking up screaming from a nightmare at three a.m. And with our son due in seven weeks, I'm a little nervous about getting involved in anything overly upsetting."

"Have the two of you picked a name yet?".

"We're going with Thomas Ethan, for Paul's favorite uncle and Dad's middle name … I wonder what Spector wanted to send us — and why?"

"Maybe it's the instructions for the secret handshake so we can join the one billion survivors?" Marci overplayed her part with a hopeful tone in her voice.

"Our department-issued laptops come with every malware protection known to man. So, just in case, I stuck the drive into a USB port in mine and scanned it for viruses. The software didn't pick up any problems. There's just a single file on the flash drive with an MP4 extension, so it's a video. Too big to e-mail, and I don't want to put it up on the department's servers."

"Want to do pizza and a movie, then? Come over to my place. Paul will be at work. I'll make alcohol-free mai tais; if the video gets too crazy, we'll shut it down and switch to something on Netflix."

"Works for me if you can make the drinks sugar-free, too." Marci laughed. "My shift ends at six — say, around seven-thirty?"

"It's a deal — the pizza will be in the oven, so don't be late," I said as menacingly as possible.

With our supper on the coffee table and drinks in hand, we leaned back into our respective ends of my couch as Marci cast the video from her work laptop to my flatscreen.

Spector appeared in the opening frame with several scratches on his face and a bandage above his right eye. The background looked like Spector's room at the Kohrmann Psychiatric Hospital. He sat in the middle of the mattress on the lower tier of a gray, metal-frame bunk bed, his feet on the floor, his head barely clearing the rails of the upper bunk.

Spector had shot the video about five months ago following Marci's and my first interview with him. It had to have been recorded after the paramilitary assault on the facility had slightly injured him but before he returned to San Diego County custody. Spector either had the camera or cell phone smuggled in or borrowed one from a hospital employee, visitor, or patient on the unsecured wing; their policies didn't allow secured clients to have electronic devices.

I knew the facility's administrator was sympathetic to Spector's story, if not the man himself. It wouldn't have surprised me to learn his staff had relaxed the rules just enough to help Spector get his message out.

As Marci and I watched the last images of Frank Spector we'd ever see, I felt a twinge of something akin to sadness or perhaps regret. I felt no connection to the serial killer other than through his story. Still, Marci and I'd spent time with him and the circumstances surrounding his activities. We'd been thrown into a lockdown situation together. You can't help but become at least a little familiar with someone that way. As I looked upon Spector's visage again, knowing he'd paid a high price by committing self-murder helped cover for at least some of his sins and made him more relatable.

"I assume that I'm long gone by the time you see this," Spector's narration began, "but I hope this tape finds its way to you. You and Dr. Luft were among the few who took the time to listen to what I had to say, and I appreciate that. In return, I wanted you and your loved ones to have a heads-up about something I didn't share with you or, for that matter, anyone else."

OK, something more than an apology, then…

"If you understand and accept what will happen, you'll want to get the word out to others. I suppose it's self-serving to use the two of you as better messengers than I proved to be; I hope the day will come when no one questions the truth about what I was trying to say or do.

"You'd think PWW and the Hodin federation would've cut off my access immediately the day I escaped Chris Patterson's office building. Why they didn't, I'll never know. But as soon as I got to a location where I could feel safe, catch my breath, and get a decent cup of coffee, I made a secure call to my team.

"I lied to them. What else could I do? Once the coalition began chasing me, I knew it was over — I couldn't trust anyone. It was clear law enforcement had no interest in a depopulation campaign scaled to rid the earth of seven billion souls. And no matter what happened, I was going down for the serial killings. The police wouldn't bother checking out the Hodin coalition once they had me for those. No one would be willing or able to stop the federation and their dedication to terminating most of us."

Something was wrong. Spector's first words suggested he was heading toward the apologetic mea culpa I expected. Yet, his tone wasn't quite right. Here was a man who'd just barely evaded an assassination attempt by well-armed mercenaries while he sat helplessly locked in a room at the psychiatric unit. He should be in fear for his life, panicked about his options, remorseful, even supplicating.

Instead, his demeanor brought to mind a player holding a pat poker hand in a Thursday night game. I looked at Marci — her years of experience reading people as a police officer made her a reliable barometer. Her face showed genuine concern as we listened to what Spector had to say.

My heart had begun pounding in my chest; apprehension was taking over. There weren't many things a long-gone homicidal sociopath might say to make me break into tears whenever I thought of my brand-new son's life and future. But trust the ever-resourceful Frank Spector to find the words.

"My lie? I told my federation team we'd had a significant breakthrough; I said I had, in my hands, the antidote system we'd been trying to develop to protect intended survivors from our microplastics chemistry initiative. Our Holy Grail, as it were.

"I put everything I knew about advertising into spinning that story. I not only told my employees the antidote met the immediate need, I cranked it up a notch. I convinced them it was in the form of a universal AI mini-lab that could cover almost any toxin.

"As the ruse went, you'd simply provide it with a reference blood sample from a period before you were infected, along with a current draw of your blood. The mini-lab could detect the differences between the samples. It would then generate or direct you to the antidote necessary to stimulate your immune system to produce the cells and chemistry that would return your blood to its prior state.

"I told my assistant we could quickly reproduce the system at any scale we needed. I gave him just enough details to make it believable, something I've practiced all my life."

Spector paused, and his eyes seemed to lock with mine.

"The trick is avoiding the temptation to oversell it."

Book Three — Chapter 12

I hit the pause button on the laptop's video player. Spector's presentation wasn't at all what I was expecting.

I looked over at Marci and saw that her complexion had gone ashen. Her eyes had narrowed and were fixated on the screen, her hands on each side of her mouth as she slowly swung her head from side to side, as though she knew what was coming.

Marci turned toward me, and our eyes met. I realized we had no choice but to see this through, and I hit the play button.

Spector leaned forward and appeared for a moment to be talking to the ceiling.

"And why shouldn't they believe me?"

His tone was quietly obstinate.

"My family and I would be just as dependent upon a working antidote for our survival as anyone else. They knew we'd gotten far enough along we were doing live human trials. We'd been pulling people off the street and testing them in real-world environments for three years. No one but me knew the actual results, of course.

"Other than the fine civil servants who buried the bodies for us, that is. They certainly weren't going to risk their badges or freedom saying anything.

"For all anyone would ever know, those antidotes worked."

It took a second for what he was saying to sink in. It hit Marci at that exact moment.

You son-of-a-bitch.... I fought to suppress the urge to scream at the flat screen as I paused the playback.

"*This* is the asshole responsible for killing Alma? And our missing homeless?" The pitch of Marci's voice had gone higher, her face shoved forward, and her eyebrows arched. And then, a few seconds later, her tone flattened, and her volume went lower. "And I'll bet it's not just here in San Diego."

I was up and pacing at this point, upset at myself that I hadn't seen the connection.

It took me a while to realize no one could have put the big picture together, not in time to have made any real difference.

The DA had been content to run with hatred for the down-and-out and city officials going rogue to solve the homeless problem as the motives for those murders out in the desert. I'd seen it myself all too often with officer-involved crimes: politicians want to rush them out the door to get rid of the bothersome media attention they attract.

Pursuing the pathologist's suspicion of medical experimentation would open a serious can of worms for the DA - neither **Crabtree** nor any of the bad cops had any known association with the medical community. That meant the experiments would have been at the behest of someone outside their group.

But making a leap from there to the Hodin cabal would have been impossible — at the time, local officials knew nothing of the organization. Until Danny Boy was gutted and left on my car's hood, the cabal interviews had, in my mind, been about circumstances thousands of miles away. Both stories falling into my lap around the same time was the only tie I knew of between them. How could I expect anyone else to see the connection if *I'd* missed it?

Calmer now, I plopped back down on the couch. I looked at Marci, and she nodded back. I pressed the play chevron on the laptop.

"I'd talked with my crew a lot over the years about the distribution challenges for this initiative," Spector continued.

"We knew that even in a best-case scenario, it would take time for everything to come together in our supply network, get our products established in the food chain, and see them circulating in human bodies.

"So, my team understood that once we had an antidote system, we'd need to act quickly. The microplastics chemistry initiative would have to get into the hands of the depopulation directors for immediate execution.

"My escape to that coffee shop bought me the opportunity I needed. I asked my federation assistant to ride herd on the distribution effort while I was out of pocket. Jeremy Hansen was one of our better hires, and I knew I could count on him to see things through. Once in their hands, the implementation directors would take it from there."

Now Spector was coming off as almost cocky.

"To hedge my bet, I called our federation embed in Germany and ensured he believed we had that antidote system ready to go. His team managed the antidote program before I created a focus group under my direction to take over that part of the problem. My goal was to get the U.S. and German teams to cross-confirm the antidote's development with one another. Once they did that, they'd accept the news as legitimate."

This asshole is so *proud of himself,* I thought. *It's almost like having locks on the door and bars on the window of Spector's room in a psychiatric hospital wasn't even relevant to him.*

Spector had dropped his forearms to rest on his thighs. He was slowly shaking his head as he looked down at the floor.

"I'd done what I could, but there was no guarantee it'd work. Once in jail, I had no way to monitor things. There was a period when I thought it was all for naught."

I glanced over at Marci. Wholly immersed in Spector's presentation, her eyes were wide open with an uncharacteristic deer-in-the-headlights look.

I reached for her hand. Lost in reverie, she was startled by my touch and jumped, knocking her open water bottle off the end table. The quarter-full bottle bounced as it hit the hardwood floor, splattering liquid all around as it rolled and then spun to a stop.

"Oh, my God, I'm so sorry!" Marci yelped apologetically, "I'll clean it up." But before she could stand, I was already on my feet and waved her off.

"It's alright, I got this, Marci — my bad, I didn't mean to catch you by surprise."

I paused the video and headed to the kitchen to grab the Swiffer and a roll of paper towels. Marci insisted on mopping up the worst of the spill. Dropping to my knees, I chased down the last water droplets with wadded-up paper towels. I picked up hers and my empty water bottles and returned to the kitchen with the used towels. Seeing my trash container overflowing, I let Marci know I was extending my break from our video session. I walked the bag out to my building's garbage chute.

With everything again dry and just as it was, Marci and I returned to our seats, and I resumed the video.

Spector had leaned back into the shadow cast by the upper bunk. When he brought his head and shoulders forward toward the camera, his expression was one of confident satisfaction.

"A couple of days ago, I got an e-mail from one of my old Boston neighbors. To her, I was just someone she chatted with across our backyard fence. She didn't know about my legal challenges or the events surrounding me. The e-mail allowed her to brag a little — her daughter had graduated from Harvard.

"She signed off with a 'by the way' that made my day. I'd told her at some point about a new startup I had among my clients at PWW. She remembered the brand name and wanted to congratulate me on my success. She noticed the first batch of the federation's discounted waters, sports drinks, and nutrition bars landing on Walmart, Target, and CVS store shelves two weeks beforehand.

"I'd had no reason to mention anything to her about the microplastic binder payloads or carcinogens in them. She expressed genuine happiness that my new enterprise had launched so successfully.

"The coalition's distribution team had seen their tasks through after all."

Spector looked to the side as a metallic noise off-camera caught his attention and then quickly returned his focus to the camera.

"I saw in the business trades this morning that one of the federation's front companies purchased a national office water delivery business. That would have been the next logical step once they successfully removed anything you could see or taste from our additives."

He paused.

"It's a safe bet that the initiative will soon be in everything you can consume. That the coalition is so far along means the world has about six months before the hospitals begin to fill and the bodies start piling up. I wish I could see the faces within the federation when the left hand realizes the right has no antidote."

Out of nowhere, my heart suddenly fell into my stomach.

Something Spector said a moment ago had just sunk in, and I panicked.

"Jesus, Marci, what was the … "

The playback of the recording was still going.

As I tried to get Marci's attention, she sat there utterly oblivious to me, transfixed by the image on the screen.

Instinctively following her eyes back to the TV, I caught the final video snippet that hypnotized her.

Spector had leaned forward on the edge of the mattress, his hands loosely clasped in front of him, just below his waist.

He pursed his lips as he glanced without focus to the far wall for a brief moment.

Then he brought his head back up and cocked it to one side, looking directly into the camera, a wry smile slowly crossing his face even as his eyes remained steely and resolute.

"Screw their one billion," he said, his tone flashing defiance.

Then, another tiny pause, his face pushing forward, his upper lip curling, and his eyes spitting venom.

"Fuck all of you."

Momentarily taken aback, Marci and I stared at one another, our eyes wide open.

It took but an instant for me to snap back into reality, now honestly freaked.

My heart was pounding like a jackhammer as I grabbed my friend by her shoulders, shaking her as I nearly screamed in her face.

"What was the brand on that bottle we spilled?"

THE WRITINGS OF
AVRIL MARIA SERENE

Did you enjoy reading *The Hodin Cabal: Choices*? Would you be willing to leave a review?

Honest reviews from you and others who have read my work help me write the kinds of books you will enjoy. I write to earn kudos from my readers, and your comments keep me on the right track – I appreciate your input more than you know. Your reviews also help new readers find quality books they will like. Please follow this link to leave your review:

https://www.amazon.com/review/create-review/?ie=UTF8&channel=glance-detail&asin=B0F628CBLM

Thank you,

Avril Maria Serene

THE WRITINGS OF
AVRIL MARIA SERENE

HIGHLIGHT REEL

THE WRITINGS OF
AVRIL MARIA SERENE

JOHN MASTERS'S/ FRANK SPECTOR'S DIGITAL HIGHLIGHT REEL

1. **Backgrounder: General cybercrime reference**
   Link: https://en.wikipedia.org/wiki/Cybercrime
   Website title: "Cybercrime"
   Source: *Wikipedia*
   Relevance: This article explains the potential of, and the means for, exploiting cybercrime, a primary resource for funding Hodin federation operations.

2. **Backgrounder: U.S. government cybercrime estimates (losses only)**
   Link: https://www.usaid.gov/digital-development/cybersecurity/economic-growth-briefer#:~:text=cybersecurity%20as%20the%20single%20greatest,top%20%248%20trillion%20in%202023.
   Website title: "Cybersecurity Briefer: Economic Growth and Trade"
   Source: *United States Agency for International Development*
   Relevance: This article describes the losses to the world economy from cybercrime (as opposed to economic impact generally, which are much larger numbers).

3. **Backgrounder: American business and Silicon Valley steal massive amounts of data from citizens and consumers**
   Link: https://www.cbsnews.com/news/amazon-facebook-youtube-federal-trade-commission-privacy-children/
   Website title: "Social media companies, video streaming services engage in "vast surveillance" of users, FTC says"
   Source: *CBS News*
   Relevance: American businesses and Silicon Valley have become so dependent upon stealing personal data from and compromising the privacy of citizens and consumers that they can no longer function without it.

4. **Backgrounder: Inefficiency of war as a population reduction tool - statistics on World War II casualties**
   Link: https://en.wikipedia.org/wiki/World_War_II_casualties
   Website title: "World War II casualties"
   Source: *Wikipedia*
   Relevance: Though armed conflict is a significant component of the

Hodin federation's efforts to reduce population, it is not reliable or efficient enough to independently produce the desired results at scale.

5. **Backgrounder: India unreliable reporting population data**
   Link: https://www.bbc.com/news/world-asia-india-60981318
   Website title: "Why India's real Covid toll may never be known"
   Source: *BBC News*
   Relevance: The Hodin federation has decided to release its initiatives in India as the last targeted region. India's official reporting of population counts and more detailed accounting describing births, deaths, fertility rates, and other data is unreliable, and production is slow. The inaccuracy and delay make India unsuitable for experimentation with initiatives because it is challenging to gauge efficacy without accurate starting and ending numbers.

6. **Backgrounder: One of every six Indian residents lives in a slum**
   Link: https://www.sandiegouniontribune.com/sdut-census-1-in-6-india-city-residents-lives-in-slums-2013mar22-story.html
   Website title: "Census: 1 in 6 India city residents lives in slums"
   Source: *San Diego Union-Tribune*
   Relevance: Despite the challenges experimenting with new Hodin federation initiatives in India due to poor official reporting, the federation expects the application of initiatives tested elsewhere to perform well, in part because so many Indians live in densely packed cities where spreading biologics, aerosols, contaminants, poisons, heavy metals, and chemicals is relatively easy and inexpensive.

7. **Backgrounder: About the Ganges**
   Link: https://www.wwf.org.uk/where-we-work/ganges
   Website title: "The Ganges"
   Source: *World Wildlife Fund*
   Relevance: One of the factors that makes India a much easier target for Hodin federation initiatives than other countries is their absolute dependence upon the Ganges River. The Ganges is very vulnerable, accessible from a wide variety of locations upstream where the coalition can introduce any number of pollutants, contaminants, chemicals, and biologics into its flow.

8. **Backgrounder: Over eighty percent of the future population will live in Asia or Africa**
   Link: https://ourworldindata.org/region-population-2100#:~:text=Here%20we%20see%20that%20today,live%20in%20Asia%20or%20Africa.

Website title: "More than 8 out of 10 people in the world will live in Asia or Africa by 2100"
Source: *Our World in Data*
Relevance: This article explains why the Hodin federation assigns significant importance to having a well-developed depopulation strategy and implementation plan for addressing Asia and Africa.

9. **Backgrounder: Africa's susceptibility to drought, floods, and poor farming and land usage**
   Link: https://www.tomorrow.city/what-causes-the-drought-cycles-in-africa/
   Website title: "What causes the drought cycles in Africa?"
   Source: *Tomorrow.City*
   Relevance: This article explains why the Hodin federation is comfortable leaving the implementation of its initiatives targeting Africa until they've refined them in more extensive and affluent regions of the world. Africa's natural vulnerabilities to depopulation efforts render it relatively defenseless, and spillover from geographically non-specific initiatives like those directed at global warming and pollution may significantly reduce the African population beforehand.

10. **Backgrounder: COVID-19 and SARS origins**
    Link: https://www.news-medical.net/health/How-Does-the-SARS-Virus-Genome-Compare-to-Other-Viruses.aspx
    Website title: "How Does the SARS-CoV-2 Genome Compare to Other Viruses?"
    Source: *News Medical | Life Sciences*
    Relevance: This highly technical article describes COVID-19's origins from its likely parentage and includes information about possible modifications to increase its transmissibility and lethality.

11. **Backgrounder: How presumably good things happening to a member can destroy human social circles**
    Link: https://en.wikipedia.org/wiki/Abraham_Shakespeare
    Website title: "Abraham Shakespeare"
    Source: *Wikipedia*
    Relevance: This article illustrates that Hodin federation initiatives can harness events and circumstances otherwise considered positive to cause harm and even death. This approach is especially pertinent to their social media initiatives.

12. **Backgrounder: Martin Shkreli pharmaceutical fraud and conspiracy**
    Link: https://en.wikipedia.org/wiki/Martin_Shkreli

Website title: "Martin Shkreli"
Source: *Wikipedia*
Relevance: Shkreli's long run of getting away with the most egregious, even obscene, exercises in pharmaceutical greed and chutzpah illustrates the abuses in play that make the U.S. healthcare system one of the worst among industrialized nations. Hodin federation initiatives encourage and reward such behaviors to reduce lifespan and the population count.

13. **Backgrounder: The FDA allows thousands of untested chemicals into U.S. food supply**
    Link: https://www.cbsnews.com/news/fda-chemicals-food-supply/
    Website title: "How the FDA lets chemicals pour into America's food supply"
    Source: *CBS News*
    Relevance: U.S. citizens assume the FDA is safeguarding our food supply. Nothing could be further from the truth, especially where industry profiteering overrides health concerns.

14. **Backgrounder: Responsibilities of the prefrontal cortex**
    Link: https://www.linkedin.com/pulse/nine-functions-prefrontal-cortex-neurotherapy-dr-judith
    Website title: "Nine Functions of the Prefrontal Cortex: Neurotherapy — Dysfunctional to Functional"
    Source: *LinkedIn*
    Relevance: The Hodin federation is actively investigating, creating, and deploying several initiatives based on modifying the prefrontal cortex. The goal is to make living, walking remotely controlled time bombs induceable on demand with triggers to perform a variety of tasks on behalf of depopulation.

15. **Backgrounder: Stray dogs overwhelm poorer nations, with millions of the animals at large**
    Link: https://www.humanesociety.org/sites/default/files/docs/slum-dogs--by-the-millions.pdf
    Website title: "Slum Dogs by the Millions"
    Source: *Humane Society*
    Relevance: The sheer number of stray animals in poorer countries affords an excellent opportunity for the federation's animal-to-human disease transmission incentives.

16. **Federation resource: CRISPR gene-editing capabilities**
    Link: https://innovativegenomics.org/what-is-crispr/
    Website title: "What is CRISPR?"

Source: *Innovative Genomics Institute*

Relevance: Gene editing is the primary tool the Hodin federation uses in their biologics initiatives — they modify the D.N.A. sequence of various organisms towards achieving their depopulation goals. This article explains why that's possible and describes how gene editing works.

17. **Federation resource: Massive garbage patch circulating in the Pacific**

    Link: https://www.latimes.com/science/sciencenow/la-sci-sn-garbage-patch-plastic-20180322-story.html

    Website title: "The Great Pacific Garbage Patch counts 1.8 trillion pieces of trash, mostly plastic"

    Source: *Los Angeles Times*

    Relevance: The microplastics chemistry initiatives are among the Hodin federation's most potent. This article demonstrates the massive size and longevity of one of many sources of microplastics for the initiative, illustrating that the supply of raw materials required is virtually infinite.

18. **Federation resource: Diseases that can transfer from other animals to humans**

    Link: https://www.dhs.wisconsin.gov/disease/zoonotic.htm

    Website title: "Zoonotic Diseases"

    Source: *Wisconsin Department of Health Services*

    Relevance: Initiatives transferring fungi, bacteria, viruses, chemicals, and poisons from animals to humans through contact, food, waste products, and water runoff is an area of intense investigation and dynamic activity within the Hodin federation.

19. **Initiative results: Warring African countries**

    Link: https://en.wikipedia.org/wiki/List_of_conflicts_in_Africa

    Website title: "List of conflicts in Africa"

    Source: *Wikipedia*

    Relevance: The Hodin federation manipulates large numbers of more minor, ongoing armed regional conflicts to achieve some measure of population control.

20. **Initiative results: Bilderbeck Group influences governmental inability to address global warming**

    Link: https://www.cnn.com/2023/09/13/world/planetary-boundaries-humanity-climate/index.html

    Website title: "Conditions on Earth may be moving outside the 'safe operating space' for humanity, according to dozens of scientists"

    Source: *CNN*

Relevance: The Bilderbeck Group provides political access and messaging, and the Hodin federation offers the tools and methods to frustrate government efforts at any level to curb climate change or its potential to reduce population.

21. **Initiative results: Global warming kicks off events and challenges that are helpful to the Hodin federation's goals and interests**
    Link: https://us.cnn.com/2023/03/20/world/ipcc-synthesis-report-climate-intl/index.html
    Website title: "The climate time-bomb is ticking: The world is running out of time to avoid catastrophe, new U.N. report warns."
    Source: *CNN*
    Relevance: The Hodin federation's broader initiatives, such as global warming and microplastics chemistry, can instigate a wide variety of more specific threats to the human population, which increases their ultimate effect.

22. **Initiative results: U.S. CO2 output, fossil fuels shipments between countries, and emissions data**
    Link: https://www.theguardian.com/commentisfree/2022/jun/02/for-50-years-governments-have-failed-to-act-on-climate-change-no-more-excuses
    Website title: "For 50 years, governments have failed to act on climate change. No more excuses"
    Source: *The Guardian*
    Relevance: The Hodin federation encourages the continued use of fossil fuels politically and economically to advance global warming, a promising opportunity and tool to reduce population.

23. **Initiative results: Nine million added deaths from pollution**
    Link: https://www.nbcnews.com/health/health-news/pollution-death-toll-high-studies-rcna29189
    Website title: "Pollution's fatal threat gains urgency after 9 million died in one year"
    Source: *NBC News*
    Relevance: This article provides affirmation in the general media for the population-reducing effects of the Hodin federation's initiatives around pollution and climate change.

24. **Initiative results: Most humans consume at least five grams of plastic every week**
    Link: https://www.wwf.mg/en/?348373/Revealed-plastic-ingestion-by-people-could-be-equating-to-a-credit-card-a-week

Website title: "Revealed: Plastic ingestion by people could be equating to a credit card a week"
Source: *World Wildlife Fund*
Relevance: This article illustrates the efficacy of the distribution process for the raw materials the Hodin federation requires to support their microplastics chemistry initiatives.

25. **Initiative results: Dangerous levels of microplastics in human testicles**
Link: https://www.cnn.com/2024/05/21/health/microplastics-testicles-study-wellness/index.html
Website title: "Tiny plastic shards found in human testicles, study says"
Source: *CNN*
Relevance: Microplastics are not only everywhere but in alarming concentrations.

26. **Initiative results: Microplastics found deep in the base of the human brain**
Link: https://www.cnn.com/2024/09/16/health/microplastics-nose-wellness/index.html
Website title: "Microplastics found in nose tissue at base of brain, study says"
Source: *CNN Life | but better*
Relevance: The ability to attach binders to microplastics embedded in the brain allows the federation a direct pathway to modifying elements of the mind.

27. **Initiative results: Microplastics in bottled water**
Link: https://people.com/nanoplastics-discovered-bottled-water-8424730
Website title: "Scientists Say They'll Cut Back on Bottled Water After Learning 1 Liter Contains a Quarter of a Million Pieces of Plastic"
Source: *People*
Relevance: This article demonstrates the reach of microplastics and their abundant presence even in highly filtered and processed products.

28. **Initiative results: Microplastics in the polar ice caps**
Link:
https://www.theatlantic.com/science/archive/2019/08/microplastic-air-pollution-real/596119/
Website title: "A Worrisome Discovery in High Arctic Snowfall"
Source: *The Atlantic*

Relevance: This article demonstrates the range of distribution of microplastics, even throughout the natural environment.

29. **Initiative results: Microplastic pollution and weather**
Link: https://www.cnn.com/2023/11/15/weather/microplastic-pollution-weather-study-climate/index.html
Website title: "Microplastics could trigger cloud formation and affect the weather, new study suggests"
Source: *CNN*
Relevance: Microplastics distribution in the atmosphere gives Hodin federation microplastics chemistry initiatives access to human lungs and suggests other initiatives based on microplastics the coalition can spread through air-breathing species other than humans.

30. **Initiative results: Microplastics found in meat, water, and plants**
Link: https://www.foxnews.com/health/microplastics-found-overwhelming-majority-american-meat-water-plants-study
Website title: "Microplastics found in overwhelming majority of American meat, water, plants: study"
Source: *Fox News | Health*
Relevance: The microplastics chemistry initiative is far and away the Hodin federation's most promising, and every element of the project, including aiding the distribution of the raw material, is a priority.

31. **Initiative results: Microplastics hide in surprising places**
Link: https://www.cnn.com/2024/04/22/health/plastics-food-wellness-scn/index.html
Website title: "Which foods have the most plastics? You may be surprised"
Source: *CNN | Life but better | Food*
Relevance: You can't escape consuming microplastics – they are indeed everywhere. Translation: You can't escape the Hodin federation, either.

32. **Initiative results: Microplastics are harmful to humans in and of themselves**
Link: https://www.ewg.org/news-insights/news/2024/03/new-study-links-microplastics-serious-health-harms-humans
Website title: "New study links microplastics to serious health harms in humans"
Source: *ewg*
Relevance: Microplastics harm humans but are not sufficiently able to achieve the population reduction the Hodin federation desires.

33. **Initiative results: Everywhere chemicals and cancer in children**
Link:
https://www.sciencedaily.com/releases/2022/03/220316145830.htm#:~
:text=Childhood%2C%20but%20not%20gestational%20(in,diagnosis%2
C%20cancer%20of%20the%20blood.
Website title: "Exposure to phthalates -- the 'everywhere chemical' --
may increase children's cancer risk"
Source: *Science Daily*
Relevance: "Everywhere" chemicals constitute one of the other legs of
the microplastics chemistry initiative, with the same scope and potential as
the microplastics component.

34. **Initiative results: Everywhere chemicals can disrupt newborn brain development**
Link: https://www.cnn.com/2025/04/02/health/phthalates-affect-
newborn-brain-development-wellness/index.html
Website title: "Exposure to phthalates during pregnancy can affect a
newborn's brain development, study finds"
Source: *CNN Health*
Relevance: "Everywhere" chemicals alter the metabolism of
neurotransmitters and amino acids involved in brain maturation.

35. **Initiative results: Thousands of chemicals can enter human bodies through food packaging**
Link: https://www.washingtonpost.com/climate-
environment/2024/09/16/more-than-3000-chemicals-food-packaging-
have-infiltrated-our-bodies/
Website title: "Scientists just figured out how many chemicals enter our
bodies from food packaging"
Source: *Washington Post*
Relevance: Food packaging has been a longtime staple for the Hodin
federation to introduce plastics, chemicals, and other substances into
human bodies.

36. **Initiative results: Forever chemicals**
Link: https://cleanwater.org/pfas-forever-chemicals
Website title: "P.F.A.S.: The Forever Chemicals"
Source: *Clean Water Action*
Relevance: "Forever" chemicals constitute the last leg of the
microplastics chemistry initiative, with the same scope and potential as the
microplastics component.

37. **Initiative results: Heavy metals are a key group of payloads for reducing lifespans and causing death**
Link: https://www.cnn.com/2024/09/20/health/heavy-metal-exposure-cardiovascular-disease-wellness/index.html
Website title: "Heavy metal exposure could increase cardiovascular disease risk, study finds"
Source: *CNN Health*
Relevance: Heavy metals are among the critical payloads for the Hodin federation's microplastics chemistry initiatives.

38. **Initiative results: Chemicals used in rocket fuel and fireworks are widespread in our food supply**
Link: https://www.cbsnews.com/news/consumer-reports-chemical-rocket-fuel-perchlorate/
Website title: "Chemical used in rocket fuel is widespread in food, Consumer Reports finds"
Source: *CBS News*
Relevance: Perchlorates are another pervasive chemical the Hodin federation can exploit to deliver its initiatives.

39. **Initiative results: Unregulated toxic chemicals**
Link: https://www.cnn.com/2024/03/14/health/toxic-unregulated-chemicals-report-wellness/index.html
Website title: "Toxic plastic chemicals number in the thousands, most are unregulated, report finds."
Source: *CNN Health | Life but better*
Relevance: The Hodin federation constantly introduces new chemicals into the environment to reduce fertility, lifespan, and population counts.

40. **Initiative results: Dangerous fumes escaping consumer products**
Link: https://www.cnn.com/2023/05/02/health/voc-levels-consumer-products-wellness/index.html
Website title: "Over 5,000 tons of dangerous fumes escaped from consumer products, study finds"
Source: *CNN*
Relevance: The general media has become aware of the effects of some of the Hodin federation's initiatives.

41. **Initiative results: U.S. life expectancy**
Link: https://www.hsph.harvard.edu/news/hsph-in-the-news/whats-behind-shocking-u-s-life-expectancy-decline-and-what-to-do-about-it/
Website title: "What's behind 'shocking' U.S. life expectancy decline — and what to do about it"

Source: Harvard's *T.H. Chan School of Public Health*

Relevance: This article affirms the reduction in life expectancy the Hodin federation (and before their origin, the Bilderbeck Group) has achieved in one of the wealthiest countries on Earth — shorter life expectancies are one of the essential components of the federation's depopulation strategy.

42. **Initiative results: U.S. life expectancy (factoring in COVID-19)**
    Link: https://www.washingtonpost.com/health/2023/11/29/life-expectancy-2022-united-states/
    Website title: "New C.D.C. life expectancy data shows painfully slow rebound from covid"
    Source: *The Washington Post*
    Relevance: This article describes movement in life expectancy as it relates to COVID-19 — shorter life expectancies are one of the critical components of the federation's depopulation strategy.

43. **Initiative results: Bilderbeck Group influences lack of political response to U.S. life expectancy dropping**
    Link: https://www.washingtonpost.com/health/2023/12/28/life-expectancy-no-political-response/
    Website title: "America has a life expectancy crisis. But it's not a political priority"
    Source: *The Washington Post*
    Relevance: The Hodin federation leverages its political influence within the Bilderbeck Group to forestall and weaken governmental attempts to shore up life expectancy — shorter life expectancies are one of the crucial components of the federation's depopulation strategy.

44. **Initiative results: The U.S. is ranked number twenty-one against other developed nations' healthcare**
    Link: https://www.usnews.com/news/best-countries/slideshows/countries-with-the-most-well-developed-public-health-care-system
    Website title: "These 10 Countries Are Seen as Having the Best Public Health Care Systems"
    Source: *U.S. News and World Report*
    Relevance: Various Hodin federation initiatives have driven U.S. healthcare rankings down to among the worst of industrialized nations despite being the costliest system in the world (causing higher death rates and population reduction).

45. **Initiative results: Influencers promote the idea that curing patients makes no business sense (their continued suffering is more**

profitable)
Link: https://www.cnbc.com/2018/04/11/goldman-asks-is-curing-patients-a-sustainable-business-model.html
Website title: "Goldman Sachs asks in biotech research report: 'Is curing patients a sustainable business model?'"
Source: *CNBC*
Relevance: Hodin federation initiatives have contributed to the pervasive greed consuming health care (which elevates death rates decreasing population) to the point that Wall Street, insurance companies, and practitioners themselves are asking why they are curing patients when it is far more profitable to torture them by subscription — that is, to keep patients chronically ill and addicted to monthly prescriptions and treatments forever, a monthly payment that patients dare not let lapse.

46. **Initiative results: Reduction in the number of reproductive-age females compared to males**
    Link: https://www.statista.com/statistics/241488/population-of-the-us-by-sex-and-age/
    Website title: "Resident population of the United States by sex and age as of July 1, 2021"
    Source: *Statista Research Department*
    Relevance: The Hodin federation's initiatives first concentrate on reducing the population of the most important demographic — females of child-bearing age — because doing so also reduces the likely number of future children.

47. **Initiative results: The fertility rate in the United States has been falling for decades, now the lowest it's been in more than a century**
    Link: https://www.cnn.com/2024/04/24/health/us-birth-rate-decline-2023-cdc/index.html
    Website title: "U.S. fertility rate dropped to lowest in a century as births dipped in 2023"
    Source: *CNN Health*
    Relevance: This article reflects the progress of the Hodin federation's efforts.

48. **Initiative results: Reduced fertility of women**
    Link: https://data.worldbank.org/indicator/SP.DYN.TFRT.IN
    Website title: "Fertility rate, total (births per woman)"
    Source: *The World Bank*
    Relevance: The Hodin federation's initiatives target female fertility as a direct means of reducing the live birth rate.

49. **Initiative results: Global fertility rate plunging at an alarming pace**
    Link: https://www.healthdata.org/news-events/newsroom/news-releases/lancet-dramatic-declines-global-fertility-rates-set-transform#:~:text=The%20global%20TFR%20has%20more,per%20female%20as%20of%202021
    Website title: "The Lancet: Dramatic declines in global fertility rates set to transform global population patterns by 2100"
    Source: *CNN*
    Relevance: The Hodin federation has already managed to drop global fertility rates to barely above the replacement rate, and they will be intensifying their efforts.

50. **Initiative results: Birth control pills make sex less enjoyable for women**
    Link: https://www.cnn.com/2023/03/19/health/birth-control-sex-drive-wellness/index.html#:~:text=Most%20people%20taking%20birth%20control,pleasure%20and%20protection%2C%20Gordon%20said.
    Website title: "Is your birth control messing with your sex life? Experts explain"
    Source: *CNN Life, but better: Relationships*
    Relevance: The Hodin federation's initiatives to reduce sexual pleasure for women directly result in lower birth rates, especially unplanned pregnancies.

51. **Initiative results: Shocking levels of chemicals in male sperm**
    Link: https://www.euronews.com/health/2022/06/10/research-into-falling-sperm-counts-finds-alarming-levels-of-chemicals-in-male-urine-sample
    Website title: "Research into falling sperm counts finds 'alarming' levels of chemicals in male urine samples"
    Source: *euronews*
    Relevance: The Hodin federation's initiatives to add chemicals to semen decrease the number of births and the likelihood of viable offspring reaching child-bearing age or producing children of their own.

52. **Initiative results: Rapid drop in sperm counts**
    Link: https://www.euronews.com/health/2022/11/15/sperm-count-drop-is-accelerating-worldwide-and-threatens-the-future-of-mankind-study-warns
    Website title: "Sperm count drop is accelerating worldwide and threatens the future of mankind, study warns"

Source: *euronews*
Relevance: Hodin federation initiatives targeting sperm counts help reduce viable birth rates. Fertility treatments are expensive, and those who counter the effects tend to be better educated and have higher incomes, indicators for successful individuals, and superior candidates for depopulation survival.

53. **Initiative results: One-sixth of the humans on Earth are infertile**
Link: https://www.cnn.com/2023/04/03/health/infertility-global-prevalence-who-report/index.html#:~:text=%E2%80%9CIn%20our%20analysis%2C%20the%20global,research%20at%20WHO%2C%20said%20Monday.
Website title: "Infertility affects a 'staggering' 1 in 6 people worldwide, WHO says"
Source: *CNN Health*
Relevance: Hodin federation initiatives focusing on infertility reduce birth rates now and in the future.

54. **Initiative results: The U.S. has the highest infant mortality rate at the highest cost, while Norway's is the lowest**
Link: https://www.ajmc.com/view/us-has-highest-infant-maternal-mortality-rates-despite-the-most-health-care-spending
Website title: "U.S. Has Highest Infant, Maternal Mortality Rates Despite the Most Health Care Spending"
Source: *American Journal of Managed Care.*
Relevance: Hodin federation initiatives significantly increase the dangers to the child (and mother) during birth and keep the birthrate down.

55. **Initiative results: Infant mortality in the U.S. on the rise again**
Link: https://abcnews.go.com/Health/infant-mortality-us-rose-3-2022-marking-2nd/story?id=112225772
Website title: "Infant mortality in the U.S. rose 3% in 2022, marking 1st significant increase since 2002: C.D.C."
Source: *ABC News*
Relevance: The worst among industrialized countries, the U.S. birth mortality rate has been dropping but is once again on the rise.

56. **Initiative results: U.S. maternal mortality rate is three times that of other developed countries and rising, twice that bad for blacks**
Link: https://www.cdc.gov/nchs/data/hestat/maternal-mortality/2021/maternal-mortality-rates-2021.htm
Website title: "Maternal Mortality Rates in the United States, 2021"
Source: *CDC's National Center for Health Statistics*

Relevance: Hodin federation initiatives that increase maternal mortality rates lower the population count immediately and reduce future birth rates by making fewer females of reproducing age available.

57. **Initiative results: U.S. infant mortality rate comparison to other countries**
Link: https://www.commonwealthfund.org/blog/2022/us-maternal-mortality-crisis-continues-worsen-international-comparison
Website title: "The U.S. Maternal Mortality Crisis Continues to Worsen: An International Comparison"
Source: *The Commonwealth Fund*
Relevance: Hodin federation initiatives that increase maternal mortality rates lower the population count immediately and reduce future birth rates by making fewer females of reproducing age available.

58. **Initiative results: U.S. birth rate continues to fall to record levels**
Link: https://www.cnn.com/2024/08/20/health/us-birth-rate-fertility-final-data-2023/index.html
Website title: "U.S. fertility rate dropped to record low in 2023, C.D.C. data shows"
Source: *CNN Health*
Relevance: The Hodin federation's efforts to lower the birth rate continue to demonstrate success.

59. **Initiative results: U.S. population growth dropped to between one-third and a half of a percent, with gains coming from immigration, not births**
Link: https://www.macrotrends.net/global-metrics/countries/USA/united-states/population-growth-rate
Website title: "U.S. Population Growth Rate 1950 2023"
Source: *macrotrends*
Relevance: This article affirms the combined effects of Hodin federation initiatives on population numbers.

60. **Initiative results: Why population declines aren't yet evident in the U.S.**
Link: https://www.cnn.com/2024/05/09/opinions/us-population-shrinking-immigration-census-gest/index.html
Website title: "Opinion: The one reason America's population isn't about to start shrinking"
Source: *CNN*
Relevance: This article explains why some aspects of the Hodin federation's work aren't yet more apparent.

61. **Initiative results: China's population is in decline**
Link: https://www.cnn.com/2023/01/18/china/china-population-drop-explainer-intl-hnk/index.html
Website title: "China's population is shrinking. The impact will be felt around the world"
Source: *CNN*
Relevance: Before the formation of the Hodin federation and after its inception, the Bilderbeck Group has been able to manipulate politically China's development and implementation of its one-child policy. Their success has created unexpected side effects, serving the Hodin federation's goals.

62. **Initiative results: Bilderbeck Group's influence over China's one-child policy and resulting issues**
Link: https://www.pewresearch.org/short-reads/2022/12/05/key-facts-about-chinas-declining-population/
Website title: "Key facts about China's declining population"
Source: *Pew Research Center*
Relevance: Before the formation of the Hodin federation and after its inception, the Bilderbeck Group has been able to manipulate politically China's development and implementation of its one-child policy. Their success has created unexpected side effects, serving the Hodin federation's goals.

63. **Initiative results: China's one-child policy and millions of 'missing girls'**
Link: https://www.scmp.com/news/china/politics/article/3144225/we-had-no-choice-chinas-one-child-policy-and-millions-missing
Website title: "'We had no choice': China's one-child policy and the millions of 'missing girls'"
Source: *South China Morning Post*
Relevance: Before the formation of the Hodin federation and after its inception, the Bilderbeck Group has been able to manipulate politically China's development and implementation of its one-child policy. Their success has created unexpected side effects. One of them, the significantly smaller number of girls, serves the Hodin federation's goals particularly well because it inhibits future population growth.

64. **Initiative results: China struggles to reverse its one-child policy**
Link: https://www.cnn.com/2024/08/18/china/china-one-child-policy-hangover-intl-hnk/index.html
Website title: "China's one-child policy hangover: Scarred women

dismiss Beijing's pro-birth agenda"
Source: *CNN | World | China*
Relevance: As China tries to reverse its old one-child policy, it must fight its past mistakes, citizen attitudes, and Hodin federation influencer campaigns.

65. **Initiative results: Japan's drop in population to all-time lows**
Link: https://www.cnn.com/2023/03/01/asia/japan-births-2022-record-low-intl-hnk/index.html
Website title: "Japan births fall to record low as population crisis deepens"
Source: *CNN*
Relevance: Japan was the first Asian country in which the Hodin federation experimented with various initiatives, including social engineering. This article validates the success of those initiatives.

66. **Initiative results: South Korea has the world's lowest fertility rate**
Link: https://www.cnn.com/2022/08/26/asia/south-korea-worlds-lowest-fertility-rate-intl-hnk/index.html
Website title: "South Korea records world's lowest fertility rate — again"
Source: *CNN*
Relevance: South Korea was the second Asian country in which the Hodin federation experimented with various initiatives, including social engineering, applying lessons learned in Japan. This article validates the success of the fertility reduction initiatives.

67. **Initiative results: South Korea's birth rate falls below the death rate**
Link:
https://koreajoongangdaily.joins.com/2021/12/14/opinion/fountain/births-Korea-pandemic/20211214194332790.html
Website title: "The death cross"
Source: *Korea JoongAng Daily*
Relevance: South Korea was the second Asian country in which the Hodin federation experimented with various initiatives, including social engineering, applying lessons learned in Japan. This article validates the success of the birth rate reduction initiatives.

68. **Initiative results: Population declines in Europe**
Link: https://www.euronews.com/next/2023/04/04/china-sees-first-population-decline-in-six-decades-where-does-the-eu-stand#:~:text=The%20estimates%20from%20Eurostat%20signal,the%20start%20of%20this%20year.
Website title: "In data: The E.U. faces a major demographic decline with

27.3 million fewer people by 2100"
Source: *euronews*
Relevance: This article includes projections that validate the effects of specific Hodin federation's initiatives on future European and other countries' population counts.

69. **Initiative results: Europe's population recedes to early twentieth-century levels**
    Link: https://www.intellinews.com/population-decline-to-take-emerging-europe-back-to-the-early-20th-century-253068/
    Website title: "Population decline to take Emerging Europe back to the early 20th century"
    Source: *bne Intellinews*
    Relevance: This article includes projections that validate the effects of the Hodin federation's initiatives on specific European countries.

70. **Initiative results: Recent and current population data**
    Link: https://www.worldometers.info
    Website title: "worldometer"
    Source: *Worldometers*
    Relevance: The data displayed within this website and its descendant pages, subject to analysis and interpretation, shows dramatically slowing population growth generally (a population that had doubled in forty years now projects to grow only twenty-five percent in the next thirty-six), and population declines in the specific areas targeted by the Hodin federation's initiatives.

71. **Initiative results: World population growth (detailed)**
    Link: https://ourworldindata.org/population-growth-over-time
    Website title: "How has world population growth changed over time?"
    Source: *Our World in Data*
    Relevance: The data and their representations, especially charts, show dramatically both the problem the Hodin federation is solving and their success with their solution. As to the latter, the chart entitled "World population growth, 1700-2100" provides a stark portrayal. The Hodin federation's progress (and before their formation, the Bilderbeck Group's) is shown clearly in the purple line labeled "Annual growth rate of the world population." As to how the overpopulation problem came to be, the charts entitled "Time for the world population to double, 1495 to 2078" and "Time for the world population to increase by one billion" offer additional insights.

72. Initiative results: Obesity trends
Link: https://www.hsph.harvard.edu/obesity-prevention-source/obesity-trends/
Website title: "Obesity Prevention Source | Obesity Trends"
Source: Harvard's *T.H. Chan School of Public Health*
Relevance: Several of the Hodin federation's initiatives enable and promote obesity as a proven means to reduce population.

73. Initiative results: Distribution of poisons as weight loss supplements
Link: https://www.nbcnews.com/health/health-news/weight-loss-supplements-contain-hidden-poisonous-ingredient-rcna105032
Website title: "Two purported weight loss supplements may contain a hidden, poisonous ingredient"
Source: *NBC News*
Relevance: Though rarely, Hodin federation initiatives are occasionally detected before they have the intended effect. In this case, several of our partners saw that there was also a financial benefit to replacing one product with another (the deadly substitute was cheaper), and they got greedy. While we would prefer that these incidents didn't happen, they prove that our initiatives are out there for anyone who doubts our capabilities.

74. Initiative results: Artificial sweeteners made from stevia or monk fruit
Link: https://www.cnn.com/2023/02/27/health/zero-calorie-sweetener-heart-attack-stroke-wellness/index.html
Website title: "Erythritol, an ingredient in stevia, linked to heart attack and stroke, study finds"
Source: *National Institutes of Health*
Relevance: Beginning before and continuing after the formation of the Hodin federation, members and partners of the Bilderbeck Group were responsible for the development of efficient yeast-based fermentation, introduction, and promotion of erythritol after its harmful effects became known to its researchers.

75. Initiative results: Weight-loss drug manufacturers gouge American consumers with prices 15 times what they charge in Great Britain
Link: https://www.nbcnews.com/health/health-news/ozempic-maker-defends-high-us-price-s-helping-reduce-cost-obesity-rcna161175
Website title: "Ozempic maker defends high U.S. price: It's 'helping' reduce the cost of obesity"

Source: *NBC News*

Relevance: Arbitrary pricing serves two goals – generating gross and undeserved profits for pharmaceutical companies and ensuring that access to successful regimens is limited to the Hodin federation's desired survivors.

76. **Initiative results: How the Hodin federation made it possible for food manufacturers, not the FDA, to determine what additives are safe**

    Link: https://www.cbsnews.com/news/ultra-processed-foods-fda-health-safety/

    Website title: "The federal loophole that allows food companies to decide what's safe for you to eat"

    Source: *CBS News*

    Relevance: Regulations and regulating agencies are not burdensome for the Hodin federation to work around.

77. **Initiative results: Spreading disease through bone dust**

    Link:
    https://www.ncbi.nlm.nih.gov/pmc/articles/PMC7090790/#:~:text=When%20an%20electric%20oscillating%20saw,used%20to%20minimize%20aerosol%20production.

    Website title: "Minimizing aerosol bone dust during autopsies"

    Source: *National Library of Medicine's National Center for Biotechnology*

    Relevance: Media awareness of a problem processing cadavers inspired Hodin federation initiatives for distributing infected bone dust in various forms worldwide.

78. **Initiative results: Power and potential of animal-to-human transfer**

    Link: https://www.nbcnews.com/science/science-news/rare-strain-parasite-killed-4-otters-california-pose-danger-humans-res-rcna76461

    Website title: "Rare strain of parasite that killed 4 otters in California could pose danger to humans, researchers say"

    Source: *NBC News*

    Relevance: Another example of a Hodin federation initiative implementation where samples escaped and found their way into public media, this article demonstrates the federation's investment in zoonotic diseases and transmission.

79. **Initiative results: *Chytridiomycosis* among amphibians in Africa**

    Link: https://www.cnn.com/2023/03/24/world/fungus-pandemic-frogs-amphibians-scn/index.html

    Website title: "A terrifying fungal disease is infecting frogs in Africa.

Here's why it matters"
Source: *CNN*
Relevance: Another example of a Hodin federation initiative
implementation where samples escaped and found their way into public
media, this article demonstrates the federation's investment in zoonotic
diseases and transmission. In this case, the fungi samples were highly
successful in the wild, killing amphibians in large numbers.

80. **Initiative results: Mass extinctions of non-human species**
    Link: https://www.cnn.com/2023/12/23/world/mass-extinctions-
    explained-scn-climate/index.html
    Website title: "What is a mass extinction, and why do scientists think
    we're in the middle of one?"
    Source: *CNN Space + Science*
    Relevance: The Hodin federation doesn't expressly target species other
    than humans, except for its animal-to-human transfer initiatives.
    However, it welcomes the side effects that can often occur among non-
    humans. As apex predators, humanity is susceptible to the challenges that
    arise when their prey becomes unavailable, hazardous to consume, or
    more difficult to capture and control.

81. **Initiative results: Fatal fungus infections increasing**
    Link: https://www.cnn.com/2023/03/20/health/fungus-candida-auris-
    increase/index.html
    Website title: "An emerging fungal threat spread at an alarming rate in
    U.S. health care facilities, study says"
    Source: *CNN*
    Relevance: The Hodin federation's candida auris fungus initiative is one
    of its most successful.

82. **Initiative results: Antibiotic-resistant infections increasing**
    Link: https://www.cnn.com/2024/09/16/health/antibiotic-resistant-
    superbug-infections-2050-wellness/index.html
    Website title: "Superbug crisis could get worse, killing nearly 40 million
    people by 2050, study estimates"
    Source: *CNN Health*
    Relevance: The Hodin federation is rapidly developing an increasing
    inventory of new biological weapons resistant to antibiotics.

83. **Initiative results: Cancers in patients under 50 increasing globally**
    Link: https://www.health.com/news/cancer-under-50-rising-globally
    Website title: "Cancer Among Those Under 50 Is Rising Dramatically —
    Study Examines Causes and Risk Factors"

Source: *Health.com*

Relevance: The Hodin federation has released many cancer-related initiatives and works constantly to develop new and more aggressive carcinogens.

84. **Initiative results: Cancer rates for men about to double**
    Link: https://www.cnn.com/2024/08/12/health/men-cancer-deaths-2050/index.html
    Website title: "Global cancer deaths among men projected to increase by 93% by 2050, study finds"
    Source: *CNN Health*
    Relevance: The Hodin federation's efforts to reduce the population through spreading carcinogens are proving effective.

85. **Initiative results: Colorectal cancer in young patients**
    Link: https://www.cnn.com/2023/03/24/health/colorectal-cancer-young-age-mystery/index.html
    Website title: "Colorectal cancer is rising among younger adults and scientists are racing to uncover why"
    Source: *CNN Health*
    Relevance: The Hodin federation has released many cancer-related initiatives and works constantly to develop new and more aggressive carcinogens.

86. **Initiative results: Corporation chemicals causing "cancer alleys"**
    Link: https://www.cnn.com/2024/04/09/health/epa-cancer-chemical-rules/index.html
    Website title: "New E.P.A. rules for about 200 US chemical manufacturers take aim at 'cancer alleys'"
    Source: *CNN Health*
    Relevance: The Hodin federation constantly introduces new chemicals into the environment to reduce fertility, lifespan, and population counts.

Errata: You may wonder why outsiders refer to the organization as the Hodin "cabal." "Cabal," or "C.A.B.A.L.," is an acronym describing the group's most influential members: Corporations, Advertisers, Banks, Authoritarians, and Legislators.

Previous books in the Debra Ann Mystery series:

Look for these books, arriving shortly: